Tales And Novels

Vol. IV

Containing
Castle Rackrent; An Essay On Irish Bulls; An Essay On The Noble Science Of Self-Justification; Ennui; And The Dun

by

Maria Edgeworth

Tales And Novels
Vol. IV
by Maria Edgeworth

ISBN: 978-93-68097-12-9

Published by

DOUBLE 9 BOOKS

2/13-B, Ansari Road
Daryaganj, New Delhi – 110002
info@double9books.com
www.double9books.com
Tel. 011-40042856

ABOUT THE AUTHOR

Maria Edgeworth was an Irish novelist and educationalist, born in 1768, she is best known for her contributions to children's literature and her novels that explore social issues and moral themes, particularly in works like "Tales and Novels." This collection includes stories designed to impart moral lessons through engaging narratives, showcasing her belief in the importance of education and character development.

Edgeworth's writing is characterized by its realism, wit, and keen observation of human behavior. Her most notable works, such as "Castle Rackrent," employ innovative narrative techniques that reflect the complexities of Irish society. She often focused on themes of gender roles and the moral responsibilities of individuals within their communities. In addition to fiction, Edgeworth wrote essays on education and social reform, advocating for improved educational opportunities, especially for women. Her influence extended beyond her lifetime, and she remains an important figure in both Irish and British literature, celebrated for her insights into character and society.

CONTENTS

PREFACE

The prevailing taste of the public for anecdote has been censured and ridiculed by critics who aspire to the character of superior wisdom; but if we consider it in a proper point of view, this taste is an incontestable proof of the good sense and profoundly philosophic temper of the present times. Of the numbers who study, or at least who read history, how few derive any advantage from their labours! The heroes of history are so decked out by the fine fancy of the professed historian; they talk in such measured prose, and act from such sublime or such diabolical motives, that few have sufficient taste, wickedness, or heroism, to sympathize in their fate. Besides, there is much uncertainty even in the best authenticated ancient or modern histories; and that love of truth, which in some minds is innate and immutable, necessarily leads to a love of secret memoirs and private anecdotes. We cannot judge either of the feelings or of the characters of men with perfect accuracy, from their actions or their appearance in public; it is from their careless conversations, their half-finished sentences, that we may hope with the greatest probability of success to discover their real characters. The life of a great or of a little man written by himself, the familiar letters, the diary of any individual published by his friends or by his enemies, after his decease, are esteemed important literary curiosities. We are surely justified, in this eager desire, to collect the most minute facts relative to the domestic lives, not only of the great and good, but even of the worthless and insignificant, since it is only by a comparison of their actual happiness or misery in the privacy of domestic life that we can form a just estimate of the real reward of virtue, or the real punishment of vice. That the great are not as happy as they seem, that the external circumstances of fortune and rank do not constitute felicity, is asserted by every moralist: the historian can seldom, consistently with his dignity, pause to illustrate this truth: it is therefore to the biographer we must have recourse. After we have beheld splendid characters playing their parts on the great theatre of the world, with all the advantages of stage effect and decoration, we anxiously beg to be admitted behind the scenes, that we may take a nearer view of the actors and actresses.

Some may perhaps imagine, that the value of biography depends upon the judgment and taste of the biographer: but on the contrary it may be maintained, that the merits of a biographer are inversely as the extent of his intellectual powers and of his literary talents. A plain unvarnished tale is preferable to the most highly ornamented narrative. Where we see that a man has the power, we may naturally suspect that he has the will to deceive us; and those who are used to literary manufacture know how much is often sacrificed to the rounding of a period, or the pointing of an antithesis.

That the ignorant may have their prejudices as well as the learned cannot be disputed; but we see and despise vulgar errors: we never bow to the authority of him who has no great name to sanction his absurdities. The partiality which blinds a biographer to the defects of his hero, in proportion as it is gross, ceases to be dangerous; but if it be concealed by the appearance of candour, which men of great abilities best know how to assume, it endangers our judgment sometimes, and sometimes our morals. If her grace the Duchess of Newcastle, instead of penning her lord's elaborate eulogium, had undertaken to write the life of Savage, we should not have been in any danger of mistaking an idle, ungrateful libertine, for a man of genius and virtue. The talents of a biographer are often fatal to his reader. For these reasons the public often judiciously countenance those who, without sagacity to discriminate character, without elegance of style to relieve the tediousness of narrative, without enlargement of mind to draw any conclusions from the facts they relate, simply pour forth anecdotes, and retail conversations, with all the minute prolixity of a gossip in a country town.

The author of the following Memoirs has upon these grounds fair claims to the public favour and attention; he was an illiterate old steward, whose partiality to *the family*, in which he was bred and born, must be obvious to the reader. He tells the history of the Rackrent family in his vernacular idiom, and in the full confidence that Sir Patrick, Sir Murtagh, Sir Kit, and Sir Condy Rackrent's affairs will be as interesting to all the world as they were to himself. Those who were acquainted with the manners of a certain class of the gentry of Ireland some years ago, will want no evidence of the truth of honest Thady's narrative: to those who are totally unacquainted with Ireland, the following Memoirs will perhaps be scarcely intelligible, or probably they may appear perfectly incredible. For the information of the *ignorant* English reader, a few notes have been subjoined by the editor, and he had it once in contemplation to translate the language of Thady into plain English; but Thady's idiom is incapable of translation, and, besides, the authenticity of his story would have been more exposed to doubt if it were not told in his own characteristic manner. Several years ago he related to the editor the history of the Rackrent family, and it was with some difficulty that he was persuaded to have it committed to writing; however, his feelings for "*the honour of the family,*" as he expressed himself, prevailed over his habitual laziness, and he at length completed the narrative which is now aid before the public.

The editor hopes his readers will observe that these are "tales of other times:" that the manners depicted in the following pages are not those of the present age: the race of the Rackrents has long since been extinct in Ireland; and the drunken Sir Patrick, the litigious Sir Murtagh, the fighting Sir Kit, and the slovenly Sir Condy, are characters which could no more be met with at present in Ireland, than Squire Western or Parson Trulliber in England. There is a time when individuals can bear to be rallied for their past follies and absurdities, after they have acquired new habits and a new consciousness. Nations, as well as individuals, gradually lose attachment to their identity, and the present generation is amused, rather than offended, by the ridicule that is thrown upon its ancestors.

Probably we shall soon have it in our power, in a hundred instances, to verify the truth of these observations.

When Ireland loses her identity by an union with Great Britain, she will look back, with a smile of good-humoured complacency, on the Sir Kits and Sir Condys of her former existence.

CASTLE RACKRENT

Monday Morning.[A]

Having, out of friendship for the family, upon whose estate, praised be Heaven! I and mine have lived rent-free, time out of mind, voluntarily undertaken to publish the MEMOIRS of the RACKRENT FAMILY, I think it my duty to say a few words, in the first place, concerning myself. My real name is Thady Quirk, though in the family I have always been known by no other than "*honest Thady*" —afterward, in the time of Sir Murtagh, deceased, I remember to hear them calling me "*old Thady*," and now I'm come to "poor Thady;" for I wear a long great coat1 winter and summer, which is very handy, as I never put my arms into the sleeves; they are as good as new, though come Holantide next I've had it these seven years; it holds on by a single button round my neck, cloak fashion. To look at me, you would hardly think "poor Thady" was the father of attorney Quirk; he is a high gentleman, and never minds what poor Thady says, and having better than fifteen hundred a year, landed estate, looks down upon honest Thady; but I wash my hands of his doings, and as I have lived so will I die, true and loyal to the family. The family of the Rackrents is, I am proud to say, one of the most ancient in the kingdom. Every body knows this is not the old family name, which was O'Shaughlin, related to the kings of Ireland—but that was before my time. My grandfather was driver to the great Sir Patrick O'Shaughlin, and I heard him, when I was a boy, telling how the Castle Rackrent estate came to Sir Patrick; Sir Tallyhoo Rackrent was cousin-german to him, and had a fine estate of his own, only never a gate upon it, it being his maxim that a car was the best gate. Poor gentleman! he lost a fine hunter and his life, at last, by it, all in one day's hunt. But I ought to bless that day, for the estate came straight into *the* family, upon one condition, which Sir Patrick O'Shaughlin at the time took sadly to heart, they say, but thought better of it afterwards, seeing how large a stake depended upon it, that he should, by act of parliament, take and bear the surname and arms of Rackrent.

Now it was that the world was to see what was *in* Sir Patrick. On coming into the estate, he gave the finest entertainment ever was heard of in the country; not a man could stand after supper but Sir Patrick himself, who could sit out the best man in Ireland, let alone the three kingdoms itself.

[B] He had his house, from one year's end to another, as full of company as ever it could hold, and fuller; for rather than be left out of the parties at Castle Rackrent, many gentlemen, and those men of the first consequence and landed estates in the country, such as the O'Neils of Ballynagrotty, and the Moueygawls of Mount Juliet's Town, and O'Shannons of New Town Tullyhog, made it their choice, often and often, when there was no room to be had for love nor money, in long winter nights, to sleep in the chicken-house, which Sir Patrick had fitted up for the purpose of accommodating his friends and the public in general, who honoured him with their company unexpectedly at Castle Rackrent; and this went on, I can't tell you how long—the whole country rang with his praises!—Long life to him! I'm sure I love to look upon his picture, now opposite to me; though I never saw him, he must have been a portly gentleman—his neck something short, and remarkable for the largest pimple on his nose, which, by his particular desire, is still extant in his picture, said to be a striking likeness, though taken when young. He is said also to be the inventor of raspberry whiskey, which is very likely, as nobody has ever appeared to dispute it with him, and as there still exists a broken punch-bowl at Castle Rackrent, in the garret, with an inscription to that effect—a great curiosity. A few days before his death he was very merry; it being his honour's birth-day, he called my grandfather in, God bless him! to drink the company's health, and filled a bumper himself, but could not carry it to his head, on account of the great shake in his hand; on this he cast his joke, saying, "What would my poor father say to me if he was to pop out of the grave, and see me now? I remember when I was a little boy, the first bumper of claret he gave me after dinner, how he praised me for carrying it so steady to my mouth. Here's my thanks to him—a bumper toast." Then he fell to singing the favourite song he learned from his father—for the last time, poor gentleman—he sung it that night as loud and as hearty as ever with a chorus:

"He that goes to bed, and goes to bed sober,
Falls as the leaves do, falls as the leaves do, and dies in October;
But he that goes to bed, and goes to bed mellow,
Lives as he ought to do, lives as he ought to do, and dies an
honest fellow."

Sir Patrick died that night: just as the company rose to drink his health with three cheers, he fell down in a sort of fit, and was carried off; they sat it out, and were surprised, on inquiry, in the morning, to find that it was all over with poor Sir Patrick. Never did any gentleman live and die more beloved in the country by rich and poor. His funeral was such a one as was never known before or since in the county! All the gentlemen in the three counties were at it; far and near, how they flocked! my great grandfather said, that to see all the women even in their red cloaks, you would have taken them for the army drawn out. Then such a fine whillaluh![C] you might have heard it to the farthest end of the county, and happy the man who could get but a sight of the hearse! But who'd have thought it? just as all was going on right, through his own town they were passing, when the body was seized for debt—a rescue was apprehended from the mob; but the heir who attended the funeral was against that, for fear of consequences, seeing that those villains who came to serve acted under the disguise of the law: so, to be sure, the law must take its course, and little gain had the creditors for their pains. First and foremost, they had the curses of the country: and Sir Murtagh Rackrent, the new heir, in the next place, on account of this affront to the body, refused to pay a shilling of the debts, in which he was countenanced by all the best gentlemen of property, and others of his acquaintance; Sir Murtagh alleging in all companies, that he all along meant to pay his father's debts of honour, but the moment the law was taken of him, there was an end of honour to be sure. It was whispered (but none but the enemies of the family believe it), that this was all a sham seizure to get quit of the debts, which he had bound himself to pay in honour.

It's a long time ago, there's no saying how it was, but this for certain, the new man did not take at all after the old gentleman; the cellars were never filled after his death, and no open house, or any thing as it used to be; the tenants even were sent away without their whiskey.[D] I was ashamed myself, and knew not what to say for the honour of the family; but I made the best of a bad case, and laid it all at my lady's door, for I did not like her any how, nor any body else; she was of the family of the Skinflints, and a widow; it was a strange match for Sir Murtagh; the people in the country thought he demeaned himself greatly,[E] but I said nothing: I knew how it was; Sir Murtagh was a great lawyer, and looked to the great Skinflint estate; there, however, he overshot himself; for though one of the co-heiresses, he was never the better for her, for she outlived him many's the long day— he could not see that to be sure when he married her. I must say for her, she made him the best of wives, being a very notable, stirring woman, and looking close to every thing. But I always suspected she had Scotch blood in her veins; any thing else I could have looked over in her from a regard to the family. She was a strict observer for self and servants of Lent, and all fast days, but not holidays. One of the maids having fainted three times the last day of Lent, to keep soul and body together, we put a morsel of roast beef into her mouth, which came from Sir Murtagh's dinner, who never fasted, not he; but somehow or other it unfortunately reached my lady's ears, and the priest of the parish had a complaint made of it the next day, and the poor girl was forced, as soon as she could walk, to do penance for it, before she could get any peace or absolution, in the house or out of it. However, my lady was very charitable in her own way. She had a charity school for poor children, where they were taught to read and write gratis, and where they were kept well to spinning gratis for my lady in return; for she had always heaps of duty yarn from the tenants, and got all her household linen out of the estate from first to last; for after the spinning, the weavers on the estate took it in hand for nothing, because of the looms my lady's interest could get from the Linen Board to distribute gratis. Then there was a bleach-yard near us, and the tenant dare refuse my lady nothing, for fear of a law-suit Sir Murtagh kept hanging over him about the water-course. With these ways of managing, 'tis surprising how cheap my lady got things done, and how proud she was of it. Her table the same way, kept for next to nothing;[F] duty fowls, and duty turkeys, and duty geese, came as fast as we could eat 'em, for my lady kept a sharp look-out, and knew to a tub of butter every thing the tenants had, all round. They knew her way, and what with fear of driving for rent and Sir Murtagh's lawsuits, they were kept in such good order, they never thought of coming near Castle Rackrent without a present of something or other—nothing too much or too little for my lady—eggs, honey, butter, meal, fish, game, grouse, and herrings, fresh or salt, all went for something. As for their young pigs, we had them, and the best bacon and hams they could make up, with all young chickens in spring; but they were a set of poor wretches, and we had nothing but misfortunes with them, always breaking and running away. This, Sir Murtagh and my lady said, was all their former landlord Sir Patrick's fault, who let 'em all get the half year's rent into arrear; there was something in that to be sure. But Sir Murtagh was as much the contrary way; for let alone making English tenants[G] of them, every soul, he was always driving and driving, and pounding and pounding, and canting[H] and canting, and replevying and replevying, and he made a good living of trespassing cattle; there was always some tenant's pig, or horse, or cow, or calf, or goose, trespassing, which was so great a gain to Sir Murtagh, that he did not like to hear me talk of repairing fences. Then his heriots and duty-work[I] brought him in something, his turf was cut, his potatoes set and dug, his hay brought home, and, in short, all the work about his house done for nothing; for in all our leases there were strict clauses heavy with penalties, which Sir Murtagh knew well how to enforce; so many days' duty work of man and horse, from every tenant, he was to have, and had, every year; and when a man vexed him, why the finest day he could pitch on, when the cratur was getting in his own harvest, or thatching his cabin, Sir Murtagh made it a principle to call upon him and his horse; so he taught 'em all, as he said, to know the law of landlord and tenant. As for law, I believe no man, dead or alive, ever loved it so well as Sir Murtagh. He had once sixteen suits pending at a time, and I never saw him so much himself; roads, lanes, bogs, wells, ponds, eel-wires, orchards, trees, tithes, vagrants, gravelpits, sandpits, dunghills, and nuisances, every thing upon the face of the earth furnished him good matter for a suit. He used to boast that he had a lawsuit for every letter in the alphabet. How I used to wonder to see Sir Murtagh in the midst of the papers in his office! Why he could hardly turn about for them. I made bold to shrug my shoulders once in his presence, and thanked my stars I was not born a gentleman to so much toil and trouble; but Sir Murtagh took me up short with his old proverb, "learning is better than house or land." Out of forty-nine suits which he had, he never lost one but seventeen;[J] the rest he gained with costs, double costs, treble costs sometimes; but even that did not pay. He was a very learned man in the law, and had the character of it; but how it was I can't tell, these suits that he carried cost him a power of money; in the end he sold some hundreds a year of the family estate; but he was a very learned man in the law, and I know nothing of the matter, except having a great regard for the family; and I could not help grieving when he sent me to post up notices of the sale of the fee-simple of the lands and appurtenances of Timoleague. "I know, honest Thady," says he, to comfort me, "what I'm about better than you do; I'm only selling to get the ready money wanting to carry on my suit with spirit with the Nugents of Carrickashaughlin."

He was very sanguine about that suit with the Nugents of Carrickashaughlin. He could have gained it, they say, for certain, had it pleased Heaven to have spared him to us, and it would have been at the least a plump two thousand a-year in his way; but things were ordered otherwise, for the best to be sure. He dug up a fairy-mount2 against my advice, and had no luck afterwards. Though a learned man in the law, he was a little too incredulous in other matters. I warned him that I heard the very Banshee3 that my grandfather heard under Sir Patrick's window a few days before his death. But Sir Murtagh thought nothing of the Banshee, nor of his cough, with a spitting of blood, brought on, I understand, by catching cold in attending the courts, and overstraining his chest with making himself heard in one of his favourite causes. He was a great speaker with a powerful voice; but his last speech was not in the courts at all. He and my lady, though both of the same way of thinking in some things, and though she was as good a wife and great economist as you could see, and he the best of husbands, as to looking into his affairs, and making money for his family; yet I don't know how it was, they had a great deal of sparring and jarring between them. My lady had her privy purse—and she had her weed ashes,[L] and her sealing money[M] upon the signing of all the leases, with something to buy gloves besides; and, besides, again often took money from the tenants, if offered properly, to speak for them to Sir Murtagh about abatements and renewals. Now the weed ashes and the glove money he allowed her clear perquisites; though once when he saw her in a new gown saved out of the weed ashes, he told her to my face (for he could say a sharp thing), that she should not put on her weeds before her husband's death. But in a dispute about an abatement, my lady would have the last word, and Sir Murtagh grew mad;[N] I was within hearing of the door, and now I wish I had made bold to step in. He spoke so loud, the whole kitchen was out on the stairs. [O] All on a sudden he stopped and my lady too. Something has surely happened, thought I—and so it was, for Sir Murtagh in his passion broke a blood-vessel, and all the law in the land could do nothing in that case. My lady sent for five physicians, but Sir Murtagh died, and was buried. She had a fine jointure settled upon her, and took herself away to the great joy of the tenantry. I never said any thing one way or the other, whilst she was part of the family, but got up to see her go at three o'clock in the morning. "It's a fine morning, honest Thady," says she; "good bye to ye," and into the carriage she stepped, without a word more, good or bad, or even half-a-crown; but I made my bow, and stood to see her safe out of sight for the sake of the family.

Then we were all bustle in the house, which made me keep out of the way, for I walk slow and hate a bustle; but the house was all hurry-skurry, preparing for my new master. Sir Murtagh, I forgot to notice, had no childer;4 so the Rackrent estate went to his younger brother, a young dashing officer, who came amongst us before I knew for the life of me where-abouts I was, in a gig or some of them things, with another spark along with him, and led horses, and servants, and dogs, and scarce a place to put any Christian of them into; for my late lady had sent all the feather-beds off before her, and blankets and household linen, down to the very knife cloths, on the cars to Dublin, which were all her own, lawfully paid for out of her own money. So the house was quite bare, and my young master, the moment ever he set foot in it out of his gig, thought all those things must come of themselves, I believe, for he never looked after any thing at all, but harum-scarum called for every thing as if we were conjurers, or he in a public-house. For my part, I could not bestir myself any how; I had been so much used to my late master and mistress, all was upside down with me, and the new servants in the servants' hall were quite out of my way; I had nobody to talk to, and if it had not been for my pipe and tobacco, should, I verily believe, have broke my heart for poor Sir Murtagh.

But one morning my new master caught a glimpse of me as I was looking at his horse's heels, in hopes of a word from him. "And is that old Thady?" says he, as he got into his gig: I loved him from that day to this, his voice was so like the family; and he threw me a guinea out of his waistcoat pocket, as he drew up the reins with the other hand, his horse rearing too; I thought I never set my eyes on a finer figure of a man, quite another sort from Sir Murtagh, though withal, *to me*, a family likeness. A fine life we should have led, had he stayed amongst us, God bless him! He valued a guinea as little as any man: money to him was no more than dirt, and his gentleman and groom, and all belonging to him, the same; but the sporting season over, he grew tired of the place, and having got down a great architect for the house, and an improver for the grounds, and seen their plans and elevations, he fixed a day for settling with the tenants, but went off in a whirlwind to town, just as some of them came into the yard in the morning. A circular letter came next post from the new agent, with news that the master was sailed for England, and he must remit 500*l*. to Bath for his use before a fortnight was at an end; bad news still for the poor tenants, no change still for the better with them. Sir Kit Rackrent, my young master, left all to the agent; and though he had the spirit of a prince, and lived away to the honour of his country abroad, which I was proud to hear of, what were we the better for that at home? The agent was one of your middle men,5 who grind the face of the poor, and can never bear a man with a hat upon his head: he ferreted the tenants out of their lives; not a week without a call for money, drafts upon drafts from Sir Kit; but I laid it all to the fault of the agent; for, says I, what can Sir Kit do with so much cash, and he a single man? but still it went. Rents must be all paid up to the day, and afore; no allowance for improving tenants, no consideration for those who had built upon their farms: no sooner was a lease out, but the land was advertised to the highest bidder, all the old tenants turned out, when they spent their substance in the hope and trust of a renewal from the landlord. All was now let at the highest penny to a parcel of poor wretches, who meant to run away, and did so, after taking two crops out of the ground. Then fining down the year's rent came into fashion,[P] any thing for the ready penny; and with all this, and presents to the agent and the driver,[Q] there was no such thing as standing it. I said nothing, for I had a regard for the family; but I walked about thinking if his honour Sir Kit knew all this, it would go hard with him, but he'd see us righted; not that I had any thing for my own share to complain of, for the agent was always very civil to me, when he came down into the country, and took a great deal of notice of my son Jason. Jason Quirk, though he be my son, I must say, was a good scholar from his birth, and a very 'cute lad: I thought to make him a priest,[R] but he did better for himself: seeing how he was as good a clerk as any in the county, the agent gave him his rent accounts to copy, which he did first of all for the pleasure of obliging the gentleman, and would take nothing at all for his trouble, but was always proud to serve the family. By-and-by a good farm bounding us to the east fell into his honour's hands, and my son put in a proposal for it:

why shouldn't he, as well as another? The proposals all went over to the master at the Bath, who knowing no more of the land than the child unborn, only having once been out a grousing on it before he went to England; and the value of lands, as the agent informed him, falling every year in Ireland, his honour wrote over in all haste a bit of a letter, saying he left it all to the agent, and that he must let it as well as he could to the best bidder, to be sure, and send him over 200*l.*, by return of post: with this the agent gave me a hint, and I spoke a good word for my son, and gave out in the country that nobody need bid against us. So his proposal was just the thing, and he a good tenant; and he got a promise of an abatement in the rent, after the first year, for advancing the half year's rent at signing the lease, which was wanting to complete the agent's 200*l.*, by the return of the post, with all which my master wrote back he was well satisfied. About this time we learned from the agent as a great secret, how the money went so fast, and the reason of the thick coming of the master's drafts: he was a little too fond of play; and Bath, they say, was no place for a young man of his fortune, where there were so many of his own countrymen too hunting him up and down, day and night, who had nothing to lose. At last, at Christmas, the agent wrote over to stop the drafts, for he could raise no more money on bond or mortgage, or from the tenants, or any how, nor had he any more to lend himself, and desired at the same time to decline the agency for the future, wishing Sir Kit his health and happiness, and the compliments of the season, for I saw the letter before ever it was sealed, when my son copied it. When the answer came, there was a new turn in affairs, and the agent was turned out; and my son Jason, who had corresponded privately with his honour occasionally on business, was forthwith desired by his honour to take the accounts into his own hands, and look them over till further orders. It was a very spirited letter to be sure: Sir Kit sent his service, and the compliments of the season, in return to the agent, and he would fight him with pleasure to-morrow, or any day, for sending him such a letter, if he was born a gentleman, which he was sorry (for both their sakes) to find (too late) he was not. Then, in a private postscript, he condescended to tell us, that all would be speedily settled to his satisfaction, and we should turn over a new leaf, for he was going to be married in a fortnight to the grandest heiress in England, and had only immediate occasion at present for 200*l.*, as he would not choose to touch his lady's fortune for travelling expenses home to Castle Rackrent, where he intended to be, wind and weather permitting, early in the next month; and desired fires, and the house to be painted, and the new building to go on as fast as possible, for the reception of him and his lady before that time; with several words besides in the letter, which we could not make out, because, God bless him! he wrote in such a flurry. My heart warmed to my new lady when I read this; I was almost afraid it was too good news to be true; but the girls fell to scouring, and it was well they did, for we soon saw his marriage in the paper, to a lady with I don't know how many tens of thousand pounds to her fortune: then I watched the post-office for his landing; and the news came to my son of his and the bride being in Dublin, and on the way home to Castle Rackrent. We had bonfires all over the country, expecting him down the next day, and we had his coming of age still to celebrate, which he had not time to do properly before he left the country; therefore a great ball was expected, and great doings upon his coming, as it were, fresh to take possession of his ancestors' estate. I never shall forget the day he came home: we had waited and waited all day long till eleven o'clock at night, and I was thinking of sending the boy to lock the gates, and giving them up for that night, when there came the carriages thundering up to the great hall door. I got the first sight of the bride; for when the carriage door opened, just as she had her foot on the steps, I held the flam[S] full in her face to light her, at which she shut her eyes, but I had a full view of the rest, of her, and greatly shocked I was, for by that light she was little better than a blackamoor, and seemed crippled, but that was only sitting so long in the chariot. "You're kindly welcome to Castle Rackrent, my lady," says I (recollecting who she was); "did your honour hear of the bonfires?" His honour spoke never a word, nor so much as handed her up the steps—he looked to me no more like himself than nothing at all; I know I took him for the skeleton of his honour: I was not sure what to say next to one or t'other, but seeing she was a stranger in a foreign country, I thought it but right to speak cheerful to her, so I went back again to the bonfires. "My lady," says I, as she crossed the hall, "there would have been fifty times as many, but for fear of the horses, and frightening your ladyship: Jason and I forbid them, please your honour." With that she looked at me a little bewildered. "Will I have a fire lighted in the state-room to-night?" was the next question I put to her, but never a word she answered, so I concluded she could not speak a word of English, and was from foreign parts. The short and the long of it was, I couldn't tell what to make of her; so I left her to herself, and went straight down to the servants' hall to learn something for certain about her. Sir Kit's own man was tired, but the groom set him a talking at last, and we had it all out before ever I closed my eyes that night. The bride might well be a great fortune— she was a *Jewish* by all accounts, who are famous for their great riches. I had never seen any of that tribe or nation before, and could only gather, that she spoke a strange kind of English of her own, that she could not abide pork or sausages, and went neither to church or mass. Mercy upon his honour's poor soul, thought I; what will become of him and his, and all of us, with his heretic blackamoor at the head of the Castle Rackrent estate! I never slept a wink all night for thinking of it: but before the servants I put my pipe in my mouth, and kept my mind to myself; for I had a great regard for the family; and after this, when strange gentlemen's servants came to the house, and would begin to talk about the bride, I took care to put the best foot foremost, and passed her for a nabob in the kitchen, which accounted for her dark complexion and every thing.

The very morning after they came home, however, I saw plain enough how things were between Sir Kit and my lady, though they were walking together arm in arm after breakfast, looking at the new building and the improvements. "Old Thady," said my master, just as he used to do, "how do you do?" "Very well, I thank your honour's honour," said I; but I saw he was not well pleased, and my heart was in my mouth as I walked along after him. "Is the large room damp, Thady?" said his honour. "Oh, damp, your honour! how should it but be as dry as a bone," says I, "after all the fires we have kept in it day and night? it's the barrack-room[T] your honour's talking on." "And what is a barrack-room, pray, my dear?" were the first words I ever heard out of my lady's lips. "No matter, my dear!" said he, and went on talking to me, ashamed like I should witness her ignorance. To be sure, to hear her talk one might have taken her for an innocent,[U] for it was, "what's this, Sir Kit? and what's that, Sir Kit?" all the way we went. To be sure, Sir Kit had enough to do to answer her. "And what do you call that, Sir Kit?" said she, "that, that looks like a pile of black bricks, pray, Sir Kit?" "My turf stack, my dear," said my master, and bit his lip. Where have you lived, my lady, all your life, not to know a turf stack when you see it? thought I, but I said nothing. Then, by-and-by, she takes out her glass, and begins spying over the country. "And what's all that black swamp out yonder, Sir Kit?" says she. "My bog, my dear," says he, and went on whistling. "It's a very ugly prospect, my dear," says she. "You don't see it, my dear," says he, "for we've planted it out, when the trees grow up in summer time," says he. "Where are the trees," said she, "my dear?" still looking through her glass. "You are blind, my dear," says he; "what are these under your eyes?" "These shrubs," said she. "Trees," said he. "May be they are what you call trees in Ireland, my dear," said she; "but they are not a yard high, are they?" "They were planted out but last year, my lady," says I, to soften matters between them, for I saw she was going the way to make his honour mad with her: "they are very well grown for their age, and you'll not see the bog of Allyballycarricko'shaughlin at-all-at-all through the skreen, when once the leaves come out. But, my lady, you must not quarrel with any part or parcel of Allyballycarricko'shaughlin, for you don't know how many hundred years that same bit of bog has been in the family; we would not part with the bog of Allyballycarricko'shaughlin upon no account at all; it cost the late Sir Murtagh two hundred good pounds to defend his title to it and boundaries against the O'Learys, who cut a road through it." Now one would have thought this would have been hint enough for my lady, but she fell to laughing like one out of their right mind, and made me say the name of the bog over for her to get it by heart, a dozen times—then she must ask me how to spell it, and what was the meaning of it in English—Sir Kit standing by whistling all the while; I verily believed she laid the corner stone of all her future misfortunes at that very instant; but I said no more, only looked at Sir Kit.

There were no balls, no dinners, no doings; the country was all disappointed—Sir Kit's gentleman said in a whisper to me, it was all my lady's own fault, because she was so obstinate about the cross. "What cross?" says I; "is it about her being a heretic?" "Oh, no such matter," says he; "my master does not mind her heresies, but her diamond cross, it's worth I can't tell you how much; and she has thousands of English pounds concealed in diamonds about her, which she as good as promised to give up to my master before he married, but now she won't part with any of them, and she must take the consequences."

Her honey-moon, at least her Irish honey-moon, was scarcely well over, when his honour one morning said to me, "Thady, buy me a pig!" and then the sausages were ordered, and here was the first open breaking-out of my lady's troubles. My lady came down herself into the kitchen, to speak to the cook about the sausages, and desired never to see them more at her table. Now my master had ordered them, and my lady knew that. The cook took my lady's part, because she never came down into the kitchen, and was young and innocent in housekeeping, which raised her pity; besides, said she, at her own table, surely, my lady should order and disorder what she pleases; but the cook soon changed her note, for my master made it a principle to have the sausages, and swore at her for a Jew herself, till he drove her fairly out of the kitchen; then, for fear of her place, and because he threatened that my lady should give her no discharge without the sausages, she gave up, and from that day forward always sausages, or bacon, or pig meat in some shape or other, went up to table; upon which my lady shut herself up in her own room, and my master said she might stay there, with an oath: and to make sure of her, he turned the key in the door, and kept it ever after in his pocket. We none of us ever saw or heard her speak for seven years after that:6 he carried her dinner himself. Then his honour had a great deal of company to dine with him, and balls in the house, and was as gay and gallant, and as much himself as before he was married; and at dinner he always drank my Lady Rackrent's good health, and so did the company, and he sent out always a servant, with his compliments to my Lady Rackrent, and the company was drinking her ladyship's health, and begged to know if there was any thing at table he might send her; and the man came back, after the sham errand, with my Lady Rackrent's compliments, and she was very much obliged to Sir Kit—she did not wish for any thing, but drank the company's health. The country, to be sure, talked and wondered at my lady's being shut up, but nobody chose to interfere or ask any impertinent questions, for they knew my master was a man very apt to give a short answer himself, and likely to call a man out for it afterwards; he was a famous shot; had killed his man before he came of age, and nobody scarce dared look at him whilst at Bath. Sir Kit's character was so well known in the country, that he lived in peace and quietness ever after, and was a great favourite with the ladies, especially when in process of time, in the fifth year of her confinement, my Lady Rackrent fell ill, and took entirely to her bed, and he gave out that she was now skin and bone, and could not last through the winter. In this he had two physicians' opinions to back him (for now he called in two physicians for her), and tried all his arts to get the diamond cross from her on her death-bed, and to get her to make a will in his favour of her separate possessions; but there she was too tough for him. He used to swear at her behind her back, after kneeling to her to her face, and call her in the presence of his gentleman his stiff-necked Israelite, though before he married her, that same gentleman told me he used to call her (how he could bring it out, I don't know) "my pretty Jessica!" To be sure it must have been hard for her to guess what sort of a husband he reckoned to make her. When she was lying, to all expectation, on her death-bed of a broken heart, I could not but pity her, though she was a Jewish; and considering too it was no fault of hers to be taken with my master so young as she was at the Bath, and so fine a gentleman as Sir Kit was when he courted her; and considering too, after all they had heard and seen of him as a husband, there were now no less than three ladies in our county talked of for his second wife, all at daggers drawn with each other, as his gentleman swore, at the balls, for Sir Kit for their partner,—I could not but think them bewitched; but they all reasoned with themselves, that Sir Kit would make a good husband to any Christian but a Jewish, I suppose, and especially as he was now a reformed rake; and it was not known how my lady's fortune was settled in her will, nor how the Castle Rackrent estate was all mortgaged, and bonds out against him, for he was never cured of his gaming tricks; but that was the only fault he had, God bless him!

My lady had a sort of fit, and it was given out she was dead, by mistake: this brought things to a sad crisis for my poor master,—one of the three ladies showed his letters to her brother, and claimed his promises, whilst another did the same. I don't mention names. Sir Kit, in his defence, said he would meet any man who dared to question his conduct, and as to the ladies, they must settle it amongst them who was to be his second, and his third, and his fourth, whilst his first was still alive, to his mortification and theirs. Upon this, as upon all former occasions, he had the voice of the country with him, on account of the great spirit and propriety he acted with. He met and shot the first lady's brother; the next day he called out the second, who had a wooden-leg; and their place of meeting by appointment being in a new ploughed field, the wooden-leg man stuck fast in it. Sir Kit, seeing his situation, with great candour fired his pistol over his head; upon which the seconds interposed, and convinced the parties there had been a slight misunderstanding between them; thereupon they shook hands cordially, and went home to dinner together. This gentleman, to show the world how they stood together, and by the advice of the friends of both parties, to re-establish his sister's injured reputation, went out with Sir Kit as his second, and carried his message next day to the last of his adversaries: I never saw him in such fine spirits as that day he went out—sure enough he was within ames-ace of getting quit handsomely of all his enemies; but unluckily, after hitting the tooth-pick out of his adversary's finger and thumb, he received a ball in a vital part, and was brought home, in little better than an hour after the affair, speechless on a hand-barrow, to my lady. We got the key out of his pocket the first thing we did, and my son Jason ran to unlock the barrack-room, where my lady had been shut up for seven years, to acquaint her with the fatal accident. The surprise bereaved her of her senses at first, nor would she believe but we were putting some new trick upon her, to entrap her out of her jewels, for a great while, till Jason bethought himself of taking her to the window, and showed her the men bringing Sir Kit up the avenue upon the hand-barrow, which had immediately the desired effect; for directly she burst into tears, and pulling her cross from her bosom, she kissed it with as great devotion as ever I witnessed; and lifting up her eyes to heaven, uttered some ejaculation, which none present heard; but I take the sense of it to be, she returned thanks for this unexpected interposition in her favour when she had least reason to expect it. My master was greatly lamented: there was no life in him when we lifted him off the barrow, so he was laid out immediately, and *waked* the same night. The country was all in an uproar about him, and not a soul but cried shame upon his murderer; who would have been hanged surely, if he could have been brought to his trial, whilst the gentlemen in the country were up about it; but he very prudently withdrew himself to the continent before the affair was made public. As for the young lady, who was the immediate cause of the fatal accident, however innocently, she could never show her head after at the balls in the county or any place; and by the advice of her friends and physicians, she was ordered soon after to Bath, where it was expected, if any where on this side of the grave, she would meet with the recovery of her health and lost peace of mind. As a proof of his great popularity, I need only add, that there was a song made upon my master's untimely death in the newspapers, which was in every body's mouth, singing up and down through the country, even down to the mountains, only three days after his unhappy exit. He was also greatly bemoaned at the Curragh,[V] where his cattle were well known; and all who had taken up his bets were particularly inconsolable for his loss to society. His stud sold at the cant[X] at the greatest price ever known in the county; his favourite horses were chiefly disposed of amongst his particular friends, who would give any price for them for his sake; but no ready money was required by the new heir, who wished not to displease any of the gentlemen of the neighbourhood just upon his coming to settle amongst them; so a long credit was given where requisite, and the cash has never been gathered in from that day to this.

But to return to my lady:—She got surprisingly well after my master's decease. No sooner was it known for certain that he was dead, than all the gentlemen within twenty miles of us came in a body, as it were, to set my lady at liberty, and to protest against her confinement, which they now for the first time understood was against her own consent The ladies too were as attentive as possible, striving who should be foremost with their morning visits; and they that saw the diamonds spoke very handsomely of them, but thought it a pity they were not bestowed, if it had so pleased God, upon a lady who would have become them better. All these civilities wrought little with my lady, for she had taken an unaccountable prejudice against the country, and every thing belonging to it, and was so partial to her native land, that after parting with the cook, which she did immediately upon my master's decease, I never knew her easy one instant, night or day, but when she was packing up to leave us. Had she meant to make any stay in Ireland, I stood a great chance of being a great favourite with her; for when she found I understood the weathercock, she was always finding some pretence to be talking to me, and asking me which way the wind blew, and was it likely, did I think, to continue fair for England. But when I saw she had made up her mind to spend the rest of her days upon her own income and jewels in England, I considered her quite as a foreigner, and not at all any longer as part of the family. She gave no vails to the servants at Castle Rackrent at parting, notwithstanding the old proverb of "*as rich as a Jew*," which she being a Jewish, they built upon with reason. But from first to last she brought nothing but misfortunes amongst us; and if it had not been all along with her, his honour, Sir Kit, would have been now alive in all appearance. Her diamond cross was, they say, at the bottom of it all; and it was a shame for her, being his wife, not to show more duty, and to have given it up when he condescended to ask so often for such a bit of a trifle in his distresses, especially when he all along made it no secret he married for money. But we will not bestow another thought upon her. This much I thought it lay upon my conscience to say, in justice to my poor master's memory.

'Tis an ill wind that blows nobody no good—the same wind that took the Jew Lady Rackrent over to England, brought over the new heir to Castle Rackrent.

Here let me pause for breath in my story, for though I had a great regard for every member of the family, yet without compare Sir Conolly, commonly called, for short, amongst his friends, Sir Condy Rackrent, was ever my great favourite, and, indeed, the most universally beloved man I had ever seen or heard of, not excepting his great ancestor Sir Patrick, to whose memory he, amongst other instances of generosity, erected a handsome marble stone in the church of Castle Rackrent, setting forth in large letters his age, birth, parentage, and many other virtues, concluding with the compliment so justly due, that "Sir Patrick Rackrent lived and died a monument of old Irish hospitality."

CONTINUATION OF THE MEMOIRS OF THE RACKRENT FAMILY

HISTORY OF SIR CONOLLY RACKRENT

Sir Condy Rackrent, by the grace of God heir-at-law to the Castle Rackrent estate, was a remote branch of the family: born to little or no fortune of his own, he was bred to the bar; at which, having many friends to push him, and no mean natural abilities of his own, he doubtless would, in process of time, if he could have borne the drudgery of that study, have been rapidly made king's counsel, at the least; but things were disposed of otherwise, and he never went the circuit but twice, and then made no figure for want of a fee, and being unable to speak in public. He received his education chiefly in the college of Dublin; but before he came to years of discretion lived in the country, in a small but slated house, within view of the end of the avenue. I remember him bare footed and headed, running through the street of O'Shaughlin's town, and playing at pitch and toss, ball, marbles, and what not, with the boys of the town, amongst whom my son Jason was a great favourite with him. As for me, he was ever my white-headed boy: often's the time when I would call in at his father's, where I was always made welcome; he would slip down to me in the kitchen, and love to sit on my knee, whilst I told him stories of the family, and the blood from which he was sprung, and how he might look forward, if the *then* present man should die without childer, to being at the head of the Castle Rackrent estate. This was then spoke quite and clear at random to please the child, but it pleased Heaven to accomplish my prophecy afterwards, which gave him a great opinion of my judgment in business. He went to a little grammar-school with many others, and my son amongst the rest, who was in his class, and not a little useful to him in his book learning, which he acknowledged with gratitude ever after. These rudiments of his education thus completed, he got a-horseback, to which exercise he was ever addicted, and used to gallop over the country while yet but a slip of a boy, under the care of Sir Kit's huntsman, who was very fond of him, and often lent him his gun, and took him out a-shooting under his own eye. By these means he became well acquainted and popular amongst the poor in the neighbourhood early; for there was not a cabin at which he had not stopped some morning or other, along with the huntsman, to drink a glass of burnt whiskey out of an eggshell, to do him good and warm his heart, and drive the cold out of his stomach. The old people always told him he was a great likeness of Sir Patrick; which made him first have an ambition to take after him, as far as his fortune should allow. He left us when of an age to enter the college, and there completed his education and nineteenth year; for as he was not born to an estate, his friends thought it incumbent on them to give him the best education which could be had for love or money; and a great deal of money consequently was spent upon him at College and temple. He was a very little altered for the worse by what he saw there of the great world; for when he came down into the country, to pay us a visit, we thought him just the same man as ever, hand and glove with every one, and as far from high, though not without his own proper share of family pride, as any man ever you see. Latterly, seeing how Sir Kit and the Jewish lived together, and that there was no one between him and the Castle Rackrent estate, he neglected to apply to the law as much as was expected of him; and secretly many of the tenants, and others, advanced him cash upon his note of hand value received, promising bargains of leases and lawful interest, should he ever come into the estate. All this was kept a great secret, for fear the present man, hearing of it, should take it into his head to take it ill of poor Condy, and so should cut him off for ever, by levying a fine, and suffering a recovery to dock the entail.[Y] Sir Murtagh would have been the man for that; but Sir Kit was too much taken up philandering to consider the law in this case, or any other. These practices I have mentioned, to account for the state of his affairs, I mean Sir Condy's, upon his coming into the Castle Rackrent estate. He could not command a penny of his first year's income; which, and keeping no accounts, and the great sight of company he did, with many other causes too numerous to mention, was the origin of his distresses. My son Jason, who was now established agent, and knew every thing, explained matters out of the face to Sir Conolly, and made him sensible of his embarrassed situation. With a great nominal rent-roll, it was almost all paid away in interest; which being for convenience suffered to run on, soon doubled the principal, and Sir Condy was obliged to pass new bonds for the interest, now grown principal, and so on. Whilst this was going on, my son requiring to be paid for his trouble, and many years' service in the family gratis, and Sir Condy not willing to take his affairs into his own hands, or to look them even in the face, he gave my son a bargain of some acres, which Jell out of lease, at a reasonable rent. Jason set the land, as soon as his lease was sealed, to under tenants, to make the rent, and got two hundred a-year profit rent; which was little enough considering his long agency. He bought the land at twelve years' purchase two years afterwards, when Sir Condy was pushed for money on an execution, and was at the same time allowed for his improvements thereon. There was a sort of hunting-lodge upon the estate, convenient to my son Jason's land, which he had his eye upon about this time; and he was a little jealous of Sir Condy, who talked of setting it to a stranger, who was just come into the country—Captain Moneygawl was the man. He was son and heir to the Moneygawls of Mount Juliet's town, who had a great estate in the next county to ours; and my master was loth to disoblige the young gentleman, whose heart was set upon the lodge; so he wrote him back, that the lodge was at his service, and if he would honour him with his company at Castle Rackrent, they could ride over together some morning, and look at it, before signing the lease. Accordingly the captain came over to us, and he and Sir Condy grew the greatest friends ever you see, and were for ever out a-shooting or hunting together, and were very merry in the evenings; and Sir Condy was invited of course to Mount Juliet's town; and the family intimacy that had been in Sir Patrick's time was now recollected, and nothing would serve Sir Condy but he must be three times a-week at the least with his new friends, which grieved me, who knew, by the captain's groom and gentleman, how they talked of him at Mount Juliet's town, making him quite, as one may say, a laughing-stock and a butt for the whole company; but they were soon cured of *that* by an accident that surprised 'em not a little, as it did me. There was a bit of a scrawl found upon the waiting-maid of old Mr. Moneygawl's youngest daughter, Miss Isabella, that laid open the whole; and her father, they say, was like *one out of his right mind*, and swore it was the last thing he ever should have thought of, when he invited my master to his house, that his daughter should think of such a match. But their talk signified not a straw, for, as Miss. Isabella's maid reported, her young mistress was fallen over head and ears in love with Sir Condy, from the first time that ever her brother brought him into the house to dinner: the servant who waited that day behind my master's chair was the first who knew it, as he says; though it's hard to believe him, for he did not tell it till a great while afterwards; but, however, it's likely enough, as the thing turned out, that he was not far out of the way; for towards the middle of dinner, as he says, they were talking of stage-plays, having a playhouse, and being great play-actors at Mount Juliet's town; and Miss Isabella turns short to my master, and says, "Have you seen the play-bill, Sir Condy?" "No, I have not," said he. "Then more shame for you," said the captain her brother, "not to know that my sister is to play Juliet to-night, who plays it better than any woman on or off the stage in all Ireland." "I am very happy to hear it," said Sir Condy; and there the matter dropped for the present. But Sir Condy all this time, and it great while afterwards, was at a terrible nonplus; for he had no liking, not he, to stage-plays, nor to Miss Isabella either; to his mind, as it came out over a bowl of whiskey-punch at home, his little Judy M'Quirk, who was daughter to a sister's son of mine, was worth twenty of Miss Isabella. He had seen her often when he stopped at her father's cabin to drink whiskey out of the egg-shell, out hunting, before he came to the estate, and, as she gave out, was under something like a promise of marriage to her. Any how, I could not but pity my poor master, who was so bothered between them, and he an easy-hearted man, that could not disoblige nobody, God bless him! To be sure, it was not his place to behave ungenerous to Miss Isabella, who had disobliged all her relations for his sake, as he remarked; and then she was locked up in her chamber, and forbid to think of him any more, which raised his spirit, because his family was, as he observed, as good as theirs at any rate, and the Rackrents a suitable match for the Moneygawls any day in the year: all which was true enough; but it grieved me to see, that upon the strength of all this, Sir Condy was growing more in the mind to carry off Miss Isabella to Scotland, in spite of her relations, as she desired.

"It's all over with our poor Judy!" said I, with a heavy sigh, making bold to speak to him one night when he was a little cheerful, and standing in the servants' hall all alone with me, as was often his custom. "Not at all," said he; "I never was fonder of Judy than at this present speaking; and to prove it to you," said he, and he took from my hand a halfpenny, change that I had just got along with my tobacco, "and to prove it to you, Thady," says he, "it's a toss up with me which I should marry this minute, her or Mr. Moneygawl of Mount Juliet's town's daughter—so it is." "Oh, boo! boo!" 7 says I, making light of it, to see what he would go on to next; "your honour's joking, to be sure; there's no compare between our poor Judy and Miss Isabella, who has a great fortune, they say." "I'm not a man to mind a fortune, nor never was," said Sir Condy, proudly, "whatever her friends may say; and to make short of it," says he, "I'm come to a determination upon the spot;" with that he swore such a terrible oath, as made me cross myself; "and by this book," said he, snatching up my ballad book, mistaking it for my prayer book, which lay in the window; "and by this book," says he, "and by all the books that ever were shut and opened, it's come to a toss-up with me, and I'll stand or fall by the toss; and so Thady, hand me over that *pin* 8 out of the ink-horn," and he makes a cross on the smooth side of the halfpenny; "Judy M'Quirk," says he, "her mark." 9 God bless him! his hand was a little unsteadied by all the whiskey punch he had taken, but it was plain to see his heart was for poor Judy. My heart was all as one as in my mouth when I saw the halfpenny up in the air, but I said nothing at all; and when it came down, I was glad I had kept myself to myself, for to be sure now it was all over with poor Judy. "Judy's out a luck," said I, striving to laugh. "I'm out a luck," said he; and I never saw a man look so cast down: he took up the halfpenny off the flag, and walked away quite sober-like by the shock. Now, though as easy a man, you would think, as any in the wide world, there was no such thing as making him unsay one of these sort of vows,10 which he had learned to reverence when young, as I well remember teaching him to toss up for bog-berries on my knee. So I saw the affair was as good as settled between him and Miss Isabella, and I had no more to say but to wish her joy, which I did the week afterwards, upon her return from Scotland with my poor master.

My new lady was young, as might be supposed of a lady that had been carried off, by her own consent, to Scotland; but I could only see her at first through her veil, which, from bashfulness or fashion, she kept over her face. "And am I to walk through all this crowd of people, my dearest love?" said she to Sir Condy, meaning us servants and tenants, who had gathered at the hack gate. "My dear," said Sir Condy, "there's nothing for it but to walk, or to let me carry you as far as the house, for you see the back road is too narrow for a carriage, and the great piers have tumbled down across the front approach; so there's no driving the right way, by reason of the ruins." "Plato, thou reasonest well!" said she, or words to that effect, which I could no ways understand; and again, when her foot stumbled against a broken bit of a car-wheel, she cried out, "Angels and ministers of grace defend us!" Well, thought I, to be sure, if she's no Jewish, like the last, she is a mad woman for certain, which is as bad: it would have been as well for my poor master to have taken up with poor Judy, who is in her right mind, any how.

She was dressed like a mad woman, moreover, more than like any one I ever saw afore or since, and I could not take my eyes off her, but still followed behind her; and her feathers on the top of her hat were broke going in at the low back door, and she pulled out her little bottle out of her pocket to smell to when she found herself in the kitchen, and said, "I shall faint with the heat of this odious, odious place." "My dear, it's only three steps across the kitchen, and there's a fine air if your veil was up," said Sir Condy, and with that threw hack her veil, so that I had then a full sight of her face; she had not at all the colour of one going to faint, but a fine complexion of her own, as I then took it to be, though her maid told me after it was all put on; but even complexion and all taken in, she was no way, in point of good looks, to compare to poor Judy; and with all she had a quality toss with her; but may be it was my over-partiality to Judy, into whose place I may say she stepped, that made me notice all this. To do her justice, however, she was, when we came to know her better, very liberal in her house-keeping, nothing at all of the skinflint in her; she left every thing to the housekeeper; and her own maid, Mrs. Jane, who went with her to Scotland, gave her the best of characters for generosity. She seldom or ever wore a thing twice the same way, Mrs. Jane told us, and was always pulling her things to pieces, and giving them away; never being used, in her father's house, to think of expense in any thing; and she reckoned, to be sure, to go on the same way at Castle Rackrent; but, when I came to inquire, I learned that her father was so mad with her for running off, after his locking her up, and forbidding her to think any more of Sir Condy, that he would not give her a farthing; and it was lucky for her she had a few thousands of her own, which had been left to her by a good grandmother, and these were very convenient to begin with. My master and my lady set out in great style; they had the finest coach and chariot, and horses and liveries, and cut the greatest dash in the county, returning their wedding visits: and it was immediately reported, that her father had undertaken to pay all my master's debts, and of course all his tradesmen gave him a new credit, and every thing went on smack smooth, and I could not but admire my lady's spirit, and was proud to see Castle Rackrent again in all its glory. My lady had a fine taste for building, and furniture, and playhouses, and she turned every thing topsy-turvy, and made the barrack-room into a theatre, as she called it, and she went on as if she had a mint of money at her elbow; and, to be sure, I thought she knew best, especially as Sir Condy said nothing to it one way or the other. All he asked, God bless him! was to live in peace and quietness, and have his bottle or his whiskey punch at night to himself. Now this was little enough, to be sure, for any gentleman; but my lady couldn't abide the smell of the whiskey punch. "My dear," says he, "you liked it well enough before we were married, and why not now?" "My dear," said she, "I never smelt it, or I assure you I should never have prevailed upon myself to marry you." "My dear, I am sorry you did not smell it; but we can't help that now," returned my master, without putting himself in a passion, or going out of his way, but just fair and easy helped himself to another glass, and drank it off to her good health. All this the butler told me, who was going backwards and forwards unnoticed with the jug, and hot water, and sugar, and all he thought wanting. Upon my master's swallowing the last glass of whiskey punch, my lady burst into tears, calling him an ungrateful, base, barbarous wretch! and went off into a fit of hysterics, as I think Mrs. Jane called it, and my poor master was greatly frightened, this being the first thing of the kind he had seen; and he fell straight on his knees before her, and, like a good-hearted cratur as he was, ordered the whiskey punch out of the room, and bid 'em throw open all the windows, and cursed himself: and then my lady came to herself again, and when she saw him kneeling there, bid him get up, and not forswear himself any more, for that she was sure he did not love her, and never had: this we learned from Mrs. Jane, who was the only person left present at all this. "My dear," returns my master, thinking, to be sure, of Judy, as well he might, "whoever told you so is an incendiary, and I'll have 'em turned out of the house this minute, if you'll only let me know which of them it was." "Told me what?" said my lady, starting upright in her chair. "Nothing at all, nothing at all," said my master, seeing he had overshot himself, and that my lady spoke at random; "but what you said just now, that I did not love you, Bella; who told you that?" "My own sense," she said, and she put her handkerchief to her face, and leant back upon Mrs. Jane, and fell to sobbing as if her heart would break. "Why now, Bella, this is very strange of you," said my poor master; "if nobody has told you—nothing, what is it you are taking on for at this rate, and exposing yourself and me for this way?" "Oh, say no more, say no more; every word you say kills me," cried my lady; and she ran on like one, as Mrs. Jane says, raving, "Oh, Sir Condy, Sir Condy! I that had hoped to find in you——" "Why now, faith, this is a little too much; do, Bella, try to recollect yourself, my dear; am not I your husband, and of your own choosing; and is not that enough?" "Oh, too much! too much!" cried my lady, wringing her hands. "Why, my dear, come to your right senses, for the love of heaven. See, is not the whiskey punch, jug and bowl, and all, gone out of the room long ago? What is it, in the wide world, you have to complain of?" But still my lady sobbed and sobbed, and called herself the most wretched of women; and among other out-of-the-way provoking things, asked my master, was he fit for company for her, and he drinking all night? This nettling him, which it was hard to do, he replied, that as to drinking all night, he was then as sober as she was herself, and that it was no matter how much a man drank, provided it did no ways affect or stagger him: that as to being fit company for her, he thought himself of a family to be fit company for any lord or lady in the land; but that he never prevented her from seeing and keeping what company she pleased, and that he had done his best to make Castle Rackrent pleasing to her since her marriage, having always had the house full of visitors, and if her own relations were not amongst them, he said that was their own fault, and their pride's fault, of which he was sorry to find her ladyship had so unbecoming a share. So concluding, he took his candle and walked off to his room, and my lady was in her tantarums for three days after; and would have been so much longer, no doubt, but some of her friends, young ladies, and cousins, and second cousins, came to Castle Rackrent, by my poor master's express invitation, to see her, and she was in a hurry to get up, as Mrs. Jane called it, a play for them, and so got well, and was as finely dressed, and as happy to look at, as ever; and all the young ladies, who used to be in her room dressing of her, said, in Mrs. Jane's hearing, that my lady was the happiest bride ever they had seen, and that to be sure a love-match was the only thing for happiness, where the parties could any way afford it.

As to affording it, God knows it was little they knew of the matter; my lady's few thousands could not last for ever, especially the way she went on with them; and letters from tradesfolk came every post thick and threefold with bills as long as my arm, of years' and years' standing: my son Jason had 'em all handed over to him, and the pressing letters were all unread by Sir Condy, who hated trouble, and could never be brought to hear talk of business, but still put it off and put it off, saying, settle it any how, or bid 'em call again to-morrow, or speak to me about it some other time. Now it was hard to find the right time to speak, for in the mornings he was a-bed, and in the evenings over his bottle, where no gentleman chooses to be disturbed. Things in a twelvemonth or so came to such a pass there was no making a shift to go on any longer, though we were all of us well enough used to live from hand to mouth at Castle Rackrent. One day, I remember, when there was a power of company, all sitting after dinner in the dusk, not to say dark, in the drawing-room, my lady having rung five times for candles, and none to go up, the housekeeper sent up the footman, who went to my mistress, and whispered behind her chair how it was. "My lady," says he, "there are no candles in the house." "Bless me," says she; "then take a horse and gallop off as fast as you can to Carrick O'Fungus, and get some." "And in the mean time tell them to step into the playhouse, and try if there are not some bits left," added Sir Condy, who happened to be within hearing. The man was sent up again to my lady, to let her know there was no horse to go, but one that wanted a shoe. "Go to Sir Condy then; I know nothing at all about the horses," said my lady; "why do you plague me with these things?" How it was settled I really forget, but to the best of my remembrance, the boy was sent down to my son Jason's to borrow candles for the night. Another time in the winter, and on a desperate cold day, there was no turf in for the parlour and above stairs, and scarce enough for the cook in the kitchen; the little *gossoon* 11 was sent off to the neighbours, to see and beg or borrow some, but none could he bring back with him for love or money; so as needs must, we were forced to trouble Sir Condy—"Well, and if there's no turf to be had in the town or country, why what signifies talking any more about it; can't ye go and cut down a tree?" "Which tree, please your honour?" I made bold to say. "Any tree at all that's good to burn," said Sir Condy; "send off smart and get one down, and the fires lighted, before my lady gets up to breakfast, or the house will be too hot to hold us." He was always very considerate in all things about my lady, and she wanted for nothing whilst he had it to give. Well, when things were tight with them about this time, my son Jason put in a word again about the lodge, and made a genteel offer to lay down the purchase-money, to relieve Sir Condy's distresses. Now Sir Condy had it from the best authority, that there were two writs come down to the sheriff against his person, and the sheriff, as ill luck would have it, was no friend of his, and talked how he must do his duty, and how he would do it, if it was against the first man in the country, or even his own brother; let alone one who had voted against him at the last election, as Sir Condy had done. So Sir Condy was fain to take the purchase-money of the lodge from my son Jason to settle matters; and sure enough it was a good bargain for both parties, for my son bought the fee-simple of a good house for him and his heirs for ever, for little or nothing, and by selling of it for that same, my master saved himself from a gaol. Every way it turned out fortunate for Sir Condy; for before the money was all gone there came a general election, and he being so well beloved in the county, and one of the oldest families, no one had a better right to stand candidate for the vacancy; and he was called upon by all his friends, and the whole county I may say, to declare himself against the old member, who had little thought of a contest. My master did not relish the thoughts of a troublesome canvass, and all the ill-will he might bring upon himself by disturbing the peace of the county, besides the expense, which was no trifle; but all his friends called upon one another to subscribe, and they formed themselves into a committee, and wrote all his circular letters for him, and engaged all his agents, and did all the business unknown to him; and he was well pleased that it should be so at last, and my lady herself was very sanguine about the election; and there was open house kept night and day at Castle Rackrent, and I thought I never saw my lady look so well in her life as she did at that time: there were grand dinners, and all the gentlemen drinking success to Sir Condy till they were carried off; and then dances and balls, and the ladies all finishing with a raking pot of tea in the morning.[Z] Indeed it was well the company made it their choice to sit up all nights, for there were not half beds enough for the sights of people that were in it, though there were shake-downs in the drawing-room always made up before sunrise for those that liked it. For my part, when I saw the doings that were going on, and the loads of claret that went down the throats of them that had no right to be asking for it, and the sights of meat that went up to table and never came down, besides what was carried off to one or t'other below stairs, I couldn't but pity my poor master, who was to pay for all; but I said nothing, for fear of gaining myself ill-will. The day of election will come some time or other, says I to myself, and all will be over; and so it did, and a glorious day it was as any I ever had the happiness to see. "Huzza! huzza! Sir Condy Rackrent for ever!" was the first thing I hears in the morning, and the same and nothing else all day, and not a soul sober only just when polling, enough to give their votes as became 'em, and to stand the browbeating of the lawyers, who came tight enough upon us; and many of our freeholders were knocked off, having never a freehold that they could safely swear to, and Sir Condy was not willing to have any man perjure himself for his sake, as was done on the other side, God knows; but no matter for that. Some of our friends were dumb-founded, by the lawyers asking them: Had they ever been upon the ground where their free-holds lay? Now, Sir Condy being tender of the consciences of them that had not been on the ground, and so could not swear to a freehold when cross-examined by them lawyers, sent out for a couple of cleaves-full of the sods of his farm of Gulteeshinnagh12 and as soon as the sods came into town, he set each man upon his sod, and so then, ever after, you know, they could fairly swear they had been upon the ground.13 We gained the day by this piece of honesty.[A2] I thought I should have died in the streets for joy when I seed my poor master chaired, and he bareheaded, and it raining as hard as it could pour; but all the crowds following him up and down, and he bowing and shaking hands with the whole town. "Is that Sir Condy Rackrent in the chair?" says a stranger man in the crowd. "The same," says I; "who else should it he? God bless him!" "And I take it, then, you belong to him?" says he. "Not at all," says I; "but I live under him, and have done so these two hundred years and upwards, me and mine." "It's lucky for you, then," rejoins he, "that he is where he is; for was he any where else but in the chair, this minute he'd be in a worse place; for I was sent down on purpose to put him up,14 and here's my order for so doing in my pocket." It was a writ that villain the wine merchant had marked against my poor master for some hundreds of an old debt, which it was a shame to be talking of at such a time as this. "Put it in your pocket again, and think no more of it any ways for seven years to come, my honest friend," says I; "he's a member of parliament now, praised be God, and such as you can't touch him: and if you'll take a fool's advice, I'd have you keep out of the way this day, or you'll run a good chance of getting your deserts amongst my master's friends, unless you choose to drink his health like every body else." "I've no objection to that in life," said he; so we went into one of the public houses kept open for my master; and we had a great deal of talk about this thing and that. "And how is it," says he, "your master keeps on so well upon his legs? I heard say he was off Holantide twelvemonth past." "Never was better or heartier in his life," said I. "It's not that I'm after speaking of," said he; "but there was a great report of his being ruined." "No matter," says I, "the sheriffs two years running were his particular friends, and the sub-sheriffs were both of them gentlemen, and were properly spoken to; and so the writs lay snug with them, and they, as I understand by my son Jason the custom in them cases is, returned the writs as they came to them to those that sent 'em; much good may it do them! with a word in Latin, that no such person as Sir Condy Rackrent, Bart., was to be found in those parts." "Oh, I understand all those ways better, no offence, than you," says he, laughing, and at the same time filling his glass to my master's good health, which convinced me he was a warm friend in his heart after all, though appearances were a little suspicious or so at first. "To be sure," says he, still cutting his joke, "when a man's over head and shoulders in debt, he may live the faster for it, and the better, if he goes the right way about it; or else how is it so many live on so well, as we see every day, after they are ruined?" "How is it," says I, being a little merry at the time; "how is it but just as you see the ducks in the chicken-yard, just after their heads are cut off by the cook, running round and round faster than when alive?" At which conceit he fell a laughing, and remarked he had never had the happiness yet to see the chicken-yard at Castle Rackrent. "It won't be long so, I hope," says I; "you'll be kindly welcome there, as every body is made by my master: there is not a freer spoken gentleman, or a better beloved, high or low, in all Ireland." And of what passed after this I'm not sensible, for we drank Sir Condy's good health and the downfall of his enemies till we could stand no longer ourselves. And little did I think at the time, or till long after, how I was harbouring my poor master's greatest of enemies myself. This fellow had the impudence, after coming to see the chicken-yard, to get me to introduce him to my son Jason; little more than the man that never was born did I guess at his meaning by this visit: he gets him a correct list fairly drawn out from my son Jason of all my master's debts, and goes straight round to the creditors and buys them all up, which he did easy enough, seeing the half of them never expected to see their money out of Sir Condy's hands. Then, when this base-minded limb of the law, as I afterward detected him in being, grew to be sole creditor over all, he takes him out a custodiam on all the denominations and sub-denominations, and every carton[B2] and half carton upon the estate; and not content with that, must have an execution against the master's goods and down to the furniture, though little worth, of Castle Rackrent itself. But this is a part of my story I'm not come to yet, and its bad to be forestalling: ill news flies fast enough all the world over.

To go back to the day of the election, which I never think of but with pleasure and tears of gratitude for those good times; after the election was quite and clean over, there comes shoals of people from all parts, claiming to have obliged my master with their votes, and putting him in mind of promises which he could never remember himself to have made: one was to have a freehold for each of his four sons; another was to have a renewal of a lease; another an abatement; one came to be paid ten guineas for a pair of silver buckles sold my master on the hustings, which turned out to be no better than copper gilt; another had a long bill for oats, the half of which never went into the granary to my certain knowledge, and the other half were not fit for the cattle to touch; but the bargain was made the week before the election, and the coach and saddle horses were got into order for the day, besides a vote fairly got by them oats; so no more reasoning on that head; but then there was no end to them that were telling Sir Condy he had engaged to make their sons excisemen, or high constables, or the like; and as for them that had bills to give in for liquor, and beds, and straw, and ribands, and horses, and postchaises for the gentlemen freeholders that came from all parts and other counties to vote for my master, and were not, to be sure, to be at any charges, there was no standing against all these; and, worse than all, the gentlemen of my master's committee, who managed all for him, and talked how they'd bring him in without costing him a penny, and subscribed by hundreds very genteelly, forgot to pay their subscriptions, and had laid out in agents' and lawyers' fees and secret service money the Lord knows how much; and my master could never ask one of them for their subscription you are sensible, nor for the price of a fine horse he had sold one of them; so it all was left at his door. He could never, God bless him again! I say, bring himself to ask a gentleman for money, despising such sort of conversation himself; but others, who were not gentlemen born, behaved very uncivil in pressing him at this very time, and all he could do to content 'em all was to take himself out of the way as fast as possible to Dublin, where my lady had taken a house fitting for him as a member of parliament, to attend his duty in there all the winter. I was very lonely when the whole family was gone, and all the things they had ordered to go, and forgot, sent after them by the car. There was then a great silence in Castle Rackrent, and I went moping from room to room, hearing the doors clap for want of right locks, and the wind through the broken windows, that the glazier never would come to mend, and the rain coming through the roof and best ceilings all over the house for want of the slater, whose bill was not paid, besides our having no slates or shingles for that part of the old building which was shingled and burnt when the chimney took fire, and had been open to the weather ever since. I took myself to the servants' hall in the evening to smoke my pipe as usual, but missed the bit of talk we used to have there sadly, and ever after was content to stay in the kitchen and boil my little potatoes,15 and put up my bed there; and every post-day I looked in the newspaper, but no news of my master in the House; he never spoke good or bad; but as the butler wrote down word to my son Jason, was very ill used by the government about a place that was promised him and never given, after his supporting them against his conscience very honourably, and being greatly abused for it, which hurt him greatly, he having the name of a great patriot in the country before. The house and living in Dublin too were not to be had for nothing, and my son Jason said, "Sir Condy must soon be looking out for a new agent, for I've done my part, and can do no more:—if my lady had the bank of Ireland to spend, it would go all in one winter, and Sir Condy would never gainsay her, though he does not care the rind of a lemon for her all the while."

Now I could not bear to hear Jason giving out after this manner against the family, and twenty people standing by in the street. Ever since he had lived at the lodge of his own, he looked down, howsomever, upon poor old Thady, and was grown quite a great gentleman, and had none of his relations near him: no wonder he was no kinder to poor Sir Condy than to his own kith or kin.16 In the spring it was the villain that got the list of the debts from him brought down the custodiam, Sir Condy still attending his duty in parliament, and I could scarcely believe my own old eyes, or the spectacles with which I read it, when I was shown my son Jason's name joined in the custodiam; but he told me it was only for form's sake, and to make things easier than if all the land was under the power of a total stranger. Well, I did not know what to think; it was hard to be talking ill of my own, and I could not but grieve for my poor master's fine estate, all torn by these vultures of the law; so I said nothing, but just looked on to see how it would all end.

It was not till the month of June that he and my lady came down to the country. My master was pleased to take me aside with him to the brewhouse that same evening, to complain to me of my son and other matters, in which he said he was confident I had neither art nor part; he said a great deal more to me, to whom he had been fond to talk ever since he was my white-headed boy, before he came to the estate; and all that he said about poor Judy I can never forget, but scorn to repeat. He did not say an unkind word of my lady, but wondered, as well he might, her relations would do nothing for him or her, and they in all this great distress. He did not take any thing long to heart, let it be as it would, and had no more malice, or thought of the like in him, than a child that can't speak; this night it was all out of his head before he went to his bed. He took his jug of whiskey punch—my lady was grown quite easy about the whiskey punch by this time, and so I did suppose all was going on right betwixt them, till I learnt the truth through Mrs. Jane, who talked over their affairs to the housekeeper, and I within hearing. The night my master came home thinking of nothing at all but just making merry, he drank his bumper toast "to the deserts of that old curmudgeon my father-in-law, and all enemies at Mount Juliet's Town." Now my lady was no longer in the mind she formerly was, and did no ways relish hearing her own friends abused in her presence, she said, "Then why don't they show themselves your friends," said my master, "and oblige me with the loan of the money I condescended, by your advice, my dear, to ask? It's now three posts since I sent off my letter, desiring in the postscript a speedy answer by the return of the post, and no account at all from them yet." "I expect they'll write to *me* next post," says my lady, and that was all that passed then; but it was easy from this to guess there was a coolness betwixt them, and with good cause.

The next morning, being post-day, I sent off the gossoon early to the post-office, to see was there any letter likely to set matters to rights, and he brought back one with the proper post-mark upon it, sure enough, and I had no time to examine, or make any conjecture more about it, for into the servants' hall pops Mrs. Jane with a blue bandbox in her hand, quite entirely mad. "Dear ma'am, and what's the matter?" says I. "Matter enough," says she; "don't you see my bandbox is wet through, and my best bonnet here spoiled, besides my lady's, and all by the rain coming in through that gallery window, that you might have got mended, if you'd had any sense, Thady, all the time we were in town in the winter?" "Sure, I could not get the glazier, ma'am," says I. "You might have stopped it up any how," says she. "So I did, ma'am, to the best of my ability; one of the panes with the old pillow-case, and the other with a piece of the old stage green curtain; sure I was as careful as possible all the time you were away, and not a drop of rain came in at that window of all the windows in the house, all winter, ma'am, when under my care; and now the family's come home, and it's summer time, I never thought no more about it, to be sure; but dear, it's a pity to think of your bonnet, ma'am; but here's what will please you, ma'am, a letter from Mount Juliet's Town for my lady." With that she snatches it from me without a word more, and runs up the back stairs to my mistress; I follows with a slate to make up the window. This window was in the long passage, or gallery, as my lady gave out orders to have it called, in the gallery leading to my master's bedchamber and hers. And when I went up with the slate, the door having no lock, and the bolt spoilt, was a-jar after Mrs. Jane, and as I was busy with the window, I heard all that was saying within.

"Well, what's in your letter, Bella, my dear?" says he: "you're a long time spelling it over." "Won't you shave this morning, Sir Condy?" says she, and put the letter into her pocket. "I shaved the day before yesterday," says he, "my dear, and that's not what I'm thinking of now; but any thing to oblige you, and to have peace and quietness, my dear"—and presently I had the glimpse of him at the cracked glass over the chimney-piece, standing up shaving himself to please my lady. But she took no notice, but went on reading her book, and Mrs. Jane doing her hair behind. "What is it you're reading there, my dear?—phoo, I've cut myself with this razor; the man's a cheat that sold it me, but I have not paid him for it yet: what is it you're reading there? did you hear me asking you, my dear?" "The Sorrows of Werter," replies my lady, as well as I could hear. "I think more of the sorrows of Sir Condy," says my master, joking like. "What news from Mount Juliet's Town?" "No news," says she, "but the old story over again, my friends all reproaching me still for what I can't help now." "Is it for marrying me?" said my master, still shaving: "what signifies, as you say, talking of that, when it can't be help'd now?"

With that she heaved a great sigh, that I heard plain enough in the passage. "And did not you use me basely, Sir Condy," says she, "not to tell me you were ruined before I married you?" "Tell you, my dear," said he; "did you ever ask me one word about it? and had not you friends enough of your own, that were telling you nothing else from morning to night, if you'd have listened to them slanders?" "No slanders, nor are my friends slanderers; and I can't bear to hear them treated with disrespect as I do," says my lady, and took out her pocket handkerchief; "they are the best of friends; and if I had taken their advice—. But my father was wrong to lock me up, I own; that was the only unkind thing I can charge him with; for if he had not locked me up, I should never have had a serious thought of running away as I did." "Well, my dear," said my master, "don't cry and make yourself uneasy about it now, when it's all over, and you have the man of your own choice, in spite of 'em all." "I was too young, I know, to make a choice at the time you ran away with me, I'm sure," says my lady, and another sigh, which made my master, half shaved as he was, turn round upon her in surprise. "Why, Bell," says he, "you can't deny what you know as well as I do, that it was at your own particular desire, and that twice under your own hand and seal expressed, that I should carry you off as I did to Scotland, and marry you there." "Well, say no more about it, Sir Condy," said my lady, pettish like—"I was a child then, you know." "And as far as I know, you're little better now, my dear Bella, to be talking in this manner to your husband's *face*; but I won't take it ill of you, for I know it's something in that letter you put into your pocket just now, that has set you against me all on a sudden, and imposed upon your understanding." "It's not so very easy as you think it, Sir Condy, to impose upon *my* understanding," said my lady. "My dear," says he, "I have, and with reason, the best opinion of your understanding of any man now breathing; and you know I have never set my own in competition with it till now, my dear Bella," says he, taking her hand from her book as kind as could be—"till now, when I have the great advantage of being quite cool, and you not; so don't believe one word your friends say against your own Sir Condy, and lend me the letter out of your pocket, till I see what it is they can have to say." "Take it then," says she, "and as you are quite cool, I hope it is a proper time to request you'll allow me to comply with the wishes of all my own friends, and return to live with my father and family, during the remainder of my wretched existence, at Mount Juliet's Town."

At this, my poor master fell back a few paces, like one that had been shot. "You're not serious, Bella," says he; "and could you find it in your heart to leave me this way in the very middle of my distresses, all alone?" But recollecting himself after his first surprise, and a moment's time for reflection, he said, with a great deal of consideration for my lady, "Well, Bella, my dear, I believe you are right; for what could you do at Castle Rackrent, and an execution against the goods coming down, and the furniture to be canted, and an auction in the house all next week? so you have my full consent to go, since that is your desire, only you must not think of my accompanying you, which I could not in honour do upon the terms I always have been, since our marriage, with your friends; besides, I have business to transact at home; so in the mean time, if we are to have any breakfast this morning, let us go down and have it for the last time in peace and comfort, Bella."

Then as I heard my master coming to the passage door, I finished fastening up my slate against the broken pane; and when he came out, I wiped down the window seat with my wig,17 and bade him a good morrow as kindly as I could, seeing he was in trouble, though he strove and thought to hide it from me. "This window is all racked and tattered," says I, "and it's what I'm striving to mend." "It *is* all racked and tattered, plain enough," says he, "and never mind mending it, honest old Thady," says he; "it will do well enough for you and I, and that's all the company we shall have left in the house by-and-by." "I'm sorry to see your honour so low this morning," says I; "but you'll be better after taking your breakfast." "Step down to the servants' hall," said he, "and bring me up the pen and ink into the parlour, and get a sheet of paper from Mrs. Jane, for I have business that can't brook to be delayed; and come into the parlour with the pen and ink yourself, Thady, for I must have you to witness my signing a paper I have to execute in a hurry." Well, while I was getting of the pen and ink-horn, and the sheet of paper, I ransacked my brains to think what could be the papers my poor master could have to execute in such a hurry, he that never thought of such a thing as doing business afore breakfast, in the whole course of his life, for any man living; but this was for my lady, as I afterwards found, and the more genteel of him after all her treatment.

I was just witnessing the paper that he had scrawled over, and was shaking the ink out of my pen upon the carpet, when my lady came in to breakfast, and she started as if it had been a ghost! as well she might, when she saw Sir Condy writing at this unseasonable hour. "That will do very well, Thady," says he to me, and took the paper I had signed to, without knowing what upon the earth it might be, out of my hands, and walked, folding it up, to my lady.

"You are concerned in this, my Lady Rackrent," said he, putting it into her hands; "and I beg you'll keep this memorandum safe, and show it to your friends the first thing you do when you get home; but put it in your pocket now, my dear, and let us eat our breakfast, in God's name." "What is all this?" said my lady, opening the paper in great curiosity. "It's only a bit of a memorandum of what I think becomes me to do whenever I am able," says my master; "you know my situation, tied hand and foot at the present time being, but that can't last always, and when I'm dead and gone, the land will be to the good, Thady, you know; and take notice, it's my intention your lady should have a clear five hundred a year jointure off the estate afore any of my debts are paid." "Oh, please your honour," says I, "I can't expect to live to see that time, being now upwards of fourscore years of age, and you a young man, and likely to continue so, by the help of God." I was vexed to see my lady so insensible too, for all she said was, "This is very genteel of you, Sir Condy. You need not wait any longer, Thady;" so I just picked up the pen and ink that had tumbled on the floor, and heard my master finish with saying, "You behaved very genteel to me, my dear, when you threw all the little you had in your own power along with yourself into my hands; and as I don't deny but what you may have had some things to complain of," — to be sure he was thinking then of Judy, or of the whiskey punch, one or t'other, or both, — "and as I don't deny but you may have had something to complain of, my dear, it is but fair you should have something in the form of compensation to look forward to agreeably in future; besides, it's an act of justice to myself, that none of your friends, my dear, may ever have it to say against me, I married for money, and not for love." "That is the last thing I should ever have thought of saying of you, Sir Condy," said my lady, looking very gracious. "Then, my dear," said Sir Condy, "we shall part as good friends as we met; so all's right."

I was greatly rejoiced to hear this, and went out of the parlour to report it all to the kitchen. The next morning my lady and Mrs. Jane set out for Mount Juliet's Town in the jaunting car: many wondered at my lady's choosing to go away, considering all things, upon the jaunting car, as if it was only a party of pleasure; but they did not know, till I told them, that the coach was all broke in the journey down, and no other vehicle but the car to be had; besides, my lady's friends were to send their coach to meet her at the cross roads; so it was all done very proper.

My poor master was in great trouble after my lady left us. The execution came down; and every thing at Castle Rackrent was seized by the gripers, and my son Jason, to his shame be it spoken, amongst them. I wondered, for the life of me, how he could harden himself to do it; but then he had been studying the law, and had made himself Attorney Quirk; so he brought down at once a heap of accounts upon my master's head. To cash lent, and to ditto, and to ditto, and to ditto, and oats, and bills paid at the milliner's and linen-draper's, and many dresses for the fancy balls in Dublin for my lady, and all the bills to the workmen and tradesmen for the scenery of the theatre, and the chandler's and grocer's bills, and tailor's, besides butcher's and baker's, and worse than all, the old one of that base wine merchant's, that wanted to arrest my poor master for the amount on the election day, for which amount Sir Condy afterwards passed his note of hand, bearing lawful interest from the date thereof; and the interest and compound interest was now mounted to a terrible deal on many other notes and bonds for money borrowed, and there was besides hush money to the sub-sheriffs, and sheets upon sheets of old and new attorneys' bills, with heavy balances, *as per former account furnished*, brought forward with interest thereon; then there was a powerful deal due to the crown for sixteen years' arrear of quit-rent of the town-lands of Carrickshaughlin, with driver's fees, and a compliment to the receiver every year for letting the quit-rent run on to oblige Sir Condy, and Sir Kit afore him. Then there were bills for spirits and ribands at the election time, and the gentlemen of the committee's accounts unsettled, and their subscription never gathered; and there were cows to be paid for, with the smith and farrier's bills to be set against the rent of the demesne, with calf and hay money; then there was all the servants' wages, since I don't know when, coming due to them, and sums advanced for them by my son Jason for clothes, and boots, and whips, and odd moneys for sundries expended by them in journeys to town and elsewhere, and pocket-money for the master continually, and messengers and postage before his being a parliament man; I can't myself tell you what besides; but this I know, that when the evening came on the which Sir Condy had appointed to settle all with my son Jason, and when he comes into the parlour, and sees the sight of bills and load of papers all gathered on the great dining-table for him, he puts his hands before both his eyes, and cried out, "Merciful Jasus! what is it I see before me?" Then I sets an arm-chair at the table for him, and with a deal of difficulty he sits him down, and my son Jason hands him over the pen and ink to sign to this man's bill and t'other man's bill, all which he did without making the least objections. Indeed, to give him his due, I never *seen* a man more fair and honest, and easy in all his dealings, from first to last, as Sir Condy, or more willing to pay every man his own as far as he was able, which is as much as any one can do. "Well," says he, joking like with Jason, "I wish we could settle it all with a stroke of my grey goose quill. What signifies making me wade through all this ocean of papers here; can't you now, who understand drawing out an account, debtor and creditor, just sit down here at the corner of the table and get it done out for me, that I may have a clear view of the balance, which is all I need be talking about, you know?" "Very true, Sir Condy; nobody understands business better than yourself," says Jason. "So I've a right to do, being born and bred to the bar," says Sir Condy. "Thady, do step out and see are they bringing in the things for the punch, for we've just done all we have to do for this evening." I goes out accordingly, and when I came back, Jason was pointing to the balance, which was a terrible sight to my poor master. "Pooh! pooh! pooh!" says he, "here's so many noughts they dazzle my eyes, so they do, and put me in mind of all I suffered, larning of my numeration table, when I was a boy at the day-school along with you, Jason—units, tens, hundreds, tens of hundreds. Is the punch ready, Thady?" says he, seeing me. "Immediately; the boy has the jug in his hand; it's coming up stairs, please your honour, as fast as possible," says I, for I saw his honour was tired out of his life; but Jason, very short and cruel, cuts me off with—"Don't be talking of punch yet a while; it's no time for punch yet a bit—units, tens, hundreds," goes he on, counting over the master's shoulder, units, tens, hundreds, thousands. "A-a-ah! hold your hand," cries my master; "where in this wide world am I to find hundreds, or units itself, let alone thousands?" "The balance has been running on too long," says Jason, sticking to him as I could not have done at the time, if you'd have given both the Indies and Cork to boot; "the balance has been running on too long, and I'm distressed myself on your account, Sir Condy, for money, and the thing must be settled now on the spot, and the balance cleared off," says Jason. "I'll thank you if you'll only show me how," says Sir Condy. "There's but one way," says Jason, "and that's ready enough: when there's no cash, what can a gentleman do, but go to the land?" "How can you go to the land, and it under custodiam to yourself already," says Sir Condy, "and another custodiam hanging over it? and no one at all can touch it, you know, but the custodees." "Sure, can't you sell, though at a loss? sure you can sell, and I've a purchaser ready for you," says Jason. "Have ye so?" said Sir Condy; "that's a great point gained; but there's a thing now beyond all, that perhaps you don't know yet, barring Thady has let you into the secret." "Sarrah bit of a secret, or any thing at all of the kind, has he learned from me these fifteen weeks come St. John's eve," says I; "for we have scarce been upon speaking terms of late: but what is it your honour means of a secret?" "Why, the secret of the little keepsake I gave my Lady Rackrent the morning she left us, that she might not go back empty-handed to her friends." "My Lady Rackrent, I'm sure, has baubles and keepsakes enough, as those bills on the table will show," says Jason; "but whatever it is," says he, taking up his pen, "we must add it to the balance, for to be sure it can't be paid for." "No, nor can't till after my decease," said Sir Condy; "that's one good thing." Then colouring up a good deal, he tells Jason of the memorandum of the five hundred a-year jointure he had settled upon my lady; at which Jason was indeed mad, and said a great deal in very high words, that it was using a gentleman, who had the management of his affairs, and was moreover his principal creditor, extremely ill, to do such a thing without consulting him, and against his knowledge and consent. To all which Sir Condy had nothing to reply, but that upon his conscience, it was in a hurry and without a moment's thought on his part, and he was very sorry for it, but if it was to do over again he would do the same; and he appealed to me, and I was ready to give my evidence, if that would do, to the truth of all he said.

So Jason with much ado was brought to agree to a compromise. "The purchaser that I have ready," says he, "will be much displeased, to be sure, at the incumbrance on the land, but I must see and manage him; here's a deed ready drawn up; we have nothing to do but to put in the consideration money and our names to it." "And how much am I going to sell?—the lands of O'Shaughlin's Town, and the lands of Gruneaghoolaghan, and the lands of Crookagnawaturgh," says he, just reading to himself,—"and—oh, murder, Jason! sure you won't put this in—the castle, stable, and appurtenances of Castle Rackrent." "Oh, murder!" says I, clapping my hands, "this is too bad, Jason." "Why so?" said Jason, "when it's all, and a great deal more to the back of it, lawfully mine, was I to push for it." "Look at him," says I, pointing to Sir Condy, who was just leaning back in his arm-chair, with his arms falling beside him like one stupified; "is it you, Jason, that can stand in his presence, and recollect all he has been to us, and all we have been to him, and yet use him so at the last?" "Who will you find to use him better, I ask you?" said Jason; "if he can get a better purchaser, I'm content; I only offer to purchase, to make things easy, and oblige him: though I don't see what compliment I am under, if you come to that; I have never had, asked, or charged more than sixpence in the pound, receiver's fees; and where would he have got an agent for a penny less?" "Oh, Jason! Jason! how will you stand to this in the face of the county and all who know you?" says I; "and what will people think and say, when they see you living here in Castle Rackrent, and the lawful owner turned out of the seat of his ancestors, without a cabin to put his head into, or so much as a potatoe to eat?" Jason, whilst I was saying this, and a great deal more, made me signs, and winks, and frowns; but I took no heed; for I was grieved and sick at heart for my poor master, and couldn't but speak.

"Here's the punch," says Jason, for the door opened; "here's the punch!" Hearing that, my master starts up in his chair, and recollects himself, and Jason uncorks the whiskey. "Set down the jug here," says he, making room for it beside the papers opposite to Sir Condy, but still not stirring the deed that was to make over all. Well, I was in great hopes he had some touch of mercy about him when I saw him making the punch, and my master took a glass; but Jason put it back as he was going to fill again, saying, "No, Sir Condy, it sha'n't be said of me, I got your signature to this deed when you were half-seas over: you know your name and hand-writing in that condition would not, if brought before the courts, benefit me a straw; wherefore let us settle all before we go deeper into the punch-bowl." "Settle all as you will," said Sir Condy, clapping his hands to his ears: "but let me hear no more; I'm bothered to death this night." "You've only to sign," said Jason, putting the pen to him. "Take all, and be content," said my master. So he signed; and the man who brought in the punch witnessed it, for I was not able, but crying like a child; and besides, Jason said, which I was glad of, that I was no fit witness, being so old and doting. It was so bad with me, I could not taste a drop of the punch itself, though my master himself, God bless him! in the midst of his trouble, poured out a glass for me, and brought it up to my lips. "Not a drop; I thank your honour's honour as much as if I took it, though," and I just set down the glass as it was, and went out, and when I got to the street-door, the neighbour's childer, who were playing at marbles there, seeing me in great trouble, left their play, and gathered about me to know what ailed me; and I told them all, for it was a great relief to me to speak to these poor childer, that seemed to have some natural feeling left in them: and when they were made sensible that Sir Condy was going to leave Castle Rackrent for good and all, they set up a whillalu that could be heard to the farthest end of the street; and one fine boy he was, that my master had given an apple to that morning, cried the loudest, but they all were the same sorry, for Sir Condy was greatly beloved amongst the childer, for letting them go a-nutting in the demesne, without saying a word to them, though my lady objected to them. The people in the town, who were the most of them standing at their doors, hearing the childer cry, would know the reason of it; and when the report was made known, the people one and all gathered in great anger against my son Jason, and terror at the notion of his coming to be landlord over them, and they cried, "No Jason! no Jason! Sir Condy! Sir Condy! Sir Condy Rackrent for ever!" and the mob grew so great and so loud, I was frightened, and made my way back to the house to warn my son to make his escape, or hide himself for fear of the consequences. Jason would not believe me till they came all round the house, and to the windows with great shouts: then he grew quite pale, and asked Sir Condy what had he best do? "I'll tell you what you'd best do," said Sir Condy, who was laughing to see his fright; "finish your glass first, then let's go to the window and show ourselves, and I'll tell 'em, or you shall, if you please, that I'm going to the Lodge for change of air for my health, and by my own desire, for the rest of my days." "Do so," said

Jason, who never meant it should have been so, but could not refuse him the Lodge at this unseasonable time. Accordingly Sir Condy threw up the sash, and explained matters, and thanked all his friends, and bid 'em look in at the punch-bowl, and observe that Jason and he had been sitting over it very good friends; so the mob was content, and he sent 'em out some whiskey to drink his health, and that was the last time his honour's health was ever drunk at Castle Rackrent.

The very next day, being too proud, as he said to me, to stay an hour longer in a house that did not belong to him, he sets off to the Lodge, and I along with him not many hours after. And there was great bemoaning through all O'Shaughlin's Town, which I stayed to witness, and gave my poor master a full account of when I got to the Lodge. He was very low, and in his bed, when I got there, and complained of a great pain about his heart, but I guessed it was only trouble, and all the business, let alone vexation, he had gone through of late; and knowing the nature of him from a boy, I took my pipe, and, whilst smoking it by the chimney, began telling him how he was beloved and regretted in the county, and it did him a deal of good to hear it. "Your honour has a great many friends yet, that you don't know of, rich and poor, in the county," says I; "for as I was coming along the road, I met two gentlemen in their own carriages, who asked after you, knowing me, and wanted to know where you was and all about you, and even how old I was: think of that." Then he wakened out of his doze, and began questioning me who the gentlemen were. And the next morning it came into my head to go, unknown to any body, with my master's compliments, round to many of the gentlemen's houses, where he and my lady used to visit, and people that I knew were his great friends, and would go to Cork to serve him any day in the year, and I made bold to try to borrow a trifle of cash from them. They all treated me very civil for the most part, and asked a great many questions very kind about my lady, and Sir Condy, and all the family, and were greatly surprised to learn from me Castle Rackrent was sold, and my master at the Lodge for health; and they all pitied him greatly, and he had their good wishes, if that would do, but money was a thing they unfortunately had not any of them at this time to spare. I had my journey for my pains, and I, not used to walking, nor supple as formerly, was greatly tired, but had the satisfaction of telling my master, when I got to the Lodge, all the civil things said by high and low.

"Thady," says he, "all you've been telling me brings a strange thought into my head: I've a notion I shall not be long for this world any how, and I've a great fancy to see my own funeral afore I die." I was greatly shocked, at the first speaking, to hear him speak so light about his funeral, and he, to all appearance, in good health, but recollecting myself, answered, "To be sure, it would be as fine a sight as one could see, I dared to say, and one I should be proud to witness, and I did not doubt his honour's would be as great a funeral as ever Sir Patrick O'Shaughlin's was, and such a one as that had never been known in the county afore or since." But I never thought he was in earnest about seeing his own funeral himself, till the next day he returns to it again. "Thady," says he, "as far as the wake18 goes, sure I might without any great trouble have the satisfaction of seeing a bit of my own funeral." "Well, since your honour's honour's so bent upon it," says I, not willing to cross him, and he in trouble, "we must see what we can do." So he fell into a sort of a sham disorder, which was easy done, as he kept his bed, and no one to see him; and I got my shister, who was an old woman very handy about the sick, and very skilful, to come up to the Lodge to nurse him; and we gave out, she knowing no better, that he was just at his latter end, and it answered beyond any thing; and there was a great throng of people, men, women, and childer, and there being only two rooms at the Lodge, except what was locked up full of Jason's furniture and things, the house was soon as full and fuller than it could hold, and the heat, and smoke, and noise wonderful great; and standing amongst them that were near the bed, but not thinking at all of the dead, I was started by the sound of my master's voice from under the great coats that had been thrown all at top, and I went close up, no one noticing. "Thady," says he, "I've had enough of this; I'm smothering, and can't hear a word of all they're saying of the deceased." "God bless you, and lie still and quiet," says I, "a bit longer, for my shister's afraid of ghosts, and would die on the spot with fright, was she to see you come to life all on a sudden this way without the least preparation." So he lays him still, though well nigh stifled, and I made all haste to tell the secret of the joke, whispering to one and t'other, and there was a great surprise, but not so great as we had laid out it would. "And aren't we to have the pipes and tobacco, after coming so far to-night?" said some; but they were all well enough pleased when his honour got up to drink with them, and sent for more spirits from a shebean-house,19 where they very civilly let him have it upon credit. So the night passed off very merrily, but, to my mind, Sir Condy was rather upon the sad order in the midst of it all, not finding there had been such a great talk about himself after his death as he had always expected to hear.

The next morning when the house was cleared of them, and none but my shister and myself left in the kitchen with Sir Condy, one opens the door, and walks in, and who should it be but Judy M'Quirk herself! I forgot to notice, that she had been married long since, whilst young Captain Moneygawl lived at the Lodge, to the captain's huntsman, who after a whilst listed and left her, and was killed in the wars. Poor Judy fell off greatly in her good looks after her being married a year or two; and being smoke-dried in the cabin, and neglecting herself like, it was hard for Sir Condy himself to know her again till she spoke; but when she says, "It's Judy M'Quirk, please your honour, don't you remember her?" "Oh, Judy, is it you?" says his honour; "yes, sure, I remember you very well; but you're greatly altered, Judy." "Sure it's time for me," says she; "and I think your honour, since I *seen* you last,—but that's a great while ago,—is altered too." "And with reason, Judy," says Sir Condy, fetching a sort of a sigh; "but how's this, Judy?" he goes on; "I take it a little amiss of you, that you were not at my wake last night." "Ah, don't be being jealous of that," says she; "I didn't hear a sentence of your honour's wake till it was all over, or it would have gone hard with me but I would have been at it sure; but I was forced to go ten miles up the country three days ago to a wedding of a relation of my own's, and didn't get home till after the wake was over; but," says she, "it won't be so, I hope, the next time,20 please your honour." "That we shall see, Judy," says his honour, "and may be sooner than you think for, for I've been very unwell this while past, and don't reckon any way I'm long for this world." At this, Judy takes up the corner of her apron, and puts it first to one eye and then to t'other, being to all appearance in great trouble; and my shister put in her word, and bid his honour have a good heart, for she was sure it was only the gout that Sir Patrick used to have flying about him, and he ought to drink a glass or a bottle extraordinary to keep it out of his stomach; and he promised to take her advice, and sent out for more spirits immediately; and Judy made a sign to me, and I went over to the door to her, and she said, "I wonder to see Sir Condy so low! has he heard the news?" "What news?" says I. "Didn't ye hear it, then?" says she; "my Lady Rackrent that was is kilt[D2] and lying for dead, and I don't doubt but it's all over with her by this time." "Mercy on us all," says I; "how was it?" "The jaunting car it was that ran away with her," says Judy. "I was coming home that same time from Biddy M'Guggin's marriage, and a great crowd of people too upon the road, coming from the fair of Crookaghnawaturgh, and I sees a jaunting car standing in the middle of the road, and with the two wheels off and all tattered. 'What's this?' says I. 'Didn't ye hear of it?' says they that were looking on; 'it's my Lady Rackrent's car, that was running away from her husband, and the horse took fright at a carrion that lay across the road, and so ran away with the jaunting car, and my Lady Rackrent and her maid screaming, and the horse ran with them against a car that was coming from the fair, with the boy asleep on it, and the lady's petticoat hanging out of the jaunting car caught, and she was dragged I can't tell you how far upon the road, and it all broken up with the stones just going to be pounded, and one of the road-makers, with his sledge-hammer in his hand, stops the horse at the last; but my Lady Rackrent was all kilt21 and smashed, and they lifted her into a cabin hard by, and the maid was found after, where she had been thrown, in the gripe of the ditch, her cap and bonnet all full of bog water, and they say my lady can't live any way.' Thady, pray now is it true what I'm told for sartain, that Sir Condy has made over all to your son Jason?" "All," says I. "All entirely?" says she again. "All entirely," says I. "Then," says she, "that's a great shame, but don't be telling Jason what I say." "And what is it you say?" cries Sir Condy, leaning over betwixt us, which made Judy start greatly. "I know the time when Judy M'Quirk would never have stayed so long talking at the door, and I in the house." "Oh!" says Judy, "for shame, Sir Condy; times are altered since then, and it's my Lady Rackrent you ought to be thinking of." "And why should I be thinking of her, that's not thinking of me now?" said Sir Condy. "No matter for that," says Judy, very properly; "it's time you should be thinking of her, if ever you mean to do it at all, for don't you know she's lying for death?" "My Lady Rackrent!" says Sir Condy, in a surprise; "why it's but two days since we parted, as you very well know, Thady, in her full health and spirits, and she and her maid along with her going to Mount Juliet's Town on her jaunting car." "She'll never ride no more on her jaunting car," said Judy, "for it has been the death of her, sure enough." "And is she dead then?" says his honour. "As good as dead, I hear," says Judy; "but there's Thady here has just learnt the whole truth of the story as I had it, and it is fitter he or any body else should be telling it you than I, Sir Condy: I must be going home to the childer." But he stops her, but rather from civility in him, as I could see very plainly, than any thing else, for Judy was, as his honour remarked at her first coming in, greatly changed, and little likely, as far as I could see—though she did not seem to be clear of it herself—little likely to be my Lady Rackrent now, should there be a second toss-up to be made. But I told him the whole story out of the face, just as Judy had told it to me, and he sent off a messenger with his compliments to Mount Juliet's Town that evening, to learn the truth of the report, and Judy bid the boy that was going call in at Tim M'Enerney's shop in O'Shaughlin's Town and buy her a new shawl. "Do so," said Sir Condy, "and tell Tim to take no money from you, for I must pay him for the shawl myself." At this my shister throws me over a look, and I says nothing, but turned the tobacco in my mouth, whilst Judy began making a many words about it, and saying how she could not be beholden for shawls to any gentleman. I left her there to consult with my shister, did she think there was any thing in it, and my shister thought I was blind to be asking her the question, and I thought my shister must see more into it than I did; and recollecting all past times and every thing, I changed my mind, and came over to her way of thinking, and we settled it that Judy was very like to be my Lady Rackrent after all, if a vacancy should have happened.

The next day, before his honour was up, somebody comes with a double knock at the door, and I was greatly surprised to see it was my son Jason. "Jason, is it you?" said I; "what brings you to the Lodge?" says I; "is it my Lady Rackrent? we know that already since yesterday." "May be so," says he, "but I must see Sir Condy about it." "You can't see him yet," says I; "sure he is not awake." "What then," says he, "can't he be wakened? and I standing at the door." "I'll not be disturbing his honour for you, Jason," says I; "many's the hour you've waited in your time, and been proud to do it, till his honour was at leisure to speak to you. His honour," says I, raising my voice, at which his honour wakens of his own accord, and calls to me from the room to know who it was I was speaking to. Jason made no more ceremony, but follows me into the room. "How are you, Sir Condy?" says he; "I'm happy to see you looking so well; I came up to know how you did to-day, and to see did you want for any thing at the Lodge." "Nothing at all, Mr. Jason, I thank you," says he; for his honour had his own share of pride, and did not choose, after all that had passed, to be beholden, I suppose, to my son; "but pray take a chair and be seated, Mr. Jason." Jason sat him down upon the chest, for chair there was none, and after he had set there some time, and a silence on all sides, "What news is there stirring in the country, Mr. Jason M'Quirk?" says Sir Condy, very easy, yet high like. "None that's news to you, Sir Condy, I hear," says Jason: "I am sorry to hear of my Lady Rackrent's accident." "I'm much obliged to you, and so is her ladyship, I'm sure," answered Sir Condy, still stiff; and there was another sort of a silence, which seemed to lie the heaviest on my son Jason.

"Sir Condy," says he at last, seeing Sir Condy disposing himself to go to sleep again, "Sir Condy, I dare say you recollect mentioning to me the little memorandum you gave to Lady Rackrent about the 500*l.* a-year jointure." "Very true," said Sir Condy; "it is all in my recollection." "But if my Lady Rackrent dies, there's an end of all jointure," says Jason. "Of course," says Sir Condy. "But it's not a matter of certainty that my Lady Rackrent won't recover," says Jason. "Very true, sir," says my master. "It's a fair speculation, then, for you to consider what the chance of the jointure on those lands, when out of custodiam, will be to you." "Just five hundred a-year, I take it, without any speculation at all," said Sir Condy. "That's supposing the life dropt, and the custodiam off, you know; begging your pardon, Sir Condy, who understands business, that is a wrong calculation." "Very likely so," said Sir Condy; "but Mr. Jason, if you have any thing to say to me this morning about it, I'd be obliged to you to say it, for I had an indifferent night's rest last night, and wouldn't be sorry to sleep a little this morning." "I have only three words to say, and those more of consequence to you, Sir Condy, than me. You are a little cool, I observe; but I hope you will not be offended at what I have brought here in my pocket," and he pulls out two long rolls, and showers down golden guineas upon the bed. "What's this?" said Sir Condy; "it's long since" —but his pride stops him, "All these are your lawful property this minute, Sir Condy, if you please," said Jason. "Not for nothing, I'm sure," said Sir Condy, and laughs a little—"nothing for nothing, or I'm under a mistake with you, Jason." "Oh, Sir Condy, we'll not be indulging ourselves in any unpleasant retrospects," says Jason; "it's my present intention to behave, as I'm sure you will, like a gentleman in this affair. Here's two hundred guineas, and a third I mean to add, if you should think proper to make over to me all your right and title to those lands that you know of." "I'll consider of it," said my master; and a great deal more, that I was tired listening to, was said by Jason, and all that, and the sight of the ready cash upon the bed worked with his honour; and the short and the long of it was, Sir Condy gathered up the golden guineas, and tied them up in a handkerchief, and signed some paper Jason brought with him as usual, and there was an end of the business: Jason took himself away, and my master turned himself round and fell asleep again.

I soon found what had put Jason in such a hurry to conclude this business. The little gossoon we had sent off the day before with my master's compliments to Mount Juliet's Town, and to know how my lady did after her accident, was stopped early this morning, coming back with his answer through O'Shaughlin's Town, at Castle Rackrent, by my son Jason, and questioned of all he knew of my lady from the servant at Mount Juliet's Town; and the gossoon told him my Lady Rackrent was not expected to live over night; so Jason thought it high time to be moving to the Lodge, to make his bargain with my master about the jointure afore it should be too late, and afore the little gossoon should reach us with the news. My master was greatly vexed, that is, I may say, as much as ever I *seen* him, when he found how he had been taken in; but it was some comfort to have the ready cash for immediate consumption in the house, any way.

And when Judy came up that evening, and brought the childer to see his honour, he unties the handkerchief, and, God bless him! whether it was little or much he had, 'twas all the same with him, he gives 'em all round guineas a-piece. "Hold up your head," says my shister to Judy, as Sir Condy was busy filling out a glass of punch for her eldest boy—"Hold up your head, Judy; for who knows but we may live to see you yet at the head of the Castle Rackrent estate?" "Maybe so," says she, "but not the way you are thinking of." I did not rightly understand which way Judy, was looking when she makes this speech, till a-while after. "Why, Thady, you were telling me yesterday, that Sir Condy had sold all entirely to Jason, and where then does all them guineas in the handkerchief come from?" "They are the purchase-money of my lady's jointure," says I. Judy looks a little bit puzzled at this. "A penny for your thoughts, Judy," says my shister; "hark, sure Sir Condy is drinking her health." He was at the table in *the room*,22 drinking with the exciseman and the gauger, who came up to see his honour, and we were standing over the fire in the kitchen. "I don't much care is he drinking my health or not," says Judy; "and it is not Sir Condy I'm thinking of, with all your jokes, whatever he is of me." "Sure you wouldn't refuse to be my Lady Rackrent, Judy, if you had the offer?" says I. "But if I could do better!" says she. "How better?" says I and my shister both at once. "How better?" says she; "why, what signifies it to be my Lady Rackrent, and no castle? sure what good is the car, and no horse to draw it?" "And where will ye get the horse, Judy?" says I. "Never mind that," says she; "may be it is your own son Jason might find that." "Jason!" says I; "don't be trusting to him, Judy. Sir Condy, as I have good reason to know, spoke well of you, when Jason spoke very indifferently of you, Judy." "No matter," says Judy; "it's often men speak the contrary just to what they think of us." "And you the same way of them, no doubt," answers I. "Nay, don't be denying it, Judy, for I think the better of ye for it, and shouldn't be proud to call ye the daughter of a shister's son of mine, if I was to hear ye talk ungrateful, and any way disrespectful of his honour." "What disrespect," says she, "to say I'd rather, if it was my luck, be the wife of another man?" "You'll have no luck, mind my words, Judy," says I; and all I remembered about my poor master's goodness in tossing up for her afore he married at all came across me, and I had a choaking in my throat that hindered me to say more. "Better luck, any how, Thady," says she, "than to be like some folk, following the fortunes of them that have none left." "Oh! King of Glory!" says I, "hear the pride and ungratitude of her, and he giving his last guineas but a minute ago to her childer, and she with the fine shawl on her he made her a present of but yesterday!" "Oh, troth, Judy, you're wrong now," says my shister, looking at the shawl. "And was not he wrong yesterday, then," says she, "to be telling me I was greatly altered, to affront me?" "But, Judy," says I, "what is it brings you here then at all in the mind you are in; is it to make Jason think the better of you?" "I'll tell you no more of my secrets, Thady," says she, "nor would have told you this much, had I taken you for such an unnatural fader as I find you are, not to wish your own son prefarred to another." "Oh, troth, *you* are wrong now, Thady," says my shister. Well, I was never so put to it in my life: between these womens, and my son and my master, and all I felt and thought just now, I could not, upon my conscience, tell which was the wrong from the right. So I said not a word more, but was only glad his honour had not the luck to hear all Judy had been saying of him, for I reckoned it would have gone nigh to break his heart; not that I was of opinion he cared for her as much as she and my shister fancied, but the ungratitude of the whole from Judy might not plase him; and he could never stand the notion of not being well spoken of or beloved like behind his back. Fortunately for all parties concerned, he was so much elevated at this time, there was no danger of his understanding any thing, even if it had reached his ears. There was a great horn at the Lodge, ever since my master and Captain Moneygawl was in together, that used to belong originally to the celebrated Sir Patrick, his ancestor; and his honour was fond often of telling the story that he learned from me when a child, how Sir Patrick drank the full of this horn without stopping, and this was what no other man afore or since could without drawing breath. Now Sir Condy challenged the gauger, who seemed to think little of the horn, to swallow the contents, and had it filled to the brim with punch; and the gauger said it was what he could not do for nothing, but he'd hold Sir Condy a hundred guineas he'd do it. "Done," says my master; "I'll lay you a hundred golden guineas to a tester23 you don't." "Done," says the gauger; and done and done's enough between two gentlemen. The gauger was cast, and my master won the bet, and thought he'd won a hundred guineas, but by the wording it was adjudged to be only a tester that was his due by the exciseman. It was all one to him; he was as well pleased, and I was glad to see him in such spirits again.

The gauger, bad luck to him! was the man that next proposed to my master to try himself could he take at a draught the contents of the great horn. "Sir Patrick's horn!" said his honour; "hand it to me: I'll hold you your own bet over again I'll swallow it." "Done," says the gauger; "I'll lay ye anything at all you do no such thing." "A hundred guineas to sixpence I do," says he: "bring me the handkerchief." I was loth, knowing he meant the handkerchief with the gold in it, to bring it out in such company, and his honour not very able to reckon it. "Bring me the handkerchief, then, Thady," says he, and stamps with his foot; so with that I pulls it out of my great coat pocket, where I had put it for safety. Oh, how it grieved me to see the guineas counting upon the table, and they the last my master had! Says Sir Condy to me, "Your hand is steadier than mine to-night, old Thady, and that's a wonder; fill you the horn for me." And so, wishing his honour success, I did; but I filled it, little thinking of what would befall him. He swallows it down, and drops like one shot. We lifts him up, and he was speechless, and quite black in the face. We put him to bed, and in a short time he wakened, raving with a fever on his brain. He was shocking either to see or hear. "Judy! Judy! have you no touch of feeling? won't you stay to help us nurse him?" says I to her, and she putting on her shawl to go out of the house. "I'm frightened to see him," says she, "and wouldn't nor couldn't stay in it; and what use? he can't last till the morning." With that she ran off. There was none but my shister and myself left near him of all the many friends he had. The fever came and went, and came and went, and lasted five days, and the sixth he was sensible for a few minutes, and said to me, knowing me very well, "I'm in burning pain all withinside of me, Thady." I could not speak, but my shister asked him would he have this thing or t'other to do him good? "No," says he, "nothing will do me good no more," and he gave a terrible screech with the torture he was in—then again a minute's ease—"brought to this by drink," says he; "where are all the friends?—where's Judy?—Gone, hey? Ay, Sir Condy has been a fool all his days," said he; and there was the last word he spoke, and died. He had but a very poor funeral, after all.

If you want to know any more, I'm not very well able to tell you; but my Lady Rackrent did not die, as was expected of her, but was only disfigured in the face ever after by the fall and bruises she got; and she and Jason, immediately after my poor master's death, set about going to law about that jointure; the memorandum not being on stamped paper, some say it is worth nothing, others again it may do; others say, Jason won't have the lands at any rate; many wishes it so: for my part, I'm tired wishing for any thing in this world, after all I've seen in it—but I'll say nothing; it would be a folly to be getting myself ill-will in my old age. Jason did not marry, nor think of marrying Judy, as I prophesied, and I am not sorry for it; who is? As for all I have here set down from memory and hearsay of the family, there's nothing but truth in it from beginning to end: that you may depend upon; for where's the use of telling lies about the things which every body knows as well as I do?

The Editor could have readily made the catastrophe of Sir Condy's history more dramatic and more pathetic, if he thought it allowable to varnish the plain round tale of faithful Thady. He lays it before the English reader as a specimen of manners and characters, which are, perhaps, unknown in England. Indeed, the domestic habits of no nation in Europe were less known to the English than those of their sister country, till within these few years.

Mr. Young's picture of Ireland, in his tour through that country, was the first faithful portrait of its inhabitants. All the features in the foregoing sketch were taken from the life, and they are characteristic of that mixture of quickness, simplicity, cunning, carelessness, dissipation, disinterestedness, shrewdness, and blunder, which, in different forms, and with various success, has been brought upon the stage, or delineated in novels.

It is a problem of difficult solution to determine, whether an Union will hasten or retard the amelioration of this country. The few gentlemen of education, who now reside in this country, will resort to England: they are few, but they are in nothing inferior to men of the same rank in Great Britain. The best that can happen will be the introduction of British manufacturers in their places.

Did the Warwickshire militia, who were chiefly artisans, teach the Irish to drink beer? or did they learn from the Irish to drink whiskey?

1800

GLOSSARY

Some friends, who have seen Thady's history since it has been printed, have suggested to the Editor, that many of the terms and idiomatic phrases, with which it abounds, could not be intelligible to the English reader without further explanation. The Editor has therefore furnished the following Glossary.

[A] *Monday morning,*—Thady begins his memoirs of the Rackrent Family by dating *Monday morning,* because no great undertaking can be auspiciously commenced in Ireland on any morning but *Monday morning.* "Oh, please God we live till Monday morning, we'll set the slater to mend the roof of the house. On Monday morning we'll fall to, and cut the turf. On Monday morning we'll see and begin mowing. On Monday morning, please your honour, we'll begin and dig the potatoes," &c.

All the intermediate days, between the making of such speeches and the ensuing Monday, are wasted: and when Monday morning comes, it is ten to one that the business is deferred to *the next* Monday morning. The Editor knew a gentleman, who, to counteract this prejudice, made his workmen and labourers begin all new pieces of work upon a Saturday.

[B] *Let alone the three kingdoms itself.*—*Let alone,* in this sentence, means *put out of consideration.* The phrase, *let alone,* which is now used as the imperative of a verb, may in time become a conjunction, and may exercise the ingenuity of some future etymologist. The celebrated Horne Tooke has proved most satisfactorily, that the conjunction *but* comes from the imperative of the Anglo-Saxon verb *(beoutan) to be out*; also, that *if* comes from *gif,* the imperative of the Anglo-Saxon verb which signifies *to give,* &c.

[C] *Whillaluh.*—Ullaloo, Gol, or lamentation over the dead—

"*Magnoque ululante tumultu.*"—*VIRGIL.*

"*Ululatibus omne*

Implevere nemus."—*OVID.*

A full account of the Irish Gol, or Ullaloo, and of the Caoinan or Irish funeral song, with its first semichorus, second semichorus, full chorus of sighs and groans, together with the Irish words and music, may be found in the fourth volume of the transactions of the Royal Irish Academy. For the advantage of *lazy* readers, who would rather read a page than walk a yard, and from compassion, not to say sympathy, with their infirmity, the Editor transcribes the following passages:

"The Irish have been always remarkable for their funeral lamentations; and this peculiarity has been noticed by almost every traveller who visited them; and it seems derived from their Celtic ancestors, the primaeval inhabitants of this isle ... ...

"It has been affirmed of the Irish, that to cry was more natural to them than to any other nation, and at length the Irish cry became proverbial.... ... ...

"Cambrensis in the twelfth century says, the Irish then musically expressed their griefs; that is, they applied the musical art, in which they excelled all others, to the orderly celebration of funeral obsequies, by dividing the mourners into two bodies, each alternately singing their part, and the whole at times joining in full chorus.... ... The body of the deceased, dressed in grave clothes, and ornamented with flowers, was placed on a bier, or some elevated spot. The relations and keepers (*singing mourners*) ranged themselves in two divisions, one at the head, and the other at the feet of the corpse. The bards and croteries had before prepared the funeral Caoinan. The chief bard of the head chorus began by singing the first stanza, in a low, doleful tone, which was softly accompanied by the harp: at the conclusion, the foot semichorus began the lamentation, or Ullaloo, from the final note of the preceding stanza, in which they were answered by the head semichorus; then both united in one general chorus. The chorus of the first stanza being ended, the chief bard of the foot semichorus began the second Gol or lamentation, in which he was answered by that of the head; and then, as before, both united in the general full chorus. Thus alternately were the song and choruses performed during the night. The genealogy, rank, possessions, the virtues and vices of the dead were rehearsed, and a number of interrogations were addressed to the deceased; as, Why did he die? If married, whether his wife was faithful to him, his sons dutiful, or good hunters or warriors? If a woman, whether her daughters were fair or chaste? If a young man, whether he had been crossed in love; or if the blue-eyed maids of Erin treated him with scorn?"

We are told, that formerly the feet (the metrical feet) of the Caoinan were much attended to; but on the decline of the Irish bards these feet were gradually neglected, and the Caoinan fell into a sort of slipshod metre amongst women. Each province had different Caoinans, or at least different imitations of the original. There was the Munster cry, the Ulster cry, &c. It became an extempore performance, and every set of keepers varied the melody according to their own fancy.

It is curious to observe how customs and ceremonies degenerate. The present Irish cry, or howl, cannot boast of such melody, nor is the funeral procession conducted with much dignity. The crowd of people who assemble at these funerals sometimes amounts to a thousand, often to four or five hundred. They gather as the bearers of the hearse proceed on their way, and when they pass through any village, or when they come near any houses, they begin to cry—Oh! Oh! Oh! Oh! Oh! Agh! Agh! raising their notes from the first *Oh!* to the last *Agh!* in a kind of mournful howl. This gives notice to the inhabitants of the village that *a funeral is passing*, and immediately they flock out to follow it. In the province of Munster it is a common thing for the women to follow a funeral, to join in the universal cry with all their might and main for some time, and then to turn and ask—"Arrah! who is it that's dead?—who is it we're crying for?" Even the poorest people have their own burying-places, that is, spots of ground in the church-yards where they say that their ancestors have been buried ever since the wars of Ireland; and if these burial-places are ten miles from the place where a man dies, his friends and neighbours take care to carry his corpse thither. Always one priest, often five or six priests, attend these funerals; each priest repeats a mass, for which he is paid, sometimes a shilling, sometimes half-a-crown, sometimes half-a-guinea, or a guinea, according to their circumstances, or, as they say, according to the *ability* of the deceased. After the burial of any very poor man, who has left a widow or children, the priest makes what is called *a collection* for the widow; he goes round to every person present, and each contributes sixpence or a shilling, or what they please. The reader will find in the note upon the word *Wake*, more particulars respecting the conclusion of the Irish funerals.

Certain old women, who cry particularly loud and well, are in great request, and, as a man said to the Editor, "Every one would wish and be proud to have such at his funeral, or at that of his friends." The lower Irish are wonderfully eager to attend the funerals of their friends and relations, and they make their relationships branch out to a great extent. The proof that a poor man has been well beloved during his life is his having a crowded funeral. To attend a neighbour's funeral is a cheap proof of humanity, but it does not, as some imagine, cost nothing. The time spent in attending funerals may be safely valued at half a million to the Irish nation; the Editor thinks that double that sum would not be too high an estimate. The habits of profligacy and drunkenness which are acquired at *wakes*, are here put out of the question. When a labourer, a carpenter, or a smith, is not at his work, which frequently happens, ask where he is gone, and ten to one the answer is—"Oh, faith, please your honour, he couldn't do a stroke to-day, for he's gone to *the* funeral."

Even beggars, when they grow old, go about begging *for their own funerals*; that is, begging for money to buy a coffin, candles, pipes, and tobacco. For the use of the candles, pipes, and tobacco, see *Wake*.

Those who value customs in proportion to their antiquity, and nations in proportion to their adherence to ancient customs, will doubtless, admire the Irish *Ullaloo*, and the Irish nation, for persevering in this usage from time immemorial. The Editor, however, has observed some alarming symptoms, which seem to prognosticate the declining taste for the Ullaloo in Ireland. In a comic theatrical entertainment, represented not long since on the Dublin stage, a chorus of old women was introduced, who set up the Irish howl round the relics of a physician, who is supposed to have fallen under the wooden sword of Harlequin. After the old women have continued their Ullaloo for a decent time, with all the necessary accompaniments of wringing their hands, wiping or rubbing their eyes with the corners of their gowns or aprons, &c. one of the mourners suddenly suspends her lamentable cries, and, turning to her neighbour, asks, "Arrah now, honey, who is it we're crying for?"

[D] *The tenants were sent away without their whiskey.*—It is usual with some landlords to give their inferior tenants a glass of whiskey when they pay their rents. Thady calls it *their* whiskey; not that the whiskey is actually the property of the tenants, but that it becomes their *right* after it has been often given to them. In this general mode of reasoning respecting *rights* the lower Irish are not singular, but they are peculiarly quick and tenacious in claiming these rights. "Last year your honour gave me some straw for the roof of my house and I *expect* your honour will be after doing the same this year." In this manner gifts are frequently turned into tributes. The high and low are not always dissimilar in their habits. It is said, that the Sublime Ottoman Porte is very apt to claim gifts as tributes: thus it is dangerous to send the Grand Seignor a fine horse on his birthday one year, lest on his next birthday he should expect a similar present, and should proceed to demonstrate the reasonableness of his expectations.

[E] *He demeaned himself greatly*—means, he lowered or disgraced himself much.

[F] *Duty fowls, duty turkeys, and duty geese.*—In many leases in Ireland, tenants were *formerly* bound to supply an inordinate quantity of poultry to their landlords. The Editor knew of thirty turkeys being reserved in one lease of a small farm.

[G] *English tenants.*—An English tenant does not mean a tenant who is an Englishman, but a tenant who pays his rent the day that it is due. It is a common prejudice in Ireland, amongst the poorer classes of people, to believe that all tenants in England pay their rents on the very day when they become due. An Irishman, when he goes to take a farm, if he wants to prove to his landlord that he is a substantial man, offers to become an *English tenant*. If a tenant disobliges his landlord by voting against him, or against his opinion, at an election, the tenant is immediately informed by the agent, that he must become an *English tenant*. This threat does not imply that he is to change his language or his country, but that he must pay all the arrear of rent which he owes, and that he must thenceforward pay his rent on that day when it becomes due.

[H] *Canting*—does not mean talking or writing hypocritical nonsense, but selling substantially by auction.

[I] *Duty work.*—It was formerly common in Ireland to insert clauses in leases, binding tenants to furnish their landlords with labourers and horses for several days in the year. Much petty tyranny and oppression have resulted from this feudal custom. Whenever a poor man disobliged his landlord, the agent sent to him for his duty work; and Thady does not exaggerate when he says, that the tenants were often called from their own work to do that of their landlord. Thus the very means of earning their rent were taken from them: whilst they were getting home their landlord's harvest, their own was often ruined, and yet their rents were expected to be paid as punctually as if their time had been at their own disposal. This appears the height of absurd injustice.

In Esthonia, amongst the poor Sclavonian race of peasant slaves, they pay tributes to their lords, not under the name of duty work, duty geese, duty turkeys, &c., but under the name of *righteousnesses*. The following ballad is a curious specimen of Esthonian poetry:—

> "*This is the cause that the country is ruined,*
> *And the straw of the thatch is eaten away,*
> *The gentry are come to live in the land—*
> *Chimneys between the village,*
> *And the proprietor upon the white floor!*
> *The sheep brings forth a lamb with a white forehead,*
> *This is paid to the lord for a righteousness sheep.*
> *The sow farrows pigs,*
> *They go to the spit of the lord.*
> *The hen lays eggs,*
> *They go into the lord's frying-pan.*

The cow drops a male calf,

That goes into the lord's herd as a bull.

The mare foals a horse foal,

That must be for my lord's nag.

The boor's wife has sons,

They must go to look after my lord's poultry."

[J] *Out of forty-nine suits which he had, he never lost one but seventeen,* — Thady's language in this instance is a specimen of a mode of rhetoric common in Ireland. An astonishing assertion is made in the beginning of a sentence, which ceases to be in the least surprising, when you hear the qualifying explanation that follows. Thus a man who is in the last stage of staggering drunkenness will, if he can articulate, swear to you — "Upon his conscience now, and may he never stir from the spot alive if he is telling a lie, upon his conscience he has not tasted a drop of any thing, good or bad, since morning at-all-at-all, but half a pint of whiskey, please your honour."

[K] *Fairy Mounts* — Barrows. It is said that these high mounts were of great service to the natives of Ireland when Ireland was invaded by the Danes. Watch was always kept on them, and upon the approach of an enemy a fire was lighted to give notice to the next watch, and thus the intelligence was quickly communicated through the country. *Some years ago,* the common people believed that these barrows were inhabited by fairies, or, as they called them, by the *good people.* "Oh, troth, to the best of my belief, and to the best of my judgment and opinion," said an elderly man to the Editor, "it was only the old people that had nothing to do, and got together, and were telling stories about them fairies, but to the best of my judgment there's nothing in it. Only this I heard myself not very many years back from a decent kind of a man, a grazier, that as he was coming just *fair and easy (quietly)* from the fair, with some cattle and sheep, that he had not sold, just at the church of — —, at an angle of the road like, he was met by a good-looking man, who asked him where he was going? And he answered, 'Oh, far enough, I must be going all night.' 'No, that you mustn't nor won't (says the man), you'll sleep with me the night, and you'll want for nothing, nor your cattle nor sheep neither, nor your *beast (horse);* so come along with me.' With that the grazier *lit (alighted)* from his horse, and it was dark night; but presently he finds himself, he does not know in the wide world how, in a fine house, and plenty of every thing to eat and drink; nothing at all wanting that he could wish for or think of. And he does not *mind (recollect or know)* how at last he falls asleep; and in the morning he finds himself lying, not in ever a bed or a house at all, but just in the angle of the road where first he met the strange man: there he finds himself lying on his back on the grass, and all his sheep feeding as quiet as ever all round about him, and his horse the same way, and the bridle of the beast over his wrist. And I asked him what he thought of it; and from first to last he could think of nothing, but for certain sure it must have been the fairies that entertained him so well. For there was no house to see any where nigh hand, or any building, or barn, or place at all, but only the church and the *mote (barrow)*. There's another odd thing enough that they tell about this same church, that if any person's corpse, that had not a right to be buried in that church-yard, went to be burying there in it, no, not all the men, women, or childer in all Ireland could get the corpse any way into the church-yard; but as they would be trying to go into the church-yard, their feet would seem to be going backwards instead of forwards; ay, continually backwards the whole funeral would seem to go; and they would never set foot with the corpse in the church-yard. Now they say that it is the fairies do all this; but it is my opinion it is all idle talk, and people are after being wiser now."

The country people in Ireland certainly *had* great admiration mixed with reverence, if not dread, of fairies. They believed that beneath these fairy mounts were spacious subterraneous palaces, inhabited by *the good people*, who must not on any account be disturbed. When the wind raises a little eddy of dust upon the road, the poor people believe that it is raised by the fairies, that it is a sign that they are journeying from one of the fairies' mounts to another, and they say to the fairies, or to the dust as it passes, "God speed ye, gentlemen; God speed ye." This averts any evil that *the good people* might be inclined to do them. There are innumerable stories told of the friendly and unfriendly feats of these busy fairies; some of these tales are ludicrous, and some romantic enough for poetry. It is a pity that poets should lose such convenient, though diminutive machinery. By-the-bye, Parnell, who showed himself so deeply "skilled in faerie lore," was an Irishman; and though he has presented his fairies to the world in the ancient English dress of "Britain's isle, and Arthur's days," it is probable that his first acquaintance with them began in his native country.

Some remote origin for the most superstitious or romantic popular illusions or vulgar errors may often be discovered. In Ireland, the old churches and church-yards have been usually fixed upon as the scenes of wonders. Now antiquaries tell us, that near the ancient churches in that kingdom caves of various constructions have from time to time been discovered, which were formerly used as granaries or magazines by the ancient inhabitants, and as places to which they retreated in time of danger. There is (p. 84 of the R.I.A. Transactions for 1789) a particular account of a number of these artificial caves at the west end of the church of Killossy, in the county of Kildare. Under a rising ground, in a dry sandy soil, these subterraneous dwellings were found: they have pediment roofs, and they communicate with each other by small apertures. In the Brehon laws these are mentioned, and there are fines inflicted by those laws upon persons who steal from the subterraneous granaries. All these things show that there was a real foundation for the stories which were told of the appearance of lights, and of the sounds of voices, near these places. The persons who had property concealed there, very willingly countenanced every wonderful relation that tended to make these places objects of sacred awe or superstitious terror.

[L] *Weed-ashes.*—By ancient usage in Ireland, all the weeds on a farm belonged to the farmer's wife, or to the wife of the squire who holds the ground in his own hands. The great demand for alkaline salts in bleaching rendered these ashes no inconsiderable perquisite.

[M] *Sealing money.*—Formerly it was the custom in Ireland for tenants to give the squire's lady from two to fifty guineas as a perquisite upon the sealing of their leases. The Editor not very long since knew of a baronet's lady accepting fifty guineas as sealing money, upon closing a bargain for a considerable farm.

[N] *Sir Murtagh grew mad.*—Sir Murtagh grew angry.

[O] *The whole kitchen was out on the stairs*—means that all the inhabitants of the kitchen came out of the kitchen, and stood upon the stairs. These, and similar expressions, show how much the Irish are disposed to metaphor and amplification.

[P] *Fining down the year's rent.*—When an Irish gentleman, like Sir Kit Rackrent, has lived beyond his income, and finds himself distressed for ready money, tenants obligingly offer to take his land at a rent far below the value, and to pay him a small sum of money in hand, which they call fining down the yearly rent. The temptation of this ready cash often blinds the landlord to his future interest.

[Q] *Driver.*—A man who is employed to drive tenants for rent; that is, to drive the cattle belonging to tenants to pound. The office of driver is by no means a sinecure.

[R] *I thought to make him a priest.*—It was customary amongst those of Thady's rank in Ireland, whenever they could get a little money, to send their sons abroad to St. Omer's, or to Spain, to be educated as priests. Now they are educated at Maynooth. The Editor has lately known a young lad, who began by being a post-boy, afterwards turn into a carpenter, then quit his plane and work-bench to study his *Humanities*, as he said, at the college of Maynooth; but after he had gone through his course of Humanities, he determined to be a soldier instead of a priest.

[S] *Flam.*—Short for flambeau.

[T] *Barrack-room.*—Formerly it was customary, in gentlemen's houses in Ireland, to fit up one large bedchamber with a number of beds for the reception of occasional visitors. These rooms were called Barrack-rooms.

[U] *An innocent*—in Ireland, means a simpleton, an idiot.

[V] *The Curragh*—is the Newmarket of Ireland.

[X] *The cant.*—The auction.

[Y] *And so should cut him off for ever, by levying a fine, and suffering a recovery to dock the entail.*—The English reader may perhaps be surprised at the extent of Thady's legal knowledge, and at the fluency with which he pours forth law-terms; but almost every poor man in Ireland, be he farmer, weaver, shopkeeper, or steward, is, besides his other occupations, occasionally a lawyer. The nature of processes, ejectments, custodiams, injunctions, replevins, &c. is perfectly known to them, and the terms as familiar to them as to any attorney. They all love law. It is a kind of lottery, in which every man, staking his own wit or cunning against his neighbour's property, feels that he has little to lose, and much to gain.

"I'll have the law of you, so I will!" is the saying of an Englishman who expects justice. "I'll have you before his honour," is the threat of an Irishman who hopes for partiality. Miserable is the life of a justice of the peace in Ireland the day after a fair, especially if he resides near a small town. The multitude of the *kilt* (*kilt* does not mean *killed*, but hurt) and wounded who come before his honour with black eyes or bloody heads is astonishing: but more astonishing is the number of those who, though they are scarcely able by daily labour to procure daily food, will nevertheless, without the least reluctance, waste six or seven hours of the day lounging in the yard or court of a justice of the peace, waiting to make some complaint about—nothing. It is impossible to convince them that *time is money.* They do not set any value upon their own time, and they think that others estimate theirs at less than nothing. Hence they make no scruple of telling a justice of the peace a story of an hour long about a *tester* (sixpence); and if he grows impatient, they attribute it to some secret prejudice which he entertains against them.

Their method is to get a story completely by heart, and to tell it, as they call it, *out of the face,* that is, from the beginning to the end, without interruption.

"Well, my good friend, I have seen you lounging about these three hours in the yard; what is your business?"

"Please your honour, it is what I want to speak one word to your honour."

"Speak then, but be quick—What is the matter?"

"The matter, please your honour, is nothing at-all-at-all, only just about the grazing of a horse, please your honour, that this man here sold me at the fair of Gurtishannon last Shrove fair, which lay down three times with myself, please your honour, and *kilt* me; not to be telling your honour of how, no later back than yesterday night, he lay down in the house there within, and all the childer standing round, and it was God's mercy he did not fall a-top of them, or into the fire to burn himself. So please your honour, to-day I took him back to this man, which owned him, and after a great deal to do, I got the mare again I *swopped (exchanged)* him for; but he won't pay the grazing of the horse for the time I had him, though he promised to pay the grazing in case the horse didn't answer; and he never did a day's work, good or bad, please your honour, all the time he was with me, and I had the doctor to him five times any how. And so, please your honour, it is what I expect your honour will stand my friend, for I'd sooner come to your honour for justice than to any other in all Ireland. And so I brought him here before your honour, and expect your honour will make him pay me the grazing, or tell me, can I process him for it at the next assizes, please your honour?"

The defendant now turning a quid of tobacco with his tongue into some secret cavern in his mouth, begins his defence with—

"Please your honour, under favour, and saving your honour's presence, there's not a word of truth in all this man has been saying from beginning to end, upon my conscience, and I wouldn't for the value of the horse itself, grazing and all, be after telling your honour a lie. For, please your honour, I have a dependence upon your honour that you'll do me justice, and not be listening to him or the like of him. Please your honour, it's what he has brought me before your honour, because he had a spite against me about some oats I sold your honour, which he was jealous of, and a shawl his wife got at my shister's shop there without, and never paid for; so I offered to set the shawl against the grazing, and give him a receipt in full of all demands, but he wouldn't out of spite, please your honour; so he brought me before your honour, expecting your honour was mad with me for cutting down the tree in the horse park, which was none of my doing, please your honour—ill luck to them that went and belied me to your honour behind my back! So if your honour is pleasing, I'll tell you the whole truth about the horse that he swopped against my mare out of the face. Last Shrove fair I met this man, Jemmy Duffy, please your honour, just at the corner of the road, where the bridge is broken down, that your honour is to have the presentment for this year—long life to you for it! And he was at that time coming from the fair of Gurtishannon, and I the same way. 'How are you, Jemmy?' says I. 'Very well, I thank ye kindly, Bryan,' says he; 'shall we turn back to Paddy Salmon's and take a naggin of whiskey to our better acquaintance?' 'I don't care if I did, Jemmy,' says I; 'only it is what I can't take the whiskey, because I'm under an oath against it for a month.' Ever since, please your honour, the day your honour met me on the road, and observed to me I could hardly stand, I had taken so much; though upon my conscience your honour wronged me greatly that same time—ill luck to them that belied me behind my back to your honour! Well, please your honour, as I was telling you, as he was taking the whiskey, and we talking of one thing or t'other, he makes me an offer to swop his mare that he couldn't sell at the fair of Gurtishannon, because nobody would be troubled with the beast, please your honour, against my horse, and to oblige him I took the mare—sorrow take her! and him along with her! She kicked me a new car, that was worth three pounds ten, to tatters the first time I ever put her into it, and I expect your honour will make him pay me the price of the car, any how, before I pay the grazing, which I've no right to pay at-all-at-all, only to oblige him. But I leave it all to your honour; and the whole grazing he ought to be charging for the beast is but two and eight pence halfpenny, any how, please your honour. So I'll abide by what your honour says, good or bad. I'll leave it all to your honour."

I'll leave *it* all to your honour—literally means, I'll leave all the trouble to your honour.

The Editor knew a justice of the peace in Ireland, who had such a dread of *having it all left to his honour*, that he frequently gave the complainants the sum about which they were disputing, to make peace between them, and to get rid of the trouble of hearing their stories *out of the face*. But he was soon cured of this method of buying off disputes, by the increasing multitude of those who, out of pure regard to his honour, came "to get justice from him, because they would sooner come before him than before any man in all Ireland."

[Z] *A raking pot of tea.*—We should observe, this custom has long since been banished from the higher orders of Irish gentry. The mysteries of a raking pot of tea, like those of the Bona Dea, are supposed to be sacred to females; but now and then it has happened, that some of the male species, who were either more audacious, or more highly favoured than the rest of their sex, have been admitted by stealth to these orgies. The time when the festive ceremony begins varies according to circumstances, but it is never earlier than twelve o'clock at night; the joys of a raking pot of tea depending on its being made in secret, and at an unseasonable hour. After a ball, when the more discreet part of the company has departed to rest, a few chosen female spirits, who have footed it till they can foot it no longer, and till the sleepy notes expire under the slurring hand of the musician, retire to a bedchamber, call the favourite maid, who alone is admitted, bid her *put down the kettle*, lock the door, and amidst as much giggling and scrambling as possible, they get round a tea-table, on which all manner of things are huddled together. Then begin mutual railleries and mutual confidences amongst the young ladies, and the faint scream and the loud laugh is heard, and the romping for letters and pocket-books begins, and gentlemen are called by their surnames, or by the general name of fellows! pleasant fellows! charming fellows! odious fellows! abominable fellows! and then all prudish decorums are forgotten, and then we might be convinced how much the satirical poet was mistaken when he said,

"*There is no woman where there's no reserve.*"

The merit of the original idea of a raking pot of tea evidently belongs to the washerwoman and the laundry-maid. But why should not we have *Low life above stairs* as well as *High life below stairs*?

[A2] *We gained the day by this piece of honesty.*—In a dispute which occurred some years ago in Ireland, between Mr. E. and Mr. M., about the boundaries of a farm, an old tenant of Mr. M.'s cut a *sod* from Mr. M.'s land, and inserted it in a spot prepared for its reception in Mr. E.'s land; so nicely was it inserted, that no eye could detect the junction of the grass. The old man, who was to give his evidence as to the property, stood upon the inserted sod when the *viewers* came, and swore that the ground he *then stood upon* belonged to his landlord, Mr. M.

The Editor had flattered himself that the ingenious contrivance which Thady records, and the similar subterfuge of this old Irishman, in the dispute concerning boundaries, were instances of 'cuteness unparalleled in all but Irish story: an English friend, however, has just mortified the Editor's national vanity by an account of the following custom, which prevails in part of Shropshire. It is discreditable for women to appear abroad after the birth of their children till they have been *churched*. To avoid this reproach, and at the same time to enjoy the pleasure of gadding, whenever a woman goes abroad before she has been to church, she takes a tile from the roof of her house, and puts it upon her head: wearing this panoply all the time she pays her visits, her conscience is perfectly at ease; for she can afterwards safely declare to the clergyman, that she "has never been from under her own roof till she came to be churched."

[B2] *Carton, and half carton.*—Thady means cartron, and half cartron. "According to the old record in the black book of Dublin, a *cantred* is said to contain 30 *villatas terras*, which are also called *quarters* of land (quarterons, cartrons); every one of which quarters must contain so much ground as will pasture 400 cows, and 17 plough-lands. A knight's fee was composed of 8 hydes, which amount to 160 acres, and that is generally deemed about a *ploughland*."

The Editor was favoured by a learned friend with the above extract, from a MS. of Lord Totness's in the Lambeth library.

[C2] *Wake.*—A wake in England means a festival held upon the anniversary of the saint of the parish. At these wakes, rustic games, rustic conviviality, and rustic courtship, are pursued with all the ardour and all the appetite which accompany such pleasures as occur but seldom. In Ireland a wake is a midnight meeting, held professedly for the indulgence of holy sorrow, but usually it is converted into orgies of unholy joy. When an Irish man or woman of the lower order dies, the straw which composed the bed, whether it has been contained in a bag to form a mattress, or simply spread upon the earthen floor, is immediately taken out of the house, and burned before the cabin door, the family at the same time setting up the death howl. The ears and eyes of the neighbours being thus alarmed, they flock to the house of the deceased, and by their vociferous sympathy excite and at the same time soothe the sorrows of the family.

It is curious to observe how good and bad are mingled in human institutions. In countries which were thinly inhabited, this custom prevented private attempts against the lives of individuals, and formed a kind of coroner's inquest upon the body which had recently expired, and burning the straw upon which the sick man lay became a simple preservative against infection. At night the dead body is waked, that is to say, all the friends and neighbours of the deceased collect in a barn or stable, where the corpse is laid upon some boards, or an unhinged door, supported upon stools, the face exposed, the rest of the body covered with a white sheet. Bound the body are stuck in brass candlesticks, which have been borrowed perhaps at five miles' distance, as many candles as the poor person can beg or borrow, observing always to have an odd number. Pipes and tobacco are first distributed, and then, according to the *ability* of the deceased, cakes and ale, and sometimes whiskey, are *dealt* to the company:

> "Deal on, deal on, my merry men all,
> Deal on your cakes and your wine,
> For whatever is dealt at her funeral to-day
> Shall be dealt to-morrow at mine."

After a fit of universal sorrow, and the comfort of a universal dram, the scandal of the neighbourhood, as in higher circles, occupies the company. The young lads and lasses romp with one another, and when the fathers and mothers are at last overcome with sleep and whiskey (*vino et somno*), the youth become more enterprising, and are frequently successful. It is said that more matches are made at wakes than at weddings.

[D2] *Kilt.*—This word frequently occurs in the preceding pages, where it means not *killed*, but much *hurt*. In Ireland, not only cowards, but the brave "die many times before their death." — There killing is no murder.

ESSAY ON IRISH BULLS

Summos posse viros, et magna exempla daturos, Vervecum in patria,
crassoque sub aëre nasci. JUVENAL.

IRISH BULLS

INTRODUCTION

What mortal, what fashionable mortal, is there who has not, in the midst of a formidable circle, been reduced to the embarrassment of having nothing to say? Who is there that has not felt those oppressive fits of silence which ensue after the weather, and the fashions, and the politics, and the scandal, and all the common-place topics of the day have been utterly exhausted? Who is there that, at such a time, has not tried in vain to call up an idea, and found that *none would come when they did call*, or that all that came were impertinent, and must be rejected, some as too grave, others too gay, some too vulgar, some too refined for the hearers, some relating to persons, others to circumstances that must not be mentioned? Not one will do! and all this time the silence lasts, and the difficulty of breaking it increases every instant in an incalculable proportion.

Let it be some comfort to those whose polite sensibility has laboured under such distress to be assured, that they need never henceforward fear to be reduced to similar dilemmas. They may be insured for ever against such dangers at the slight premium and upon the easy condition of perusing the following little volume. It will satisfy them that there is a subject which still affords inexhausted and inexhaustible sources of conversation, suited to all tastes, all ranks, all individuals, democratic, aristocratic, commercial, or philosophic; suited to every company which can be combined, purposely or fortuitously, in this great metropolis, or in any of the most remote parts of England, Wales, or Scotland. There is a subject which dilates the heart of every true Briton, which relaxes his muscles, however rigid, to a smile,— which opens his lips, however closed, to conversation. There is a subject "which frets another's spleen to cure our own," and which makes even the angelic part of the creation *laugh themselves mortal*. For who can forbear to laugh at the bare idea of an Irish bull?

Nor let any one apprehend that this subject can ever become trite and vulgar. Custom cannot stale its infinite variety. It is in the main obvious, and palpable enough for every common understanding; yet it leads to disquisitions of exquisite subtlety, it branches into innumerable ramifications, and involves consequences of surprising importance; it may exercise the ingenuity of the subtlest wit, the fancy of the oddest humourist, the imagination of the finest poet, and the judgment of the most profound metaphysician. Moreover, this happy subject is enveloped in all that doubt and confusion which are so favourable to the reputation of disputants, and which secures the glorious possibility of talking incessantly, without being stopped short by a definition or a demonstration. For much as we have all heard and talked of Irish bulls, it has never yet been decided what it is that constitutes a bull. *Incongruity of ideas,* says one. But this supposition touches too closely upon the definition of wit, which, according to the best authorities, Locke, Burke, and Stewart, consists in an unexpected assemblage of ideas, apparently discordant, but in which some point of resemblance or aptitude is suddenly discovered.

Then, perhaps, says another, the essence of a bull lies in *confusion of ideas.* This sounds plausible in theory, but it will not apply in practice; for confusion of ideas is common to both countries: for instance, was there not some slight confusion of ideas in the mind of that English student, who, when he was asked what progress he had made in the study of medicine, replied, "I hope I shall soon be qualified to be a physician, for I think I am now able to cure a child?"

To amend our bill, suppose we insert the word laughable, and say that a *laughable confusion of ideas* constitutes a bull. But have we not a laughable confusion of ideas in our English poet Blackmore's famous lines in Prince Arthur?—

> "A painted vest prince Vortigern had on,
>
> Which from a naked Pict his grandsire won."

We are sensible that, to many people, the most vulgar Irish bull would appear more laughable merely from its being Irish,—therefore we cannot make the propensity to laughter in one man the criterion of what is ridiculous in another; though we have a precedent for this mode of judging in the laws of England, which are allowed to be the perfection of human reason. If a man swear that his neighbour has put him in bodily fear, he may have the cause of his terror sent to gaol; thus the feelings of the plaintiff become the measure of the defendant's guilt. As we cannot extend this convenient principle to all matters of taste, and all subjects of risibility, we are still compelled to acknowledge that no accurate definition of a bull has yet been given. The essence of an Irish bull must be of the most ethereal nature, for notwithstanding the most indefatigable research, it has hitherto escaped from analysis. The crucible always breaks in the long-expected moment of projection: we have nevertheless the courage to recommence the process in a new mode. Perhaps by ascertaining what it is not, we may at last discover what it is: we must distinguish the genuine from the spurious, the original from all imitations, the indigenous from the exotic; in short, it must be determined in what an Irish bull essentially differs from a blunder, or in what Irish blunders specifically differ from English blunders, and from those of all other nations. To elucidate these points, or to prove to the satisfaction of all competent judges that they are beyond the reach of the human understanding, is the object of the following *Essay concerning the Nature of Bulls and Blunders.*

CHAPTER I
ORIGINALITY OF IRISH BULLS EXAMINED

The difficulty of selecting from the vulgar herd of Irish bulls one that shall be entitled to the prize, from the united merits of pre-eminent absurdity, and indisputable originality, is greater than hasty judges may imagine. Many bulls, reputed to be bred and born in Ireland, are of foreign extraction; and many more, supposed to be unrivalled in their kind, may be matched in all their capital *points*: for instance, there is not a more celebrated bull than Paddy Blake's. When Paddy heard an English gentleman speaking of the fine echo at the lake of Killarney, which repeats the sound forty times, he very promptly observed, "Faith, that's nothing at all to the echo in my father's garden, in the county of Galway: if you say to it, 'How do you do, Paddy Blake?' it will answer, 'Pretty well, I thank you, sir.'"

Now this echo of Paddy Blake's, which has long been the admiration of the world, is not a prodigy *unique* in its kind; it can be matched by one recorded in the immortal works of the great Lord Verulam.24

"I remember well," says this father of philosophy, "that when I went to the echo at Port Charenton, there was an old Parisian that took it to be the work of spirits, and of good spirits, 'for,' said he, 'call Satan, and the echo will not deliver back the devil's name, but will say, 'Va t'en.'"

The Parisian echo is surely superior to the Hibernian! Paddy Blake's simply understood and practised the common rules of good-breeding; but the Port Charenton echo is "instinct with spirit," and endowed with a nice moral sense.

Amongst the famous bulls recorded by the illustrious Joe Miller, there is one which has been continually quoted as an example of original Irish genius. An English gentleman was writing a letter in a coffee-house, and perceiving that an Irishman stationed behind him was taking that liberty which Hephaestion used with his friend Alexander, instead of putting his seal upon the lips of the *curious impertinent*, the English gentleman thought proper to reprove the Hibernian, if not with delicacy, at least with poetical justice: he concluded writing his letter in these words: "I would say more, but a damned tall Irishman is reading over my shoulder every word I write."

"You lie, you scoundrel!" said the self-convicted Hibernian.

This blunder is unquestionably excellent; but it is not originally Irish: it comes, with other riches, from the East, as the reader may find by looking into a book by M. Galland, entitled, "The Remarkable Sayings of the Eastern Nations."

"A learned man was writing to a friend; a troublesome fellow was beside him, who was looking over his shoulder at what he was writing. The learned man, who perceived this, continued writing in these words, 'If an impertinent chap, who stands beside me, were not looking at what I write, I would write many other things to you, which should be known only to you and to me.'

"The troublesome fellow, who was reading on, now thought it incumbent upon him to speak, and said, 'I swear to you, that I have not read or looked at what you are writing.'

"The learned man replied, 'Blockhead, as you are, why then do you say to me what you are now saying?'" 25

Making allowance for the difference of manners in eastern and northern nations, there is, certainly, such a similarity between this oriental anecdote and Joe Miller's story, that we may conclude the latter is stolen from the former. Now, an *Irish* bull must be a species of blunder *peculiar* to Ireland; those that we have hitherto examined, though they may be called Irish bulls by the ignorant vulgar, have no right, title, or claim to such a distinction. We should invariably exclude from that class all blunders which can be found in another country. For instance, a speech of the celebrated Irish beauty, Lady C——, has been called a bull; but as a parallel can be produced in the speech of an English nobleman, *it tells for nothing*. When her ladyship was presented at court, his majesty, George the Second, politely hoped, "that, since her arrival in England, she had been entertained with the gaieties of London."

"Oh, yes, please your majesty, I have seen every sight in London worth seeing, except a coronation."

This *naïveté* is certainly not equal to that of the English earl marshal, who, when his king found fault with some arrangement at his coronation, said, "Please your majesty, I hope it will be better next time."

A *naïveté* of the same species entailed a heavy tax upon the inhabitants of Beaune, in France. Beaune is famous for burgundy; and Henry the Fourth, passing through his kingdom, stopped there, and was well entertained by his loyal subjects. His Majesty praised the burgundy which they set before him—"It was excellent! it was admirable!"

"Oh, sire!" cried they, "do you think this excellent? *we have much finer burgundy than this.*"

"Have you so? then you can afford to pay for it," replied Harry the Fourth; and he laid a double tax thenceforward upon the burgundy of Beaune.

Of the same class of blunders is the following speech, which we actually heard not long ago from an Irishman:—

"Please your worship, he sent me to the devil, and I came straight to your honour."

We thought this an original Irish blunder, till we recollected its prototype in Marmontel's Annette and Lubin. Lubin concludes his harangue with, "The bailiff sent us to the devil, and we come to put ourselves under your protection, my lord." 26

The French, at least in former times, were celebrated for politeness; yet we meet with a *naïve* compliment of a Frenchman, which would have been accounted a bull if it had been found in Ireland.

A gentleman was complimenting Madame Denis on the manner in which she had just acted Zaire. "To act that part," said she, "a person should be young and handsome." "Ah, madam!" replied the complimenter *naïvement*, "you are a complete proof of the contrary." 27

We know not any original Irish blunder superior to this, unless it be that which Lord Orford pronounced to be the best bull that he ever heard.

"I hate that woman," said a gentleman, looking at one who had been his nurse; "I hate that woman, for she changed me at nurse."

Lord Orford particularly admires this bull, because in the confusion of the blunderer's ideas he is not clear even of his personal identity. Philosophers will not perhaps be so ready as his lordship has been to call this a blunder of the first magnitude. Those who have never been initiated into the mysteries of metaphysics may have the presumptuous ignorance to fancy that they understand what is meant by the common words *I*, or *me*; but the able metaphysician knows better than Lord Orford's changeling how to prove, to our satisfaction, that we know nothing of the matter.

"Personal identity," says Locke, "consists not in the identity of substance, but in the identity of consciousness, wherein Socrates and the present mayor of Queenborough agree they are the same person: if the same Socrates, sleeping and waking, do not partake of the same consciousness, Socrates waking and sleeping is not the same person; and to punish Socrates waking for what sleeping Socrates thought, and waking Socrates was never conscious of, would be no more of right than to punish one twin for what his brother twin did, whereof he knew nothing, because their outsides are so like that they could not be distinguished; for such twins have been seen." 28

We may presume that our Hibernian's consciousness could not retrograde to the time when he was changed at nurse; consequently there was no continuity of identity between the infant and the man who expressed his hatred of the nurse for perpetrating the fraud. At all events, the confusion of identity which excited Lord Orford's admiration in our Hibernian is by no means unprecedented in France, England, or ancient Greece, and consequently it cannot be an instance of national idiosyncracy, or an Irish bull. We find a similar blunder in Spain, in the time of Cervantes:—

"Pray tell me, squire," says the duchess, in Don Quixote, "is not your master the person whose history is printed under the name of the sage Hidalgo Don Quixote de la Mancha, who professes himself the admirer of one Dulcinea del Toboso?"

"The very same, my lady," answered Sancho; "and I myself am that very squire of his, who is mentioned, or ought to be mentioned, in that history, *unless they have changed me in the cradle.*"

In Molière's Amphitrion there is a dialogue between Mercure and Sosie, evidently taken from the *Attic* Lucian. Sosie being completely puzzled out of his personal identity, if not out of his senses, says literally, "of my being myself I begin to doubt in good earnest; yet when I feel myself, and when I recollect myself, it seems to me that *I am I.*" 29

We see that the puzzle about identity proves at last to be of Grecian origin. It is really edifying to observe how those things which have long been objects of popular admiration shrink and fade when exposed to the light of strict examination. An experienced critic proposed that a work should be written to inquire into the pretensions of modern writers to original invention, to trace their thefts, and to restore the property to the ancient owners. Such a work would require powers and erudition beyond what can be expected from any ordinary individual; the labour must be shared amongst numbers, and we are proud to assist in ascertaining the rightful property even of bulls and blunders; though without pretending, like some literary blood-hounds, to follow up a plagiarism, where common sagacity is at a fault.

CHAPTER II
IRISH NEWSPAPERS

We presume that we have successfully disputed the claims imposed upon the public, in behalf of certain spurious alien blunders, pretending to be native, original Irish bulls; and we shall now with pleasure proceed to examine those which have better titles to notice. Even nonsense ceases to be worthy of attention and public favour, unless it be original.

"Dear Lady Emily," says Miss Allscrip, in the excellent comedy of the Heiress—"Dear Lady Emily, don't you dote upon folly?"

"To ecstasy!" replies her ladyship; "I only despair of seeing it well kept up."

We flatter ourselves, "there is no great danger of that," for we have the Irish newspapers before us, where, no doubt, we shall find a fresh harvest of indigenous absurdity ripe for the sickle.

The first advertisement that meets our eye is promising.

It is the late proclamation of an Irish mayor, in which we are informed, that certain business is to be transacted in that city "every Monday (Easter Sunday only excepted)." This seems rather an unnecessary exception; but it is not an inadvertency, caused by any hurry of business in his worship; it is deliberately copied from a precedent, set in England, by a baronet formerly well known in parliament, who, in the preamble to a bill, proposed that certain regulations should take place "on every Monday (Tuesday excepted)." We fear, also, that an English mayor has been known to blunder. Some years ago the mayor of a capital English city published a proclamation and advertisement, previous to the races, "that no gentleman will be allowed to ride on the course, but *the horses* that are to run." A mayor's blundering proclamation is not, however, worth half so much in the eye of ridicule as a lord lieutenant's.

"A saint in crape is twice a saint in lawn."

A bull on the throne is worth twice as much as a bull in the chair.

"By the lord lieutenant and council of Ireland.

A proclamation.

— — —,

"Whereas the greatest economy is necessary in the consumption of all species of grain, and especially in the consumption of potatoes, &c.

"Given at the council chamber in Dublin."

This is the first time we have been informed, by authority, that potatoes are a species of grain; but we must accede to this new botanical arrangement, when published under such splendid auspices. The assertion certainly is not made in distinct terms: but all who understand the construction of language must imply the conclusion that we draw from these premises. A general position is in the first member of the sentence laid down, *"that the greatest economy is necessary in the consumption of all species of grain."* A particular exemplification of the principle is made in the next clause, *"especially in the consumption of potatoes."*

The inference is as plain as can be made.

The next article in our newspaper is an advertisement of lands to be let to *an improving tenant:* — "A few miles from Cork, in *a most sporting country,* bounded by an *uncommon fine* turf bog, on the verge of which there are a number of fine *lime kilns,* where *that manure* may be had on very moderate terms, the distance for carriage not being many hundred yards. The whole lands being now in great heart, and completely laid down, entirely surrounded, and divided by *impenetrable furze ditches, made of quarried stones laid edgeways."*

It will be a matter of difficulty to the untravelled English reader to comprehend how furze ditches can be made of quarried stones laid edgeways, or any way; and we fear that we should only puzzle his intellects still more if we should attempt to explain to him the mysteries of Irish ditching in the technical terms of the country. With the face of a ditch he may be acquainted, but to *the back* and *gripe,* and bottom of the gripe, and top of the back of a ditch, we fear he is still to be introduced.

We can never sufficiently admire these furze ditches made of quarried stones; they can, indeed, be found only in Ireland; but we have heard in England of things almost as extraordinary. Dr. Grey, in his erudite and entertaining notes on Hudibras, records the deposition of a lawyer, who, in an action of battery, told the judge "that the defendant beat his client with a certain *wooden instrument* called *an iron pestle."* Nay, to go further still, a wise annotator on the Pentateuch, named Peter Harrison, observed of Moses' two *tables of stone,* that they were made of *shittim-wood.* The stone furze ditches are scarcely bolder instances of the catachresis than the stone tables of shittim-wood. This bold figure of rhetoric in an Irish advertisement of an estate may lead us to expect that Hibernian advertisers may, in time, emulate the fame of Christie, the prince of auctioneers, whose fine descriptive powers can make more of an estate on paper than ever was made of it in any other shape, except in the form of an ejectment. The fictions of law, indeed, surpass even the auctioneer's imagination; and a man may be said never to know the extent of his own possessions until he is served with a process of ejectment. He then finds himself required to give up the possession of a multitude of barns, orchards, fish-ponds, horse-ponds, dwelling-houses, pigeon-houses, dove-cotes, out-houses, and appurtenances, which he never saw or heard of, and which are nowhere to be found upon the surface of the habitable globe; so that we cannot really express this English legal transaction without being guilty of an Irish bull, and saying that the person ejected is *ousted* from places which he never entered.

To proceed with our newspapers.—The next advertisement is from a schoolmaster: but we shall not descant upon its grammatical errors, because they are not blunders peculiar to Irish schoolmasters. We have frequently observed that the advertisements of schoolmasters, even in England, are seldom free from solecisms: too much care in writing, it seems, is almost as bad as too little. In the preface of the dictionary of the French Academy, there are, as it is computed by an able French critic, no less than sixteen faults; and in Harris, the celebrated grammarian's dedication of his Hermes, there is one bull, and almost as many faults as lines. It appears as if the most precise and learned writers sometimes, like the ladies in one of Congreve's plays, "run into the danger to avoid the apprehension."

After a careful scrutiny of the Hibernian advertisements, we are compelled to confess that we have not met with any blunders that more nearly resemble our notion of an Irish bull than one which, some years ago, appeared in our English papers. It was the title to an advertisement of a washing machine, in these words: "Every *Man* his own *Washerwoman!*" We have this day, Nov. 19, 1807, seen the following: "This day were published, Memoirs of the Life of Mrs. Elizabeth Carter, with a *new edition* of her Poems, some of which have *never* before appeared." And an eye-witness assures us, that lately he saw an advertisement in the following terms stuck up on the walls of an English coffee-house: "This coffee-house removed up-stairs!"

A Roman emperor used to draw his stairs up after him every night into his bedchamber, and we have heard of throwing a house out of the windows; but drawing a whole house up into itself is new.

How can we account for such a blunder, in an advertisement on the wall of an English coffee-house, except by supposing that it was penned by an Irish waiter? If that were the case, it would an admirable example of an Irish bull! and therefore we had best take it for granted.

Let not any conscientious person be startled at the mode of reasoning by which we have convicted an imaginary Irish waiter of a real bull: it is at least as good, if not better logic, than that which was successfully employed in the time of the *popish plot*, to convict an Irish physician of forgery. The matter is thus recorded by L'Estrange. The Irish physician "was charged with writing a treasonable libel, but denied the thing, and appealed to the unlikeness of the characters. It was agreed that there was no resemblance at all in the hands; but asserted that the doctor had two hands; his *physic hand* and his *plot hand*, and the one not a jot like the other. Now this was the doctor's plot hand, and it was insisted that, because it was not like one of his hands, it must be like the other."

By this convenient mode of reasoning, an Irishman may, at any time, be convicted of any crime, or of any absurdity.

But what have we next in our newspaper?—"Murder, Robbery, and Reward." This seems a strange connexion of things, according to our vulgar notions of distributive justice; but we are told that the wicked shall have their *reward* even in this world; and we suppose it is upon this principle, that over the stocks in a town in Ireland there appears this inscription: "A reward for vagabonds."

Upon proceeding further in our advertisement, which begins with "Murder, Robbery, and Reward," we find, however, that contrary to the just expectations raised by the title, the reward is promised, not to the robbers and murderers, but to those who shall discover and prosecute them to conviction. Here we were led into error by that hasty mode of elision which sometimes obtains in the titles even of our English law processes; as sci-fa, fi-fa, qui-tam, &c.; names which, to preserve the glorious uncertainty of the law, never refer to the sense, but to the first words of the writs.

In our newspaper, a formidable list of unanimous resolutions of various committees and corps succeeds to the advertisement of murder, robbery, and reward; and we have, at the close of each day's business, thanksgivings, in various formulas, for the very proper, upright, or spirited behaviour of our worthy, gallant, or respected chairman. Now that a man may behave properly, or sit upright in a chair, we can readily comprehend; but what are we to understand by a *spirited* behaviour in a chair? Perhaps it alludes to the famous duel fought by a gouty Irish gentleman in his arm chair. As the gallant chairman actually in that position shot his adversary, it behoves us to *understand* the meaning of spirited behaviour in the chair.

We may, however, venture to hint, fas est et ab hoste doceri, that in the publication of corps and committees, this formula should be omitted— "Resolved *unanimously* (with only *one* dissentient voice)." Here the obloquy, meant to rest on the one dissentient voice, unfortunately falls upon the publishers of the disgrace, exposing them to the ridicule of resolving an Irish bull. If this be a bull, however, we are concerned to find it is matched by that of the government of Munich, who published a catalogue of forbidden books, and afterwards, under heavy penalties, forbade the reading of the catalogue. But this might be done in the hurry occasioned by the just dread of revolutionary principles.

What shall we say for the blunder of a French academician, in a time of profound peace, who gave it as his opinion, that nothing should be read in the public sittings of the academy "par dela ce qui est imposé par les statuts: il motivait son avis en disant—En fait *d'inutilités* il ne faut que *le nécessaire.*" If this speech had been made by a member of the Royal Irish academy, it would have had the honour to be noticed all over England as a bull. *The honour to be noticed*, we say, in imitation of the exquisitely polite expression of a correspondent of the English Royal Society, who talks of "the earthquake that had the honour to be noticed by the Royal Society."

It will, we fear, be long before the Irish emerge so far from barbarism as to write in this style. The Irish are, however, we are happy to observe, making some little approaches to a refined and courtly style; kings, and in imitation of them, great men, and all who think themselves great—a numerous class—speak and write as much as possible in the plural number instead of the singular. Instead of *I*, they always say *we*; instead of *my, our*, according to the Italian idiom, which flatters this humour so far as to make it a point of indispensable politeness. It is, doubtless, in humble imitation of such illustrious examples, that an Irishman of the lowest class, when he means to express that he is a member of a committee, says, *I am a committee*; thus consolidating the power, wisdom, and virtue of a whole committee in his own person. Superior even to the Indian, who believes that he shall inherit the powers and virtues of his enemies after he has destroyed them;30 this committee-man takes possession of the faculties of his living friends and associates. When some of the *united men,* as they called themselves, were examined, they frequently answered to the questions, who, or what are you? I am a com'mittéé.

However extraordinary it may at first sound, to hear one man assert that he is a whole committee, it is not more wonderful than that the whole parliament of Bordeaux should be found in a one-horse chair.31

We forbear to descant further upon Irish committee-men, lest we should call to mind, merely by the similarity of name, the times when England had her committee-men, who were not perfectly free from all tinge of absurdity. It is remarkable, that in times of popular ferment, a variety of new terms are coined to serve purposes and passions of the moment. In the days of the English committee-men this practice had risen to such a height, that it was fair game for ridicule. Accordingly, Sir John Birkenhead, about that time, found it necessary to publish, *"The Children's Dictionary; an exact Collection of all New Words born since Nov. 3, 1640, in Speeches, Prayers, and Sermons, as well those that signify something as nothing."* We observe that it has been likewise found necessary to publish, in France, *un Dictionnaire néologique,* a dictionary of the new terms adopted since the revolution.

It must be supposed, that during the late disturbances in Ireland, many *cant* terms have been brought into use, which are not yet to be reckoned amongst the acknowledged terms of the country. However absurd these may be, they are not for our purpose proper subjects of animadversion. Some countries have their birds of passage, and some their follies of passage, which it is scarcely worth while to shoot as they fly. It has been often said, that the language of a people is a just criterion of their progress in civilization; but we must not take a specimen of their vocabulary during the immediate prevalence of any transient passion or prejudice. It is to be hoped, that all party barbarisms in language will now be disused and forgotten; for some time has elapsed since we read the following article of country intelligence in a Dublin paper:—

"General — — scoured the country yesterday, but had not the good fortune to meet with a single rebel."

The author of this paragraph seems to have been a keen sportsman; he regrets the not meeting with a single rebel, as he would the not meeting with a single hare or partridge; and he justly considers the human biped as fair game, to be hunted down by all who are properly qualified and licensed by government. To the English, perhaps, it may seem a strange subject of lamentation, that a general could not meet with a single rebel in the county of Wicklow, when they have so lately been informed, from the high authority of a noble lord, that Ireland was so disturbed, that whenever he went out, he called as regularly for his pistols as for his hat and gloves. Possibly, however, this was only a figure of speech, like that of Bishop Wilkins, who prophesied that the time would come when gentlemen, when they were to go a journey, would call for their wings as regularly as they call for their boots. — We *believe* that the hyperboles of the privy-counsellor and the bishop are of equal magnitude.

CHAPTER III
THE CRIMINAL LAW OF BULLS
AND BLUNDERS

Madame de Sevigné observes, that there are few people sufficiently candid, or sufficiently enlightened, to distinguish, in their judgments of others, between those faults and mistakes which proceed from *manque d'esprit*, and those which arise merely from *manque d'usage*. We cannot appreciate the talents or character of foreigners, without making allowance for their ignorance of our manners, of the idiom of our language, and the multifarious significations of some of our words. A French gentleman, who dined in London, in company with the celebrated author of the Rambler, wishing to show him a mark of peculiar respect, drank Dr. Johnson's health in these words: "Your health, Mr. Vagabond." Assuredly no well-judging Englishman would undervalue the Frenchman's abilities, because he mistook the meaning of the words Vagabond and Rambler; he would recollect, that in old English and modern French authors, vagabond means wanderer: des eaux vagabondes is a phrase far from inelegant. But independently of this consideration, no well-bred gentleman would put a foreigner out of countenance by openly laughing at such a mistake: he would imitate the politeness of the Frenchman, who, when Dr. Moore said, "I am afraid the expression I have just used is not French," replied, "Non, monsieur—mais il mérite bien de l'être." It would, indeed, be a great stretch of politeness to extend this to our Irish neighbours: for no Irishism can ever deserve to be Anglicised, though so many Gallicisms have of late not only been naturalized in England, but even adopted by the most fashionable speakers and writers. The mistaking a feminine for a masculine noun, or a masculine for a feminine, must, in all probability, have happened to every Englishman that ever opened his lips in Paris; yet without losing his reputation for common sense. But when a poor Irish haymaker, who had but just learned a few phrases of the English language by rote, mistook a feminine for a masculine noun, and began his speech in a court of justice with these words: "My lord, I am a poor widow," instead of, "My lord, I am a poor widower;" it was sufficient to throw a grave judge and jury into convulsions of laughter. It was formerly, in law, no murder to kill a *merus Hibernicus;* and it is to this day no offence against good manners to laugh at any of this species. It is of a thousand times more consequence to have the laugh than the argument on our side, as all those know full well who have any experience in the management of the great or little vulgar. By the common custom and courtesy of England we *have* the laugh on our side: let us keep it by all means. All means are justifiable to obtain a great end, as all great men maintain in practice, if not in theory. We need not, in imitating them, have any scruples of conscience; we need not apprehend, that to ridicule our Hibernian neighbours unmercifully is unfriendly or ungenerous. Nations, it has been well observed, are never generous in their conduct towards each other. We must follow the common *custom* of nations where we have no *law* to guide our proceedings. We must therefore carefully continue the laudable practice of ridiculing the blunders, whether real or imaginary, of Irishmen. In conversation, Englishmen are permitted sometimes to blunder, but without ever being called blunderers. It would, indeed, be an intolerable restraint upon social intercourse, if every man were subject to be taxed for each inaccuracy of language—if he were compelled to talk, upon all occasions, as if he were amenable to a star-chamber of criticism, and surrounded by informers.

Much must be allowed in England for the licence of conversation; but by no means must this conversation-licence be extended to the Irish. If, for instance, at the convivial hour of dinner, when men are not usually intent upon grammatical or mathematical niceties, an Irish gentleman desires him "who rules the roast," to cut the sirloin of beef *horizontally downwards*, let the mistake immediately be set down in our note-books, and conned over, and got by heart; and let it be repeated to all eternity as a bull. But if an English lady observe, when the candles have long stood unsnuffed, that "those odious long wicks will soon grow up to the ceiling," she can be accused only of an error of vision. We conjure our readers to attend to these distinctions in their intercourse with their Hibernian neighbours: it must be done habitually and technically; and we must not listen to what is called reason; we must not enter into any argument, pro or con, but silence every Irish opponent, if we can, with a laugh.

The Abbé Girard, in his accurate work, "Synonymes François," makes a *plausible* distinction between *un âne* et *un ignorant*; he says, "On est âne par disposition: on est ignorant par défaut d'instruction." An ignorant person may certainly, even in the very circumstances which betray his ignorance, evince considerable ability. For instance, the native Indian, who for the first time saw a bottle of porter uncorked, and who expressed great astonishment at the quantity of froth which he saw burst from the bottle, and much curiosity to know whether it could all be put in again, showed even in his ignorance a degree of capacity, which in different situations might have saved his life, or have made his fortune. In the situation of the poor fisher-man, and the great giant of smoke, who issued from the small vessel, well known to all versed in the Arabian Tales, such acuteness would have saved his life; and a similar spirit of inquiry, applied to chemistry, might, in modern times, have made his fortune. Even where no positive abilities are displayed at the time by those who manifest ignorance, we should not (*except the culprits be natives of Ireland*) hastily give them up. Ignorance of the most common objects is not only incident to certain situations, but absolutely unavoidable; and the individuals placed in those situations are no more blameable than they would be for becoming blind in the snows of Lapland, or for having goitres amongst the Cretins of Le Vallais. Would you blame the ignorant nuns who, insensible of the danger of an eruption of Mount Vesuvius,32 warmed themselves at the burning lava which flowed up to the windows of their cells? or would you think the French canoness an idiot who, at the age of fifty, was, on account of her health, to go out of her convent, and asked, when she met a cow for the first time, what strange animal that was? or would you think that those poor children deserved to be stigmatized as fools, who, after being confined for a couple of years in an English workhouse, actually at eight years old had forgotten the names of a pig and a calf?33 their ignorance was surely more deplorable than ridiculous. When the London young lady kept a collection of chicken-bones on her plate at dinner, as a bonne-bouche for her brother's horse,34 Dr. Johnson would not suffer her to be called an idiot, but very judiciously defended her, by maintaining, that her action merely demonstrated her ignorant of points of natural history, on which a London miss had no immediate opportunity of obtaining information. Had the world always judged upon such subjects with similar candour, the reproachful cant term of *cockney* would never have been disgracefully naturalized in the English language. This word, as we are informed by a learned philologist, originated from the mistake of a learned citizen's son, who having been bred up entirely in the metropolis, was so gloriously ignorant of country life and country animals, that the first time he heard a *cock* crow, he called it *neighing*. If such a mistake had been made by an Irishman, it would surely have been called a bull: it has, at least, as good pretensions to the title as many mistakes made by ignorant Hibernians; for instance, the well-known blunder relative to the sphinx:—An uninformed Irishman, hearing the sphinx alluded to in company whispered to a friend, "The sphinx! who is that now?"

"A monster-man."

"Oh, a *Munster*-man: I thought he was from Connaught," replied our Irishman, determined not to seem totally unacquainted with the family.

Gross and ridiculous as this blunder appears, we are compelled by candour to allow, that the affectation of showing knowledge has betrayed to shame men far superior to our Hibernian, both in reputation and in the means of acquiring knowledge.

Cardinal Richelieu, the Maecenas or would-be Maecenas of France, once mistook the name of a noted grammarian, *Maurus Terentianus*, for a play of Terence's. This is called by the French writer who records it, "une *bévue* bien grossière." However gross, a mistake can never be made into a bull. We find *bévues* French, English, Italian, German, Latin, and Greek, of theologians, historians, antiquaries, poets, critics, and translators, without end. The learned Budaeus takes Sir Thomas More's Utopia for a true history; and proposes sending missionaries to work the conversion of so wise a people as the Utopians. An English antiquary35 mistakes a tomb in a Gothic cathedral for the tomb of Hector. Pope, our great poet, and prince of translators, mistakes *Dec. the 8th, Nov. the 5th*, of Cinthio, for Dec. 8th, Nov. 5th; and Warburton, his learned critic, improves upon the blunder, by afterward writing the words December and November at full length. Better still, because more comic, is the blunder of a Frenchman, who, puzzled by the title of one of Cibber's plays, "Love's Last Shift," translates it "La Dernière Chemise de l'Amour." We laugh at these mistakes, and forget them; but who can forget the blunder of the Cork almanack-maker, who informs the world that the principal republics in *Europe*, are Venice, Holland, and *America*?

The blunders of men of all countries, except Ireland, do not affix an indelible stigma upon individual or national character. A free pardon is, and ought to be, granted by every Englishman to the vernacular and literary errors of those who have the happiness to be born subjects of Great Britain. What enviable privileges are annexed to the birth of an Englishman! and what a misfortune it is to be a native of Ireland!

CHAPTER IV
LITTLE DOMINICK

We have laid down the general law of bulls and blunders; but, as there is no rule without an exception, we may perhaps allow an exception in favour of little Dominick.

Little Dominick was born at Fort-Reilly, in Ireland, and bred nowhere until his tenth year, when he was sent to Wales to learn manners and grammar at the school of Mr. Owen ap Davies ap Jenkins ap Jones. This gentleman had reason to think himself the greatest of men; for he had over his chimney-piece a well-smoked genealogy, duly attested, tracing his ancestry in a direct line up to Noah; and moreover he was nearly related to the learned etymologist, who, in the time of Queen Elizabeth, wrote a folio to prove that the language of Adam and Eve in Paradise was pure Welsh. With such causes to be proud, Mr. Owen ap Davies ap Jenkins ap Jones was excusable for sometimes seeming to forget that a schoolmaster is but a man. He, however, sometimes entirely forgot that a boy is but a boy; and this happened most frequently with respect to little Dominick.

This unlucky wight was flogged every morning by his master, not for his vices, but for his vicious constructions, and laughed at by his companions every evening for his idiomatic absurdities. They would probably have been inclined to sympathize in his misfortunes, but that he was the only Irish boy at school; and as he was at a distance from all his relations, and without a friend to take his part, he was a just object of obloquy and derision. Every sentence he spoke was a bull; every two words he put together proved a false concord; and every sound he articulated betrayed the brogue. But as he possessed some of the characteristic boldness of those who have been dipped in the Shannon, he showed himself able and willing to fight his own battles with the host of foes by whom he was encompassed. Some of these, it was said, were of nearly twice his stature. This may be exaggerated, but it is certain that our hero sometimes ventured with sly Irish humour to revenge himself upon his most powerful tyrant by mimicking the Welsh accent, in which Mr. Owen ap Jones said to him, "Cot pless me, you plockit, and shall I never *learn* you Enclish crammer?"

It was whispered in the ear of this Dionysius, that our little hero was a mimick; and he was treated with increased severity.

The midsummer holydays approached; but he feared that they would shine no holydays for him. He had written to his mother to tell her that school would break up the 21st, and to beg an answer, without fail, by return of post; but no answer came.

It was now nearly two months since he had heard from his dear mother or any of his friends in Ireland. His spirits began to sink under the pressure of these accumulated misfortunes: he slept little, ate less, and played not at all; indeed nobody would play with him upon equal terms, because he was nobody's equal; his schoolfellows continued to consider him as a being, if not of a different species, at least of a different *caste* from themselves.

Mr. Owen ap Jones's triumph over the little Irish plockit was nearly complete, for the boy's heart was almost broken, when there came to the school a new scholar—oh, how unlike the others! His name was Edwards; he was the son of a neighbouring Welsh gentleman; and he had himself the spirit of a gentleman. When he saw how poor Dominick was persecuted, he took him under his protection, fought his battles with the Welsh boys, and, instead of laughing at him for speaking Irish, he endeavoured to teach him to speak English. In his answers to the first question Edwards ever asked him, little Dominick made two blunders, which set all his other companions in a roar; yet Edwards would not allow them to be genuine bulls.

In answer to the question, "Who is your father?" Dominick said, with a deep sigh, "I have no father—I am an orphan36—I have only a mother."

"Have you any brothers and sisters?"

"No; I wish I had; perhaps they would love me, and not laugh at me," said Dominick, with tears in his eyes; "but I have no brothers but myself."

One day Mr. Jones came into the schoolroom with an open letter in his hand, saying, "Here, you little Irish plockit, here's a letter from your mother."

The little Irish blockhead started from his form, and, throwing his grammar on the floor, leaped up higher than he or any boy in the school had ever been seen to leap before, and, clapping his hands, he exclaimed, "A letter from my mother! And *will* I hear the letter? And *will* I see her once more? And *will* I go home these holydays? Oh, then I will be too happy!"

"There's no tanger of that," said Mr. Owen ap Jones; "for your mother, like a wise ooman, writes me here, that py the atvice of your cardian, to oom she is coing to be married, she will not pring you home to Ireland till I send her word you are perfect in your Enclish crammer at least."

"I have my lesson perfect, sir," said Dominick, taking his grammar up from the floor; "*will* I say it now?"

"*Will* I say it now? No, you plockit, no; and I will write your mother word you have proke Priscian's head four times this tay, since her letter came. You Irish plockit!" continued the relentless grammarian, "will you never learn the tifference between *shall* and *will*? *Will* I hear the letter, and *will* I see her once more? What Enclish is this, plockit?"

The Welsh boys all grinned, except Edwards, who hummed, loud enough to be heard, two lines of the good old English song,

"*And will I see him once again?*

And will I hear him speak?"

Many of the boys were fortunately too ignorant to feel the force of the quotation; but Mr. Owen ap Jones understood it, turned upon his heel, and walked off. Soon afterwards he summoned Dominick to his awful desk; and, pointing with his ruler to the following page in Harris's Hermes, bade him "reat it, and understant it, if he could." Little Dominick read, but could not understand.

"Then read it loud, you plockit."

Dominick read aloud —

"There is *nothing appears so clearly* an object of the mind or intellect only as *the future* does, since we can find no place for its existence any where else: not but the same, if we consider, is *equally true* of the past —"

"Well, co on — What stops the plockit? Can't you reat Enclish now?"

"Yes, sir; but I was trying to understand it. I was considering, that this is like what they would call an Irish bull, if I had said it."

Little Dominick could not explain what he meant in English, that Mr. Owen ap Jones *would* understand; and, to punish him for his impertinent observation, the boy was doomed to learn all that Harris and Lowth have written to explain the nature of *shall* and *will*. The reader, if he be desirous of knowing the full extent of the penance enjoined, may consult Lowth's Grammar, p. 52, ed. 1799, and Harris's Hermes, p. 10, 11, and 12, 4th edition. Undismayed at the length of his task, little Dominick only said, "I hope, if I say it all without missing a word, you will not give my mother a bad account of me and my grammar studies, sir."

"Say it all first, without missing a word, and then I shall see what I shall say," replied Mr. Owen ap Jones.

Even the encouragement of this oracular answer excited the boy's fond hopes so keenly, that he lent his little soul to the task, learned it perfectly, said it at night, without missing one word, to his friend Edwards, and said it the next morning, without missing one word, to his master.

"And now, sir," said the boy, looking up, "will you write to my mother? And *shall* I see her? And *shall* I go home?"

"Tell me first, whether you understant all this that you have learnt so cliply," said Mr. Owen ap Jones.

That was more than his bond. Our hero's countenance fell: and he acknowledged that he did not understand it perfectly.

"Then I cannot write a coot account of you and your crammer studies to your mother; my conscience coes against it," said the conscientious Mr. Owen ap Jones.

No entreaties could move him. Dominick never saw the letter that was written to his mother; but he felt the consequence. She wrote word this time punctually *by return of the post*, that she was sorry that she could not send for him home these holydays, as she heard so bad an account from Mr. Jones, &c. and as she thought it her duty not to interrupt the course of his education, especially his grammar studies. Little Dominick heaved many a sigh when he saw the packings-up of all his school-fellows, and dropped a few tears as he looked out of the window, and saw them, one after another, get on their Welsh ponies, and gallop off towards their homes.

"I have no home to go to," said he.

"Yes, you have," cried Edwards; "and *our* horses are at the door to carry us there."

"To Ireland? me!—the horses!" said the poor boy, quite bewildered: "and will they bring me to Ireland?"

"No; the horses cannot carry you to Ireland," said Edwards, laughing good-naturedly, "but you have a home now in England. I asked my father to let me *take* you home with me; and he says 'Yes,' like a dear, good father, and has sent the horses. Come, let's away."

"But will Mr. Jones let me go?"

"Yes; he dare not refuse; for my father has a living in his gift that Jones wants, and which he will not have, if he do not change his tone to you."

Little Dominick could not speak one word, his heart was so full. No boy could be happier than he was during these holydays: "the genial current of his soul," which had been frozen by unkindness, flowed with all its natural freedom and force. When Dominick returned to school after these holydays were over, Mr. Owen ap Jones, who now found that the Irish boy had an English protector with a living in his gift, changed his tone. He never more complained unjustly that Dominick broke Priscian's head, seldom called him Irish plockit, and once would have flogged a Welsh boy for taking up this cast-off expression of the master's, but the Irish blockhead begged the culprit off.

Little Dominick sprang forward rapidly in his studies: he soon surpassed every boy in the school, his friend Edwards only excepted. In process of time his guardian removed him to a higher seminary of education. Edwards had a tutor at home. The friends separated. Afterwards they followed different professions in distant parts of the world; and they neither saw nor heard any more of each other for many years. From boys they grew into men, and Dominick, now no longer little Dominick, went over to India as private secretary to one of our commanders in chief. How he got into this situation, or by what gradations he rose in the world, we are not exactly informed: we know only that he was the reputed author of a much-admired pamphlet on Indian affairs; that the despatches of the general to whom he was secretary were remarkably well written, and that Dominick O'Reilly, Esq. returned to England, after several years' absence, not miraculously rich, but with a fortune equal to his wishes. His wishes were not extravagant: his utmost ambition was to return to his native country with a fortune that should enable him to live independently of all the world, especially of some of his relations, who had not used him well. His mother was no more.

Upon his arrival in London, one of the first things he did was to read the Irish newspapers.—To his inexpressible joy, he saw the estate of Fort-Reilly advertised to be sold—the very estate which had formerly belonged to his own family. Away he posted directly to an attorney's who was empowered to dispose of the land.

When this attorney produced a map of the well-known pleasure-ground, and an elevation of that house in which he had spent the happiest hours of his infancy, his heart was so touched, that he was on the point of paying down more for an old ruin than a good new house would cost. The attorney acted *honestly by his client*, and seized this moment to exhibit a plan of the stabling and offices, which, as sometimes is the case in Ireland, were in a style far superior to the dwelling-house. Our hero surveyed these with transport. He rapidly planned various improvements in imagination, and planted certain favourite spots in the pleasure-ground. During this time the attorney was giving directions to a clerk about some other business: suddenly the name of *Owen ap Jones* struck his ear—He started.

"Let him wait in the front parlour; his money is not forthcoming," said the attorney; "and if he keep Edwards in gaol till he rots."

"Edwards! Good heavens!—in gaol! What Edwards?" exclaimed our hero.

It was his friend Edwards.

The attorney told him that Mr. Edwards had been involved in great distress by taking upon himself his father's debts, which had been incurred in exploring a mine in Wales; that of all the creditors none had refused to compound, except a Welsh parson, who had been presented to his living by old Edwards; and that this Mr. Owen ap Jones had thrown young Mr. Edwards into gaol for the debt.

"What is the rascal's demand? He shall be paid off this instant," cried Dominick, throwing down the plan of Fort-Reilly: "send for him up, and let me pay him off upon the spot."

"Had not we best finish our business first, about the O'Reilly estate, sir?" said the attorney.

"No, sir; damn the O'Reilly estate," cried he, huddling the maps together on the desk, and taking up the bank notes, which he had begun to reckon for the purchase money. "I beg your pardon, sir. If you knew the facts, you would excuse me. Why does not this rascal come up to be paid?"

The attorney, thunderstruck by this Hibernian impetuosity, had not yet found time to take his pen out of his mouth. As he sat transfixed in his arm-chair, O'Reilly ran to the head of the stairs, and called out in a stentorian voice, "Here, you Mr. Owen ap Jones; come up and be paid off this instant, or you shall never be paid *at all*."

Up stairs hobbled the old schoolmaster, as fast as the gout and Welsh ale would let him. "Cot pless me, that voice," he began—

"Where's your bond, sir?" said the attorney.

"Safe here, Cot be praised," said the terrified Owen ap Jones, pulling out of his bosom, first a blue pocket-handkerchief, and then a tattered Welsh grammar, which O'Reilly kicked to the farther end of the room.

"Here is my bond," said he, "in the crammer," which he gathered from the ground; then fumbling over the leaves, he at length unfolded the precious deposit.

O'Reilly saw the bond, seized it, looked at the sum, paid it into the attorney's hands, tore the seal from the bond; then, without looking at old Jones, whom he dared not trust himself to speak to, he clapped his hat upon his head, and rushed out of the room. Arrived at the King's Bench prison, he hurried to the apartment where Edwards was confined. The bolts flew back; for even the turnkeys seemed to catch our hero's enthusiasm.

"Edwards, my dear boy! how do you do? Here's a bond debt, justly due to you for my education. Oh, never mind asking any unnecessary questions; only just make haste out of this undeserved abode: our old rascal is paid off—Owen ap Jones, you know.—Well, how the man stares! Why, now, will you have the assurance to pretend to forget who I am? and must I *spake*," continued he, assuming the tone of his childhood, "and must I *spake* to you again in my ould Irish brogue before you will ricollict your own *little Dominick?*"

When his friend Edwards was out of prison, and when our hero had leisure to look into business, he returned to the attorney to see that Mr. Owen ap Jones had been legally satisfied.

"Sir," said the attorney, "I have paid the plaintiff in this suit; and he is satisfied: but I must say," added he, with a contemptuous smile, "that you Irish gentlemen are rather in too great a hurry in doing business: business, sir, is a thing that must be done slowly to be done well."

"I am ready now to do business as slowly as you please; but when my friend was in prison, I thought the quicker I did his business the better. Now tell me what mistake I have made, and I will rectify it instantly."

"*Instantly!* 'Tis well, sir, with your promptitude, that you have to deal with what prejudice thinks uncommon—an honest attorney. Here are some bank notes of yours, sir, amounting to a good round sum. You made a little blunder in this business: you left me the penalty, instead of the principal, of the bond—just twice as much as you should have done."

"Just twice as much as was in the bond, but not twice as much as I should have done, nor half as much as I should have done, in my opinion," said O'Reilly; "but whatever I did was with my eyes open: I was persuaded you were an honest man; in which you see I was not mistaken; and as a man of business, I knew you would pay Jones only his due. The remainder of the money I meant, and mean, should lie in your hands for my friend Edwards's use. I feared he would not have taken it from my hands: I therefore left it in yours. To have taken my friend out of prison merely to let him go back again to-day, for want of money to keep himself clear with the world, would have been a blunder indeed, but not an Irish blunder: our Irish blunders are never blunders of the heart."

CHAPTER V
THE BLISS OF IGNORANCE

No *well-informed* Englishman would laugh at the blunders of such a character as little Dominick; but there are people who justify the assertion, that laughter always arises from a sense of real or imaginary superiority. Now if it be true, that laughter has its source in vanity, as the most ignorant are generally the most vain, they must enjoy this pleasure in its highest perfection. Unconscious of their own deficiencies, and consequently fearless of becoming in their turn the objects of ridicule, they enjoy in full security the delight of humbling their superiors. How much are they to be admired for the courage with which they apply, on all occasions, their test of truth! Wise men may be struck with admiration, respect, doubt, or humility; but the ignorant, happily unconscious that they know nothing, can be checked in their merriment by no consideration, human or divine. Theirs is the sly sneer, the dry joke, and the horse laugh: theirs the comprehensive range of ridicule, which takes "every creature in, of every kind." No fastidious delicacy spoils their sports of fancy: though ten times told, the tale to them never can be tedious; though dull "as the fat weed that grows on Lethe's bank," the jest for them has all the poignancy of satire: on the very offals, the garbage of wit, they can feed and batten. Happy they who can find in every jester the wit of Sterne or Swift; who else can wade through hundreds of thickly-printed pages to obtain for their reward such witticisms as the following:—

"Two Irishmen having travelled on foot from Chester to Barnet, were confoundedly tired and fatigued by their journey; and the more so when they were told that they had still about ten miles to go. 'By my shoul and St. Patrick,' cries one of them, 'it is but five miles a-piece.'"

Here, notwithstanding the promise of a jest held forth by the words, "By my shoul and St. Patrick," we are ultimately cheated of our hopes. To the ignorant, indeed, the word of promise is kept to the mind as well as to the ear; but others perceive that, instead of a bull, they have only a piece of sentimental arithmetic, founded upon the elegant theorem, that friendship doubles all our pleasures, and divides all our pains.

We must not, from false delicacy to our countrymen, here omit a piece of advice to English retailers or inventors of Irish blunders. Let them beware of such prefatory exclamations as—"*By my shoul and St. Patrick! By Jasus! Arrah, honey! My dear joy!*" &c., because all such phrases, besides being absolutely out of date and fashion in Ireland, raise too high an expectation in the minds of a British audience, operating as much to the disadvantage of the story-teller as the dangerous exordium of—"I'll tell you an excellent story;" an exordium ever to be avoided by all prudent wits.

Another caution should be given to well-meaning ignorance. Never produce that as an Irish bull for which any person of common literature can immediately supply a precedent from our best authors. Never be at the pains, for instance, of telling, from Joe Miller, a *good* story of an *Irish* sailor, who *travelled* with Captain Cook *round* the world, and afterwards swore to his companions that it was as flat as a table.

This anecdote, however excellent, immediately finds a parallel in Pope:

"*Mad Mathesis alone was unconfined,*

Too mad for mere material chains to bind;

Now to pure space lifts her ecstatic stare,

Now running round the circle finds it square."

Pope was led into the blunder of representing Mad Mathesis running *round the circle*, and finding it *square* by a confused notion that mathematicians had considered the circle as composed of straight lines. His mathematical friends could have told him, that though it was talked of as a polygon, it was not supposed to be a square; but *polygon* would not have rhymed to *stare*; and poets, when they launch into the ocean of words, must have an eye to the helm; at all events a poet, who is not supposed to be a student of the exact sciences, may be forgiven for a mathematical blunder. This affair of squaring the circle seems to be peculiarly liable to error; for even an accurate mathematician cannot speak of it without committing something very like a bull.

Dr. Hutton, in his Treatise on Mensuration, p. 119, says, "As the *famous* quadrature of the late Mr. John Machin, professor of astronomy in Gresham College, is extremely expeditious and *but little known*, I shall take this opportunity of explaining it."

It is to be presumed, that the doctor here uses the word *famous* in that acceptation in which it is daily and hourly employed by our Bond-street loungers, by city apprentices, and men of the ton. "That was a *famous* good joke;" "He is a *famous* whip;" "We had a *famous* hop," &c. Now it cannot be supposed that any of these things are in themselves entitled to fame; but they may, indeed, by the courtesy of England, be at once *famous*, and but little known. It is unnecessary to enter into the defence either of Dr. Hutton or of Pope, for they were not born in Ireland, therefore they cannot make bulls; and assuredly their mistakes will not, in the opinion of any person of common sense or candour, derogate from their reputation.

"Never strike till you are sure to wound," is a maxim well known to the polite37 and politic part of the world. "Never laugh when the laugh can be turned against you," should be the maxim of those who find their chief pleasure in making others ridiculous. This principle, if applied to our subject, would lead, however, to a very extensive and troublesome system of mutual forbearance; troublesome in proportion to the good or ill humour of the parties concerned; extensive in proportion to their knowledge and acquirements. A man of cultivated parts will foresee the possibility of the retort courteous, where an ignorant man will enjoy the fearless bliss of ignorance. For example, an illiterate person may enjoy a hearty laugh at the common story of an old Irish beggar-man, who, pretending to be dumb, was thrown off his guard by the question, "How many years have you been dumb?" and answered, "Five years last St. John's Eve, please your honour."

But our triumph over the Irishman abates, when we recollect in the History of England, and in Shakspeare, the case of Saunder Simcox, who pretended to be miraculously and instantaneously cured of blindness at St. Alban's shrine.

Since we have bestowed so much criticism on the blunder of a beggar-man, a word or two must be permitted on the blunder of a thief. It is natural for ignorant people to laugh at the Hibernian who said that he had stolen a pound of chocolate *to make tea of*. But philosophers are disposed to abstain from the laugh of superiority when they recollect that the Irishman could probably make as good tea from chocolate as the chemist could make butter, sugar, and cream, from antimony, sulphur, and tartar. The absurdities in the ancient chemical nomenclature could not be surpassed by any in the Hibernian catalogue. If the reader should think this a rash and unwarrantable assertion, we refer him to an essay,38 in which the flagrant abuses of speech in the old language of chemistry are admirably exposed and ridiculed. Could an Irishman confer a more appropriate appellation upon a white powder than that of *beautiful black*?

It is really provoking to perceive, that as our knowledge of science or literature extends, we are in more danger of finding, in our own and foreign languages, parallels and precedents for Irish blunders; so that a very well informed man can scarcely with any grace or conscience smile, where a booby squire might enjoy a long and loud horse-laugh of contempt.

What crowds were collected to see the Irish bottle conjuror39 get into a quart bottle; but Dr. Desaguliers had prepared the English to think such a condensation of animal particles not impossible. He says, vol. i. p. 5, of his Lectures on Natural Philosophy, "that the nature of things should last, and their natural course continue the same; all the changes made in bodies must arise only from the various separations, new conjunctions, and motions, of these original particles. *These must be imagined of an unconceivable smallness,* but by the union of them there are made bigger lumps," &c.

Indeed things are now come to such a lamentable pass, that without either literary or scientific acquirements, mere local knowledge, such as can be obtained from a finger-post, may sometimes prevent us from the full enjoyment of the Boeotian absurdity of our neighbours. What can, at first view, appear a grosser blunder than that of the Irishman who begged a friend to look over his library, to find for him the history of the world before the creation? Yet this anachronism of ideas is not unparalleled; it is matched, though on a more contracted scale, by an inscription on a British finger-post—

"Had you seen these roads before they were made,

You'd lift up your eyes, and bless Marshal Wade!"

There is, however, a rabbi, mentioned by Bayle, who far exceeds both the Irishman and the finger-post. He asserts, that Providence questioned Adam concerning the creation before he was born; and that Adam knew more of the matter than the angels who had laughed at him.

Those who see things in a philosophical light must have observed more frequently than others, that there is in this world a continual recurrence or rotation of ideas, events, and blunders. With his utmost ingenuity, or his utmost absurdity, a man, in modern days, cannot contrive to produce a system for which there is no prototype in antiquity, or to commit a blunder for which there is no precedent. For example: during the late rebellion in Ireland, at the military execution of some wretched rebel, the cord broke, and the criminal, who had been only half hanged, fell to the ground. The Major, who was superintending the execution, exclaimed, "You rascal, if you do that again, I'll kill you, as sure as you breathe."

Now this is by no means an original idea. In an old French book, called "La Charlatanerie des Savans," is the following note:—"D'autres ont proposé et résolu en même tems des questions ridicules; par exemple celle-ci: Devroit-on faire souffrir une seconde fois le même genre de mort à un criminel, qui après avoir eu la tête coupée viendroit à résusciter?" —*Finkelth*, Praef. ad Observationes Pract. num. 12.

The passionate major, instead of being a mere Irish *blunderer*, was, without knowing it, a learned casuist; for he was capable of deciding, in one word, a question, which, it seems, had puzzled the understandings of the ablest lawyers of France, or which had appalled their conscientious sensibility.

Alas! there is nothing new under the sun.

"Where ignorance is bliss, 'tis folly to be wise."

CHAPTER VI
"THOUGHTS THAT BREATHE,
AND WORDS THAT BURN"

We lamented, in our last chapter, that there is nothing new under the sun; yet, perhaps, the thoughts and phraseology of the following story may not be familiar to the English.

"Plase your honour," says a man, whose head is bound up with a garter, in token and commemoration of his having been at a fair the preceding night—"Plase your honour, it's what I am striving since six o'clock and before, this morning, becàase I'd sooner trouble your honour's honour than any man in all Ireland, on account of your character, and having lived under your family, me and mine, twenty years, aye, say forty again to the back o' that, in the old gentleman's time, as I well remember before I was born; that same time I heard tell of your own honour's riding a little horse in green with your gun before you, a grousing over our town-lands, which was the mill and abbey of Ballynagobogg, though 'tis now set away from me (owing to them that belied my father) to Christy Salmon, becàase he's an Orangeman—or his wife—though he was once (let him deny it who can), to *my certain knowledge*, behind the haystack in Tullygore, *sworn* in a United man by Captain Alick, who was hanged——Pace to the dead any how!——Well, not to be talking too much of that now, only for this Christy Salmon, I should be still living under your honour."

"Very likely; but what has all this to do with the present business? If you have any complaint to make against Christy Salmon, make it—if not, let me go to dinner."

"Oh, it would be too bad to be keeping your honour from your dinner, but I'll make your honour sinsible immadiately. It is not of Christy Salmon at-all-at-all I'm talking. May be your honour is not sinsible yet who I am—I am Paddy M'Doole, of the Curragh, and I've been a flax-dresser and dealer since I parted your honour's land, and was last night at the fair of Clonaghkilty, where I went just in a quiet way thinking of nothing at all, as any man might, and had my little yarn along with me, my wife's and the girl's year's spinning, and all just hoping to bring them back a few honest shillings as they desarved—none better!—Well, plase your honour, my beast lost a shoe, which brought me late to the fair, but not so late but what it was as throng as ever; you could have walked over the heads of the men, women, and childer, a foot and a horseback, all buying and selling; so I to be sure thought no harm of doing the like; so I makes the best bargain I could of the little hanks for my wife and the girl, and the man I sold them to was just weighing them at the crane, and I standing forenent him—'Success to myself!' said I, looking at the shillings I was putting into my waistcoat pocket for my poor family, when up comes the inspector, whom I did not know, I'll take my oath, from Adam, nor couldn't know, becááse he was the deputy inspector, and had been but just made, of which I was ignorant, by this book and all the books that ever were shut and opened—but no matter for that; he seizes my hanks out of the scales that I had just sold, saying they were unlawful and forfeit, becááse by his watch it was past four o'clock, which I denied to be possible, plase your honour, becááse not one, nor two, nor three, but all the town and country were selling the same as myself in broad day, only when the deputy came up they stopped, which I could not, by rason I did not know him.—'Sir,' says I (very civil), 'if I had known you, it would have been another case, but any how I hope no jantleman will be making it a crime to a poor man to sell his little matter of yarn for his wife and childer after four o'clock, when he did not know it was contrary to law at-all-at-all.'

"'I gave you notice that it was contrary to law at the fair of Edgerstown,' said he.—'I axe your pardon, sir,' said I, 'it was my brother, for I was by.' With that he calls me liar, and what not, and takes a grip40 of me, and I a grip of my flax, and he had a shilala41 and I had none; so he gave it me over the head, I crying 'murder! murder!' and clinging to the scales to save me, and they set a swinging and I with them, plase your honour, till the bame comes down a'top o' the back o' my head, and *kilt* me, as your honour sees."

"I see that you are alive still, I think."

"It's not his fault if I am, plase your honour, for he left me for dead, and I am as good as dead still: if it be plasing to your honour to examine my head, you'll be sinsible I'm telling nothing but the truth. Your honour never *seen* a man kilt as I was and am—all which I'm ready (when convanient) to swear before your honour." 42

The reiterated assurances which this hero gives us of his being killed, and the composure with which he offers to swear to his own assassination and decease, appear rather surprising and ludicrous to those who are not aware that *kilt* is here used in a metaphorical sense, and that it has not the full force of our word killed. But we have been informed by a lady of unquestionable veracity, that she very lately received a petition worded in this manner—

"To the Right Hon. Lady E — — P — —.

"Humbly showeth;

"That your poor petitioner is now lying dead in a ditch," &c.

This poor Irish petitioner's expression, however preposterous it sounds, might perhaps be justified, if we were inclined to justify an Irishman by the example, not only of poets comic and tragic, but of prose writers of various nations. The evidence in favour both of the fact and the belief, that people can speak and walk after they are dead, is attested by stout warriors and grave historians. Let us listen to the solemn voice of a princess, who comes sweeping in the sceptred pall of gorgeous tragedy, to inform us that half herself has buried the other half.

"Weep, eyes; melt into tears these cheeks to lave:

*One half myself lays t'other in the grave." 43_*

For six such lines as these Corneille received six thousand livres, and the admiration of the French court and people during the Augustan age of French literature. But an Italian is not content with killing by halves. Here is a man from Italy who goes on fighting, not like Witherington, upon his stumps, but fairly after he is dead.

"Nor yet perceived the vital spirit fled,

*But still fought on, nor knew that he was dead." 44_*

Common sense is somewhat shocked at this single instance of an individual fighting after he is dead; but we shall, doubtless, be reconciled to the idea by the example of a gallant and modern commander, who has declared his opinion, that nothing is more feasible than for a garrison to fight, or at least to surrender, after they are dead, nay, after they are buried.—Witness this public document.

"Liberty and Equality.

"May 29th, | Garrison of Ostend.

30th Floréal, 6 |

"Muscar, commandant of Ostend, to the commandant in

chief of his British majesty.

"General,

"The council of war was sitting when I received the honour of
your letters. We have unanimously resolved not to surrender the
place until we shall have been buried in its ruins," &c.

One step further in hyperbole is reserved for him, who, being buried,
carries about his own sepulchre.

"To live a life half dead, a living death,

And buried; but oh, yet more miserable!

Myself my sepulchre, a moving grave!"

No person, if he heard this passage for the first time from the lips of an
Irishman, could hesitate to call it a series of bulls; yet these lines are part of
the beautiful complaint of Samson Agonistes on his blindness. Such are the
hyperboles sanctioned by the genius, or, what with some judges may have
more influence, the name of Milton. The bounds which separate sublimity
from bombast, and absurdity from wit, are as fugitive as the boundaries
of taste. Only those who are accustomed to examine and appraise literary
goods are sensible of the prodigious change that can be made in their
apparent value by a slight change in the manufacture. The absurdity of a
man's swearing he was killed, or declaring that he is now dead in a ditch, is
revolting to common sense; yet the *living death* of Dapperwit, in the "Rape
of the Lock," is not absurd, but witty; and representing men as dying many
times before their death is in Shakspeare sublime:

"Cowards die many times before their death; The brave can never taste
of death but once."

The most direct contradictions in words do not (*in English writers*)
destroy the eflect of irony, wit, pathos, or sublimity.

In the classic ode on Eton College, the poet exclaims —

"To each their sufferings, all are men

Condemned alike to groan;

The feeling for another's pain,

Th' unfeeling for their own."

Who but a half-witted dunce would ask how those that are unfeeling
can have sufferings? When Milton in melodious verse inquires,

"Who shall tempt with wandering feet

The dark unbottom'd infinite abyss,

And through the palpable obscure find out

His uncouth way!" —

what Zoilus shall dare interrupt this flow of poetry to object to the palpable obscure, or to ask how feet can wander upon that which has no bottom?

It is easy, as Tully has long ago observed, to fix the brand of ridicule upon the *verbum ardens* of orators and poets—the "Thoughts that breathe, and words that burn."

CHAPTER VII
PRACTICAL BULLS

As we have not hitherto been successful in finding original Irish bulls in language, we must now look for them in conduct. A person may be guilty of a solecism without uttering a single syllable—"That man has been guilty of a solecism with his hand," an ancient critic said of an actor, who had pointed his hand upwards when invoking the infernal gods. "You may act a lie as well as speak one," says Wollaston. Upon the same, principle, the Irish may be said to act, as well as to utter bulls. We shall give some instances of their practical bulls, which we hope to find unmatched by the blunders of all other nations. Most people, whether they be savage or civilized, can contrive to revenge themselves upon their enemies without blundering; but the Irish are exceptions. They cannot even do this without *a bull.* During the late Irish rebellion, there was a banker to whom they had a peculiar dislike, and on whom they had vowed vengeance: accordingly they got possession of as many of his bank-notes as they could, and made a bonfire of them! This might have been called a feu de joie, perhaps, but certainly not un feu d'artifice; for nothing could show less art than burning a banker's notes in order to destroy his credit. How much better do the English understand the arts of vengeance! Captain Drinkwater45 informs us, that during the siege of Gibraltar, the English, being half famished, were most violently enraged against the Jews, who withheld their stores of provision, and made money of the public distress—a crime *never committed except by Jews:* at length the fleet relieved the besieged, and as soon as the provisions were given out, the English soldiers and sailors, to revenge themselves upon the Jews, burst open their stores, and actually roasted a pig at a fire made of cinnamon. There are other persons, as well as the Irish, who do not always understand their own interests where their passions are concerned. That great warrior, Hyder Ali, once lost a battle by a practical bull. Being encamped within sight of the British, he resolved to give them a high idea of his forces and of his artillery; for this purpose, before the engagement,46 he ordered his army to march early, and conveying some large pieces of cannon to the top of a hill, he caused them to be pointed at the English camp, which they reached admirably well, and occasioned a kind of disorder and haste in striking and removing tents, &c. Hyder, delighted at having thus insulted the English, caused all his artillery, even the very smallest pieces, to be drawn up the hill for the purpose of making a vain parade, though the greater part of the balls could never reach the English: he imagined he should give the enemy a high idea of his forces, and intimidate them by showing all his artillery, and the vivacity with which it was worked; and in order that his intention might be answered, he encouraged the soldiers himself, by giving money to the cannoneers of those pieces that appeared to be the best served.

The English presently, after this farce was over, obliged Hyder to come down from labour-in-vain hill and to give them battle in earnest. As the historian observes, "The ridiculous cannonade at the top of the hill had exhausted his ammunition, his great guns were useless to him, and he lost the day by his premature rejoicings before the battle." A still more ancient precedent for this preposterous practical bull, of rejoicing for an anticipated victory, was given by Xerxes, we believe, who brought with him an immense block of marble, on which he intended to inscribe the date and manner of his victory over the Greeks. When Xerxes was defeated, the Greeks dedicated this stone to Nemesis, the goddess of vengeance. But Xerxes was in the habit of making practical bulls, such as whipping the sea, and begging pardon for it afterwards; throwing fetters into the Hellespont as a token of subjugation, and afterwards expiating his offence by an offering of a golden cup and Persian scimetar.

To such blunders can the passions betray the most renowned heroes, although they had not the misfortune to have been born in Ireland.

The impatience which induced Hyder Ali to anticipate victory is not confined to military men and warlike operations; if we descend to common life and vulgar business, we shall find the same disposition even in the precincts of Change-alley: those who bargained for South Sea stock, that was not actually forthcoming, were called *bears*, in allusion to the practice of the hunters of bears in Canada, who were accustomed to bargain for the skin of the bear before it was caught; but whence the correlative term *bull* is derived we are at a loss to determine, and we must also leave it to the mercantile speculators of England to explain why gentlemen call themselves bulls of wheat and bulls of coals: all we can say is, that these are not Irish bulls. There is one distinguished peculiarity of the Irish bull—*its horns are tipped with brass*.47 It is generally supposed that persons who have been dipped in the Shannon48 are ever afterwards endowed with a supernatural portion of what is called, by enemies, impudence or assurance, by friends, self-possession or *civil courage*. These invulnerable mortals are never oppressed with *mauvaise honte*, that malady which keeps the faculties of the soul under imaginary imprisonment. A well-dipped Irishman, on the contrary, can move, speak, think, like Demosthenes, with as much ease, when the eyes of numbers are upon him, as if the spectators were so many cabbage-stalks. This virtue of *civil courage* is of inestimable value in the opinion of the best judges. The great Lord Verulam—no one, by-the-by, could be a better judge of its value than he, who wanted it so much—the great Lord Verulam declares, that if he were asked what is the first, second, and third thing necessary to success in public business, he should answer boldness, boldness, boldness. Success to the nation which possesses it in perfection! Bacon was too acute and candid a philosopher not to acknowledge, that like all the other goods of life this same boldness has its countervailing disadvantages.

"Certainly," says he, "to men of great judgment, bold persons are a sport to behold; nay, and to the vulgar, boldness hath somewhat of the ridiculous; for if absurdity be the subject of laughter, doubt you not but great boldness is seldom without some absurdity; especially it is a sport to see when a bold fellow is out of countenance, for that puts his face into a most shrunken and wooden posture, as needs it must."

The man, however, who possesses boldness in perfection, can never be put out of countenance, and consequently can never exhibit, for the sport of his enemies, a face in this wooden posture. It is the deficiency, and not the excess of this quality, that is to be feared. Civil boldness without military courage would, indeed, be somewhat ridiculous: but we cannot accuse the Irish of any want of military courage; on the contrary, it is supposed in England, that an Irishman is always ready *to give any gentleman satisfaction*, even when none is desired.

At the close of the American war, as a noble lord of high naval character was returning home to his family after various escapes from danger, he was detained a day at Holyhead by contrary winds. Reading in a summer-house, he heard the well-known sound of bullets whistling near him: he looked about, and found that two balls had just passed through the door close beside him; he looked out of the window, and saw two gentlemen who were just charging their pistols again, and, as he guessed that they had been shooting at a mark upon the door, he rushed out, and very civilly remonstrated with them on the imprudence of firing at the door of a house without having previously examined whether any one was withinside. One of them immediately answered, in a tone which proclaimed at once his disposition and his country, "Sir, I did not know you were within there, and I don't know who you are now; but if I've given offence, I am willing," said he, holding out the ready-charged pistols, "to give you the *satisfaction of a gentleman*—take your choice."

With his usual presence of mind the noble lord seized hold of both the pistols, and said to his astonished countryman, "Do me the justice, sir, to go into that summer-house, shut the door, and let me have two shots at you; then we shall be upon equal terms, and I shall be quite at your service to give or receive the *satisfaction of a gentleman.*"

There was an air of drollery and of superiority in his manner which at once struck and pleased the Hibernian. "Upon my conscience, sir, I believe you are a very honest fellow," said he, looking him earnestly in the face, "and I have a great mind to shake hands with you. Will you only just tell me who you are?"

The nobleman told his name—a name dear to every Briton and every Irishman.

"I beg your pardon, and that's what no man ever accused me of doing before," cried the gallant Hibernian; "and had I known who you were, I would as soon have *shot my own soul* as have fired at the door. But how could I tell who was withinside?"

"That is the very thing of which I complain," said his lordship.

His candid opponent admitted the justice of the complaint as soon as he understood it, and he promised never more to be guilty of such a practical bull.

CHAPTER VIII
THE DUBLIN SHOEBLACK

Upon looking over our last chapter on practical bulls, we were much concerned to find that we have so few Irish and so many foreign blunders. It is with still more regret we perceive, that notwithstanding our utmost diligence, we have not yet been able to point out the distinguishing characteristic of an Irish bull. But to compensate for this disappointment we have devised a syllogism, which some people may prefer to an à priori argument, to prove irrefragably, that the Irish are blunderers.

After the instances we have produced, chapter 6th, of the *verbum ardens* of English and foreign poets, and after the resemblance that we have pointed out betwixt certain figures of rhetoric and the Irish bull, we have little reason to fear that the candid and enlightened reader should object to our major.

Major.—Those who use figurative language are disposed to make bulls.

Minor.—The Irish use figurative language.

Conclusion.—Therefore the Irish are disposed to make bulls.

We proceed to establish the truth of our minor, and the first evidence we shall call is a Dublin shoeblack. He is not in circumstances peculiarly favourable for the display of figurative language; he is in a court of justice, upon his trial for life or death. A quarrel happened between two shoeblacks, who were playing at what in England is called pitch-farthing, or heads and tails, and in Ireland, head or harp. One of the combatants threw a small paving stone at his opponent, who drew out the knife with which he used to scrape shoes, and plunged it up to the hilt in his companion's breast. It is necessary for our story to say, that near the hilt of this knife was stamped the name of Lamprey, an eminent cutler in Dublin. The shoeblack was brought to trial. With a number of significant gestures, which on his audience had all the powers that Demosthenes ascribes to action, he, in a language not purely Attic, gave the following account of the affair to his judge.

"Why, my lard, as I was going past the Royal Exchange I meets Billy. 'Billy,' says I, 'will you sky a copper?' 'Done,' says he; 'Done,' says I; and done and done's enough between two jantlemen. With that I ranged them fair and even with my hook-em-snivey—up they go. 'Music!' says he—'Skulls!' says I; and down they come, three brown mazards. 'By the holy! you flesh'd 'em,' says he. 'You lie,' says I. With that he ups with a lump of a two year old, and lets drive at me. I outs with my bread-earner, and gives it him up to Lamprey in the bread-basket."

To make this intelligible to the English, some comments are necessary. Let us follow the text, step by step, and it will afford our readers, as Lord Kames says of Blair's Dissertation on Ossian, a delicious morsel of criticism.

As I was going past the Royal Exchange I meets Billy.

In this apparently simple exordium, the scene and the meeting with Billy are brought before the eye by the judicious use of the present tense.

Billy, says I, will you sky a copper?

A copper! genus pro specie! the generic name of copper for the base individual halfpenny.

Sky a copper.

To *sky* is a new verb, which none but a master hand could have coined: a more splendid metonymy could not be applied upon a more trivial occasion; the lofty idea of raising a metal to the skies is substituted for the mean thought of tossing up a halfpenny. Our orator compresses his hyperbole into a single word. Thus the mind is prevented from dwelling long enough upon the figure to perceive its enormity. This is the perfection of the art. Let the genius of French exaggeration and of eastern hyperbole hide their diminished heads—Virgil is scarcely more sublime.

"*Ingrediturque solo, et caput inter nubila condit.*"

"*Her feet on earth, her head amidst the clouds.*"

Up they go, continues our orator.

Music! says he—Skulls! says I.

Metaphor continually: on one side of an Irish halfpenny there is a harp; this is expressed by the general term music, which is finely contrasted with the word skull.

Down they come, three brown mazards.

Mazards! how the diction of our orator is enriched from the vocabulary of Shakspeare! the word head, instead of being changed for a more general term, is here brought distinctly to the eye by the term mazard, or face, which is more appropriate to his majesty's profile than the word skull or head.

By the holy! you flesh'd 'em, says he.

By the holy! is an oath in which more is meant than meets the ear; it is an ellipsis—an abridgment of an oath. The full formula runs thus—By the holy poker of hell! This instrument is of Irish invention or imagination. It seems a useful piece of furniture in the place for which it is intended, to stir the devouring flames, and thus to increase the torments of the damned. Great judgment is necessary to direct an orator how to suit his terms to his auditors, so as not to shock their feelings either by what is too much above or too much below common life. In the use of oaths, where the passions are warm, this must be particularly attended to, else they lose their effect, and seem more the result of the head than the heart. But to proceed:—

By the holy! you flesh'd 'em.

To *flesh* is another verb of Irish coinage; it means, in shoeblack dialect, to touch a halfpenny, as it goes up into the air, with the fleshy part of the thumb, so as to turn it which way you please, and thus to cheat your opponent. What an intricate explanation saved by one word!

You lie, says I.

Here no periphrasis would do the business.

With that he ups with a lump of a two year old, and lets drive at me.

He ups with.—A verb is here formed of two prepositions—a novelty in grammar. Conjunctions, we all know, are corrupted Anglo-Saxon verbs; but prepositions, according to Horne Tooke, derive only from Anglo-Saxon nouns.

All this time it is possible that the mere English reader may not be able to guess what it is that our orator ups with or takes up. He should be apprised, that a lump of a two year old is a middle-sized stone. This is a metaphor, borrowed partly from the grazier's vocabulary, and partly from the arithmetician's vade-mecum. A stone, to come under the denomination of a lump of a two year old, must be to a less stone as a two year old calf is to a yearling; or it must be to a larger stone than itself, as a two year old calf is to an ox. Here the scholar sees that there must be two statements, one in the rule of three direct and one in the rule of three inverse, to obtain precisely the thing required; yet the untutored Irishman, without suspecting the necessity of this operose process, arrives at the solution of the problem by some short cut of his own, as he clearly evinces by the propriety of his metaphor. To be sure, there seems some incongruity in his throwing this lump of a two year old calf at his adversary. No arm but that of Milo could be strong enough for such a feat. Upon recollection, however, bold as this figure may seem, there are precedents for its use.

"We read in a certain author," says Beattie, "of a giant, who, in his wrath, tore off the top of the promontory, and flung it at the enemy; and so huge was the mass, that you might, says he, have seen goats browsing on it as it flew through the air." Compared with this, our orator's figure is cold and tame.

"I outs with my bread-earner," continues he.

We forbear to comment on *outs with*, because the intelligent critic immediately perceives that it has the same sort of merit ascribed to *ups with*. What our hero dignifies with the name of his bread-earner is the knife with which, by scraping shoes, he earned his bread. Pope's ingenious critic, Mr. Warton, bestows judicious praise upon the art with which this poet, in the Rape of the Lock, has used many "periphrases and uncommon expressions," to avoid mentioning the name of *scissars*, which would sound too vulgar for epic dignity—fatal engine, forfex, meeting-points, &c. Though the metonymy of *bread-earner* for a shoeblack's knife may not equal these in elegance, it perhaps surpasses them in ingenuity.

*I gives it him up to Lamprey in the bread-basket.*49

Homer is happy in his description of wounds, but this surpasses him in the characteristic choice of circumstance. *Up to Lamprey*, gives us at once a complete idea of the length, breadth, and thickness of the wound, without the assistance of the coroner. It reminds us of a passage in Virgil—

"Cervice orantis capulo tenus abdidit ensem."

"Up to the hilt his shining falchion sheathed."

Let us now compare the Irish shoeblack's metaphorical language with the sober *slang* of an English blackguard, who, fortunately for the fairness of the comparison, was placed somewhat in similar circumstances.

Lord Mansfield, examining a man who was a witness in the court of King's Bench, asked him what he knew of the defendant.

"Oh, my lord, I knew him. *I was up to him.*"

"Up to him!" says his lordship; "what do you mean by being up to him?"

"Mean, my lord! why, *I was down upon him.*"

"Up to him, and down upon him!" says his lordship, turning to Counsellor Dunning, "what does the fellow mean?"

"Why, I mean, my lord, as deep as he thought himself, *I stagged him.*"

"I cannot conceive, friend," says his lordship, "what you mean by this sort of language; I do not understand it."

"Not understand it!" rejoined the fellow, with surprise: "*Lord, what a flat you must be!*"

Though he undervalued Lord Mansfield, this man does not seem to have been a very bright genius. In his cant words, "*up to him, down upon him, stagged him,*" there are no metaphors; and we confess ourselves to be as great *flats* as his lordship, for we do not understand this sort of language.

"*True no meaning puzzles more than wit,*"

as we may see in another English example. Proverbs have been called the wisdom of nations; therefore it is fair to have recourse to them in estimating national abilities. Now there is an old English proverb, "Tenterden steeple is the cause of Goodwin sands."

"This proverb," says Mr. Ray, "is used when an absurd and ridiculous reason is given of any thing in question; an account of the original whereof, I find in one of Bishop Latimer's sermons in these words—'Mr. Moore was once sent with commission into Kent to try out, if it might be, what was the cause of Goodwin sands, and the shelf which stopped up Sandwich haven. Thither cometh Mr. Moore, and calleth all the country before him, such as were thought to be men of experience, and men that could, of all likelihood, best satisfy him of the matter concerning the stopping of Sandwich haven. Among the rest came in before him an old man with a white head, and one that was thought to be little less than a hundred years old. When Mr. Moore saw this aged man, he thought it expedient to hear him say his mind in this matter (for being so old a man, it was likely that he knew the most in that presence or company); so Mr. Moore called this old aged man unto him and said, 'Father,' said he, 'tell me, if you can, what is the cause of the great arising of the sands and shelves here about this haven, which stop it up so that no ships can arrive here. You are the oldest man I can espy in all the company, so that if any man can tell any cause of it, you, of all likelihood, can say most to it, or, at leastwise, more than any man here assembled.'

"'Yea, forsooth, good Mr. Moore,' quoth this old man, 'for I am well nigh a hundred years old, and no man here in this company any thing near my age.'

"'Well then,' quoth Mr. Moore, 'how say you to this matter? What think you to be the cause of these shelves and sands which stop up Sandwich haven?'

"'Forsooth, sir,' quoth he, 'I am an old man; I think that, Tenterden steeple is the cause of Goodwin sands. For I am an old man, sir,' quoth he, 'I may remember the building of Tenterden steeple, and I may remember when there was no steeple at all there; and before that Tenterden or *Totterden* steeple was in building, there was no manner of talking of any flats or sands that stopped up the haven, and therefore I think that Tenterden steeple is the cause of the decay and destroying of Sandwich haven.'" 50—Thus far the bishop.

The prolix pertinacity with which this *old aged* man adheres to the opinion that he had formed, without any intelligible reason, is characteristic of an English peasant; but however absurd his mode of judging may be, and however confused and incongruous his ideas, his species of absurdity surely bears no resemblance to an Hibernian blunder. We cannot even suspect it to be possible that a man of this slow, circumspect character could be in any danger of making an Irish bull; and we congratulate the English peasantry and populace, as a body, upon their possessing that temper which

"*Wisely rests content with sober sense,*

Nor makes to dangerous wit a vain pretence."

Even the *slang* of English pickpockets and coiners is, as we may see in Colquhoun's View of the Metropolis, free from all seducing mixture of wit and humour. What Englishman would ever have thought of calling persons in the pillory *the babes in the wood*? This is a common cant phrase amongst Dublin reprobates. Undoubtedly such phrases tend to lessen the power of shame and the effect of punishment, and a witty rogue will lead numbers to the gallows. English morality is not in so much danger as Irish manners must be from these humourous talents in their knights of industry. If, nevertheless, there be frequent executions for capital crimes in England, we must account for this in the words of the old Lord Chief Justice Fortescue—"More men," says his lordship, "are hanged in *Englonde* in one year than *in Fraunce* in seven, *because the English have better hartes;* the *Scotchmenne* likewise never *dare rob,* but only commit larcenies." At all events, the phlegmatic temper of *Englonde* secures her from making bulls. The propensity to this species of blunder exists in minds of a totally different cast; in those who are quick and enthusiastic, who are confounded by the rapidity and force with which undisciplined multitudes of ideas crowd for utterance. Persons of such intellectual characters are apt to make elisions in speaking, which they trust the capacities of their audience will supply:

passing rapidly over a long chain of thought, they sometimes forget the intermediate links, and no one but those of equally rapid habits can follow them successfully.

We hope that the evidence of the Dublin shoeblack has, in some degree, tended to prove our *minor*, that the Irish are disposed to use figurative language: we shall not, however, rest our cause on a single evidence, however respectable; but before we summon our other witnesses, we beg to relieve the reader's attention, which must have been fatigued by such a chapter of criticism. They shall now have the tale of a mendicant. A specimen of city rhetoric is given in the shoeblack; the country mendicant's eloquence is of a totally different species.

CHAPTER IX
THE HIBERNIAN MENDICANT

Perhaps the reader may wish to see as well as hear the petitioner. At first view you might have taken him for a Spaniard. He was tall; and if he had been a gentleman, you would have said that there was an air of dignity in his figure. He seemed very old, yet he appeared more worn by sorrow than by time. Leaning upon a thick oaken stick as he took off his hat to ask for alms, his white hair was blown by the wind.

"Health and long life to you!" said he. "Give an old man something to help to bury him. He is past his labour, and cannot trouble this world long any way."

He held his hat towards us, with nothing importunate in his manner, but rather with a look of confidence in us, mixed with habitual resignation. His thanks were: "Heaven bless you!—Long life and success to you! to you and yours! and may you never want a friend, as I do."

The last words were spoken low. He laid his hand upon his heart as he bowed to us, and walked slowly away. We called him back; and upon our questioning him farther, he gave the following account of himself:—

"I was bred and born—but no matter where such a one as I was bred and born, no more than where I may die and be buried. I, that have neither son, nor daughter, nor kin, nor friend on the wide earth, to mourn over my grave when I am laid in it, as I soon must. Well! when it pleases God to take me, I shall never be missed out of this world, so much as by a dog: and why should I?—having never in my time done good to any—but evil—which I have lived to repent me of, many's the long day and night, and ever shall whilst I have sense and reason left. In my youthful days God was too good to me: I had friends, and a little home of my own to go to—a pretty spot of land for a farm, as you could see, with a snug cabin, and every thing complete, and all to be mine; for I was the only one my father and mother had, and accordingly was made much of, too much; for I grew headstrong upon it, and high, and thought nothing of any man, and little of any woman, but one. That one I surely did think of; and well worth thinking of she was. Beauty, they say, is all fancy; but she was a girl every man might fancy.

Never was one more sought after. She was then just in her prime, and full of life and spirits; but nothing light in her behaviour—quite modest—yet obliging. She was too good for me to be thinking of, no doubt; but 'faint heart never won fair lady,' so I made bold to speak to Rose, for that was her name, and after a world of pains, I began to gain upon her good liking, but couldn't get her to say more than that she never *seen* the man she should fancy so well. This was a great deal from her, for she was coy and proud-like, as she had a good right to be; and, besides being young, loved her little innocent pleasure, and could not easy be brought to give up her sway. No fault of hers: but all very natural. Well! I always considered she never would have held out so long, nor have been so stiff with me, had it not been for an old aunt Honour of hers—God rest her soul! One should not be talking ill of the dead; but she was more out of my way than enough; yet the cratur had no malice in her against me, only meaning her child's good, as she called it, but mistook it, and thought to make Rose happy by some greater match than me, counting her fondness for me, which she could not but see something of, childishness, that she would soon be broke of. Now there was a party of English soldiers quartered in our town, and there was a sergeant amongst them that had money, and a pretty place, as they said, in his own country. He courted Rose, and the aunt favoured him. He and I could never relish one another at all. He was a handsome portly man, but very proud, and looked upon me as dirt under his feet, because I was an Irishman; and at every word would say, 'That's an Irish, bull!' or 'Do you hear Paddy's brogue?'' at which his fellow-soldiers, being all English, would look greatly delighted. Now all this I could have taken in good part from any but him, for I was not an ill-humoured fellow; but there was a spite in him I plainly saw against me, and I could not, nor would not take a word from him against me or my country, especially when Rose was by, who did not like me the worse for having a proper spirit. She little thought what would come of it. Whilst all this was going on, her aunt Honour found to object against me, that I was wild, and given to drink; both which charges were false and malicious, and I knew could come from none other than the sergeant, which enraged me the more against him for speaking *so mean* behind my back. Now I knew, that though the sergeant did not drink spirits, he drank plenty of beer. Rose took it, however, to heart, and talked very serious upon it, observing she could never think to marry a man given to drink, and that the sergeant was remarkably sober and staid, therefore most like, as her aunt Honour said, to make a good husband. The words went straight to my heart, along with Rose's look. I said not a word, but went out, resolving, before I slept, to take an oath against spirits, of all sorts, for Rose's sweet sake. That evening I fell in with some boys of the neighbours, who would have had me along with them, but I *denied myself* and them; and all I would taste was one parting glass, and then made my vow in the presence of the priest, forswearing spirits for two years. Then I went straight to her house to tell her what I had done, not being sensible that I was that same time a little elevated with the parting glass I had taken. The first thing I noticed on going into the room was the man I least wished to see there, and least looked for at this minute: he was in high talk with the aunt, and Rose sitting on the other side of him, no way strange towards him, as I fancied; but that was only fancy, and effect of the liquor I had drunk, which made me see things wrong. I went up, and put my head between them, asking Rose, did she know what I had been about?

"'Yes; too well!' said she, drawing back from my breath. And the aunt looked at her, and she at the aunt, and the sergeant stopped his nose, saying he had not been long enough in Ireland to love the smell of whiskey. I observed, that was an uncivil remark in the present company, and added, that I had not taken a drop that night, but one glass. At which he sneered, and said that was a bull and a blunder, but no wonder, as I was an Irishman. I replied in defence of myself and country. We went on from one smart word to another; and some of his soldiermen being of the company, he had the laugh against me still. I was vexed to see Rose bear so well what I could not bear myself. And the talk grew higher and higher; and from talking of blunders and such trifles, we got, I cannot myself tell you how, on to great party matters, and politics, and religion. And I was a catholic, and he a protestant; and there he had the thing still against me. The company seeing matters not agreeable, dropped off till none were left but the sergeant, and the aunt, and Rose, and myself. The aunt gave me a hint to part, but I would not take it; for I could not bear to go away worsted, and borne down as it were by the English faction, and Rose by to judge. The aunt was called out by one who wanted her to go to a funeral next day: the Englishman then let fall something about our Irish howl, and savages, which Rose herself said was uncivil, she being an Irish woman, which he, thinking only of making game on me, had forgot. I knocked him down, telling him that it was he that was the savage to affront a lady. As he got up he said that he'd have the law of me, if any law was to be had in Ireland.

"'The law!' said I, 'and you a soldier!'

"'Do you mean to call me coward?' said he. 'This is what an English soldier must not bear.' With that he snatches at his arms that were beside him, asking me again, did I mean to call an Englishman coward?

"'Tell me first,' said I, 'did you mean to call us Irish savages?'

"'That's no answer to *my* question,' says he, 'or only an Irish answer.'

"'It is not the worse for that, may be," says I, very coolly, despising the man now, and just took up a knife, that was on the table, to cut off a button that was hanging at my knee. As I was opening of the knife he asks me, was I going to stab at him with my Irish knife, and directly fixes a bayonet at me; on which I seizes a musket and bayonet one of his men had left, telling him I knew the use of it as well as he or any Englishman, and better; for that I should never have gone, as he did, to charge it against an unarmed man.

"'You had your knife,' said he, drawing back.

"' If I had, it was not thinking of you,' said I, throwing the knife away. 'See! I'm armed like yourself now: fight me like a man and a soldier, if you dare," says I.

"'Fight me, if you dare,' says he.

"Rose calls to me to stop; but we were both out of ourselves at the minute. We thrust at each other—he missed me—I hit him. Rose ran in between us to get the musket from my hand: it was loaded, and went off in the struggle, and the ball lodged in her body. She fell! and what happened next I cannot tell, for the sight left my eyes, and all sense forsook me. When I came to myself the house was full of people, going to and fro, some whispering, some crying; and till the words reached my ears, 'Is she quite dead?' I could not understand where I was, or what had happened. I wished to forget again, but could not. The whole truth came upon me, and yet I could not shed a tear; but just pushed my way through the crowd into the inner room, and up to the side of the bed. There she lay stretched, almost a corpse—quite still! Her sweet eyes closed, and no colour in her cheeks, that had been so rosy! I took hold of one of her hands, that hung down, and she then opens her eyes, and knew me directly, and smiles upon me, and says, 'It was no fault of yours: take notice, all of you, it was no fault of his if I die; but *that* I won't do for his sake, if I can help it!'—that was the word she spoke. I thinking, from her speaking so strong, that she was not badly hurt, knelt down to whisper her, that if my breath did smell of spirits, it was the parting glass I had tasted before making the vow I had done against drink for her sake; and that there was nothing I would not do for her, if it would please God to spare her to me. She just pressed my hand, to show me she was sensible. The priest came in, and they forced our hands asunder, and carried me away out of the room. Presently there was a great cry, and I knew all was over."

Here the old man's voice failed, and he turned his face from us. When he had somewhat recovered himself, to change the course of his thoughts, we asked whether he were prosecuted for his assault on the English sergeant, and what became of him?

"Oh! to do him justice, as one should do to every one," said the old man, "he behaved very handsome to me when I was brought to trial; and told the whole truth, only blamed himself more than I would have done, and said it was all his fault for laughing at me and my nation more than a man could bear, situated as I was. They acquitted me through his means. We shook hands, and he hoped all would go right with me, he said; but nothing ever went right with me after. I took little note ever after of worldly matters: all belonging to me went to rack and ruin. The hand of God was upon me: I could not help myself, nor settle mind or body to any thing. I heard them say sometimes I was a little touched in my head: however that might be I cannot say. But at the last I found it was as good for me to give all that was left to my friends, who were better able to manage, and more eager for it than I; and fancying a roving life would agree with me best, I quitted the place, taking nothing with me, but resolved to walk the world, and just trust to the charity of good Christians, or die, as it should please God. How I have lived so long He only knows, and his will be done."

CHAPTER X
IRISH WIT AND ELOQUENCE

"Wild wit, invention ever new," appear in high perfection amongst even the youngest inhabitants of an Irish cottage. The word *wit*, amongst the lower classes of Ireland, means not only quickness of repartee, but cleverness in action; it implies invention and address, with no slight mixture of cunning; all which is expressed in their dialect by the single word *'cuteness* (acuteness). Examples will give a better notion of this than can be conveyed by any definition.

An Irish boy (a 'cute lad) saw a train of his companions leading their cars, loaded with kishes51 of turf, coming towards his father's cabin; his father had no turf, and the question was how some should be obtained. To beg he was ashamed; to dig he was unwilling—but his head went to work directly. He took up a turf which had fallen from one of the cars the preceding day, and stuck it on the top of a pole near the cabin. When the cars were passing, he appeared throwing turf at the mark. "Boys!" cried he, "which of ye will hit?" Each leader of the car, as he passed, could not forbear to fling a turf at the mark; the turf fell at the foot of the pole, and when all the cars had passed, there was a heap left sufficient to reward the ingenuity of our little Spartan.

The same 'cuteness which appears in youth continues and improves in old age. When General V—— was quartered in a small town in Ireland, he and his lady were regularly besieged, whenever they got into their carriage, by an old beggar-woman, who kept her post at the door, assailing them daily with fresh importunities and fresh tales of distress. At last the lady's charity, and the general's patience, were nearly exhausted, but their petitioner's wit was still in its pristine vigour. One morning, at the accustomed hour, when the lady was getting into her carriage, the old woman began—"Agh! my lady; success to your ladyship, and success to your honour's honour, this morning, of all days in the year; for sure didn't I dream last night that her ladyship gave me a pound of tea, and that your honour gave me a pound of tobacco?"

"But, my good woman," said the general, "do not you know that dreams always go by the rule of contrary?"

"Do they so, plase your honour?" rejoined the old woman. "Then it must be your honour that will give me the tea, and her ladyship that will give me the tobacco?"

The general being of Sterne's opinion, that a bon-mot is always worth more than a pinch of snuff, gave the ingenious dreamer the value of her dream.

Innumerable instances might be quoted of the Hibernian genius, not merely for repartee, but for what the Italians call pasquinade. We shall cite only one, which is already so well known in Ireland, that we cannot be found guilty of *publishing* a libel. Over the ostentatious front of a nobleman's house in Dublin, the owner had this motto cut in stone:—

"Otium cum dignitate.—Leisure with dignity."

In process of time his lordship changed his residence; or, since we must descend to plebeian language, was committed to Newgate, and immediately there appeared over the front of his apartment his chosen motto, as large as the life, in white chalk,

"Otium cum dignitate."

Mixed with keen satire, the Irish often show a sort of cool good sense and dry humour, which gives not only effect, but value to their impromptus. Of this class is the observation made by the Irish hackney coachman, upon seeing a man of the ton driving four-in-hand down Bond-street.

"That fellow," said our observer, "looks like a coachman, but drives like a gentleman."

As an instance of humour mixed with sophistry, we beg the reader to recollect the popular story of the Irishman who was run over by a troop of horse, and miraculously escaped unhurt.

"Down upon your knees and thank God, you reprobate," said one of the spectators.

"Thank God! for what? Is it for letting a troop of horse run over me?"

In this speech there is the same sort of humour and sophistry that appears in the Irishman's celebrated question: "What has posterity done for me, that I should do so much for posterity?"

The Irish nation, from the highest to the lowest, in daily conversation about the ordinary affairs of life, employ a superfluity of wit and metaphor which would be astonishing and unintelligible to a majority of the respectable body of English yeomen. Even the cutters of turf and drawers of whiskey are orators; even the *cottiers* and *gossoons* speak in trope and figure. Ask an Irish gossoon to go early in the morning, on an errand, and he answers,

"I'll be off at the flight of night."

If an Irish cottager would express to his landlord that he wishes for a long lease of his land, he says, —

"I would be proud to live on your honour's land as long as grass grows or water runs."

One of our English poets has nearly the same idea: —

> *"As long as streams in silver mazes run,*
>
> *Or spring with annual green renews the grove."*

Without the advantages of a classical education, the lower Irish sometimes make similes that bear a near resemblance to those of the admired poets of antiquity. A loyalist, during the late rebellion, was describing to us the number of the rebels who had gathered on one spot, and were dispersed by the king's army; rallied, and were again put to flight.

"They were," said he, "like swarms of flies on a summer's day, that you brush away with your hand, and still they will be returning."

There is a simile of Homer's which, literally translated, runs thus: "As the numerous troops of flies about a shepherd's cottage in the spring, when the milk moistens the pails, such numbers of Greeks stood in the field against the Trojans." Lord Kames observes, that it is false taste to condemn such comparisons for the lowness of the images introduced. In fact, great objects cannot be degraded by comparison with small ones in these similes, because the only point of resemblance is number; the mind instantly perceives this, and therefore requires no other species of similitude.

When we attempt to judge of the genius of the lower classes of the people, we must take care that we are not under the influence of any prejudice of an aristocratic or literary nature. But this is no easy effort of liberty.

"*Agk! Dublin, sweet Jasus be wid you!*" exclaimed a poor Irishman, as he stood on the deck of a vessel, which was carrying him out of the bay of Dublin. The pathos of this poor fellow will not probably affect delicate sensibility, because he says *wid* instead of *with*, and *Jasus* instead of *Jesus*. Adam Smith is certainly right in his theory, that the sufferings of those in exalted stations have generally most power to command our sympathy. The very same sentiment of sorrow at leaving his country, which was expressed so awkwardly by the poor Irishman, appears, to every reader of taste, exquisitely pathetic from the lips of Mary queen of Scots.

"Farewell, France! Farewell, beloved country! which I shall never more behold!" 52

In anger as well as in sorrow the Irishman is eloquent. A gentleman who was lately riding through the county of — —, in Ireland, to canvass, called to ask a vote from a poor man, who was planting willows in a little garden by the road side.

"You have a vote, my good sir, I am told," said the candidate, in an insinuating tone.

The poor man stuck the willow which he had in his hand into the ground, and with a deliberate pace came towards the candidate to parley with him.

"Please your honour," said he, gravely, "I have a vote, and I have not a vote."

"How can that be?"

"I will tell you, sir," said he, leaning, or rather lying down slowly upon the back of the ditch facing the road, so that the gentleman, who was on horseback, could see only his head and arms.

"Sir," said he, "out of this little garden, with my five acres of land and my own labour, I once had a freehold; but I have been robbed of my freehold: and who do you think has robbed me? why, that man!" pointing to his landlord's steward, who stood beside the candidate. "With my own hands I sowed my own ground with oats, and a fine crop I expected—but I never reaped that crop: not a bushel, no, nor half a bushel, did I ever see; for into my little place comes this man, with I don't know how many more, with their shovels and their barrows, and their horses and their cars, and to work they fell, and they ran a road straight through the best part of my land, turning all to heaps of rubbish, and a bad road it was, and a bad time of year to make it! But where was I when he did this? not where I am now," said the orator, raising himself up and standing firm; "not as you see me now, but lying on my back in my bed in a fever. When I got up I was not able to make my rent out of my land. Besides myself, I had my five children to support. I sold my clothes, and have never been able to buy any since but such as a recruit could sell, who was in haste to get into regimentals—such clothes as these," said he, looking down at his black rags. "Soon I had nothing to eat: but that's not all. I am a weaver, sir: for my rent they seized my two looms; then I had nothing to do. But of all this I do not complain. There was an election some time ago in this county, and a man rode up to me in this garden as you do now, and asked me for my vote, but I refused him, for I was steady to my landlord. The gentleman observed I was a poor man, and asked if I wanted for nothing? but all did not signify; so he rode on gently, and at the corner of the road, within view of my garden, I saw him drop a purse, and I knew, by his looking at me, it was on purpose for me to pick it up. After a while he came back, thinking, to be sure, I had taken up the purse, and had changed my mind, but he found his purse where he left it. My landlord knew all this, and he promised to see justice done me, but he forgot. Then, as for the candidate's lady, before the election nothing was too fair-speaking for me; but afterward, in my distress, when I applied to her to get me a loom, which she could have had from *the Linen Board* by only asking for it, her answer to me was, 'I don't know that I shall ever want a vote again in the county.'

"Now, sir," continued he, "when justice is done to me (and no sooner), I shall be glad to assist my landlord or his friend. I know who *you* are, sir, very well: you bear a good character: success to you! but I have no vote to give to you or any man."

"If I were to attempt to make you any amends for what you have suffered," replied the candidate, "I should do you an injury; it would be said that I had bribed you; but I will repeat your story where it will meet with attention. I cannot, however, tell it so well as you have told it."

"No, sir," was his answer, "for you cannot feel it as I do."

This is almost in terms the conclusion of Pope's epistle from Eloisa to Abelard:—

> "He best can paint them who shall feel them most."

In objurgation and pathetic remonstrancing eloquence, the females of the lower class in Ireland are not inferior to the men. A thin tall woman wrapped in a long cloak, the hood of which was drawn over her head, and shaded her pale face, came to a gentleman to complain of the cruelty of her landlord.

"He is the most hard-hearted man alive, so he is, sir," said she; "he has just seized all I have, which, God knows, is little enough! and has driven my cow to pound, the only cow I have, and only dependence I have for a drop of milk to drink; and the cow itself too standing there starving in the pound, for not a wisp of hay would he give to cow or Christian to save their lives, if it was ever so! And the rent for which he is driving me, please your honour, has not been due but one week: a hard master he is; but these *middle* men are all so, one and all. Oh! if it had been but my lot to be a tenant to a *gentleman born*, like your honour, who is the poor man's friend, and the orphan's, and the widow's—the friend of them that have none other. Long life to you! and long may you live to reign over us! Would you but speak three words to my landlord, to let my cow out of pound, and give me a fortnight's time, that I might see and fatten her to sell against the fair, I could pay him then all honestly, and not be racked entirely, and he would be ashamed to refuse your honour, and afraid to disoblige the like of you, or get your ill-will. May the blessing of Heaven be upon you, if you'll just send and speak to him three words for the poor woman and widow, that has none other to speak for her in the wide world!"

Moved by this lamentable story, the effect of which the woman's whole miserable appearance corroborated and heightened, the gentleman sent immediately for her hard-hearted landlord. The landlord appeared; not a gentleman, not a rich man, as the term landlord might denote, but a stout, square, stubbed, thick-limbed, grey-eyed man, who seemed to have come smoking hot from hard labour. The gentleman repeated the charge made against him by the poor widow, and mildly remonstrated on his cruelty: the man heard all that was said with a calm but unmoved countenance.

"And now have you done?" said he, turning to the woman, who had recommenced her lamentations. "Look at her standing there, sir. It's easy for her to put on her long cloak, and to tell her long story, and to make her poor mouth to your honour; but if you are willing to hear, I'll tell you what she is, and what I am. She is one that has none but herself in this world to provide for; she is one that is able to afford herself a glass of whiskey when she pleases, and she pleases it often; she is one that never denies herself the bit of *staggering bob* 53 when in season; she is one that has a snug house well thatched to live in all the year round, and nothing to do or nothing that she does; and this is the way of her life, and this is what she is. And what am I? I am the father of eight children, and I have a wife and myself to provide for. I am a man that is at hard labour of one kind or another from sunrise to sunset. The straw that thatched the house she lives in I brought two miles on my back; the walls of the house she lives in I built with my own hands; I did the same by five other houses, and they are all sound and dry, and good to live in, summer or winter. I set them for rent to put bread into my children's mouth, and after all I cannot get it! And to support my eight children, and my wife, and myself, what have I in this world," cried he, striding suddenly with colossal firmness upon his sturdy legs, and raising to heaven arms which looked like fore-shortenings of the limbs of Hercules; "what have *I* in this wide world but these four bones?" 54

No provocation could have worked up a phlegmatic English countryman to this pitch of eloquence. He never suffers his anger to evaporate in idle figures of speech: it is always concentrated in a few words, which he repeats in reply to every argument, persuasive, or invective, that can be employed to irritate or to assuage his wrath. We recollect having once been present at a scene between an English gentleman and a churchwarden, whose feelings were grievously hurt by the disturbance that had been given to certain bones in levelling a wall which separated the churchyard from the pleasure ground of the lord of the manor. The bones belonged, as the churchwarden believed or averred, to his great great grandmother, though how they were identified it might be difficult to explain to an indifferent judge; yet we are to suppose that the confirmation of the suspicion was strong and satisfactory to the party concerned. The pious great great grandson's feelings were all in arms, but *indignation* did not inspire him with a single poetic idea or expression. In his eloquence, indeed, there was the principal requisite, action: in reply to all that could be said, he repeatedly struck his long oak stick perpendicularly upon the floor, and reiterated these words—

"It's death, sir! death by the law! It's sacrilege, sir! sacrilege by act of parliament! It's death, sir! death by the law! and the law I'll have of him, for it's lawful to have the law."

This was the whole range of his ideas, even when the passions had tumbled them all out of their dormitories.

Innumerable fresh instances of Irish eloquence and wit crowd upon our recollection, but we forbear. The examples we have cited are taken from real life, and given without alteration or embellishment.

CHAPTER XI
THE BROGUE

Having proved by a perfect syllogism that the Irish must blunder, we might rest satisfied with our labours; but there are minds of so perverse a sort, that they will not yield their understandings to the torturing power of syllogism.

It may be waste of time to address ourselves to persons of such a cast; we shall therefore change our ground, and adapt our arguments to the level of vulgar capacities. Much of the comic effect of Irish bulls, or of such speeches as are mistaken for bulls, has depended upon the tone, or *brogue*, as it is called, with which they are uttered. The first Irish blunders that we hear are made or repeated in this peculiar tone, and afterward, from the power of association, whenever we hear the tone we expect the blunder. Now there is little danger that the Irish should be cured of their brogue; and consequently there is no great reason to apprehend that we should cease to think or call them blunderers.

Of the powerful effect of any peculiarity of pronunciation to prepossess the mind against the speaker, nay, even to excite dislike amounting to antipathy, we have an instance attested by an eye-witness, or rather an ear-witness.

"In the year 1755," says the Rev. James Adams, "I attended a public disputation in a foreign university, when at least 400 Frenchmen literally hissed a grave and learned *English* doctor, not by way of insult, but irresistibly provoked by the quaintness of the repetition of sh. The thesis was, the concurrence of God *in actionibus viciosis*: the whole hall resounded with the hissing cry of sh, and its continual occurrence in *actio, actione, viciosa*, &c."

It is curious that Shibboleth should so long continue a criterion among nations!

What must have been the degree of irritation that could so far get the better of the politeness of 400 Frenchmen as to make them hiss in the days of *l'ancien régime*! The dread of being the object of that species of antipathy or ridicule, which is excited by unfashionable peculiarity of accent, has induced many of the *misguided* natives of Ireland to affect what they imagine to be the English pronunciation. They are seldom successful in this attempt, for they generally overdo the business. We are told by Theophrastus, that a *barbarian*, who had taken some pains to attain the true Attic dialect, was discovered to be a foreigner by his speaking the Attic dialect with a greater degree of precision and purity than was usual amongst the Athenians themselves. To avoid the imputation of committing barbarisms, people sometimes run into solecisms, which are yet more ridiculous. Affectation is always more ridiculous than ignorance.

There are Irish ladies, who, ashamed of their country, betray themselves by mincing out their abjuration, by calling tables *teebles*, and chairs *cheers*! To such renegadoes we prefer the honest quixotism of a modern champion55 for the Scottish accent, who boldly asserted that "the broad dialect rises above reproach, scorn, and laughter," enters the lists, as he says of himself, in Tartan dress and armour, and throws down the gauntlet to the most prejudiced antagonist. "How weak is prejudice!" pursues this patriotic enthusiast. "The sight of the Highland kelt, the flowing plaid, the buskined leg, provokes my antagonist to laugh! Is this dress ridiculous in the eyes of reason and common sense? No; nor is the dialect of speech: both are characteristic and national distinctions.

"The arguments of general vindication," continues he, "rise powerful before my sight, like the Highland bands in full array. A louder strain of apologetic speech swells my words. What if it should rise high as the unconquered summits of Scotia's hills, and call back, with voice sweet as Caledonian song, the days of ancient Scotish heroes; or attempt the powerful speech of the Latian orator, or his of Greece! The subject, methinks, would well accord with the attempt: *Cupidum, Scotia optima, vires deficiunt.* I leave this to the *king of songs*, Dunbar and Dunkeld, Douglas in *Virgilian* strains, and later poets, Ramsay, Ferguson, and Burns, awake from your graves; you have already immortalized the Scotish dialect in raptured melody! Lend me your golden target and well-pointed spear, that I might victoriously pursue, to the extremity of South Britain, reproachful ignorance and scorn still lurking there: let impartial candour seize their usurped throne. Great, then, is the birth of this national dialect," &c.

So far so good. We have some sympathy with the rhapsodist, whose enthusiasm kindles at the names of Allan Ramsay and of Burns; nay, we are willing to hear (with a grain of allowance) that "the manly eloquence of the Scotish bar affords a singular pleasure to the candid English hearer, and gives merit and dignity to the noble speakers, who retain so much of their own dialect and tempered propriety of English sounds, that they may be emphatically termed *British orators*." But we confess that we lose our patient decorum, and are almost provoked to laughter, when our philological Quixote seriously sets about to prove that Adam and Eve spoke broad Scotch in Paradise.

How angry has this grave patriot reason to be with his ingenious countryman Beattie,56 the celebrated champion of *Truth*, who acknowledges that he never could, when a boy or man, look at a certain translation of Ajax's speech into one of the vulgar Scotch dialects without laughing!

We shall now with boldness, similar to that of the Scotch champion, try the risible muscles of our English reader; we are not, indeed, inclined to go quite such lengths as he has gone: he insists that the Scotch dialect ought to be adopted all over England; we are only going candidly to confess, that we think the Irish, in general, speak *better English* than is commonly spoken by the natives of England. To limit this proposition so as to make it appear less absurd, we should observe, that we allude to the lower classes of the people in both countries. In some counties in Ireland, a few of the poorest labourers and cottagers do not understand English, they speak only Irish, as in Wales there are vast numbers who speak only Welsh; but amongst those who speak English we find fewer vulgarisms than amongst the same rank of persons in England. The English which they speak is chiefly such as has been traditional in their families from the time of the early settlers in the island. During the reign of Elizabeth and the reign of Shakspeare, numbers of English migrated to Ireland; and whoever attends to the phraseology of the lower Irish may, at this day, hear many of the phrases and expressions used by Shakspeare. Their vocabulary has been preserved nearly in its pristine purity since that time, because they have not had intercourse with those counties in England which have made for themselves a jargon unlike to any language under heaven. The Irish *brogue* is a great and shameful defect, but it does not render the English language absolutely unintelligible. There are but a few variations of the brogue, such as the long and the short, the Thady brogue and Paddy brogue, which differ much in tone, and but little in phraseology; but in England, almost all of our fifty-two counties have peculiar vulgarisms, dialects, and brogues, unintelligible to their neighbours. Herodotus tells us that some of the nations of Greece, though they used the same language, spoke it so differently, that they could not understand each other's conversation. This is literally the case at present between the provincial inhabitants of remote parts of England. Indeed the language peculiar to the metropolis, or the *cockney* dialect, is proverbially ridiculous. The Londoners, who look down with contempt upon all that have not been *bred and born* within the sound of Bow, talk with unconscious absurdity of *w*eal and *w*inegar, and *v*ine and *v*indors, and idears, and ask you *ow* you do? and *'ave ye bin taking* the *h*air in 'yde park? and *'as* your 'orse 'ad any *h*oats, &c.? aspirating always where they should not, and never aspirating where they should.

The *Zummerzetzheer* dialect, full of broad *oos* and eternal *zeds*, supplies never-failing laughter when brought upon the stage. Even a cockney audience relishes the broad pronunciation of John Moody, in the Journey to London, or of Sim in Wild Oats.

The cant of Suffolk, the vulgarisms of Shropshire, the uncouth phraseology of the three ridings of Yorkshire, amaze and bewilder foreigners, who perhaps imagine that they do not understand English, when they are in company with those who cannot speak it. The patois of Languedoc and Champagne, such as *"Mein fis sest ai bai via,"* Mon fils c'est un beau veau, exercises, it is true, the ingenuity of travellers, and renders many scenes of Molière and Marivaux difficult, if not unintelligible, to those who have never resided in the French provinces; but no French patois is more unintelligible than the following specimen of *Tummas* and *Meary's* Lancashire dialogue:—

Thomas. "Whau, but I startit up to goa to th' tits, on slurr'd deawn to th' lower part o' th' heymough, on by th' maskins, lord! whot dust think? boh leet hump stridd'n up o' summot ot felt meety heury, on it startit weh meh on its back, deawn th' lower part o' th' mough it jumpt, crost th' leath, eaw't o' th' dur whimmey it took, on into th' weturing poo, os if th' dule o' hell had driv'n it, on there it threw meh en, or I fell off, I connaw tell whether, for th' life o' meh, into the poo."

Mary. "Whoo-wo, whoo-wo, whoo! whot, ith neme o' God! widneh sey?"

Thomas. "If it wur naw Owd Nick, he wur th' orderer on't, to be shure——. Weh mitch powlering I geet eawt o' th' poo, 'lieve57 meh, as to list, I could na tell whether i'r in a sleawm or wak'n, till eh groapt ot meh een; I crope under a wough and stode like o' gawmbling,58 or o parfit neatril, till welly day," &c.

Let us now listen to a conversation which we hope will not be quite so unintelligible.

CHAPTER XII
BATH COACH CONVERSATION

In one of the coaches which travel between Bath and London, an Irish, a Scotch, and an English gentleman happened to be passengers. They were well informed and well-bred, had seen the world, had lived in good company, and were consequently superior to local and national prejudice. As their conversation was illustrative of our subject, we shall make no apology for relating it. We pass the usual preliminary compliments, and the observations upon the weather and the roads. The Irish gentleman first started a more interesting subject—the Union; its probable advantages and disadvantages were fully discussed, and, at last, the Irishman said, "Whatever our political opinions may be, there is one wish in which we shall all agree, that the Union may make us better acquainted with one another."

"It is surprising," said the Englishman, "how ignorant we English in general are of Ireland: to be sure we do not now, as in the times of Bacon and Spenser, believe that wild Irishmen have wings; nor do we all of us give credit, to Mr. Twiss's assertion, that if you look at an Irish lady, she answers, '*port if you please.*'"

Scotchman.—"That traveller seems to be almost as liberal as he who defined *oats*—food for horses in England, and for men in Scotland: such illiberal notions die away of themselves."

Irishman.—"Or they are contradicted by more liberal travellers. I am sure my country has great obligations to the gallant English and Scotch military, not only for so readily assisting to defend and quiet us, but for spreading in England a juster notion of Ireland. Within these few months, I suppose, more real knowledge of the state and manners of that kingdom has been diffused in England by their means, than had been obtained during a whole century."

Scotchman.—"Indeed, I do not recollect having read any author of note who has given me a notion of Ireland since Spenser and Davies, except Arthur Young."

Englishman.—"What little knowledge I have of Ireland has been drawn more from observation than from books. I remember when I first went over there, I did not expect to see twenty trees in the whole island: I imagined that I should have nothing to drink but whiskey, that I should have nothing to eat but potatoes, that I should sleep in mud-walled cabins; that I should, when awake, hear nothing but the Irish howl, the Irish brogue, Irish answers, and Irish bulls; and that if I smiled at any of these things, a hundred pistols would fly from their holsters to *give* or *demand* satisfaction. But experience taught me better things: I found that the stories I had heard were *tales of other times*. Their hospitality, indeed, continues to this day."

Irishman.—"It does, I believe; but of later days, as we have been honoured with the visits of a greater number of foreigners, our hospitality has become less extravagant."

Englishman.—"Not less agreeable: Irish hospitality, I speak from experience, does not now consist merely in pushing about the bottle; the Irish are convivial, but their conviviality is seasoned with wit and humour; they have plenty of good conversation as well as good cheer for their guests; and they not only have wit themselves, but they love it in others; they can take as well as give a joke. I never lived with a more good-humoured, generous, open-hearted people than the Irish."

Irishman.—"I wish Englishmen, in general, were half as partial to poor Ireland as you are, sir."

Englishman.—"Or rather you wish that they knew the country as well, and then they would do it as much justice."

Irishman.—"You do it something more than justice, I fear. There are little peculiarities in my countrymen which will long be justly the subject of ridicule in England."

Scotchman.—"Not among well-bred and well-informed people: those who have seen or read of great varieties of customs and manners are never apt to laugh at all that may differ from their own. As the sensible author of the Government of the Tongue says, 'Half-witted people are always the bitterest revilers.'"

Irishman.—"You are very indulgent, gentlemen; but in spite of all your politeness, you must allow, or, at least, I must confess, that there are little defects in the Irish government of the tongue at which even *whole*-witted people must laugh."

Scotchman.—"The well-educated people in all countries, I believe, escape the particular accent, and avoid the idiom, that are characteristic of the vulgar."

Irishman.—"But even when we escape Irish brogue, we cannot escape Irish bulls."

Englishman.—"You need not say *Irish* bulls with such emphasis; for bulls are not peculiar to Ireland. I have been informed by a person of unquestionable authority, that there is a town in Germany, Hirschau, in the Upper Palatinate, where the inhabitants are famous for making bulls."

Irishman.—"I am truly glad to hear we have companions in disgrace. Numbers certainly lessen the effect of ridicule as well as of shame: but, after all, the Irish idiom is peculiarly unfortunate, for it leads perpetually to blunder."

Scotchman.—"I have heard the same remarked of the Hebrew. I am told that the Hebrew and Irish idiom are much alike."

Irishman (laughing).—"That is a great comfort to us, certainly, particularly to those amongst us who are fond of tracing our origin up to the remotest antiquity; but still there are many who would willingly give up the honour of this high alliance to avoid its inconveniences; for my own part, if I could ensure myself and my countrymen from all future danger of making bulls and blunders, I would this instant give up all Hebrew roots; and even the Ogham character itself I would renounce, 'to make assurance doubly sure.'"

Englishman.—"'To make *assurance doubly sure.*' Now there is an example in our great Shakspeare of what I have often observed, that we English allow our poets and ourselves a licence of speech that we deny to our Hibernian neighbours. If an Irishman, instead of Shakspeare, had talked of making 'assurance doubly sure,' we should have asked how that could be. The vulgar in England are too apt to catch at every slip of the tongue made by Irishmen. I remember once being present when an Irish nobleman, of talents and literature, was actually hissed from the hustings at a Middlesex election because in his speech he happened to say, 'We have laid the root to the axe of the tree of liberty,' instead of 'we have laid the axe to the root of the tree.'"

Scotchman,—"A lapsus linguae, that might have been made by the greatest orators, ancient or modern; by Cicero or Chatham, by Burke, or by 'the fluent Murray.'"

Englishman,—"Upon another occasion I have heard that an Irish orator was silenced with '*inextinguishable* laughter' merely for saying, 'I am sorry to hear my honourable friend stand mute.'"

Scotchman.—"If I am not mistaken, that very same Irish orator made an allusion at which no one could laugh. 'The protection,' said he, 'which Britain affords to Ireland in the day of adversity, is like that which the oak affords to the ignorant countryman, who flies to it for shelter in the storm; it draws down upon his head the lightning of heaven:' may be I do not repeat the words exactly, but I could not forget the idea."

Englishman.—"I would with all my heart bear the ridicule of a hundred blunders for the honour of having made such a simile: after all, his saying, 'I am sorry to hear my honourable friend stand *mute*,' if it be a bull, is justified by Homer; one of the charms in the cestus of Venus is,

'*Silence that speaks, and eloquence of eyes.*'"

Scotchman.—"Silence that speaks, sir, is, I am afraid, an English, not a Grecian charm. It is not in the Greek; it is one of those beautiful liberties which Mr. Pope has taken with his original. But silence that speaks can be found in France as well as in England. Voltaire, in his chef-d'oeuvre, his Oedipus, makes Jocasta say,

'*Tout parle centre nous jusqu'à notre silence.*'" 59_

Englishman.—"And in our own Milton, Samson Agonistes makes as good, indeed a better bull; for he not only makes the mute speak, but speak loud:—

'*The deeds themselves, though mute, spoke loud the doer.*'

And in Paradise Lost we have, to speak in *fashionable* language, two *famous* bulls. Talking of Satan, Milton says,

'*God and his Son except,*

Created thing nought valued he nor shunn'd.'

And speaking of Adam and Eve, and their sons and daughters, he confounds them all together in a manner for which any Irishman would have been laughed to scorn:—

'*Adam, the goodliest man of men since born,*

His sons; the fairest of her daughters Eve.'

Yet Addison, who notices these blunders, calls them only little blemishes."

Scotchman.—"He does so; and he quotes Horace, who tells us we should impute such venial errors to a pardonable inadvertency; and, as I recollect, Addison makes another very just remark, that the ancients, who were actuated by a spirit of candour, not of cavilling, invented a variety of figures of speech, on purpose to palliate little errors of this nature."

"Really, gentlemen," interrupted the Hibernian, who had sat all this time in silence that spoke his grateful sense of the politeness of his companions, "you will put the finishing stroke to my obligations to you, if you will prove that the ancient figures of speech were invented to palliate Irish blunders."

Englishman.—"No matter for what purpose they were invented; if we can make so good a use of them we shall be satisfied, especially if you are pleased. I will, however, leave the burden of the proof upon my friend here, who has detected me already in quoting from Pope's Iliad instead of Homer's. I am sure he will manage the ancient figures of rhetoric better than I should; however, if I can fight behind his shield I shall not shun the combat."

Scotchman.—"I stand corrected for quoting Greek. Now I will not go to Longinus for my tropes and figures; I have just met with a little book on the subject, which I put into my pocket to-day, intending to finish it on my journey, but I have been better employed."

He drew from his pocket a book, called, "Deinology; or, the Union of Reason and Elegance." "Look," said he, "look at this long list of tropes and figures; amongst them we could find apologies for every species of Irish bulls; but in mercy, I will select, from 'the twenty chief and most moving figures of speech,' only the oxymoron, as it is a favourite with Irish orators. In the oxymoron contradictions meet: to reconcile these, Irish ingenuity delights. I will further spare four out of the seven figures of less note: emphasis, enallage, and the hysteron proteron you must have; because emphasis graces Irish diction, enallage unbinds it from strict grammatical fetters, and hysteron proteron allows it sometimes to put the cart before the horse. Of the eleven grammatical figures, Ireland delights chiefly in the antimeria, or changing one part of speech for another, and in the ellipsis or defect. Of the remaining long list of figures, the Irish are particularly disposed to the epizeuxis, as 'indeed, indeed—at all, at all,' and antanaclasis, or double meaning. The tautotes, or repetition of the same thing, is, I think, full as common amongst the English. The hyperbole and catachresis are so nearly related to a bull, that I shall dwell upon them with pleasure. You must listen to the definition of a catachresis:—'A catachresis is the boldest of any trope. *Necessity makes it borrow and employ an expression or term contrary to the thing it means to express.*'"

"Upon my word this is something like a description of an Irish bull," interrupted the Hibernian.

Scotchman.—"For instance, it has been said, *Equitare in arundine longá*, to ride on horseback on a stick. Reason condemns the contradiction, but necessity has allowed it, and use has made it intelligible. The same trope is employed in the following metaphorical expression:—the seeds of the Gospel have been *watered* by the *blood* of the martyrs."

Englishman.—"That does seem an absurdity, I grant; but you know great orators *trample on impossibilities.*" 60

Scotchman.—"And great poets get the letter of them. You recollect Shakspeare says,

> 'Now bid me run,
>
> And I will strive with things impossible,
>
> Yea, get the better of them.'"

Englishman.—"And Corneille, in the Cid, I believe, makes his hero a compliment upon his having performed impossibilities—'Vos mains seules ont le droit de vaincre un invincible.'" 61

Scotchman.—"Ay, that would be a bull in an Irishman, but it is only an hyperbole in a Frenchman."

Irishman.—"Indeed this line of Corneille's *out-hyperboles* the hyperbole, considered in any but a prophetic light; as a prophecy, it exactly foretels the taking of Bonaparte's *invincible* standard by the glorious forty-second regiment of the British: 'Your hands alone *have a right* to vanquish the invincible.' By-the-by, the phrase *ont le droit* cannot, I believe, be literally translated into English; but the Scotch and Irish, *have a right*, translates it exactly. But do not let me interrupt my country's defence, gentlemen; I am heartily glad to find Irish blunderers may shelter themselves in such good company in the ancient sanctuary of the hyperbole. But I am afraid you must deny admittance to the poor mason, who said, 'This house will stand as long as the world, and longer.'"

Scotchman.—"Why should we 'shut the gates of mercy' upon him when we pardon his betters for more flagrant sins? For instance, Mr. Pope, who, in his Essay on Criticism, makes a blunder, or rather uses an hyperbole, stronger than that of your poor Irish mason:—

> 'When first young Maro in his noble mind
>
> A work t'outlast immortal Rome design'd.'

And to give you a more modern case, I lately heard an English shopkeeper say to a lady in recommendation of his goods, 'Ma'am, it will wear for ever, and make you a petticoat afterwards.'"

Irishman.—"Upon my word, I did not think you could have found a match for the mason; but what will you say to my countryman, who, on meeting an acquaintance, accosted him with this ambiguous compliment—'When first I saw you I thought it was you, but now I see it is your brother.'"

Scotchman.—"If I were not afraid you would take me for a pedant, I should quote a sentence from Cicero that is not far behind this blunder."

Irishman.—"I can take you for nothing but a friend: pray let us have the Latin."

Scotchman.—"It is one of Cicero's compliments to Caesar—'Qui, cum ipse imperator in toto imperio populi Romani unus esset, esse me alterum passus est.'62 Perhaps," continued the Scotchman, "my way of pronouncing Latin sounds strangely to you, gentlemen?"

Irishman.—"And perhaps ours would be unintelligible to Cicero himself, if he were to overhear us: I fancy we are all so far from right, that we need not dispute about degrees of wrong."

The coach stopped at this instant, and the conversation was interrupted.

CHAPTER XIII
BATH COACH CONVERSATION

After our travellers had dined, the conversation was renewed by the English gentleman's repeating Goldsmith's celebrated lines on Burke:

"Who, too deep for his hearers, still went on refining,

And thought of convincing, whilst they thought of dining;

In short, 'twas his fate, unemployed or in place, sir,

To eat mutton cold, and cut blocks with a razor."

"What humour and wit there are in that poem of Goldsmith's! and where is there any thing equal to his 'Traveller?'"

Irishman.—"Yet this is the man who used to be the butt of the company for his bulls."

Englishman.—"No, not for his bulls, but for *blurting* out opinions in conversation that could not stand the test of Dr. Johnson's critical powers. But what would become of the freedom of wit and humour if every word that came out of our mouths were subject to the tax of a professed critic's censure, or if every sentence were to undergo a logical examination? It would be well for Englishmen if they were a little more inclined, like your open-hearted countrymen, to *blurt* out their opinions freely."

Scotchman,—"I cannot forgive Dr. Johnson for calling Goldsmith an inspired idiot; I confess I see no idiotism, but much inspiration, in his works."

Irishman.—"But we must remember, that if Johnson did laugh at Goldsmith, he would let no one else laugh at him, and he was his most sincere and active friend. The world would, perhaps, never have seen the 'Vicar of Wakefield' if Johnson had not recommended it to a bookseller; and Goldsmith might have died in jail if the doctor had not got him a hundred pounds for it, when poor Goldsmith did not know it was worth a shilling. When we recollect this, we must forgive the doctor for calling him, in jest, an inspired idiot."

Scotchman.—"Especially as Goldsmith has wit enough to bear him up against a thousand such jests."

Englishman.—"It is curious to observe how nearly wit and absurdity are allied. We may forgive the genius of Ireland if he sometimes

'Leap his light courser o'er the bounds of taste.'

Even English genius is not always to be restrained within the strict limits of common sense. For instance, Young is witty when he says,

'How would a miser startle to be told

Of such a wonder as insolvent gold.'

But Johnson is, I am afraid, absurd when he says,

'Turn from the glittering bribe your scornful eye,

Nor sell for gold what gold can never buy.'"

"One case, to be sure, must be excepted," said the Irishman; "a patriot may sell his reputation, and the purchaser get nothing by it. But, gentlemen, I have just recollected an example of an Irish bull in which are all the happy requisites, incongruity, confusion, and laughable confusion, both in thought and expression. When Sir Richard Steele was asked, how it happened that his countrymen made so many bulls, he replied, 'It is the effect of climate, sir; if an Englishman were born in Ireland, he would make as many.'"

Scotchman.—"This is an excellent bull, I allow; but I think I can match it."

Englishman.—"And if he can, you will allow yourself to be fairly vanquished?"

Irishman.—"Most willingly."

Scotchman.—"Then I shall owe my victory to our friend Dr. Johnson, the leviathan of English literature. In his celebrated preface to Shakspeare he says, that 'he has not only shown human nature as it acts in real exigencies, but as it *would be found in situations to which it cannot be exposed.'* These are his own words; I think I remember them accurately."

The English gentleman smiled, and our Hibernian acknowledged that the Scotchman had fairly gained the victory. "My friends," added he, "as I cannot pretend to be 'convinced against my will,' I certainly am not 'of the same opinion still.' But stay—there are such things as practical bulls: did you never hear of the Irishman who ordered a painter to draw his picture, and to represent him standing behind a tree?"

Englishman.—"No: but I have heard the very same story told of an Englishman. The dealers in *good jokes* give them first to one nation and then to another, first to one celebrated character and then to another, as it suits the demand and fashion of the day: just as our printsellers, with a few touches, change the portrait of General Washington into the head of the king of France, and a capital print of Sir Joshua Reynolds into a striking likeness of *the Monster*.

"But I can give you an instance of a practical bull that is not only indisputably English, but was made by one of the greatest men that England ever produced, Sir Isaac Newton, who, after he had made a large hole in his study-door for his cat to creep through, made a small hole beside it for the kitten. You will acknowledge, sir, that this is a good practical bull."

"Pardon me," said the Hibernian, "we have still some miles further to go, and, if you will give me leave, I will relate 'an Hibernian tale,' which exemplifies some of the opinions held in this conversation."

The Scotch and English gentlemen begged to hear the story, and he began in the following manner.

CHAPTER XIV
THE IRISH INCOGNITO

Sir John Bull was a native of Ireland, *bred* and *born* in the city of Cork. His real name was Phelim O'Mooney, and he was by profession a *stocah*, or walking gentleman; that is, a person who is too proud to earn his bread, and too poor to have bread without earning it. He had always been told that none of his ancestors had ever been in trade or business of any kind, and he resolved, when a boy, never to *demean* himself and family, as his elder brother had done, by becoming a rich merchant. When he grew up to be a young man, he kept this spirited resolution as long as he had a relation or friend in the world who would let him hang upon them; but when he was shaken off by all, what could he do but go into business? He chose the most genteel, however; he became a wine merchant. I'm *only* a wine merchant, said he to himself, and that is next door to being nothing at all. His brother furnished his cellars; and Mr. Phelim O'Mooney, upon the strength of the wine that he had in his cellars, and of the money he expected to make of it, immediately married a wife, set up a gig, and gave excellent dinners to men who were ten times richer than he even ever expected to be. In return for these excellent dinners, his new friends bought all their wine from Mr. O'Mooney, and never paid for it; he lived upon credit himself, and gave all his friends credit, till he became a bankrupt. Then nobody came to dine with him, and every body found out that he had been very imprudent; and he was obliged to sell his gig, but not before it had broken his wife's neck; so that when accounts came to be finally settled, he was not much worse than when he began the world, the loss falling upon his creditors, and he being, as he observed, free to begin life again, with the advantage of being once more a bachelor. He was such a good-natured, free-hearted fellow, that every body liked him, even his creditors. His wife's relations made up the sum of five hundred pounds for him, and his brother offered to take him into his firm as partner; but O'Mooney preferred, he said, going to try, or rather to make, his fortune in England, as he did not doubt but he should by marriage, being, as he did not scruple to acknowledge, a personable, clever-looking man, and a great favourite with the sex.

"My last wife I married for love, my next I expect will do the same by me, and of course the money must come on her side this time," said our hero, half jesting, half in earnest. His elder and wiser brother, the merchant, whom he still held in more than sufficient contempt, ventured to hint some slight objections to this scheme of Phelim's seeking fortune in England. He observed that so many had gone upon this plan already, that there was rather a prejudice in England against Irish adventurers.

This could not affect *him* any ways, Phelim replied, because he did not mean to appear in England as an Irishman at all.

"How then?"

"As an Englishman, since that is most agreeable."

"How can that be?"

"Who should hinder it?"

His brother, hesitatingly, said "Yourself."

"Myself!—What part of myself? Is it my tongue?—You'll acknowledge, brother, that I do not speak with the brogue."

It was true that Phelim did not speak with any Irish brogue: his mother was an English woman, and he had lived much with English officers in Cork, and he had studied and imitated their manner of speaking so successfully, that no one, merely by his accent, could have guessed that he was an Irishman.

"Hey! brother, I say!" continued Phelim, in a triumphant English tone; "I never was taken for an Irishman in my life. Colonel Broadman told me the other day, I spoke English better than the English themselves; that he should take me for an Englishman, in any part of the known world, the moment I opened my lips. You must allow that not the smallest particle of brogue is discernible on my tongue."

His brother allowed that not the smallest particle of brogue was to be discerned upon Phelim's tongue, but feared that some Irish idiom might be perceived in his conversation. And then the name of O'Mooney!

"Oh, as to that, I need not trouble an act of parliament, or even a king's letter, just to change my name for a season; at the worst, I can travel and appear incognito."

"Always?"

"No: only just till I'm upon good terms with the lady — — Mrs. Phelim O'Mooney, that is to be, God willing. Never fear, nor shake your head, brother; *you* men of business are out of this line, and not proper judges: I beg your pardon for saying so, but as you are my own brother, and nobody by, you'll excuse me."

His brother did excuse him, but continued silent for some minutes; he was pondering upon the means of persuading Phelim to give up this scheme.

"I would lay you any wager, my dear Phelim," said he, "that you could not continue four days in England incognito."

"Done!" cried Phelim. "Done for a hundred pounds; done for a thousand pounds, and welcome."

"But if you lose, how will you pay?"

"Faith! that's the last thing I thought of, being sure of winning."

"Then you will not object to any mode of payment I shall propose."

"None: only remembering always, that I was a bankrupt last week, and shall be little better till I'm married; but then I'll pay you honestly if I lose."

"No, if you lose I must be paid before that time, my good sir," said his brother, laughing. "My bet is this:—I will lay you one hundred guineas that you do not remain four days in England incognito; be upon honour with me, and promise, that if you lose, you will, instead of laying down a hundred guineas, come back immediately, and settle quietly again to business."

The word *business* was always odious to our hero's proud ears; but he thought himself so secure of winning his wager, that he willingly bound himself in a penalty which he believed would never become due; and his generous brother, at parting, made the bet still more favourable, by allowing that Phelim should not be deemed the loser unless he was, in the course of the first four days after he touched English ground, detected eight times in being an Irishman.

"Eight times!" cried Phelim. "Good bye to a hundred guineas, brother, you may say."

"You may say," echoed his brother, and so they parted.

Mr. Phelim O'Mooney the next morning sailed from Cork harbour with a prosperous gale, and with a confidence in his own success which supplied the place of auspicious omens. He embarked at Cork, to go by long sea to London, and was driven into Deal, where Julius Caesar once landed before him, and with the same resolution to see and conquer. It was early in the morning; having been very sea-sick, he was impatient, as soon as he got into the inn, for his breakfast: he was shown into a room where three ladies were waiting to go by the stage; his air of easy confidence was the best possible introduction.

"Would any of the company choose eggs?" said the waiter.

"I never touch an egg for my share," said O'Mooney, carelessly; he knew that it was supposed to be an Irish custom to eat eggs at breakfast; and when the malicious waiter afterwards set a plate full of eggs in salt upon the table, our hero magnanimously abstained from them; he even laughed heartily at a story told by one of the ladies, of an Hibernian at Buxton, who declared that "no English hen ever laid a fresh egg."

O'Mooney got through breakfast much to his own satisfaction, and to that of the ladies, whom he had taken a proper occasion to call the *three graces*, and whom he had informed that he was an *old* baronet of an English family, and that his name was Sir John Bull. The youngest of the graces civilly observed, "that whatever else he might be, she should never have taken him for an *old* baronet." The lady who made this speech was pretty, but O'Mooney had penetration enough to discover, in the course of the conversation, that she and her companions were far from being divinities; his three graces were a greengrocer's wife, a tallowchandler's widow, and a milliner. When he found that these ladies were likely to be his companions if he were to travel in the coach, he changed his plan, and ordered a postchaise and four.

O'Mooney was not in danger of making any vulgar Irish blunders in paying his bill at an inn. No landlord or waiter could have suspected him, especially as he always left them to settle the matter first, and then looked over the bill and money with a careless gentility, saying, "Very right," or "Very well, sir;" wisely calculating, that it was better to lose a few shillings on the road, than to lose a hundred pounds by the risk of Hibernian miscalculation.

Whilst the chaise was getting ready he went to the custom-house to look after his baggage. He found a red-hot countryman of his own there, roaring about four and fourpence, and fighting the battle of his trunks, in which he was ready to make affidavit there was not, nor never had been, any thing contraband; and when the custom-house officer replied by pulling out of one of them a piece of Irish poplin, the Hibernian fell immediately upon the Union, which he swore was Disunion, as the custom-house officers managed it. Sir John Bull appeared to much advantage all this time, maintaining a dignified silence; from his quiet appearance and deportment, the custom-house officers took it for granted that he was an Englishman. He was in no hurry; he begged *that* gentleman's business might be settled first; he would wait the officer's leisure, and as he spoke he played so dexterously with half-a-guinea between his fingers, as to make it visible only where he wished. The custom-house officer was his humble servant immediately; but the Hibernian would have been his enemy, if he had not conciliated him by observing, "that even Englishmen must allow there was something very like a bull in professing to make a complete identification of the two kingdoms, whilst, at the same time, certain regulations continued in full force to divide the countries by art, even more than the British Channel does by nature."

Sir John talked so plausibly, and, above all, so candidly and coolly on Irish and English politics, that the custom-house officer conversed with him for a quarter of an hour without guessing of what country he was, till in an unlucky moment Phelim's heart got the better of his head. Joining in the praises bestowed by all parties on the conduct of a distinguished patriot of his country, he, in the height of his enthusiasm, inadvertently called him the *Speaker*.

"The Speaker!" said the officer.

"Yes, the Speaker—*our* Speaker!" cried Phelim, with exultation. He was not aware how he had betrayed himself, till the officer smiled and said—

"Sir, I really never should have found out that you were an Irishman but from the manner in which you named your countryman, who is as highly thought of by all parties in this country as in yours: your enthusiasm does honour to your heart."

"And to my head, I'm sure," said our hero, laughing with the best grace imaginable. "Well, I am glad you have found me out in this manner, though I lose the eighth part of a bet of a hundred guineas by it."

He explained the wager, and begged the custom-house officer to keep his secret, which he promised to do faithfully, and assured him, "that he should be happy to do any thing in his power to serve him." Whilst he was uttering these last words, there came in a snug, but soft-looking Englishman, who opining from the words "happy to do any thing in my power to serve you," that O'Mooney was a friend of the custom-house officer's, and encouraged by something affable and good-natured in our hero's countenance, crept up to him, and whispered a request—"Could you tell a body, sir, how to get out of the custom-house a very valuable box of Sèvre china that has been *laying* in the custom-house three weeks, and which I was commissioned to get out if I could, and bring up to town for a lady."

As a lady was in the case, O'Mooney's gallantry instantly made his good-nature effective. The box of Sèvre china was produced, and opened only as a matter of form, and only as a matter of curiosity its contents were examined—a beautiful set of Sèvre china and a pendule, said to have belonged to M. Egalité! "These things must be intended," said Phelim, "for some lady of superior taste or fortune."

As Phelim was a proficient in the Socratic art of putting judicious interrogatories, he was soon happily master of the principal points it concerned him to know: he learnt that the lady was rich—a spinster—of full age—at her own disposal—living with a single female companion at Blackheath—furnishing a house there in a superior style—had two carriages—her Christian name Mary—her surname Sharperson.

O'Mooney, by the blessing of God, it shall soon he, thought Phelim. He politely offered the Englishman a place in his chaise for himself and Sèvre china, as it was for a lady, and would run great hazard in the stage, which besides was full. Mr. Queasy, for that was our soft Englishman's name, was astonished by our hero's condescension and affability, especially as he heard him called Sir John: he bowed sundry times as low as the fear of losing his wig would permit, and accepted the polite offer with many thanks for himself and the lady concerned.

Sir John Bull's chaise and four was soon ready; and Queasy seated in the corner of it, and the Sèvre china safely stowed between his knees. Captain Murray, a Scotch officer, was standing at the inn-door, with his eyes intently fixed on the letters that were worked in nails on the top of Sir John's trunk; the letters were P. O'M. Our hero, whose eyes were at least as quick as the Scotchman's, was alarmed lest this should lead to a second detection. He called instantly, with his usual presence of mind, to the ostler, and desired him to uncord *that* trunk, as it was not to go with him; raising his voice loud enough for all *the yard* to hear, he added—"It is not mine at all; it belongs to my friend, Mr. O'Mooney: let it be sent after me, at leisure, by the waggon, as directed, to the care of Sir John Bull."

Our hero was now giving his invention a prodigious quantity of superfluous trouble; and upon this occasion, as upon most others, he was more in danger from excess than deficiency of ingenuity: he was like the man in the fairy tale, who was obliged to tie his legs lest he should outrun the object of which he was in pursuit. The Scotch officer, though his eyes were fixed on the letters PO'S., had none of the suspicions which Phelim was counteracting; he was only considering how he could ask for the third place in Sir John's chaise during the next stage, as he was in great haste to get to town upon particular business, and there were no other horses at the inn. When he heard that the heavy baggage was to go by the waggon, he took courage and made his request. It was instantly granted by the good-natured Hibernian, who showed as much hospitality about his chaise as if it had been his house. Away they drove as fast as they could. Fresh dangers awaited him at the next inn. He left his hat upon the table in the hall whilst he went into the parlour, and when he returned, he heard some person inquiring what Irish gentleman was there. Our hero was terribly alarmed, for he saw that his hat was in the inquirers hand, and he recollected that the name of Phelim O'Mooney was written in it. This the inquisitive gentleman did not see, for it was written in no very legible characters on the leather withinside of the front; but "F. Guest, hatter, Damestreet, Dublin," was a printed advertisement that could not be mistaken, and *that* was pasted within the crown. O'Mooney's presence of mind did not forsake him upon this emergency.

"My good sir," said he, turning to Queasy, who, without hearing one word of what was passing, was coming out of the parlour, with his own hat and gloves in his hand; "My good sir," continued he, loading him with parcels, "will you have the goodness to see these put into my carriage? Ill take care of your hat and gloves," added O'Mooney, in a low voice. Queasy surrendered his hat and gloves instantly, unknowing wherefore; then squeezed forward with his load through the crowd, crying—"Waiter! hostler! pray, somebody put these into Sir John Bull's chaise."

Sir John Bull, equipped with Queasy's hat, marched deliberately through the defile, bowing with the air of at least an English county member to this side and to that, as way was made for him to his carriage. No one suspected that the hat did not belong to him; no one, indeed, thought of the hat, for all eyes were fixed upon the man. Seated in the carriage, he threw money to the waiter, hostler, and boots, and drew up the glass, bidding the postilions drive on. By this cool self-possession our hero effected his retreat with successful generalship, leaving his new Dublin beaver behind him, without regret, as bona waviata. Queasy, before whose eyes things passed continually without his seeing them, thanked Sir John for the care he had taken of his hat, drew on his gloves, and calculated aloud how long they should be going to the next stage. At the first town they passed through, O'Mooney bought a new hat, and Queasy deplored the unaccountable mistake by which Sir John's hat had been forgotten. No further *mistakes* happened upon the journey. The travellers rattled on, and neither 'stinted nor stayed' till they arrived at Blackheath, at Miss Sharperson's. Sir John sat Queasy down without having given him the least hint of his designs upon the lady; but as he helped him out with the Sèvre china, he looked through the large opening double doors of the hall, and slightly said—"Upon my word, this seems to be a handsome house: it would be worth looking at, if the family were not at home."

"I am morally sure, Sir John," said the soft Queasy, "that Miss Sharperson would be happy to let you see the house tonight, and this minute, if she knew you were at the door, and who you were, and all your civility about me and the china.—Do, pray, walk in."

"Not for the world: a gentleman could not do such a thing without an invitation from the lady of the house herself."

"Oh, if that's all, I'll step up myself to the young lady; I'm certain she'll be proud——"

"Mr. Queasy, by no means; I would not have the lady disturbed for the world at this unseasonable hour.—It is too late—quite too late."

"Not at all, begging pardon, Sir John," said Queasy, taking out his watch: "only just tea-time by me.—Not at all unseasonable for any body; besides, the message is of my own head:—all, you know, if not well taken——"

Up the great staircase he made bold to go on his mission, as he thought, in defiance of Sir John's better judgment. He returned in a few minutes with a face of self-complacent exultation, *and* Miss Sharperson's compliments, and begs Sir John Bull will walk up and rest himself with a dish of tea, and has her thanks to him for the china.

Now Queasy, who had the highest possible opinion of Sir John Bull and of Miss Sharperson, whom he thought the two people of the greatest consequence and affability, had formed the notion that they were made for each other, and that it must be a match if they could but meet. The meeting he had now happily contrived and effected; and he had done his part for his friend Sir John, with Miss Sharperson, by as many exaggerations as he could utter in five minutes, concerning his perdigious politeness and courage, his fine person and carriage, his ancient family, and vast connexions and importance wherever he appeared on the road, at inns, and over all England. He had previously, during the journey, done his part for his friend Miss Sharperson with Sir John, by stating that "she had a large fortune left her by her mother, and was to have twice as much from her grandmother; that she had thousands upon thousands in the funds, and an estate of two thousand a year, called Rascàlly, in Scotland, besides plate and jewels without end."

Thus prepared, how could this lady and gentleman meet without falling desperately in love with each other!

Though a servant in handsome livery appeared ready to show Sir John up the great staircase, Mr. Queasy acted as a gentleman usher, or rather as showman. He nodded to Sir John as they passed across a long gallery and through an ante-chamber, threw open the doors of various apartments as he went along, crying—"Peep in! peep in! peep in here! peep in there!—

Is not this spacious? Is not this elegant! Is not that grand? Did I say too much?" continued he, rubbing his hands with delight. "Did you ever see so magnificent and such highly-polished steel grates out of Lon'on?"

Sir John, conscious that the servant's eyes were upon him, smiled at this question, "looked superior down;" and though with reluctant complaisance he leaned his body to this side or to that, as Queasy pulled or swayed, yet he appeared totally regardless of the man's vulgar reflections. He had seen every thing as he passed, and was surprised at all he saw; but evinced not the slightest symptom of astonishment. He was now ushered into a spacious, well-lighted apartment: he entered with the easy, unembarrassed air of a man who was perfectly accustomed to such a home. His quick coup-d'oeil took in the whole at a single glance. Two magnificent candelabras stood on Egyptian tables at the farther end of the room, and the lights were reflected on all sides from mirrors of no common size. Nothing seemed worthy to attract our hero's attention but the lady of the house, whom he approached with an air of distinguished respect. She was reclining on a Turkish sofa, her companion seated beside her, tuning a harp. Miss Sharperson half rose to receive Sir John: he paid his compliments with an easy, yet respectful air. He was thanked for his civilities to *the person* who had been commissioned to bring the box of Sèvre china from Deal.

"Vastly sorry it should have been so troublesome," Miss Sharperson said, in a voice fashionably unintelligible, and with a most becoming yet intimidating nonchalance of manner. Intimidating it might have been to any man but our hero; he, who had the happy talent of catching, wherever he went, the reigning manner of the place, replied to the lady in equal strains; and she, in her turn, seemed to look upon him more as her equal. Tea and coffee were served. *Nothings* were talked of quite easily by Sir John. He practised the art "not to admire," so as to give a justly high opinion of his taste, consequence, and knowledge of the world. Miss Sharperson, though her nonchalance was much diminished, continued to maintain a certain dignified reserve; whilst her companion, Miss Felicia Flat, condescended to ask Sir John, who had doubtless seen every fine house in England and on the continent, his opinion with respect to the furniture and finishing of the room, the placing of the Egyptian tables and the candelabras.

No mortal could have guessed by Sir John Bull's air, when he heard this question, that he had never seen a candelabra before in his life. He was so much, and yet seemingly so little upon his guard, he dealt so dexterously in generals, and evaded particulars so delicately, that he went through this dangerous conversation triumphantly. Careful not to protract his visit beyond the bounds of propriety, he soon rose to take leave, and he mingled "intrusion, regret, late hour, happiness, and honour," so charmingly in his parting compliment, as to leave the most favourable impression on the minds of both the ladies, and to procure for himself an invitation to see the house next morning.

The first day was now ended, and our hero had been detected but once. He went to rest this night well satisfied with himself, but much more occupied with the hopes of marrying the heiress of Rascàlly than of winning a paltry bet.

The next day he waited upon the ladies in high spirits. Neither of them was *visible*, but Mr. Queasy had orders to show him the house, which he did with much exultation, dwelling particularly in his praises on the beautiful high polish of the steel grates. Queasy boasted that it was he who had recommended the ironmonger who furnished the house in that line; and that his bill, as he was proud to state, amounted to *many, many* hundreds. Sir John, who did not attend to one word Queasy said, went to examine the map of the Rascàlly estate, which was unrolled, and he had leisure to count the number of lords' and ladies' visiting tickets which lay upon the chimney-piece. He saw names of the people of first quality and respectability: it was plain that Miss Sharperson must be a lady of high family as well as large fortune, else she would not be visited by persons of such distinction. Our hero's passion for her increased every moment. Her companion, Miss Flat, now appeared, and entered very freely into conversation with Sir John; and as he perceived that she was commissioned to sit in judgment upon him, he evaded all her leading questions with the skill of an Irish witness, but without giving any Hibernian answers. She was fairly at a fault. Miss Sharperson at length appeared, elegantly dressed; her person was genteel, and her face rather pretty. Sir John, at this instant, thought her beautiful, or seemed to think so. The ladies interchanged looks, and afterwards Sir John found a softness in his fair one's manner, a languishing tenderness in her eyes, in the tone of her voice, and at the same time a modest perplexity and reserve about her, which altogether persuaded him that he was quite right, and his brother quite wrong *en fait d'amour*. Miss Flat appeared now to have the most self-possession of the three, and Miss Sharperson looked at her from time to time, as if she asked leave to be in love. Sir John's visit lasted a full half hour before he was sensible of having been five minutes engaged in this delightful conversation.

Miss Sharperson's coach now came to the door: he handed her into it, and she gave him a parting look, which satisfied him all was yet safe in her heart. Miss Flat, as he handed her into the carriage, said, "Perhaps they should meet Sir John at Tunbridge, where they were going in a few days." She added some words as she seated herself, which he scarcely noticed at the time, but they recurred afterwards disagreeably to his memory. The words were, "I'm so glad we've a roomy coach, for of all things it annoys me to be *squeedged* in a carriage."

This word *squeedged*, as he had not been used to it in Ireland, sounded to him extremely vulgar, and gave him suspicions of the most painful nature. He had the precaution, before he left Blackheath, to go into several shops, and to inquire something more concerning his fair ladies. All he heard was much to their advantage; that is, much to the advantage of Miss Sharperson's fortune. All agreed that she was a rich Scotch heiress. A rich Scotch heiress, Sir John wisely considered, might have an humble companion who spoke bad English. He concluded that *squeedged* was Scotch, blamed himself for his suspicions, and was more in love with his mistress and with himself than ever. As he returned to town, he framed the outline of a triumphant letter to his brother on his approaching marriage. The bet was a matter, at present, totally beneath his consideration. However, we must do him the justice to say, that like a man of honour he resolved that, as soon as he had won the lady's heart, he would *candidly* tell her his circumstances, and then leave her the choice either to marry him or break her heart, as she pleased. Just as he had formed this generous resolution, at a sudden turn of the road he overtook Miss Sharperson's coach: he bowed and looked in as he passed, when, to his astonishment, he saw, *squeedged* up in the corner by Miss Felicia, Mr. Queasy. He thought that this was a blunder in etiquette that would never have been made in Ireland. Perhaps his mistress was of the same opinion, for she hastily pulled down the blind as Sir John passed. A cold qualm came over the lover's heart. He lost no time in idle doubts and suspicions, but galloped on to town as fast as he could, and went immediately to call upon the Scotch officer with whom he had travelled, and whom he knew to be keen and prudent. He recollected the map of the Rascàlly estate, which he saw in Miss Sharperson's breakfast-room, and he remembered that the lands were said to lie in that part of Scotland from which Captain Murray came; from him he resolved to inquire into the state of the premises, before he should offer himself as tenant for life. Captain Murray assured him that there was no such place as Rascàlly in that part of Scotland; that he had never heard of any such person as Miss Sharperson, though he was acquainted with every family and every estate in the neighbourhood where she fabled hers to be. O'Mooney drew from memory, the map of the Rascàlly estate. Captain Murray examined the boundaries, and assured him that his cousin the general's lands joined his own at the very spot which he described, and that unless two straight lines could enclose a space, the Rascàlly estate could not be found.

Sir John, naturally of a warm temper, proceeded, however, with prudence. The Scotch officer admired his sagacity in detecting this adventurer. Sir John waited at his hotel for Queasy, who had promised to call to let him know when the ladies f would go to Tunbridge. Queasy came. Nothing could equal his astonishment and dismay when he was told the news.

"No such place as the Rascàlly estate! Then I'm an undone man! an undone man!" cried poor Queasy, bursting into tears: "but I'm certain it's impossible; and you'll find, Sir John, you've been misinformed. I would stake my life upon it, Miss Sharperson's a rich heiress, and has a rich grandmother. Why, she's five hundred pounds in my debt, and I know of her being thousands and thousands in the books of as good men as myself, to whom I've recommended her, which I wouldn't have done for my life if I had not known her to be solid. You'll find she'll prove a rich heiress, Sir John."

Sir John hoped so, but the proofs were not yet satisfactory. Queasy determined to inquire about her payments to certain creditors at Blackheath, and promised to give a decisive answer in the morning. O'Mooney saw that this man was too great a fool to be a knave; his perturbation was evidently the perturbation of a dupe, not of an accomplice: Queasy was made to "be an anvil, not a hammer." In the midst of his own disappointment, our good-natured Hibernian really pitied this poor currier.

The next morning Sir John went early to Blackheath. All was confusion at Miss Sharperson's house; the steps covered with grates and furniture of all sorts; porters carrying out looking-glasses, Egyptian tables, and candelabras; the noise of workmen was heard in every apartment; and louder than all the rest, O'Mooney heard the curses that were denounced against his rich heiress—curses such as are bestowed on a swindler in the moment of detection by the tradesmen whom she has ruined.

Our hero, who was of a most happy temper, congratulated himself upon having, by his own wit and prudence, escaped making the practical bull of marrying a female swindler.

Now that Phelim's immediate hopes of marrying a rich heiress were over, his bet with his brother appeared to him of more consequence, and he rejoiced in the reflection that this was the third day he had spent in England, and that he had but once been detected.—The ides of March were come, but not passed!

"My lads," said he to the workmen, who were busy in carrying out the furniture from Miss Sharperson's house, "all hands are at work, I see, in saving what they can from the wreck of *the Sharperson*. She was as well-fitted out a vessel, and in as gallant trim, as any ship upon the face of the earth."

"Ship upon the face of the *yearth*.'" repeated an English porter with a sneer; "ship upon the face of the water, you should say, master; but I take it you be's an Irishman."

O'Mooney had reason to be particularly vexed at being detected by this man, who spoke a miserable jargon, and who seemed not to have a very extensive range of ideas. He was one of those half-witted geniuses who catch at the shadow of an Irish bull. In fact, Phelim had merely made a lapsus lingual, and had used an expression justifiable by the authority of the elegant and witty Lord Chesterfield, who said—no, who wrote—that the English navy is the finest navy upon the face of the earth! But it was in vain for our hero to argue the point; he was detected—no matter how or by whom. But this was only his second detection, and three of his four days of probation were past.

He dined this day at Captain Murray's. In the room in which they dined there was a picture of the captain, painted by Romney. Sir John, who happened to be seated opposite to it, observed that it was a very fine picture; the more he looked at it, the more he liked it. His admiration was at last unluckily expressed: he said, "That's an incomparable, an inimitable picture; it is absolutely *more like than the original*." 63

A keen Scotch lady in company smiled, and repeated, "*More like than the original!* Sir John, if I had not been told by my relative here that you were an Englishman, I should have set you *doon*, from that speech, for an Irishman."

This unexpected detection brought the colour, for a moment, into Sir John's face; but immediately recovering his presence of mind, he said, "That was, I acknowledge, an excellent Irish bull; but in the course of my travels I have heard as good English bulls as Irish."

To this Captain Murray politely acceded, and he produced some laughable instances in support of the assertion, which gave the conversation a new turn.

O'Mooney felt extremely obliged to the captain for this, especially as he saw, by his countenance, that he also had suspicions of the truth. The first moment he found himself alone with Murray, our hero said to him, "Murray, you are too good a fellow to impose upon, even in jest. Your keen country-woman guessed the truth—I am an Irishman, but not a swindler. You shall hear why I conceal my country and name; only keep my secret till to-morrow night, or I shall lose a hundred guineas by my frankness."

O'Mooney then explained to him the nature of his bet. "This is only my third detection, and half of it voluntary, I might say, if I chose to higgle, which I scorn to do."

Captain Murray was so much pleased by this openness, that as he shook hands with O'Mooney, he said, "Give me leave to tell you, sir, that even if you should lose your bet by this frank behaviour, you will have gained a better thing—a friend."

In the evening our hero went with his friend and a party of gentlemen to Maidenhead, near which place a battle was to be fought next day, between two famous pugilists, Bourke and Belcher. At the appointed time the combatants appeared upon the stage; the whole boxing corps and the gentlemen *amateurs* crowded to behold the spectacle. Phelim O'Mooney's heart beat for the Irish champion Bourke; but he kept a guard upon his tongue, and had even the forbearance not to bet upon his countryman's head. How many rounds were fought, and how many minutes the fight lasted, how many blows were put *in* on each side, or which was the *game man* of the two, we forbear to decide or relate, as all this has been settled in the newspapers of the day; where also it was remarked, that Bourke, who lost the battle, "was put into a post-chaise, and left *standing* half an hour, while another fight took place. This was very scandalous on the part of his friends," says the humane newspaper historian, "as the poor man might possibly be dying."

Our hero O'Mooney's heart again got the better of his head. Forgetful of his bet, forgetful of every thing but humanity, he made his way up to the chaise, where Bourke was left. "How are you, my gay fellow?" said he. "Can you *see at all with the eye that's knocked out?*"

The brutal populace, who overheard this question, set up a roar of laughter: "A bull! a bull! an Irish bull! Did you hear the question this Irish gentleman asked his countryman?"

O'Mooney was detected a fourth time, and this time he was not ashamed. There was one man in the crowd who did not join in the laugh: a poor Irishman, of the name of Terence M'Dermod. He had in former times gone out a grousing, near Cork, with our hero; and the moment he heard his voice, he sprang forward, and with uncouth but honest demonstrations of joy, exclaimed, "Ah, my dear master! my dear young master! Phelim O'Mooney, Esq. And I have found your honour alive again? By the blessing of God above, I'll never part you now till I die; and I'll go to the world's end to *sarve yees.*"

O'Mooney wished him at the world's end this instant, yet could not prevail upon himself to check this affectionate follower of the O'Mooneys. He, however, put half a crown into his hand, and hinted that if he wished really to serve him, it must be at some other time. The poor fellow threw down the money, saying, he would never leave him. "Bid me do any thing, barring that. No, you shall never part me. Do what you plase with me, still I'll be close to your heart, like your own shadow: knock me down if you will, and wilcome, ten times a day, and I'll be up again like a ninepin: only let me sarve your honour; I'll ask no wages nor take none."

There was no withstanding all this; and whether our hero's good-nature deceived him we shall not determine, but he thought it most prudent, as he could not get rid of Terence, to take him into his service, to let him into his secret, to make him swear that he would never utter the name of Phelim O'Mooney during the remainder of this day. Terence heard the secret of the bet with joy, entered into the jest with all the readiness of an Irishman, and with equal joy and readiness swore by the hind leg of the holy lamb that he would never mention, even to his own dog, the name of Phelim O'Mooney, Esq., good or bad, till past twelve o'clock; and further, that he would, till the clock should strike that hour, call his master Sir John Bull, and nothing else, to all men, women, and children, upon the floor of God's creation.

Satisfied with the fulness of this oath, O'Mooney resolved to return to town with his man Terence M'Dermod. He, however, contrived, before he got there, to make a practical bull, by which he was detected a fifth time. He got into the coach which was driving *from* London instead of that which was driving *to* London, and he would have been carried rapidly to Oxford, had not his man Terence, after they had proceeded a mile and a half on the wrong road, put his head down from the top of the coach, crying, as he looked in at the window, "Master, Sir John Bull, are you there? Do you know we're in the wrong box, going to Oxford?"

"Your master's an Irishman, dare to say, as well as yourself," said the coachman, as he let Sir John out. He walked back to Maidenhead, and took a chaise to town.

It was six o'clock when he got to London, and he went into a coffee-house to dine. He sat down beside a gentleman who was reading the newspaper. "Any news to-day, sir?"

The gentleman told him the news of the day, and then began to read aloud some paragraphs in a strong Hibernian accent. Our hero was sorry that he had met with another countryman; but he resolved to set a guard upon his lips, and he knew that his own accent could not betray him. The stranger read on till he came to a trial about a legacy which an old woman had left to her cats. O'Mooney exclaimed, "I hate cats almost as much as old women; and if I had been the English minister, I would have laid the *dog-tax* upon cats."

"If you had been the *Irish* minister, you mean," said the stranger, smiling; "for I perceive now you are a countryman of my own."

"How can you think so, sir?" said O'Mooney: "you have no reason to suppose so from my accent, I believe."

"None in life—quite the contrary; for you speak remarkably pure English—not the least note or half note of the brogue; but there's another sort of freemason sign by which we Hibernians know one another, and are known all over the globe. Whether to call it a confusion of expressions or of ideas, I can't tell. Now an Englishman, if he had been saying what you did, sir, just now, would have taken time to separate the dog and the tax, and he would have put the tax upon cats, and let the dogs go about their business." Our hero, with his usual good-humour, acknowledged himself to be fairly detected.

"Well, sir," said the stranger, "if I had not found you out before by the blunder, I should be sure now you were my countryman by your good-humour. An Irishman can take what's said to him, provided no affront's meant, with more good-humour than any man on earth."

"Ay, that he can," cried O'Mooney: "he lends himself, like the whale, to be tickled even by the fellow with the harpoon, till he finds what he is about, and then he pays away, and pitches the fellow, boat and all, to the devil. Ah, countryman! you would give me credit indeed for my good humour if you knew what danger you have put me in by detecting me for an Irishman. I have been found out six times, and if I blunder twice more before twelve o'clock this night, I shall lose a hundred guineas by it: but I will make sure of my bet; for I will go home straight this minute, lock myself up in my room, and not say a word to any mortal till the watchman cries 'past twelve o'clock,'—then the fast and long Lent of my tongue will be fairly over; and if you'll meet me, my dear friend, at the King's Arms, we will have a good supper and keep Easter for ever."

Phelim, pursuant to his resolution, returned to his hotel, and shut himself up in his room, where he remained in perfect silence and consequent safety till about nine o'clock. Suddenly he heard a great huzzaing in the street; he looked out of the window, and saw that all the houses in the street were illuminated. His landlady came bustling into his apartment, followed by waiters with candles. His spirits instantly rose, though he did not clearly know the cause of the rejoicings. "I give you joy, ma'am. What are you all illuminating for?" said he to his landlady.

"Thank you, sir, with all my heart. I am not sure. It is either for a great victory or the peace. Bob—waiter—step out and inquire for the gentleman."

The gentleman preferred stepping out to inquire for himself. The illuminations were in honour of the peace. He totally forgot his bet, his silence, and his prudence, in his sympathy with the general joy. He walked rapidly from street to street, admiring the various elegant devices. A crowd was standing before the windows of a house that was illuminated with extraordinary splendour. He inquired whose it was, and was informed that it belonged to a contractor, who had made an immense fortune by the war.

"Then I'm sure these illuminations of his for the peace are none of the most sincere," said O'Mooney. The mob were of his opinion; and Phelim, who was now, alas! worked up to the proper pitch for blundering, added, by way of pleasing his audience still more—"If this contractor had *illuminated* in character, it should have been with *dark lanterns.*"

"Should it? by Jasus! that would be an Irish illumination," cried some one. "Arrah, honey! you're an Irishman, whoever you are, and have spoke your mind in character."

Sir John Bull was vexed that the piece of wit which he had aimed at the contractor had recoiled upon himself. "It is always, as my countryman observed, by having too much wit that I blunder. The deuce take me if I sport a single bon mot more this night. This is only my seventh detection, I have an eighth blunder still *to the good;* and if I can but keep my wit to myself till I am out of purgatory, then I shall be in heaven, and may sing Io Triumphe in spite of my brother."

Fortunately, Phelim had not made it any part of his bet that he should not speak to himself an Irish idiom, or that he should not *think* a bull. Resolved to be as obstinately silent as a monk of La Trappe, he once more shut himself up in his cell, and fell fast asleep—dreamed that fat bulls of Basan encompassed him round about—that he ran down a steep bill to escape them—that his foot slipped—he rolled to the bottom—felt the bull's horns in his side—heard the bull bellowing in his—ears—wakened—and found Terence M'Dermod bellowing at his room door.

"Sir John Bull! Sir John Bull! murder! murder! my dear master, Sir John Bull! murder, robbery, and reward! let me in! for the love of the Holy Virgin! they are all after you!"

"Who? are you drunk, Terence?" said Sir John, opening the door.

"No, but they are mad—all mad."

"Who?"

"The constable. They are all mad entirely, and the lord mayor, all along with your honour's making me swear I would not tell your name. Sure they are all coming armed in a body to put you in jail for a forgery, unless I run back and tell them the truth—will I?"

"First tell me the truth, blunderer!"

"I'll make my affidavit I never blundered, plase your honour, but just went to the merchant's, as you ordered, with the draft, signed with the name I swore not to utter till past twelve. I presents the draft, and waits to be paid. 'Are you Mr. O'Mooney's servant?' says one of the clerks after a while. 'No, sir, not at all, sir,' said I; 'I'm Sir John Bull's, at your sarvice.' He puzzles and puzzles, and asks me did I bring the draft, and was that your writing at the bottom of it? I still said it was my master's writing, *Sir John Bull's*, and no other. They whispered from one up to t'other, and then said it was a forgery, as I overheard, and I must go before the mayor. With that, while the master, who was called down to be examined as to his opinion, was putting on his glasses to spell it out, I gives them, one and all, the slip, and whips out of the street door and home to give your honour notice, and have been breaking my heart at the door this half hour to make you hear — and now you have it all."

"I am in a worse dilemma now than when between the horns of the bull," thought Sir John: "I must now either tell my real name, avow myself an Irishman, and so lose my bet, or else go to jail."

He preferred going to jail. He resolved to pretend to be dumb, and he charged Terence not to betray him. The officers of justice came to take him up: Sir John resigned himself to them, making signs that he could not speak. He was carried before a magistrate. The merchant had never seen Mr. Phelim O'Mooney, but could swear to his handwriting and signature, having many of his letters and drafts. The draft in question was produced. Sir John Bull would neither acknowledge nor deny the signature, but in dumb show made signs of innocence. No art or persuasion could make him speak; he kept his fingers on his lips. One of the bailiffs offered to open Sir John's mouth. Sir John clenched his hand, in token that if they used violence he knew his remedy. To the magistrate he was all bows and respect: but the law, in spite of civility, must take its course.

Terence McDermod beat his breast, and called upon all the saints in the Irish calendar when he saw the committal actually made out, and his dear master given over to the constables. Nothing but his own oath and his master's commanding eye, which was fixed upon him at this instant, could have made him forbear to utter, what he had never in his life been before so strongly tempted to tell — the truth.

Determined to win his wager, our hero suffered himself to be carried to a lock-up house, and persisted in keeping silence till the clock struck twelve!

Then the charm was broken, and he spoke. He began talking to himself, and singing as loud as he possibly could. The next morning Terence, who was no longer bound by his oath to conceal Phelim's name, hastened to his master's correspondent in town, told the whole story, and O'Mooney was liberated. Having won his bet by his wit and steadiness, he had now the prudence to give up these adventuring schemes, to which he had so nearly become a dupe; he returned immediately to Ireland to his brother, and determined to settle quietly to business. His good brother paid him the hundred guineas most joyfully, declaring that he had never spent a hundred guineas better in his life than in recovering a brother. Phelim had now conquered his foolish dislike to trade: his brother took him into partnership, and Phelim O'Mooney never relapsed into Sir John Bull.

CONCLUSION

Unable any longer to support the tone of irony, we joyfully speak in our own characters, and explicitly declare our opinion, that the Irish are an ingenious, generous people; that the bulls and blunders of which they are accused are often imputable to their neighbours, or that they are justifiable by ancient precedents, or that they are produced by their habits of using figurative and witty language. By what their good-humour is produced we know not; but that it exists we are certain. In Ireland, the countenance and heart expand at the approach of wit and humour: the poorest labourer forgets his poverty and toil, in the pleasure of enjoying a joke. Amongst all classes of the people, provided no malice is obviously meant, none is apprehended. That such is the character of the majority of the nation there cannot *to us* be a more convincing and satisfactory proof than the manner in which a late publication64 was received in Ireland. The Irish were the first to laugh at the caricature of their ancient foibles, and it was generally taken merely as good-humoured raillery, not as insulting satire. If gratitude for this generosity has now betrayed us unawares into the language of panegyric, we may hope for pardon from the liberal of both nations. Those who are thoroughly acquainted with Ireland will most readily acknowledge the justice of our praises; those who are ignorant of the country will not, perhaps, be displeased to have their knowledge of the people of Ireland extended. Many foreign pictures of Irishmen are as grotesque and absurd as the Chinese pictures of lions: having never seen that animal, the Chinese can paint him only from the descriptions of voyagers, which are sometimes ignorantly, sometimes wantonly exaggerated.

In Voltaire's Age of Lewis the Fourteenth we find the following passage:—"Some nations seem made to be subject to others. The English have always had over the Irish the superiority of genius, wealth, and arms. The *superiority which the whites have over the negroes.*" 65 A note in a subsequent edition informs us, that the injurious expression—"*The superiority which the whites have over the negroes,*" was erased by Voltaire; and his editor subjoins his own opinion. "The nearly savage state in which Ireland was when she was conquered, her superstition, the oppression exercised by the English, the religious fanaticism which divides the Irish into two hostile nations, such were the causes which have held down this people in depression and weakness. Religious hatreds are appeased, and this country has recovered her liberty. The Irish no longer yield to the English, either in industry or in information." 66

The last sentence of this note might, if it had reached the eyes or ears of the incensed Irish historian, Mr. O'Halloran, have assuaged his wrath against Voltaire for the unguarded expression in the text; unless the amor patriae of the historian, like the amour propre of some individuals, instead of being gratified by congratulations on their improvement, should be intent upon demonstrating that there never was anything to improve. As we were neither *born nor* bred in Ireland, we cannot be supposed to possess this amor patriae in its full force: we profess to be attached to the country only for its merits; we acknowledge that it is a matter of indifference to us whether the Irish derive their origin from the Spaniards, or the Milesians, or the Welsh: we are not so violently anxious as we ought to be to determine whether or not the language spoken by the Phoenician slave, in Terence's play, was Irish; nay, we should not break our hearts if it could never be satisfactorily proved that Albion is only another name for Ireland.67 We moreover candidly confess that we are more interested in the fate of the present race of its inhabitants than in the historian of St. Patrick, St. Facharis, St. Cormuc; the renowned Brien Boru; Tireldach, king of Connaught; M'Murrough, king of Leinster; Diarmod; Righ-Damnha; Labra-Loing-seach; Tighermas; Ollamh-Foldha; the M'Giolla-Pha-draigs; or even the great William of Ogham; and by this declaration we have no fear of giving offence to any but rusty antiquaries. We think it somewhat, more to the honour of Ireland to enumerate the names of some of the men of genius whom she has produced: Milton and Shakspeare stand unrivalled; but Ireland can boast of Usher, Boyle, Denham, Congreve, Molyneux, Farquhar, Sir Richard Steele, Bickerstaff, Sir Hans Sloane, Berkeley, Orrery, Parnell, Swift, T. Sheridan, Welsham, Bryan Robinson, Goldsmith, Sterne, Johnsons68, Tickel, Brooke, Zeland, Hussey Burgh, three Hamiltons, Young, Charlemont, Macklin, Murphy, Mrs. Sheridan,69 Francis Sheridan, Kirwan, Brinsley Sheridan, and Burke.

We enter into no invidious comparisons: it is our sincere wish to conciliate both countries; and if in this slight essay we should succeed in diffusing a more just and enlarged idea of the Irish than has been generally entertained, we hope the English will deem it not an unacceptable service. Whatever might have been the policy of the English nation towards Ireland whilst she was a separate kingdom, since the union it can no longer be her wish to depreciate the talents or ridicule the language of Hibernians. One of the Czars of Russia used to take the cap and bells from his fool, and place it on the head of any of his subjects whom he wished to disgrace. The idea of extending such a punishment to a whole nation was ingenious and magnanimous; but England cannot now put it into execution towards Ireland. Would it not be a practical bull to place the bells upon her own imperial head?

1801

APPENDIX

The following collection of Foreign Bulls was given us by a man of letters, who is now father of the French Academy.

RECUEIL DE BÊTISES.

Toutes les nations ont des contes plaisans de bêtises échappées non seulement à des personnes vraiment bêtes, mais aux distractions de gens qui ne sont pas sans esprit. Les Italiens ont leurs *spropositi*, leur arlequin ses balourdises, les Anglois leurs *blunders*, les Irlandois leurs *bulls*.

Mademoiselle Maria Edgeworth ayant fait un recueil de ces derniers, je prends la liberté de lui offrir un petit recueil de nos bêtises qui méritent le nom qu'elles portent aussi bien que les *Irish bulls*. J'ai fait autrefois une dissertation où je recherchois quelle étoit la cause du rire qu'excitent les bêtises, et dans laquelle j'appuyois mon explication de beaucoup d'exemples et peut-être même du mien sans m'en appercevoir; mais la femme d'esprit à qui j'ai adressé cette folie l'a perdue, et je n'ai pas pu la recouvrir.

Je me souviens seulement que j'y prouvois *savamment* que le rire excité par les bêtises est l'effet du contraste que nous saisissons entre l'effort que fait l'homme qui dit la bêtise, et le mauvais succès de son effort. J'assimilois la marche de l'esprit dans celui qui dit une bêtise, à ce qui arrive à un homme qui cherchant à marcher légèrement sur un pavé glissant, tombe lourdement, ou aux tours mal-adroits du paillasse de la foire. Si l'on veut examiner les bêtises rassemblèes ici, on y trouvera toujours un effort manqué de ce genre.

Un homme, dont la femme avoit été saignée, interrogé le lendemain pourquoi elle ne paroissoit pas à table, répondit:—"Elle garde la chambre: Morand l'a saignée hier, et une saignée affoiblit beaucoup quand elle est faite par un habile homme."

M. de Baville, intendant du Languedoc, avoit un secrétaire fort bête: il se servoit un jour de lui pour écrire au ministre sur des affaires très importantes et dicta ces mots: "Ne soyez point surpris de ce que je me sers d'une main étrangère pour vous écrire sur cet objet. Mon secrétaire est si bête qu'à ce moment même il ne s'apperçoit pas que je vous parle de lui."

On demandoit à un abbé de Laval Montmorency quel âge avoit son frère le maréchal dont il étoit l'aîné. "Dans deux ans," dit-il, "nous serons du même âge."

On se préparoit à observer une éclipse, et le roi devoit assister à l'observation. M. de Jonville disoit à M. Cassini—"N'attendra-t-on pas le roi pour commencer l'éclipse?"

Une femme du peuple qui avoit une petite fille malade avec le transport au cerveau, disoit au médecin, "Ah, monsieur, si vous l'aviez entendu cette nuit! elle a déraisonnée comme une grande personne."

Un homme avoit parié 25 louis qu'il traverseroit le grand bassin des Thuileries par un froid très rigoureux; il alla jusqu'au milieu, renonça à son entreprise, et revint par le même chemin en disant, "J'aime mieux perdre vingt-cinq louis que d'avoir une fluxion de poitrine."

Un homme voyoit venir de loin un médecin de sa connoissance qui l'avoit traité plusieurs années auparavant dans une maladie; il se détourna, et cacha son visage pour n'être pas reconnu. On lui demandoit, "Pourquoi."— "C'est," dit-il, "que je suis honteux devant lui de ce qu'il y a fort long temps que je n'ai été malade."

On demande à un homme qui vouloit vendre un cheval, "Votre cheval est-il peureux?" "Oh, point du tout," répond-il; "il vient de passer plusieurs nuits tout seul dans son écurie."

Dans une querelle entre un père et son fils, le père reprochoit à celui-ci son ingratitude. "Je ne vous ai point d'obligations," disoit le fils; "vous m'avez fait beaucoup de tort; si vous n'étiez point né, je serois à présent l'héritier de mon grand-père."

Un avare faisant son testament, se fit lui-même son héritier.

Un homme voyoit un bateau si chargé que les bords en étoient à fleur d'eau: "Ma foi," dit-il, "si la rivière étoit un peu plus haute le bateau iroit à fond."

M. Hume, dans son histoire d'Angleterre, parlant de la conspiration attribuée aux Catholiques en 1678 sous Charles II. rapporte le mot d'un chevalier Player qui félicitoit la ville des précautions qu'elle avoit prises— "Et sans lesquelles," disoit-il, "tous les citoyens auroient couru risque de se trouver égorgés le lendemain à leur réveil."

Le maire d'une petite ville, entendant une querelle dans la rue au milieu de la nuit, se lève du lit, et ouvrant la fenêtre, crie aux passans, "Messieurs, me lèverai-je?"

Un sot faisoit compliment à une demoiselle don't la mère venoit de se marier en secondes noces avec un ancien ami de la maison—"Mademoiselle," lui dit-il, "je suis ravi de ce que monsieur votre père vient d'épouser madame votre mère."

Racine, qui avoit été toute sa vie courtisan très attentif, étoit enterré à Port Royal des Champs dont les solitaires s'étoient attirés l'indignation de Louis XIV. M. de Boissy, célèbre par ses distractions, disoit, "Racine n'auroit pas fait cela de son vivant."

On racontait dans une conversation que Monsieur de Buffon avoit disséqué une de ses cousines, et une femme se récrioit sur l'inhumanité de l'anatomiste. M. de Mairan lui dit, "Mais, madame, elle étoit morte."

On parloit avec admiration de la belle vieillesse d'un homme de quatre-vingt dix ans, quelqu'un dit—"Cela vous étonne, messieurs; si mon père n'étoit pas mort, il auroit à présent cent ans accomplis."

Mouet, de l'opera comique, conte qu'arrivant de Lyon, et ne voulant pas qu'on sut qu'il étoit à Paris, il recommanda à son laquais, supposé qu'il fut rencontré, de dire qu'il étoit à Lyon. Le laquais trouve un ami de son maitre, qui lui en demande des nouvelles. "Il est à Lyon," dit-il, "et il ne sera de retour que la semaine prochaine." "Mais," continue le questionneur, "que portez-vous là?" "Ce sont quelques provisions qu'il m'a envoyé chercher pour son diner."

Un homme examinoit un dessin représentant la coupe d'un vaisseau construit en Hollande; quelqu'un lui dit, "Est-ce que monsieur entend le Hollandois?"

Un homme de loi disoit qu'on ne pouvait pas faire une stipulation valable avec un muet. Un des écoutans lui dit, "Monsieur le docteur, et avec un boiteux, seroit-elle bonne?"

Un homme se plaignoit que la maison de son voisin lui ôtoit la vue d'une de ses fenêtres; un autre lui dit, "Vous avez un remède; faites murer cette fenêtre."

Un homme ayarit écrit à sa maitresse, avoit glissé le billet sous la porte, et puis s'avisant que la fille ne pourroit pas s'en appercevoir il en écrivit un autre en ces termes, "J'ai mis un billet sous votre porte; prenez-y garde quand vous sortirez."

Un homme étant sur le point de marier sa fille unique, se brouille avec le prétendant, et dans sa colere il dit, "Non, monsieur, vous ne serez jamais mon gendre, et quand j'aurois cent filles uniques, je ne vous en donnerois pas une."

On avoit reçu à la grande poste une lettre avec cette adresse, *à Monsieur mon fils, Rue, &c.* On alloit la mettre au rebut; un commis s'y oppose, et dit qu'on trouvera à qui la lettre s'adresse. Dix ou douze jours se passent. On voit arriver un grand benêt, qui dit, "Messieurs, je viens savoir si on n'auroit pas garde ici une lettre de mon cher père?" "Oui, monsieur," lui dit le commis, "la voilà." On prête ce trait à Bouret, fermier général.

Milord Albemarle étant aux eaux d'Aix-la-Chapelle, et ne voulant pas être connu, ordonna a un negre qui le servoit, si on lui demandoit qui étoit son maitre, de dire qu'il étoit Frangois. On ne manqua pas de faire la question an noir, qui répondit, *"Mon maître est Franpois, et mot aussi."*

Un marchand, en finissant d'écrire une lettre à un de ses correspondans, mourut subitement. Son commis ajouta en P.S. "Depuis ma lettre écrite je suis mort ce matin. Mardi an soir *7ème,*" &c.

Un petit marchand prétendoit avoir acheté trois sols ce qu'il vendoit pour deux. On lui représente que ce commerce le ruinera—"Ah," dit-il, "je me sauve sur la quantité."

Le chevalier de Lorenzi, étant à Florence, étoit allé se promener avec trois de ses amis à quelques lieues de la ville, à pied. Ils revenoient fort las; la nuit approchoit; il veut se reposer: on lui dit qu'il restoit quatres milles à faire—"Oh," dit-il, "nous sommes quatres; ce n'est qu'un mille chacun."

On pretend qu'un fermier général voulant s'éviter l'ennui ou s'épargner les frais des lettres dont on l'accabloit au nouvel an, écrivoit au mois de Décembre à tous les employés de son département qu'il les dispensoit du cérémonial, et que ceux-ci lui réponderoient pour l'assurer qu'ils se conformeroient à ses ordres.

Maupertuis faisoit instruire un perroquet par son laquais, et vouloit qu'on lui apprit des mots extraordinaires. Depuis deux ans le laquais, enseignoit à l'animal à dire *monomotapa,* et le perroquet n'en disoit que des syllabes séparées. Maupertuis faisoit des reproches au laquais; "Oh, monsieur," dit celui-ci, "cela ne va pas si vîte; je lui ai d'abord appris *mo* et puis *no.*" "Vous êtes un bête," dit Maupertuis, "il faut lui dire le mot entier." "Monsieur," reprend le laquais, "il faut lui donner le temps de comprendre."

Il y a en Italien une lettre pleine de *spropositi* assez plaisans. Un homme écrit à son ami, "Abbiamo avuto un famosissimo tremoto, che se per la misericordia di Dio avesse durato una mezza hora di piu, saremmo tutti andati al paradiso, che Dio ce ne liberi. Vi mando quatordici pere, e sono tutti boni cristiani. A questa fiéra i porci sono saliti al cielo. O ricevete, o non ricevete questa, datemene aviso."

AN ESSAY ON THE NOBLE SCIENCE
OF SELF-JUSTIFICATION

"For which an eloquence that aims to vex,

With native tropes of anger arms the sex." —Parnell.

Endowed as the fair sex indisputably are, with a natural genius for the invaluable art of self-justification, it may not be displeasing to them to see its rising perfection evinced by an attempt to reduce it to a science. Possessed, as are all the fair daughters of Eve, of an hereditary propensity, transmitted to them undiminished through succeeding generations, to be "soon moved with slightest touch of blame;" very little precept and practice will confirm them in the habit, and instruct them in all the maxims of self-justification.

Candid pupil, you will readily accede to my first and fundamental axiom—that a lady can do no wrong.

But simple as this maxim may appear, and suited to the level of the meanest capacity, the talent of applying it on all the important, but more especially on all the most trivial, occurrences of domestic life, so as to secure private peace and public dominion, has hitherto been monopolized by the female adepts in the art of self-justification.

Excuse me for insinuating by this expression, that there may yet be amongst you some novices. To these, if any such, I principally address myself.

And now, lest fired by ambition you lose all by aiming at too much, let me explain and limit my first principle, "That you can do no wrong." You must be aware that real perfection is beyond the reach of mortals, nor would I have you aim at it; indeed it is not in any degree necessary to our purpose. You have heard of the established belief in the infallibility of the sovereign pontiff, which prevailed not many centuries ago:—if man was allowed to be infallible, I see no reason why the same privilege should not be extended to woman;—but times have changed; and since the happy age of credulity is past, leave the opinions of men to their natural perversity—their actions are the best test of their faith. Instead then of a belief in your infallibility, endeavour to enforce implicit submission to your authority. This will give you infinitely less trouble, and will answer your purpose as well.

Right and wrong, if we go to the foundation of things, are, as casuists tell us, really words of very dubious signification, perpetually varying with custom and fashion, and to be adjusted ultimately by no other standards but opinion and force. Obtain power, then, by all means: power is the law of man; make it yours. But to return from a frivolous disquisition about right, let me teach you the art of defending the wrong. After having thus pointed out to you the glorious end of your labours, I must now instruct you in the equally glorious means.

For the advantage of my subject I address myself chiefly to married ladies; but those who have not as yet the good fortune to have that common enemy, a husband, to combat, may in the mean time practise my precepts upon their fathers, brothers, and female friends; with caution, however, lest by discovering their arms too soon, they preclude themselves from the power of using them to the fullest advantage hereafter. I therefore recommend it to them to prefer, with a philosophical moderation, the future to the present.

Timid brides, you have, probably, hitherto been addressed as angels. Prepare for the time when you shall again become mortal. Take the alarm at the first approach of blame; at the first hint of a discovery that you are any thing less than infallible:—contradict, debate, justify, recriminate, rage, weep, swoon, do any thing but yield to conviction.

I take it for granted that you have already acquired sufficient command of voice; you need not study its compass; going beyond its pitch has a peculiarly happy effect upon some occasions. But are you voluble enough to drown all sense in a torrent of words? Can you be loud enough to overpower the voice of all who shall attempt to interrupt or contradict you? Are you mistress of the petulant, the peevish, and the sullen tone? Have you practised the sharpness which provokes retort, and the continual monotony which by setting your adversary to sleep effectually precludes reply? an event which is always to be considered as decisive of the victory, or at least as reducing it to a drawn battle:—you and Somnus divide the prize.

Thus prepared for an engagement, you will next, if you have not already done it, study the weak part of the character of your enemy—your husband, I mean: if he be a man of high spirit, jealous of command and impatient of control, one who decides for himself, and who is little troubled with the insanity of minding what the world says of him, you must proceed with extreme circumspection; you must not dare to provoke the combined forces of the enemy to a regular engagement, but harass him with perpetual petty skirmishes: in these, though you gain little at a time, you will gradually weary the patience, and break the spirit of your opponent. If he be a man of spirit, he must also be generous; and what man of generosity will contend for trifles with a woman who submits to him in all affairs of consequence, who is in his power, who is weak, and who loves him?

"Can superior with inferior power contend?" No; the spirit of a lion is not to be roused by the teasing of an insect.

But such a man as I have described, besides being as generous as he is brave, will probably be of an active temper: then you have an inestimable advantage; for he will set a high value upon a thing for which you have none—time; he will acknowledge the force of your arguments merely from a dread of their length; he will yield to you in trifles, particularly in trifles which do not militate against his authority; not out of regard for you, but for his time; for what man can prevail upon himself to debate three hours about what could be as well decided in three minutes?

Lest amongst infinite variety the difficulty of immediate selection should at first perplex you, let me point out, that matters of *taste* will afford you, of all others, the most ample and incessant subjects of debate. Here you have no criterion to appeal to. Upon the same principle, next to matters of taste, points of opinion will afford the most constant exercise to your talents. Here you will have an opportunity of citing the opinions of all the living and dead you have ever known, besides the dear privilege of repeating continually:—"Nay, you must allow *that*." Or, "You can't deny this, for it's the universal opinion—every body says so! every body thinks so! I wonder to hear you express such an opinion! Nobody but yourself is of that way of thinking!" with innumerable other phrases, with which a slight attention to polite conversation will furnish you. This mode of opposing authority to argument, and assertion to proof, is of such universal utility, that I pray you to practise it.

If the point in dispute be some opinion relative to your character or disposition, allow in general, that "you are sure you have a great many faults;" but to every specific charge reply, "Well, I am sure I don't know, but I did not think *that* was one of my faults! nobody ever accused me of that before! Nay, I was always remarkable for the contrary; at least before I was acquainted with you, sir: in my own family I was always remarkable for the contrary: ask any of my own friends; ask any of them; they must know me best."

But if, instead of attacking the material parts of your character, your husband should merely presume to advert to your manners, to some slight personal habit which might be made more agreeable to him; prove, in the first place, that it is his fault that it is not agreeable to him; ask which is most to blame, "she who ceases to please, or he who ceases to be pleased"70—His eyes are changed, or opened. But it may perhaps have been a matter almost of indifference to him, till you undertook its defence: then make it of consequence by rising in eagerness, in proportion to the insignificance of your object; if he can draw consequences, this will be an excellent lesson: if you are so tender of blame in the veriest trifles, how impeachable must you be in matters of importance! As to personal habits, begin by denying that you have any; or in the paradoxical language of Rousseau,71 declare that the only habit you have is the habit of having none: as all personal habits, if they have been of any long standing, must have become involuntary, the unconscious culprit may assert her innocence without hazarding her veracity.

However, if you happen to be detected in the very fact, and a person cries, "Now, now, you are doing it!" submit, but declare at the same moment—"That it is the very first time in your whole life that you were ever known to be guilty of it; and therefore it can be no habit, and of course nowise reprehensible."

Extend the rage for vindication to all the objects which the most remotely concern you; take even inanimate objects under your protection. Your dress, your furniture, your property, every thing which is or has been yours, defend, and this upon the principles of the soundest philosophy: each of these things all compose a part of your personal merit (Vide Hume); all that connected the most distantly with your idea gives pleasure or pain to others, becomes an object of blame or praise, and consequently claims your support or vindication.

In the course of the management of your house, children, family, and affairs, probably some few errors of omission or commission may strike your husband's pervading eye; but these errors, admitting them to be errors, you will never, if you please, allow to be charged to any deficiency in memory, judgment, or activity, on your part.

There are surely people enough around you to divide and share the blame; send it from one to another, till at last, by universal rejection, it is proved to belong to nobody. You will say, however, that facts remain unalterable; and that in some unlucky instance, in the changes and chances of human affairs, you may be proved to have been to blame. Some stubborn evidence may appear against you; still you may prove an alibi, or balance the evidence. There is nothing equal to balancing evidence; doubt is, you know, the most philosophic state of the human mind, and it will be kind of you to keep your husband perpetually in this sceptical state.

Indeed the short method of denying absolutely all blameable facts, I should recommend to pupils as the best; and if in the beginning of their career they may startle at this mode, let them depend upon it that in their future practice it must become perfectly familiar. The nice distinction of simulation and dissimulation depends but on the trick of a syllable; palliation and extenuation are universally allowable in self-defence; prevarication inevitably follows, and falsehood "is but in the next degree."

Yet I would not destroy this nicety of conscience too soon. It may be of use in your first setting out, because you must establish credit; in proportion to your credit will be the value of your future asseverations.

In the mean time, however, argument and debate are allowed to the most rigid moralist. You can never perjure yourself by swearing to a false opinion.

I come now to the art of reasoning: don't be alarmed at the name of reasoning, fair pupils; I will explain to you my meaning.

If, instead of the fiery-tempered being I formerly described, you should fortunately be connected with a man, who, having formed a justly high opinion of your sex, should propose to treat you as his equal, and who in any little dispute which might arise between you, should desire no other arbiter than reason; triumph in his mistaken candour, regularly appeal to the decision of reason at the beginning of every contest, and deny its jurisdiction at the conclusion. I take it for granted that you will be on the wrong side of every question, and indeed, in general, I advise you to choose the wrong side of an argument to defend; whilst you are young in the science, it will afford the best exercise, and, as you improve, the best display of your talents.

If, then, reasonable pupils, you would succeed in argument, attend to the following instructions.

Begin by preventing, if possible, the specific statement of any position, or if reduced to it, use the most general terms, and take advantage of the ambiguity which all languages and which most philosophers allow. Above all things, shun definitions; they will prove fatal to you; for two persons of sense and candour, who define their terms, cannot argue long without either convincing, or being convinced, or parting in equal good-humour; to prevent which, go over and over the same ground, wander as wide as possible from the point, but always with a view to return at last precisely to the same spot from which you set out. I should remark to you, that the choice of your weapons is a circumstance much to be attended to: choose always those which your adversary cannot use. If your husband is a man of wit, you will of course undervalue a talent which is never connected with judgment: "for your part, you do not presume to contend with him in wit."

But if he be a sober-minded man, who will go link by link along the chain of an argument, follow him at first, till he grows so intent that he does not perceive whether you follow him or not; then slide back to your own station; and when with perverse patience he has at last reached the last link of the chain, with one electric shock of wit make him quit his hold, and strike him to the ground in an instant. Depend upon the sympathy of the spectators, for to one who can understand *reason*, you will find ten who admire *wit*.

But if you should not be blessed with "a ready wit," if demonstration should in the mean time stare you in the face, do not be in the least alarmed—anticipate the blow. Whilst you have it yet in your power, rise with becoming magnanimity, and cry, "I give it up! I give it up! La! let us say no more about it; I do so hate disputing about trifles. I give it up!" Before an explanation on the word trifle can take place, quit the room with flying colours.

If you are a woman of sentiment and eloquence, you have advantages of which I scarcely need apprize you. From the understanding of a man, you have always an appeal to his heart, or, if not, to his affection, to his weakness. If you have the good fortune to be married to a weak man, always choose the moment to argue with him when you have a full audience. Trust to the sublime power of numbers; it will be of use even to excite your own enthusiasm in debate; then as the scene advances, talk of his cruelty, and your sensibility, and sink with "becoming woe" into the pathos of injured innocence.

Besides the heart and the weakness of your opponent, you have still another chance, in ruffling his temper; which, in the course of a long conversation, you will have a fair opportunity of trying; and if—for philosophers will sometimes grow warm in the defence of truth—if he should grow absolutely angry, you will in the same proportion grow calm, and wonder at his rage, though you well know it has been created by your own provocation. The by-standers, seeing anger without any adequate cause, will all be of your side.

Nothing provokes an irascible man, interested in debate, and possessed of an opinion of his own eloquence, so much as to see the attention of his hearers go from him: you will then, when he flatters himself that he has just fixed your eye with his *very best* argument, suddenly grow absent:—your house affairs must call you hence—or you have directions to give to your children—or the room is too hot, or too cold—the window must be opened—or door shut—or the candle wants snuffing. Nay, without these interruptions, the simple motion of your eye may provoke a speaker; a butterfly, or the figure in a carpet may engage your attention in preference to him; or if these objects be absent, the simply averting your eye, looking through the window in quest of outward objects, will show that your mind has not been abstracted, and will display to him at least your wish of not attending. He may, however, possibly have lost the habit of watching your eye for approbation; then you may assault his ear: if all other resources fail, beat with your foot that dead march of the spirits, that incessant tattoo, which so well deserves its name. Marvellous must be the patience of the much-enduring man whom some or other of these devices do not provoke: slight causes often produce great effects; the simple scratching of a pick-axe, properly applied to certain veins in a mine, will cause the most dreadful explosions.

Hitherto we have only professed to teach the defensive; let me now recommend to you the offensive part of the art of justification. As a supplement to reasoning comes recrimination: the pleasure of proving that you are right is surely incomplete till you have proved that your adversary is wrong; this might have been a secondary, let it now become a primary object with you; rest your own defence on it for further security: you are no longer to consider yourself as obliged either to deny, palliate, argue, or declaim, but simply to justify yourself by criminating another; all merit, you know, is judged of by comparison. In the art of recrimination, your memory will be of the highest service to you; for you are to open and keep an account-current of all the faults, mistakes, neglects, unkindnesses of those you live with; these you are to state against your own: I need not tell you that the balance will always be in your favour. In stating matters or opinion, produce the words of the very same person which passed days, months, years before, in contradiction to what he is then saying. By displacing, disjointing words and sentences, by mis-understanding the whole, or quoting only a part of what has been said, you may convict any man of inconsistency, particularly if he be a man of genius and feeling; for he speaks generally from the impulse of the moment, and of all others can the least bear to be charged with paradoxes. So far for a husband.

Recriminating is also of sovereign use in the quarrels of friends; no friend is so perfectly equable, so ardent in affection, so nice in punctilio, as never to offend: then "Note his faults, and con them all by rote." Say you can forgive, but you can never forget; and surely it is much more generous to forgive and remember, than to forgive and forget. On every new alarm, call the unburied ghosts from former fields of battle; range them in tremendous array, call them one by one to witness against the conscience of your enemy, and ere the battle is begun take from him all courage to engage.

There is one case I must observe to you in which recrimination has peculiar poignancy. If you have had it in your power to confer obligations on any one, never cease reminding them of it: and let them feel that you have acquired an indefeasible right to reproach them without a possibility of their retorting. It is a maxim with some sentimental people, "To treat their servants as if they were their friends in distress."—I have observed that people of this cast make themselves amends, by treating their friends in distress as if they were their servants.

Apply this maxim—you may do it a thousand ways, especially in company. In general conversation, where every one is supposed to be on a footing, if any of your humble companions should presume to hazard an opinion contrary to yours, and should modestly begin with, "I think;" look as the man did when he said to his servant, "You think, sir—what business have you to think?"

Never fear to lose a friend by the habits which I recommend: reconciliations, as you have often heard it said—reconciliations are the cement of friendship; therefore friends should quarrel to strengthen their attachment, and offend each other for the pleasure of being reconciled.

I beg pardon for digressing: I was, I believe, talking of your husband, not of your friend—I have gone far out of the way.

If in your debates with your husband you should want "eloquence to vex him," the dull prolixity of narration, joined to the complaining monotony of voice which I formerly recommended, will supply its place, and have the desired effect: Somnus will prove propitious; then, ever and anon as the soporific charm begins to work, rouse him with interrogatories, such as, "Did not you say so? Don't you remember? Only answer me that!"

By-the-by, interrogatories artfully put may lead an unsuspicious reasoner, you know, always to your own conclusion.

In addition to the patience, philosophy, and other good things which Socrates learned from his wife, perhaps she taught him this mode of reasoning.

But, after all, the precepts of art, and even the natural susceptibility of your tempers, will avail you little in the sublime of our science, if you cannot command that ready enthusiasm which will make you enter into the part you are acting; that happy imagination which shall make you believe all you fear and all you invent.

Who is there amongst you who cannot or who will not justify when they are accused? Vulgar talent! the sublime of our science is to justify before we are accused. There is no reptile so vile but what will turn when it is trodden on; but of a nicer sense and nobler species are those whom nature has endowed with antennas, which perceive and withdraw at the distant approach of danger. Allow me another allusion: similes cannot be crowded too close for a female taste; and analogy, I have heard, my fair pupils, is your favourite mode of reasoning.

The sensitive plant is too vulgar an allusion; but if the truth of modern naturalists may be depended upon, there is a plant which, instead of receding timidly from the intrusive touch, angrily protrudes its venomous juices upon all who presume to meddle with it:—do not you think this plant would be your fittest emblem?

Let me, however, recommend it to you, nice souls, who, of the mimosa kind, "fear the dark cloud, and feel the coming storm," to take the utmost precaution lest the same susceptibility which you cherish as the dear means to torment others should insensibly become a torment to yourselves.

Distinguish then between sensibility and susceptibility; between the anxious solicitude not to give offence, and the captious eagerness of vanity to prove that it ought not to have been taken; distinguish between the desire of praise and the horror of blame: can any two things be more different than the wish to improve, and the wish to demonstrate that you have never been to blame?

Observe, I only wish you to distinguish these things in your own minds; I would by no means advise you to discontinue the laudable practice of confounding them perpetually in speaking to others.

When you have nearly exhausted human patience in explaining, justifying, vindicating; when, in spite of all the pains you have taken, you have more than half betrayed your own vanity; you have a never-failing resource, in paying tribute to that of your opponent, as thus:—

"I am sure you must be sensible that I should never take so much pains to justify myself if I were indifferent to your opinion.—I know that I ought not to disturb myself with such trifles; but nothing is a trifle to me which concerns you. I confess I am too anxious to please; I know it's a fault, but I cannot cure myself of it now.—Too quick sensibility, I am conscious, is the defect of my disposition; it would be happier for me if I could be more indifferent, I know."

Who could be so brutal as to blame so amiable, so candid a creature? Who would not submit to be tormented with kindness?

When once your captive condescends to be flattered by such arguments as these, your power is fixed; your future triumphs can be bounded only by your own moderation; they are at once secured and justified.

Forbear not, then, happy pupils; but, arrived at the summit of power, give a full scope to your genius, nor trust to genius alone: to exercise in all its extent your privileged dominion, you must acquire, or rather you must pretend to have acquired, infallible skill in the noble art of physiognomy; immediately the thoughts as well as the words of your subjects are exposed to your inquisition.

Words may flatter you, but the countenance never can deceive you; the eyes are the windows of the soul, and through them you are to watch what passes in the inmost recesses of the heart. There, if you discern the slightest ideas of doubt, blame, or displeasure; if you discover the slightest symptoms of revolt, take the alarm instantly. Conquerors must maintain their conquests; and how easily can they do this, who hold a secret correspondence with the minds of the vanquished! Be your own spies then; from the looks, gestures, slightest motions of your enemies, you are to form an alphabet, a language intelligible only to yourselves, yet by which you shall condemn them; always remembering that in sound policy suspicion justifies punishment. In vain, when you accuse your friends of the high treason of blaming you, in vain let them plead their innocence, even of the intention. "They did not say a word which could be tortured into such a meaning." No, "but they looked daggers, though they used none."

And of this you are to be the sole judge, though there were fifty witnesses to the contrary.

How should indifferent spectators pretend to know the countenance of your friend as well as you do—you, that have a nearer, a dearer interest in attending to it? So accurate have been your observations, that no thought of their souls escapes you; nay, you often can tell even what they are going to think of.

The science of divination certainly claims your attention; beyond the past and the present, it shall extend your dominion over the future; from slight words, half-finished sentences, from silence itself, you shall draw your omens and auguries.

"I know what you were going to say;" or, "I know such a thing was a sign you were inclined to be displeased with me."

In the ardour of innocence, the culprit, to clear himself from such imputations, incurs the imputation of a greater offence. Suppose, to prove that you were mistaken, to prove that he could not have meant to blame you, he should declare that at the moment you mention, "You were quite foreign to his thoughts; he was not thinking at all about you."

Then in truth you have a right to be angry. To one of your class of justificators, this is the highest offence. Possessed as you are of the firm opinion that all persons, at all times, on all occasions, are intent upon you alone, is it not less mortifying to discover that you were thought ill of, than that you were not thought of at all? "Indifference, you know, sentimental pupils, is more fatal to love than even hatred."

Thus, my dear pupils, I have endeavoured to provide precepts adapted to the display of your several talents; but if there should be any amongst you who have no talents, who can neither argue nor persuade, who have neither sentiment nor enthusiasm, I must indeed—congratulate them;—they are peculiarly qualified for the science of Self-justification: indulgent nature, often even in the weakness, provides for the protection of her creatures; just Providence, as the guard of stupidity, has enveloped it with the impenetrable armour of obstinacy.

Fair idiots! let women of sense, wit, feeling, triumph in their various arts: yours are superior. Their empire, absolute as it sometimes may be, is perpetually subject to sudden revolutions. With them, a man has some chance of equal sway: with a fool he has none. Have they hearts and understandings? Then the one may be touched, or the other in some unlucky moment convinced; even in their very power lies their greatest danger:— not so with you. In vain let the most candid of his sex attempt to reason with you; let him begin with, "Now, my dear, only listen to reason:"—you stop him at once with, "No, my dear, you know I do not pretend to reason; I only say, that's my opinion."

Let him go on to prove that yours is a mistaken opinion:—you are ready to acknowledge it long before he desires it. "You acknowledge it may be a wrong opinion; but still it is your opinion." You do not maintain it in the least, either because you believe it to be wrong or right, but merely because it is yours. Exposed as you might have been to the perpetual humiliation of being convinced, nature seems kindly to have denied you all perception of truth, or at least all sentiment of pleasure from the perception.

With an admirable humility, you are as well contented to be in the wrong as in the right; you answer all that can be said to you with a provoking humility of aspect.

"Yes; I do not doubt but what you say may be very true, but I cannot tell; I do not think myself capable of judging on these subjects; I am sure you must know much better than I do. I do not pretend to say but that your opinion is very just; but I own I am of a contrary way of thinking; I always thought so, and I always shall."

Should a man with persevering temper tell you that he is ready to adopt your sentiments if you will only explain them; should he beg only to have a reason for your opinion—no, you can give no reason. Let him urge you to say something in its defence:—no; like Queen Anne,72 you will only repeat the same thing over again, or be silent. Silence is the ornament of your sex; and in silence, if there be not wisdom, there is safety. You will, then, if you please, according to your custom, sit listening to all entreaties to explain, and speak—with a fixed immutability of posture, and a pre-determined deafness of eye, which shall put your opponent utterly out of patience; yet still by persevering with the same complacent importance of countenance, you shall half persuade people you could speak if you would; you shall keep them in doubt by that true want of meaning, "which puzzles more than wit;" even because they cannot conceive the excess of your stupidity, they shall actually begin to believe that they themselves are stupid. Ignorance and doubt are the great parents of the sublime.

Your adversary, finding you impenetrable to argument, perhaps would try wit:—but, "On the impassive ice the lightnings play." His eloquence or his kindness will avail less; when in yielding to you after a long harangue, he expects to please you, you will answer undoubtedly with the utmost propriety, "That you should be very sorry he yielded his judgment to you; that he is very good; that you are much obliged to him; but that, as to the point in dispute, it is a matter of perfect indifference to you; for your part, you have no choice at all about it; you beg that he will do just what he pleases; you know that it is the duty of a wife to submit; but you hope, however, you may have an *opinion* of your own."

Remember, all such speeches as these will lose above half their effect, if you cannot accompany them with the vacant stare, the insipid smile, the passive aspect of the humbly perverse.

Whilst I write, new precepts rush upon my recollection; but the subject is inexhaustible. I quit it with regret, though fully sensible of my presumption in having attempted to instruct those who, whilst they read, will smile in the consciousness of superior powers. Adieu! then, my fair readers: long may you prosper in the practice of an art peculiar to your sex! Long may you maintain unrivalled dominion at home and abroad; and long may your husbands rue the hour when first they made you promise *"to obey!"*

TALES OF FASHIONABLE LIFE

Tutta la gente in lieta fronte udiva
Le graziose e finte istorielle,
Ed Ì difetti altrui tosto scopriva
Ciascuno, e non i proprj espressi in quelle;
O se de' proprj sospettava, ignoti
Credeali a ciascun altro, e a se sol noti.

PREFACE

My daughter asks me for a Preface to the following volumes; from a pardonable weakness she calls upon me for parental protection: but, in fact, the public judges of every work, not from the sex, but from the merit of the author.

What we feel, and see, and hear, and read, affects our conduct from the moment when we begin, till the moment when we cease to think. It has therefore been my daughter's aim to promote, by all her writings, the progress of education from the cradle to the grave.

Miss Edgeworth's former works consist of tales for children—of stories for young men and women—and of tales suited to that great mass which does not move in the circles of fashion. The present volumes are intended to point out some of those errors to which the higher classes of society are disposed.

All the parts of this series of moral fictions bear upon the faults and excellencies of different ages and classes; and they have all arisen from that view of society which we have laid before the public in more didactic works on education. In the PARENT'S ASSISTANT, in MORAL and in POPULAR TALES, it was my daughter's aim to exemplify the principles contained in PRACTICAL EDUCATION. In these volumes, and in others which are to follow, she endeavours to disseminate, in a familiar form, some of the ideas that are unfolded in ESSAYS ON PROFESSIONAL EDUCATION.

The first of these stories is called

ENNUI.—The causes, curses, and cure of this disease are exemplified, I hope, in such a manner, as not to make the remedy worse than the disease. Thiebauld tells us, that a prize-essay on Ennui was read to the Academy of Berlin, which put all the judges to sleep.

THE DUN—is intended as a lesson against the common folly of believing that a debtor is able, by a few cant phrases, to alter the nature of right and wrong. We had once thoughts of giving to these books the title of FASHIONABLE TALES: alas! the Dun could never have found favour with fashionable readers.

MANOEUVRING—is a vice to which the little great have recourse, to show their second-rate abilities. Intrigues of gallantry upon the continent frequently lead to political intrigue: amongst us the attempts to introduce this *improvement* of our manners have not yet been successful; but there are, however, some, who, in every thing they say or do, show a predilection for "left-handed wisdom." It is hoped that the picture here represented of a *manoeuvrer* has not been made alluring.

ALMERIA—gives a view of the consequences which usually follow the substitution of the gifts of fortune in the place of merit; and shows the meanness of those who imitate manners and haunt company above their station in society.

Difference of rank is a continual excitement to laudable emulation; but those who consider the being admitted into circles of fashion as the summit of human bliss and elevation, will here find how grievously such frivolous ambition may be disappointed and chastised.

I may be permitted to add a word on the respect with which Miss Edgeworth treats the public—their former indulgence has not made her careless or presuming. The dates subjoined to these stories show that they have not been hastily intruded upon the reader.

RICHARD LOVELL EDGEWORTH

Edgeworthstown,

March, 1809.

ENNUI; OR, MEMOIRS OF THE
EARL OF GLENTHORN

"'Que faites-vous à Potzdam?' demandois-je un jour an prince Guillaume. 'Monsieur,' me répondit-il, 'nous passons notre vie à conjuguer tous le même verbe; *Je m'ennuie, tu t'ennuies, il s'ennuie, nous nous ennuyons, vous vous ennuyez, ils s'ennuient; je m'ennuyois, je m'ennuierai,'* " &c.

THIEBAULD, Mém. de Frédéric le Grand.

CHAPTER I

Bred up in luxurious indolence, I was surrounded by friends who seemed to have no business in this world but to save me the trouble of thinking or acting for myself; and I was confirmed in the pride of helplessness by being continually reminded that I was the only son and heir of the Earl of Glenthorn. My mother died a few weeks after I was born; and I lost my father when I was very young. I was left to the care of a guardian, who, in hopes of winning my affection, never controlled my wishes or even my whims: I changed schools and masters as often as I pleased, and consequently learned nothing. At last I found a private tutor who suited me exactly, for he was completely of my own opinion, "that every thing which the young Earl of Glenthorn did not know by the instinct of genius was not worth his learning." Money could purchase a reputation for talents, and with money I was immoderately supplied; for my guardian expected to bribe me with a part of my own fortune, to forbear inquiring what had become of a certain deficiency in the remainder. This tacit compact I perfectly understood: we were consequently on the most amicable terms imaginable, and the most confidential; for I thought it better to deal with my guardian than with Jews. Thus at an age when other young men are subject to some restraint, either from the necessity of their circumstances, or the discretion of their friends, I became completely master of myself and of my fortune. My companions envied me; but even their envy was not sufficient to make me happy. Whilst yet a boy, I began to feel the dreadful symptoms of that mental malady which baffles the skill of medicine, and for which wealth can purchase only temporary alleviation. For this complaint there is no precise English name; but, alas! the foreign term is now naturalized in England. Among the higher classes, whether in the wealthy or the fashionable world, who is unacquainted with *ennui*? At first I was unconscious of being subject to this disease; I felt that something was the matter with me, but I did not know what: yet the symptoms were sufficiently marked. I was afflicted with frequent fits of fidgeting, yawning, and stretching, with a constant restlessness of mind and body; an aversion to the place I was in, or the thing I was doing, or rather to that which was passing before my eyes, for I was never doing any thing; I had an utter abhorrence and an incapacity of voluntary exertion. Unless roused by external stimulus, I sank into that kind of apathy, and vacancy of ideas, vulgarly known by the name of *a brown study*. If confined in a room for more than half an hour by bad weather or other contrarieties, I would pace backwards and forwards, like the restless *cavia* in his den, with a fretful, unmeaning pertinacity. I felt an insatiable longing for something new, and a childish love of locomotion.

My physician and my guardian, not knowing what else to do with me, sent me abroad. I set out upon my travels in my eighteenth year, attended by my favourite tutor as my *companion*. We perfectly agreed in our ideas of travelling; we hurried from place to place as fast as horses and wheels, and curses and guineas, could carry us. Milord Anglois rattled over half the globe without getting one inch farther from his ennui. Three years were to be consumed before I should be of age. What sums did I spend during this interval in expedition-money to Time! but the more I tried to hasten him, the slower the rogue went. I lost my money and my temper.

At last the day for which I had so long panted arrived—I was twenty-one! and I took possession of my estate. The bells rang, the bonfires blazed, the tables were spread, the wine flowed, huzzas resounded, friends and tenants crowded about me, and nothing but the voice of joy and congratulation was to be heard. The bustle of my situation kept me awake for some weeks; the pleasure of property was new, and, as long as the novelty lasted, delightful. I cannot say that I was satisfied; but my mind was distended by the sense of the magnitude of my possessions. I had large estates in England; and in one of the remote maritime counties of Ireland, I was lord over an immense territory, annexed to the ancient castle of Glenthorn;—a noble pile of antiquity! worth ten degenerate castles of modern days. It was placed in a bold romantic situation: at least as far as I could judge of it by a picture, said to be a striking likeness, which hung in my hall at Sherwood Park in England. I was born in Ireland, and nursed, as I was told, in an Irish cabin: for my father had an idea that this would make me hardy; he left me with my Irish nurse till I was two years old, and from that time forward neither he nor I ever revisited Ireland. He had a dislike to that country, and I grew up in his prejudices. I declared that I would always reside in England. Sherwood Park, my English country-seat, had but one fault, it was completely finished. The house was magnificent, and in the modern taste; the furniture fashionably elegant, and in all the gloss of novelty. Not a single luxury omitted; not a fault could be found by the most fastidious critic. My park, my grounds, displayed all the beauties of nature and of art, judiciously combined. Majestic woods, waving their dark foliage, overhung——But I will spare my readers the description, for I remember falling asleep myself whilst a poet was reading to me an ode on the beauties of Sherwood Park. These beauties too soon became familiar to my eye; and even the idea of being the proprietor of this enchanting place soon palled upon my vanity. Every casual visitor, all the strangers, even the common people, who were allowed once a week to walk in my pleasure-grounds, enjoyed them a thousand times more than I could. I remember, that, about six weeks after I came to Sherwood Park, I one evening escaped from the crowds of *friends* who filled my house, to indulge myself in a solitary, melancholy walk. I saw at some distance a party of people, who were coming to admire the place; and to avoid meeting them I took shelter under a fine tree, the branches of which, hanging to the ground, concealed me from the view of passengers. Thus seated, I was checked in the middle of a desperate yawn, by hearing one among the party of strangers exclaiming—

"How happy the owner of this place must be!"

Yes, had I known how to enjoy the goods of life, I might have been happy; but want of occupation, and antipathy to exertion, rendered me one of the most miserable men upon earth. Still I imagined that the cause of my discontent proceeded from some external circumstance. Soon after my coming of age, business of various sorts required my attention; papers were to be signed, and lands were to be let: these things appeared to me terrible difficulties. Not even that minister of state, who so feelingly describes his horror at the first appearance of the secretary with the great portfolio, ever experienced sensations so oppressive as mine were, when my steward began to talk to me of my own affairs. In the peevishness of my indolence, I declared that I thought the pains overbalanced the pleasures of property. Captain Crawley, a friend—a sort of a friend—a humble companion of mine, a gross, unblushing, thorough-going flatterer, happened to be present when I made this declaration: he kindly undertook to stand between me and the shadow of trouble. I accepted this offer.

"Ay, Crawley," said I, "do see and settle with these people."

I had not the slightest confidence in the person into whose hands, to save myself from the labour of thinking, I thus threw all my affairs; but I satisfied my understanding, by resolving that, when I should have leisure, I would look out for an agent upon whom I could depend.

I had now been nearly two months at Sherwood Park; too long a time, I thought, to remain in any place, and I was impatient to get away. My steward, who disliked the idea of my spending my summers at home, found it easy to persuade me that the water on my estate had a brackish unwholesome taste. The man who told me this stood before me in perfect health, though he had drunk this insalubrious water all his life: but it was too laborious a task for my intellects to compare the evidence of my different senses, and I found it most easy to believe what I heard, though it was in direct opposition to what I saw. Away I hurried to a *watering-place*, after the example of many of my noble contemporaries, who leave their delightful country-seats, to pay, by the inch, for being squeezed up in lodging-houses, with all imaginable inconvenience, during the hottest months in summer. I whiled away my time at Brighton, cursing the heat of the weather, till the winter came, and then cursing the cold, and longing for the London winter.

The London winter commenced; and the young Earl of Glenthorn, and his entertainments, and his equipages, and extravagance, were the conversation of all the world, and the joy of the newspapers. The immense cost of the fruit at my desserts was recorded; the annual expense of the vast nosegays of hot-house flowers worn daily by the footmen who clung behind my coach was calculated; the hundreds of wax lights, which burned nightly in my house, were numbered by the idle admirers of folly; and it was known by every body that Lord Glenthorn suffered nothing but wax to be burned in his stables; that his servants drank nothing but claret and champagne; that his liveries, surpassing the imagination of ambassadors, vied with regal magnificence, whilst their golden trappings could have stood even the test of Chinese curiosity. My coachmaker's bill for this year, if laid before the public, would amuse and astonish sober-minded people, as much as some charges which have lately appeared in our courts of justice for *extraordinary coaches*, and *very extraordinary landaus*. I will not enter into the detail of my extravagance in minor articles of expense; these, I thought, could never be felt by such a fortune as that of the Earl of Glenthorn; but, for the information of those who have the same course to run or to avoid, I should observe, that my diurnal visits to jewellers' shops amounted, in time, to sums worth mentioning. Of the multitude of baubles that I bought, the rings, the seals, the chains, I will give no account; it would pass the belief of man, and the imagination of woman. Those who have the least value for their time have usually the greatest number of watches, and are the most anxious about the exactness of their going. I and my repeaters were my own plagues, and the profit of all the fashionable watchmakers, whose shops I regularly visited for a *lounge*. My history, at this period, would be a complete *lounger's journal*; but I will spare my readers this diary. I wish, however, as I have had ample experience, to impress it on the minds of all whom it may concern, that a lounger of fortune *must* be extravagant. I went into shops merely to pass an idle hour, but I could not help buying something; and I was ever at the mercy of tradesmen, who took advantage of my indolence, and who thought my fortune inexhaustible. I really had not any taste for expense; but I let all who dealt with me, especially my servants, do as they pleased, rather than be at the trouble of making them do as they ought. They assured me, that Lord Glenthorn must have such and such things, and must do so and so; and I quietly submitted to this imaginary necessity.

All this time I was the envy of my acquaintance; but I was more deserving of their compassion. Without anxiety or exertion, I possessed every thing they wanted; but then I had no motive—I had nothing to desire. I had an immense fortune, and I was the Earl of Glenthorn: my title and wealth were sufficient distinctions; how could I be anxious about my boots, or the cape of my coat, or any of those trifles which so happily interest and occupy the lives of fashionable young men, who have not the misfortune to possess large estates? Most of my companions had some real or imaginary grievance, some old uncle or father, some *cursed* profession to complain of; but I had none. They had hopes and fears; but I had none. I was on the pinnacle of glory, which they were endeavouring to reach; and I had nothing to do but to sit still, and enjoy the barrenness of the prospect.

In this recital I have communicated, I hope, to my readers some portion of that ennui which I endured; otherwise they cannot form an adequate idea of my temptation to become a gambler. I really had no vice, nor any of those propensities which lead to vice; but ennui produced most of the effects that are usually attributed to strong passions or a vicious disposition.

CHAPTER II

"*O! ressource assurée,*
Viens ranimer leur langueur desoeuvrée:
Leur âme vide est du moins amusée
Par l'avarice en plaisir deguisée."

Gaming relieved me from that insuperable listlessness by which I was oppressed. I became interested—I became agitated; in short, I found a new kind of stimulus, and I indulged in it most intemperately. I grew immoderately fond of that which supplied me with sensations. My days and nights were passed at the gaming-table. I remember once spending three days and three nights in the hazard-room of a well-known house in St. James's-street: the shutters were closed, the curtains down, and we had candles the whole time; even in the adjoining rooms we had candles, that when our doors were opened to bring in refreshments, no obtrusive gleam of daylight might remind us how the hours had passed. How human nature supported the fatigue, I know not. We scarcely allowed ourselves a moment's pause to take the sustenance our bodies required. At last, one of the markers, who had been in the room with us the whole time, declared that he could hold out no longer, and that sleep he must. With difficulty he obtained an hour's truce: the moment he got out of the room he fell asleep, absolutely at the very threshold of our door. By the rules of the house he was entitled to a bonus on every transfer of property at the hazard-table; and he had made, in the course of these three days, upwards of three hundred pounds. Sleep and avarice had struggled to the utmost, but, with his vulgar habits, sleep prevailed. We were wide awake. I shall never forget the figure of one of my noble associates, who sat holding his watch, his eager eyes fixed upon the minute-hand, whilst he exclaimed continually, "This hour will never be over!" Then he listened to discover whether his watch had stopped; then cursed the lazy fellow for falling asleep, protesting that, for his part, he never would again consent to such waste of time. The very instant the hour was ended, he ordered "*that dog*" to be awakened, and to work we went. At this sitting 35,000*l.* were lost and won. I was very fortunate, for I lost a mere trifle—ten thousand pounds; but I could not expect to be always so lucky.— Now we come to the old story of being ruined by play. My English John o'-the-Scales warned me that he could *advance* no more money; my Irish agent, upon whom my drafts had indeed been unmerciful, could not *oblige* me any longer, and he threw up his agency, after having made his fortune at my expense. I railed, but railing would not pay my debts of honour. I inveighed against my grandfather for having tied me up so tight; I could neither mortgage nor sell: my Irish estate would have been sold instantly, had it not been settled upon a Mr. Delamere. The pleasure of abusing him, whom I had never seen, and of whom I knew nothing but that he was to be my heir, relieved me wonderfully. He died, and left only a daughter, a mere child. My chance of possessing the estate in fee-simple increased: I sold this increased value to the Jews, and gamed on. Miss Delamere, some time afterwards, had the smallpox. Upon the event of her illness I laid bets to an amazing amount.

She recovered. No more money could be raised, and my debts were to be paid. In this dilemma I recollected that I once had a guardian, and that I had never settled accounts with him. Crawley, who continued to be my factotum and flatterer in ordinary and extraordinary, informed me, upon looking over these accounts, that there was a mine of money due to me, if I could but obtain it by law or equity. To law I went: and the anxiety of a lawsuit might have, in some degree, supplied the place of gambling, but that all my business was managed for me by Crawley, and I charged him never to mention the subject to me till a verdict should be obtained.

A verdict was obtained against me. It was proved in open court, by my own witnesses, that I was a fool; but as no judge, jury, or chancellor, could believe that I was so great a fool as my carelessness indicated, my guardian stood acquitted in equity of being so great a rogue as he really was. What was now to be done? I saw my doom. As a highwayman knows that he must come to the gallows at last, and acts accordingly, so a fashionably extravagant youth knows that, sooner or later, he must come to matrimony. No one could have more horror of this catastrophe than I felt; but it was in vain to oppose my destiny. My opinion of women had been formed from the commonplace jests of my companions, and from my own acquaintance with the worst part of the sex. I had never felt the passion of love, and, of course, believed it to be something that might have existed in former ages, but that it was in our days quite obsolete, at least, among the *knowing* part of the world. In my imagination young women were divided into two classes; those who were to be purchased, and those who were to purchase. Between these two classes, though the division was to be marked externally by a certain degree of ceremony, yet I was internally persuaded that there was no essential difference. In my feelings towards them there was some distinction; of the first class I was tired, and of the second I was afraid.

Afraid! Yes—afraid of being taken in. With these fears, and these sentiments, I was now to choose a wife. I chose her by the numeration table: Units, tens, hundreds, thousands, tens of thousands, hundreds of thousands. I was content, in the language of the newspapers, *to lead to the Hymeneal altar* any fashionable fair one whose fortune came under the sixth place of figures. No sooner were my *dispositions* known than the friends of a young heiress, who wanted to purchase a coronet, settled a match between us. My bride had one hundred wedding-dresses, elegant as a select committee of dressmakers and milliners, French and English, could devise. The least expensive of these robes, as well as I remember, cost fifty guineas: the most admired came to about five hundred pounds, and was thought, by the best judges in these matters, to be wonderfully cheap, as it was of lace such as had never before been trailed in English dust, even by the lady of a nabob. These things were shown in London as a *spectacle* for some days, by the dressmaker, who declared that she had lost many a night's rest in contriving how to make such a variety of dresses sufficiently magnificent and *distinguished*. The jewellers also requested and obtained permission to exhibit the different sets of jewels: these were so numerous that Lady Glenthorn scarcely knew them all. One day, soon after her marriage, somebody at court, observing that her diamonds were prodigiously fine, asked where she bought them. "Really," said she, "I cannot tell. I have so many sets, I declare I don't know whether *it's* my Paris, or my Hamburgh, or my London set."

Poor young creature! I believe her chief idea of happiness in marriage was the possession of the jewels and paraphernalia of a countess—I am sure it was the only hope she could have, that was likely to be realized, in marrying me. I thought it manly and fashionable to be indifferent, if not contemptuous to my wife: I considered her only as an incumbrance, that I was obliged to take along with my fortune. Besides the disagreeable ideas generally connected with the word *wife*, I had some peculiar reasons for my aversion to my Lady Glenthorn. Before her friends would suffer me to take possession of her fortune, they required from me a solemn oath against gambling: so I was compelled to abjure the hazard-table and the turf, the only two objects in life that could keep me awake. This extorted vow I set down entirely to my bride's account; and I therefore became even more averse to her than men usually are who marry for money. Yet this dislike subsided. Lady Glenthorn was only childish—I, of an easy temper. I thought her ridiculous, but it was too much trouble to tell her so continually. I let the occasions pass, and even forgot her ladyship, when she was not absolutely in my way. She was too frivolous to be hated, and the passion of hatred was not to be easily sustained in my mind. The habit of ennui was stronger than all my passions put together.

CHAPTER III

"Or realize what we think fabulous,
I' th' bill of fare of Eliogabalus."

After my marriage, my old malady rose to an insupportable height. The pleasures of the table were all that seemed left to me in life. Most of the young men of any *ton*, either were, or pretended to be, *connoisseurs* in the science of good eating. Their *talk* was of sauces and of cooks, what dishes each cook was famous for; whether his *forte* lay in white sauces or brown, in soups, *lentilles, fricandeaus, bechemele, matelotes, daubes,* &c. Then the history and genealogy of the cooks came after the discussion of the merit of the works; whom my Lord C——'s cook lived with formerly—what my Lord D—— gave his cook—where they met with these great geniuses, &c. I cannot boast that our conversation at these select dinners, from which the ladies were excluded, was very entertaining; but true good eaters detest wit at dinner-time, and sentiment at all times. I think I observed that amongst these cognoscenti there was scarcely one to whom the delicacy of taste did not daily prove a source of more pain than pleasure. There was always a cruel something that spoiled the rest; or if the dinner were excellent, beyond the power of the most fastidious palate to condemn, yet there was the hazard of being placed far from the favourite dish, or the still greater danger of being deputed to carve at the head or foot of the table. How I have seen a heavy nobleman of this set dexterously manoeuvre to avoid the dangerous honour of carving a haunch of venison! "But, good Heavens!" said I, when a confidential whisper first pointed out this to my notice, "why does he not like to carve?—he would have it in his power to help himself to his mind, which nobody else can do so well."—"No! if he carve, he must give the *nice bits* to others; every body here understands them as well as he—each knows what is upon his neighbour's plate, and what ought to be there, and what must be in the dish." I found that it was an affair of calculation—a game at which nobody can cheat without being discovered and disgraced. I emulated, and soon equalled my experienced friends. I became a perfect epicure, and gloried in the character, for it could be supported without any intellectual exertion, and it was fashionable. I cannot say that I could ever eat as much as some of my companions. One of them I once heard exclaim, after a monstrous dinner, "I wish my digestion were equal to my appetite." I would not be thought to exaggerate, therefore I shall not recount the wonders I have seen performed by these capacious heroes of the table. After what I have beheld, to say nothing of what I have achieved, I can believe any thing that is related of the capacity of the human stomach. I can credit even the account of the dinner which Madame de Bavière affirms she saw eaten by Lewis the Fourteenth; *viz.* "quatre assiettes de différentes soupes; un faisan tout entier; un perdrix; une grande assiette pleine de salade; du mouton coupé dans son jus avec de l'ail; deux bons morceaux de jambon; une assiette pleine de patisserie! du fruit et des confitures!" Nor can I doubt the accuracy of the historian, who assures us that a Roman emperor,73 one of the most moderate of those imperial gluttons, *took* for his breakfast, 500 figs, 100 peaches, 10 melons, 100 beccaficoes, and 400 oysters.

Epicurism was scarcely more prevalent during the decline of the Roman empire than it is at this day amongst some of the wealthy and noble youths of Britain. Not one of my select dinner-party but would have been worthy of a place at the *turbot consultation* immortalized by the Roman satirist. A friend of mine, a bishop, one day went into his kitchen, to look at a large turbot, which the cook was dressing. The cook had found it so large that he had cut off the fins: "What a shame!" cried the bishop; and immediately calling for the cook's apron, he spread it before his cassock, and actually sewed the fins again to the turbot with his own episcopal hands.

If I might judge from my own experience, I should attribute fashionable epicurism in a great measure to ennui. Many affect it, because they have nothing else to do; and sensual indulgences are all that exist for those who have not sufficient energy to enjoy intellectual pleasures. I dare say, that if Heliogabalus could be brought in evidence in his own case, and could be made to understand the meaning of the word ennui, he would agree with me in opinion, that it was the cause of half his vices. His offered reward for the discovery of a new pleasure is stronger evidence than any confession he could make. I thank God that I was not born an emperor, or I might have become a monster. Though not in the least inclined to cruelty, I might have acquired the taste for it, merely for desire of the emotion which real tragedies excite. Fortunately, I was only an earl and an epicure.

My indulgence in the excesses of the table injured my health; violent bodily exercise was necessary to counteract the effects of intemperance. It was my maxim, that a man could never eat or drink too much, if he would but take exercise enough. I killed fourteen horses,74 and survived; but I grew tired of killing horses, and I continued to eat immoderately. I was seized with a nervous complaint, attended with extreme melancholy. Frequently the thoughts of putting an end to my existence occurred; and I had many times determined upon the means; but very small and apparently inadequate and ridiculous motives, prevented the execution of my design. Once I was kept alive by a *piggery*, which I wanted to see finished. Another time, I delayed destroying myself, till a statue, which I had just purchased at a vast expense, should be put up in my Egyptian *salon*. By the awkwardness of the unpacker, the statue's thumb was broken. This broken thumb saved my life; it converted ennui into anger. Like Montaigne and his sausage, I had now something to complain of, and I was happy. But at last my anger subsided, the thumb would serve me no longer as a subject of conversation, and I relapsed into silence and black melancholy. I was "a'weary of the sun;" my old thoughts recurred. At this time I was just entering my twenty-fifth year. Rejoicings were preparing for my birthday. My Lady Glenthorn had prevailed upon me to spend the summer at Sherwood Park, because it was new to her. She filled the house with company and noise; but this only increased my discontent. My birthday arrived—I wished myself dead—and I resolved to shoot myself at the close of the day. I put a pistol into my pocket, and stole out towards the evening, unobserved by my jovial companions. Lady Glenthorn and her set were dancing, and I was tired of these sounds of gaiety. I took the private way to the forest, which was near the house; but one of my grooms met me with a fine horse, which an old tenant had just sent as a present on my birthday. The horse was saddled and bridled; the groom held the stirrup, and up I got. The fellow told me the private gate was locked, and I turned as he pointed to go through the grand entrance. At the outside of the gate sat upon the ground, huddled in a great red cloak, an old woman, who started up and sprang forwards the moment she saw me, stretching out her arms and her cloak with one and the same motion.

"Ogh! is it you I see?" cried she, in a strong Irish tone.

At this sound and this sight, my horse, that was shy, backed a little. I called to the woman to stand out of my way.

"Heaven bless your sweet face! I'm the nurse that suckled *yees* when ye was a baby in Ireland. Many's the day I've been longing to see you," continued she, clasping her hands, and standing her ground in the middle of the gateway, regardless of my horse, which I was pressing forward.

"Stand out of the way, for God's sake, my good woman, or I shall certainly ride over you. So! so! so!" said I, patting my restless horse.

"Oh! he's only shy, God bless him! he's as *quite* now as a lamb; and kiss one or other of *yees*, I must," cried she, throwing her arms about the horse's neck.

The horse, unaccustomed to this mode of salutation, suddenly plunged, and threw me. My head fell against the pier of the gate. The last sound I heard was the report of a pistol; but I can give no account of what happened afterwards. I was stunned by my fall, and senseless. When I opened my eyes, I found myself stretched on one of the cushions of my landau, and surrounded by a crowd of people, who seemed to be all talking at once: in the buzz of voices I could not distinguish any thing that was said, till I heard Captain Crawley's voice above the rest, saying,

"Send for a surgeon instantly: but it's all over! it's all over! Take the body the back way to the banqueting-house; I must run to Lady Glenthorn."

I perceived that they thought me dead. I did not at this moment feel that I was hurt. I was curious to know what they would all do; so I closed my eyes again before any one perceived that I had opened them. I lay motionless, and they proceeded with me, according to Captain Crawley's orders, to the banqueting-house. When we arrived there, my servants laid me on one of the Turkish sofas; and the crowd, after having satisfied their' curiosity, dropped off one by one, till I was left with a single footman and my steward.

"I don't believe he's quite dead," said the footman, "for his heart beats."

"Oh, he's the same as dead, for he does not stir hand or foot, and his skull, they say, is fractured for certain; but it will all be seen when the surgeon comes. I am sure he will never do. Crawley will have every thing his own way now, and I may as well decamp."

"Ay; and among them," said the footman, "I only hope I may get my wages."

"What a fool that Crawley made of my lord!" said the steward.

"What a fool my lord made of himself," said the footman, "to be ruled, and let all his people be ruled, by such an upstart! With your leave, Mr. Turner, I'll just run to the house to say one word to James, and be back immediately."

"No, no, you must stay, Robert, whilst I step home to lock my places, before Crawley begins to rummage."

The footman was now left alone with me. Scarcely had the steward been gone two minutes, when I heard a low voice near me saying, in a tone of great anxiety, "Is he dead?"

I half opened my eyes to see who it was that spoke. The voice came from the door which was opposite to me; and whilst the footman turned his back,

I raised my head, and beheld the figure of the old woman, who had been the cause of my accident. She was upon her knees on the threshold—her arms crossed over her breast. I never shall forget her face, it was so expressive of despair.

"Is he dead?" she repeated.

"I tell you yes," replied the footman.

"For the love of God, let me come in, if he is here," cried she.

"Come in, then, and stay here whilst I run to the house." 75

The footman ran off; and my old nurse, on seeing me, burst into an agony of grief. I did not understand one word she uttered, as she spoke in her native language; but her lamentations went to my heart, for they came from hers. She hung over me, and I felt her tears dropping upon my forehead. I could not refrain from whispering, "Don't cry—I am alive."

"Blessings on him!" exclaimed she, starting back: she then dropped down on her knees to thank God. Then calling me by every fondling name that nurses use to their children, she begged my forgiveness, and alternately cursed herself and prayed for me.

The strong affections of this poor woman touched me more than any thing I had ever yet felt in my life; she seemed to be the only person upon earth who really cared for me; and in spite of her vulgarity, and my prejudice against the tone in which she spoke, she excited in my mind emotions of tenderness and gratitude. "My good woman, if I live, I will do something for you: tell me what I can do," said I. "Live! live! God bless you, live; that's all in the wide world I want of you, my jewel; and, till you are well, let me watch over you at nights, as I used to do when you were a child, and I had you in my arms all to myself, dear."

Three or four people now ran into the room, to get before Captain Crawley, whose voice was heard at this instant at a distance. I had only time to make the poor woman understand that I wished to appear to be dead; she took the hint with surprising quickness. Captain Crawley came up the steps, talking in the tone of a master to the steward and people who followed.

"What is this old hag doing here? Where is Robert? Where is Thomas? I ordered them to stay till I came. Mr. Turner, why did not you stay? What! has not the coroner been here yet? The coroner must see the body, I tell you. Good God! What a parcel of blockheads you all are! How many times must I tell you the same thing? Nothing can be done till the coroner has seen him; then we'll talk about the funeral, Mr. Turner—one thing at a time. Every thing shall be done properly, Mr. Turner. Lady Glenthorn trusts every thing to me—Lady Glenthorn wishes that I should order every thing."

"To be sure—no doubt—very proper—I don't say against that."

"But," continued Crawley, turning towards the sofa upon which I lay, and seeing Ellinor kneeling beside me, "what keeps this old Irish witch here still? What business have you here, pray; and who are you, or what are you?"

"Plase your honour, I was his nurse formerly, and so had a nat'ral longing to see him once again before I would die."

"And did you come all the way from Ireland on this wise errand?"

"Troth I did—every inch of the way from his own sweet place."

"Why, you are little better than a fool, I think," said Crawley.

"Little better, plase your honour; but I was always so about them *childer* that I nursed."

"*Childer*! Well, get along about your business now; you see your nursing is not wanted here."

"I'll not stir out of this, while he is here," said my nurse, catching hold of the leg of the sofa, and clinging to it.

"You'll not stir, you say," cried Captain Crawley: "Turn her out!"

"Oh, sure you would not have the cru'lty to turn his old nurse out before he's even *cowld*. And won't you let me see him buried?"

"Out with her! out with her! the old Irish hag! We'll have no howling here. Out with her, John!" said Crawley to my groom.

The groom hesitated, I fancy; for Crawley repeated the order more imperiously: "Out with her! or go yourself."

"May be it's you that will go first yourself," said she.

"Go first myself!" cried Captain Crawley, furiously: "Are you insolent to *me*?"

"And are not you cru'l to me, and to my child I nursed, that lies all as one as dead before you, and was a good friend to you in his day, no doubt?"

Crawley seized hold of her: but she resisted with so much energy, that she dragged along with her the sofa to which she clung, and on which I lay.

"Stop!" cried I, starting up. There was sudden silence. I looked round, but could not utter another syllable. Now, for the first time, I was sensible that I had been really hurt by the fall. My head grew giddy, and my stomach sick. I just saw Crawley's fallen countenance, and him and the steward looking at one another; they were like hideous faces in a dream. I sunk back.

"Ay, lie down, my darling; don't be disturbing yourself for such as them," said my nurse. "Let them do what they will with me; it's little I'd care for them, if you were but once in safe hands."

I beckoned to the groom, who had hesitated to turn out Ellinor, and bid him go to the housekeeper, and have me put to bed. "She," added I, pointing to my old nurse, "is to sit up with me at night." It was all I could say. What they did with me afterwards, I do not know; but I was in my bed, and a bandage was round my temples, and my poor nurse was kneeling on one side of the bed, with a string of beads in her hand; and a surgeon and physician, and Crawley and my Lady Glenthorn were on the other side, whispering together. The curtain was drawn between me and them; but the motion I made on wakening was instantly observed by Crawley, who immediately left the room. Lady Glenthorn drew back my curtain, and began to ask me how I did: but when I fixed my eyes upon her, she sunk upon the bed, trembling violently, and could not finish her sentence. I begged her to go to rest, and she retired. The physician ordered that I should be kept quiet, and seemed to think I was in danger. I asked what was the matter with me? and the surgeon, with a very grave face, informed me that I had an ugly contusion on my head. I had heard of a concussion of the brain; but I did not know distinctly what it was, and my fears were increased by my ignorance. The life which, but a few hours before, I had been on the point of voluntarily destroying, because it was insupportably burdensome, I was now, the moment it was in danger, most anxious to preserve; and the interest which I perceived others had in getting rid of me, increased my desire to recover. My recovery was, however, for some time doubtful. I was seized with a fever, which left me in a state of alarming debility. My old nurse, whom I shall henceforward call by her name of Ellinor, attended me with the most affectionate solicitude during my illness;76 she scarcely stirred from my bedside, night or day; and, indeed, when I came to the use of my senses, she was the only person whom I really liked to have near me. I knew that she was sincere; and, however unpolished her manners, and however awkward her assistance, the good-will with which it was given, made me prefer it to the most delicate and dexterous attentions which I believed to be interested. The very want of a sense of propriety, and the freedom with which she talked to me, regardless of what was suited to her station, or due to my rank, instead of offending or disgusting me, became agreeable; besides, the novelty of her dialect, and of her turn of thought, entertained me as much as a sick man could be entertained. I remember once her telling me, that, "if it *plased* God, she would like to die on a Christmas-day, of all days; *because* the gates of Heaven, they say, will be open all that day; and who knows but a body might slip in *unknownst?*" When she sat up with me at nights she talked on eternally; for she assured me there was nothing like talking, as she had found, to put one *asy asleep.* I listened or not, just as I liked; *any way* she was *contint.* She was inexhaustible in her anecdotes of my ancestors, all tending to the honour and glory of the family; she had also an excellent memory for all the insults, or traditions of insults, which the Glenthorns had received for many ages back, even to the times of the old kings of Ireland; long and long before they stooped to be *lorded;* when their "names, which it was a pity and a murder, and moreover a burning shame, to change, was, O'Shaughnessy." She was well-stored with histories of Irish and Scotish chiefs. The story of O'Neill, the Irish blackbeard, I am sure I ought to remember, for Ellinor told it to me at least six times. Then she had a large assortment of fairies and *shadowless* witches, and *banshees;* and besides, she had legions of spirits and ghosts, and haunted castles without end, my own castle of Glenthorn not excepted, in the description of which she was extremely eloquent; she absolutely excited in my mind some desire to see it. For many a long year, she said, it had been her nightly prayer, that she might live to see me in my own castle; and often and often she was coming over to England to tell me so, only her husband, as long as he lived, would not let her set out on what he called a fool's errand: but it pleased God to take him to himself last fair day, and then she resolved that nothing should hinder her to be with her own child against his birthday: and now, could she see me in my own Castle Glenthorn, she would die *contint*—and what a pity but I should be in it! I was only a lord, as she said, in England; but I could be all as one as a king in Ireland.

Ellinor impressed me with the idea of the sort of feudal power I should possess in my vast territory, over tenants who were almost vassals, and amongst a numerous train of dependents. We resist the efforts made by those who, we think, exert authority or employ artifice to change our determinations; whilst the perverse mind insensibly yields to those who appear not to have power, or reason, or address, sufficient to obtain a victory. I should not have heard any human being with patience try to persuade me to go to Ireland, except this ignorant poor nurse, who spoke, as I thought, merely from the instinct of affection to me and to her native country. I promised her that I would, *some time or other*, visit Glenthorn Castle: but this was only a vague promise, and it was but little likely that it should be accomplished. As I regained my strength, my mind turned, or rather was turned, to other thoughts.

CHAPTER IV

One morning—it was the day after my physicians had pronounced me out of all danger—Crawley sent me a note by Ellinor, congratulating me upon my recovery, and begging to speak to me for half an hour. I refused to see him; and said, that I was not yet well enough to do business. The same morning Ellinor came with a message from Turner, my steward, who, with his humble duty, requested to see me for five minutes, to communicate to me something of importance. I consented to see Turner. He entered with a face of suppressed joy and affected melancholy.

"Sad news I am bound in duty to be the bearer of, my lord. I was determined, whatever came to pass, however, not to speak till your honour was out of danger, which, I thank Heaven, is now the case, and I am happy to be able to congratulate your lordship upon looking as well as—"

"Never mind my looks. I will excuse your congratulations, Mr. Turner," said I, impatiently; for the recollection of the banqueting-house, and the undertaker whom Turner was so eager to introduce, came full into my mind. "Go on, if you please; five minutes is all I am at present able to give to any business, and you sent me word you had something of importance to communicate."

"True, my lord; but in case your lordship is not at present well enough, or not so disposed, I will wait your lordship's leisure."

"Now or never, Mr. Turner. Speak, but speak at once."

"My lord, I would have done so long ago, but was loth to make mischief; and besides, could not believe what I heard whispered, and would scarce believe what I verily saw; though now, as I cannot reasonably have a doubt, I think it would be a sin, and a burden upon my conscience, not to speak; only that I am unwilling to shock your lordship too much, when but just recovering, for that is not the time one would wish to tell or to hear disagreeable things."

"Mr. Turner, either come to the point at once, or leave me; for I am not strong enough to bear this suspense."

"I beg pardon, my lord: why then, my lord, the point is Captain Crawley."

"What of him? I never desire to hear his name again."

"Nor I, I am sure, my lord; but there are some in the house might not be of our opinion."

"Who? you sneaking fellow; speak out, can't you?"

"My lady—my lord—Now it is out. She'll go off with him this night, if not prevented."

My surprise and indignation were as great as if I had always been the fondest and the most attentive of husbands. I was at length roused from that indifference and apathy into which I had sunk; and though I had never loved my wife, the moment I knew she was lost to me for ever was exquisitely painful. Astonishment, the sense of disgrace, the feeling of rage against that treacherous parasite by whom she had been seduced, all combined to overwhelm me. I could command my voice only enough to bid Turner leave the room, and tell no one that he had spoken to me on this subject. "Not a soul," he said, "should be told, or could guess it."

Left to my own reflections, as soon as the first emotions of anger subsided, I blamed myself for my conduct to Lady Glenthorn. I considered that she had been married to me by her friends, when she was too young and too childish to judge for herself; that from the first day of our marriage I had never made the slightest effort to win her affections, or to guide her conduct; that, on the contrary, I had shown her marked indifference, if not aversion. With fashionable airs, I had professed, that provided she left me at liberty to spend the large fortune which she brought me, and in consideration of which she enjoyed the title of Countess of Glenthorn, I cared for nothing farther. With the consequences of my neglect I now reproached myself in vain. Lady Glenthorn's immense fortune had paid my debts, and had for two years supplied my extravagance, or rather my indolence: little remained, and she was now, in her twenty-third year, to be consigned to public disgrace, and to a man whom I knew to be destitute of honour and feeling. I pitied her, and resolved to go instantly and make an effort to save her from destruction.

Ellinor, who watched all Crawley's motions, informed me, that he was gone to a neighbouring town, and had left word that he should not be home till after dinner. Lady Glenthorn was in her dressing-room, which was at a part of the house farthest from that which I now inhabited. I had never left my room since my illness, and had scarcely walked farther than from my bed to my arm-chair; but I was so much roused by my feelings at this instant, that, to Ellinor's great astonishment, I started from my chair, and, forbidding her to follow me, walked without any assistance along the corridor, which led to the back-stairs, and to Lady Glenthorn's apartment.

I opened the private door of her dressing-room suddenly—the room was in great disorder—her woman was upon her knees packing a trunk: Lady Glenthorn was standing at a table, with a parcel of open letters before her, and a diamond necklace in her hand. She started at the sight of me as if she had beheld a ghost: the maid screamed, and ran to a door at the farther end of the room, to make her escape, but that was bolted. Lady Glenthorn was pale and motionless, till I approached; and then, recollecting herself, she reddened all over, and thrust the letters into her table-drawer. Her woman, at the same instant, snatched a casket of jewels, swept up in her arms a heap of clothes, and huddled them all together into the half-packed trunk.

"Leave the room," said I to her sternly. She locked the trunk, pocketed the key, and obeyed.

I placed a chair for Lady Glenthorn, and sat down myself. We were almost equally unable to stand. We were silent for some moments. Her eyes were fixed upon the ground, and she leaned her head upon her hand in an attitude of despair. I could scarcely articulate; but making an effort to command my voice, I at last said—

"Lady Glenthorn, I blame myself more than you for all that has happened."

"For what?" said she, making a feeble attempt at evasion, yet at the same time casting a guilty look towards the drawer of letters.

"You have nothing to conceal from me," said I.

"Nothing!" said she, in a feeble voice.

"Nothing," said I; "for I know every thing"—she started—"and am willing to pardon every thing."

She looked up in my face astonished. "I am conscious," continued I, "that you have not been well treated by me. You have had much reason to complain of my neglect. To this I attribute your error. Forget the past—I will set you the example. Promise me never to see the man more, and what has happened shall never be known to the world."

She made me no answer, but burst into a flood of tears. She seemed incapable of decision, or even of thought. I felt suddenly inspired with energy.

"Write this moment," continued I, placing a pen and ink before her, "write to forbid him ever to return to this house, or ever more to appear in your presence. If he should appear in mine, I know how to chastise him, and to vindicate my own honour. To preserve your reputation, I refrain, upon these conditions, from making my contempt of him public."

I put a pen into Lady Glenthorn's hand; but she trembled so that she could not write. She made several ineffectual attempts, then tore the paper; and again giving way to tears, exclaimed, "I cannot write—I cannot think—I do not know what to say. Write what you will, and I will sign it."

"I write to Captain Crawley! Write what *I* will! Lady Glenthorn, it must be your will to write, not mine. If it be not your will, say so."

"Oh! I do not say so—I do not say *that*. Give me a moment's time. I do not know what I say. I have been very foolish—very wicked. You are very good—but it is too late: it will all be known. Crawley will betray me; he will tell it to Mrs. Mattocks: so whichever way I turn, I am undone. Oh! what *will* become of me?"

She wrung her hands and wept, and was for an hour in this state, in all the indecision and imbecility of a child. At last, she wrote a few scarcely legible lines to Crawley, forbidding him to see or think of her more. I despatched the note, and she was full of penitence, and gratitude, and tears. The next morning, when I wakened, I in my turn received a note from her ladyship.

"Since I saw you, Captain Crawley has convinced me that I am his wife, *in the eye of Heaven*, and I therefore desire a divorce, as much as your *whole conduct*, since my marriage, convinces me *you* must in your *heart*, whatever may be your motives to *pretend* otherwise. Before you receive this I shall be *out of your way* and *beyond your reach*; so do not think of pursuing one who is no longer,

"Yours,

"A. CRAWLEY"

After reading this note, I thought not of pursuing or saving Lady Glenthorn. I was as anxious for a divorce as she could be. Some months afterwards the affair was brought to a public trial. When the cause came on, so many circumstances were brought in mitigation of damages, to prove my utter carelessness respecting my wife's conduct, that a suspicion of collusion arose. From this imputation I was clear in the opinion of all who really knew me; and I repelled the charge publicly, with a degree of indignation that surprised all who knew the usual apathy of my temper. I must observe, that during the whole time my divorce-bill was pending, and whilst I was in the greatest possible anxiety, my health was perfectly good. But no sooner was the affair settled, and a decision made in my favour, than I relapsed into my old nervous complaints.

CHAPTER V

"'Twas doing nothing was his curse; —
Is there a vice can plague us worse?
The wretch who digs the mine for bread,
Or ploughs, that others may be fed,
Feels less fatigue than that decreed
To him who cannot think or read."

Illness was a sort of occupation to me, and I was always sorry to get well. When the interest of being in danger ceased, I had no other to supply its place. I fancied that I should enjoy my liberty after my divorce; but "even freedom grew tasteless." I do not recollect any thing that wakened me from my torpor, during two months after my divorce, except a violent quarrel between all my English servants and my Irish nurse. Whether she assumed too much, upon the idea that she was a favourite, or whether national prejudice was alone the cause of the hatred, that prevailed against her, I know not; but they one and all declared that they could not, and would not, live with her. She expressed the same dislike to *consorting* with them; "but would *put up* with worse, ay, with the devils themselves, to oblige my honour, and to lie under the same roof *wid* my honour."

The rest of the servants laughed at her blunders. This she could bear with good-humour; but when they seriously affected to reproach her with having, by her uncouth appearance, at her first presenting herself at Sherwood Park, endangered my life, she retorted, "And who cared for him in the wide world but I, amongst you all, when he lay for dead? I ask you that," said she.

To this there was no reply; and they hated her the more for their having been silenced by her shrewdness. I protected her as long as I could; but, for the sake of peace, I at last yielded to the combined forces of the steward's room and the servants' hall, and despatched Ellinor to Ireland, with a renewal of the promise that I would visit Glenthorn Castle this year or the next. To comfort her at parting, I would have made her a considerable present; but she would take only a few guineas, to bear her expenses back to her native place. The sacrifice I made did not procure me a peace of any continuance in my own house: — ruined by indulgence, and by my indolent, reckless temper, my servants were now my masters. In a large, ill-regulated establishment, domestics become, like spoiled children, discontented, capricious, and the tyrants over those who have not the sense or steadiness to command. I remember one delicate puppy *parted with me*, because, as he informed me, the curtains of his bed did not close at the foot; he had never been used to such a thing, and had told the housekeeper so three times, but could obtain no redress, which necessitated him to beg my permission to retire from the service.

In his stead another coxcomb came to offer himself, who, with an incomparably easy air, begged to know whether I wanted *a man of figure* or *a man of parts?* For the benefit of those to whom this fashionable classification of domestics may not be familiar, I should observe, that the department of *a man of figure* is specially and solely to announce company on gala days; the business of *the man of parts* is multifarious: to write cards of invitation, to speak to impertinent tradesmen, to carry confidential messages, et cetera. Now, where there is an et cetera in an agreement, there is always an opening for dispute. The functions of *the man of parts* not being accurately defined, I unluckily required from him some service which was not in his bond; I believe it was to go for my pocket handkerchief: "He could not possibly do it, because it was not his business;" and I, the laziest of mortals, after waiting a full quarter of an hour, whilst they were settling whose business it was to obey me, was forced to get up and go for what I wanted. I comforted myself by the recollection of the poor king of Spain and *le brasier*. With a regal precedent I could not but be satisfied. All great people, said I to myself, are obliged to submit to these inconveniences. I submitted with so good a grace, that my submission was scarcely felt to be a condescension. My *bachelor's* house soon exhibited in perfection "High Life below Stairs."

It is said that a foreign nobleman permitted his servants to take their own way so completely, that one night he and his guests being kept waiting an unconscionable time for supper, he at last went down stairs to inquire into the cause of the delay: he found the servant, whose business it was to take up supper, quietly at cards with a large party of his friends. The man coolly remonstrated, that it was impossible to leave his game unfinished. The master candidly acknowledged the force of his plea; but insisted upon the man's going up stairs to lay the cloth for supper, whilst he took his cards, sat down, and finished the game for him.

The suavity of my temper never absolutely reached this degree of complaisance. My home was disagreeable to me: I had not the resolution to remove the causes of the discontents. Every day I swore I would part with all these rascals the next morning; but still they stayed. Abroad I was not happier than at home. I was disgusted with my former companions: they had convinced me, the night of my accident at Sherwood Park, that they cared not whether I was alive or dead; and ever since that time I had been more and more struck with their selfishness as well as folly. It was inexpressibly fatiguing and irksome to me to keep up a show of good fellowship and joviality with these people, though I had not sufficient energy to make the attempt to quit them. When these *dashers* and *loungers* found that I was not always at their disposal, they discovered that Glenthorn had always something *odd* about him; that Glenthorn had always a melancholy turn; that it ran in the family, &c. Satisfied with these phrases, they let me take my own way, and forgot my existence. Public amusements had lost their charm; I had sufficient steadiness to resist the temptation to game: but, for want of stimulus, I could hardly endure the *tedium* of my days. At this period of my life, ennui was very near turning into misanthropy. I balanced between becoming a misanthrope and a democrat.

Whilst I was in this critical state of ineptitude, my attention was accidentally roused by the sight of a boxing-match. My feelings were so much excited, and the excitation was so delightful, that I was now in danger of becoming an amateur of the pugilistic art. It did not occur to me, that it was beneath the dignity of a British nobleman to learn the vulgar terms of the boxing trade. I soon began to talk very *knowingly* of *first-rate bruisers*, *game* men, and *pleasing* fighters; *making play—beating a man under the ropes— sparring—rallying—sawing—*and *chopping*. What farther proficiency I might have made in this language, or how long my interest in these feats of prize-fighters might have continued, had I been left to myself, I cannot determine; but I was unexpectedly seized with a fit of national shame, on hearing a foreigner of rank and reputation express astonishment at our taste for these savage spectacles. It was in vain that I repeated the arguments of some of the parliamentary panegyrists of boxing and bull-baiting; and asserted, that these diversions render a people hardy and courageous. My opponent replied, that he did not perceive the necessary connexion between cruelty and courage; that he did not comprehend how the standing by in safety to see two men bruise each other almost to death could evince or inspire heroic sentiments or warlike dispositions. He observed, that the Romans were most eager for the fights of gladiators during the reigns of the most effeminate and cruel emperors, and in the decline of all public spirit and virtue. These arguments would have probably made but a feeble impression on an understanding like mine, unaccustomed to general reasoning, and on a temper habituated to pursue, without thought of consequences, my immediate individual gratification; but it happened that my feelings were touched at this time by the dreadful sufferings of one of the pugilistic combatants. He died a few hours after the battle. He was an Irishman:

most of the spectators being English, and triumphing in the victory of their countryman, the poor fellow's fate was scarcely noticed. I spoke to him a little while before he died, and found that he came from my own county. His name was Michael Noonan. He made it his dying request, that I would carry half-a-guinea, the only money he possessed, to his aged father, and a silk handkerchief he had worn round his neck, to his sister. Pity for this unfortunate Irishman recalled Ireland to my thoughts. Many small reasons concurred to make me now desirous of going to that country. I should get rid at once of a tormenting establishment, and of servants, without the odium of turning them away; for most of them declined going into banishment, as they called it. Besides this, I should leave my companions, with whom I was disgusted. I was tired of England, and wanted to see something new, even if it were to be worse than what I had seen before. These were not my ostensible reasons: I professed to have more exalted motives for my journey. It was my duty, I said, to visit my Irish estate, and to encourage my tenantry, by residing some time among them. Duties often spring up to our view at a convenient opportunity. Then my promise to poor Ellinor; it was impossible for a man of honour to break a promise, even to an old woman: in short, when people are determined upon any action, they seldom fail to find arguments capable of convincing them that their resolution is reasonable. Mixed motives govern the conduct of half mankind; so I set out upon my journey to Ireland.

CHAPTER VI

"Es tu contente à la fleur de tes ans?
As tu des goûts et des amusemens?
Tu dois mener une assez douce vie.
L'autre en deux mots répondait 'Je m'ennuie.'
C'est un grand mal, dit la fée, et je crois
Qu'un beau secret est de rester chez soi." —

I was detained six days by contrary winds at Holyhead. Sick of that miserable place, in my ill-humour I cursed Ireland, and twice resolved to return to London: but the wind changed, my carriage was on board the packet; so I sailed and landly safely in Dublin. I was surprised by the excellence of the hotel at which I was lodged. I had not conceived that such accommodation could have been found in Dublin. The house had, as I was told, belonged to a nobleman: it was fitted up and appointed with a degree of elegance, and even magnificence, beyond what I had been used to in the most fashionable hotels in London.

"Ah! sir," said an Irish gentleman, who found me in admiration upon the staircase, "this is all very good, very fine, but it is too good and too fine to last; come here again in two years, and I am afraid you will see all this going to rack and ruin. This is too often the case with us in Ireland: we can project, but we can't calculate; we must have every thing upon too large a scale. We mistake a grand beginning for a good beginning. We begin like princes, and we end like beggars."

I rested only a few days in a capital in which, I took it for granted, there could be nothing worth seeing by a person who was just come from London. In driving through the streets, I was, however, surprised to see buildings, which my prejudices could scarcely believe to be Irish. I also saw some things, which recalled to my mind the observations I had heard at my hotel. I was struck with instances of grand beginnings and lamentable want of finish, with mixture of the magnificent and the paltry; of admirable and execrable taste. Though my understanding was wholly uncultivated, these things struck my eye. Of all the faculties of my mind, my taste had been most exercised, because its exercise had given me least trouble.

Impatient to see my own castle, I left Dublin. I was again astonished by the beauty of the prospects, and the excellence of the roads. I had in my ignorance believed that I was never to see a tree in Ireland, and that the roads were almost impassable. With the promptitude of credulity, I now went from one extreme to the other: I concluded that we should travel with the same celerity as upon the Bath road; and I expected, that a journey for which four days had been allotted might be performed in two. Like all those who have nothing to do any where, I was always in a prodigious hurry to get from place to place; and I ever had a noble ambition to go over as much ground as possible in a given space of time. I travelled in a light barouche, and with my own horses. My own man (an Englishman), and my cook (a Frenchman), followed in a hackney chaise; I cared not how, so that they kept up with me; the rest was their affair. At night, my gentleman complained bitterly of the Irish post carriages, and besought me to let him follow at an easier rate the next day; but to this I could by no means consent: for how could I exist without my own man and my French cook? In the morning, just as I was ready to set off, and had thrown myself back in my carriage, my Englishman and Frenchman came to the door, both in so great a rage, that the one was inarticulate and the other unintelligible. At length the object of their indignation spoke for itself. From the inn yard came a hackney chaise, in a most deplorable crazy state; the body mounted up to a prodigious height, on unbending springs, nodding forwards, one door swinging open, three blinds up, because they could not be let down, the perch tied in two places, the iron of the wheels half off, half loose, wooden pegs for linch-pins, and ropes for harness. The horses were worthy of the harness; wretched little dog-tired creatures, that looked as if they had been driven to the last gasp, and as if they had never been rubbed down in their lives; their bones starting through their skin; one lame, the other blind; one with a raw back, the other with a galled breast; one with his neck poking down over his collar, and the other with his head dragged forward by a bit of a broken bridle, held at arm's length by a man dressed like a mad beggar, in half a hat and half a wig, both awry in opposite directions; a long tattered great-coat, tied round his waist by a hay-rope; the jagged rents in the skirts of his coat showing his bare legs marbled of many colours; while something like stockings hung loose about his ankles. The noises he made by way of threatening or encouraging his steeds, I pretend not to describe.

In an indignant voice I called to the landlord, "I hope these are not the horses—I hope this is not the chaise, intended for my servants."

The innkeeper, and the pauper who was preparing to officiate as postilion, both in the same instant exclaimed, "*Sorrow* better chaise in the county!"

"*Sorrow*" said I; "what do you mean by sorrow?"

"That there's no better, plase your honour, can be seen. We have two more, to be sure; but one has no top, and the other no bottom. Any way there's no better can be seen than this same." 77

"And these horses!" cried I; "why, this horse is so lame he can hardly stand."

"Oh, plase your honour, tho' he can't stand, he'll *go* fast enough. He has a great deal of the rogue in him, plase your honour. He's always that way at first setting out."

"And that wretched animal with the galled breast!"

"He's all the better for it, when once he warms; it's he that will go with the speed of light, plase your honour. Sure, is not he Knockecroghery? and didn't I give fifteen guineas for him, barring the luck penny, at the fair of Knockecroghery, and he rising four year old at the same time?"

I could not avoid smiling at this speech: but my *gentleman*, maintaining his angry gravity, declared, in a sullen tone, that he would be cursed if he went with such horses; and the Frenchman, with abundance of gesticulation, made a prodigious chattering, which no mortal understood.

"Then I'll tell you what you'll do," said Paddy; "you'll take four, as becomes gentlemen of your quality, and you'll see how we'll powder along."

And straight he put the knuckle of his fore-finger in his mouth, and whistled shrill and strong; and, in a moment, a whistle somewhere out in the fields answered him.

I protested against these proceedings, but in vain; before the first pair of horses were fastened to the chaise, up came a little boy with the others *fresh* from the plough. They were quick enough in putting these to; yet how they managed it with their tackle, I know not. "Now we're fixed handsomely," said Paddy.

"But this chaise will break down the first mile."

"Is it this chaise, plase your honour? I'll engage it will go the world's end. The universe wouldn't break it down now; sure it was mended but last night."

Then seizing his whip and reins in one hand, he clawed up his stockings with the other: so with one easy step he got into his place, and seated himself, coachman-like, upon a well-worn bar of wood, that served as a coach-box. "Throw me the loan of a trusty Bartly, for a cushion," said he. A frieze coat was thrown up over the horses' heads—Paddy caught it. "Where are you,

Hosey?" cried he. "Sure I'm only rowling a wisp of straw on my leg," replied Hosey. "Throw me up," added this paragon of postilions, turning to one of the crowd of idle bystanders. "Arrah, push me up, can't ye?"

A man took hold of his knee, and threw him upon the horse: he was in his seat in a trice; then clinging by the mane of his horse, he scrambled for the bridle, which was under the other horse's feet—reached it, and, well satisfied with himself, looked round at Paddy, who looked back to the chaise-door at my angry servants, "secure in the last event of things." In vain the Englishman in monotonous anger, and the Frenchman in every note of the gamut, abused Paddy: necessity and wit were on Paddy's side; he parried all that was said against his chaise, his horses, himself, and his country, with invincible comic dexterity, till at last, both his adversaries, dumb-foundered, clambered into the vehicle, where they were instantly shut up in straw and darkness. Paddy, in a triumphant tone, called to *my* postilions, bidding them "get on, and not be stopping the way any longer."

Without uttering a syllable, they drove on; but they could not, nor could I, refrain from looking back to see how those fellows would manage. We saw the fore-horses make towards the right, then to the left, and every way but straight forwards; whilst Paddy bawled to Hosey—"Keep the middle of the road, can't ye? I don't want ye to draw a pound at-all-at-all."

At last, by dint of whipping, the four horses were compelled to set off in a lame gallop; but they stopped short at a hill near the end of the town, whilst a shouting troop of ragged boys followed, and pushed them fairly to the top. Half an hour afterwards, as we were putting on our drag-chain to go down another steep hill,—to my utter astonishment, Paddy, with his horses in full gallop, came rattling and *chehupping* past us. My people called to warn him that he had no *drag*: but still he cried "Never fear!" and shaking the long reins, and stamping with his foot, on he went thundering down the hill. My Englishmen were aghast.

"The turn yonder below, at the bottom of the hill, is as sharp and ugly as ever I see," said my postilion, after a moment's stupified silence. "He will break their necks, as sure as my name is John."

Quite the contrary: when we had dragged and undragged, and came up to Paddy, we found him safe on his legs, mending some of his tackle very quietly.

"If that had broken as you were going down the steep hill," said I, "it would have been all over with you, Paddy."

"That's true, plase your honour: but it never happened me going down hill—nor never will, by the blessing of God, if I've any luck."

With this mixed confidence in a special providence, and in his own good luck, Paddy went on, much to my amusement. It was his glory to keep before us; and he rattled on till he came to a narrow part of the road, where they were rebuilding a bridge. Here there was a dead stop. Paddy lashed his horses, and called them all manner of names; but the wheel horse, Knockecroghery, was restive, and at last began to kick most furiously. It seemed inevitable that the first kick which should reach the splinter-bar, at which it was aimed, must demolish it instantly. My English gentleman and my Frenchman both put their heads out of the only window which was pervious, and called most manfully to be let out. "Never fear," said Paddy. To open the door for themselves was beyond their force or skill. One of the hind wheels, which had belonged to another carriage, was too high to suffer the door to be opened, and the blind at the other side prevented their attempts, so they were close prisoners. The men who had been at work on the broken bridge came forward, and rested on their spades to see the battle. As my carriage could not pass, I was also compelled to be a spectator of this contest between man and horse.

"Never fear," reiterated Paddy; "I'll engage I'll be up wid him. Now for it, Knockecroghery! Oh, the rogue, he thinks he has me at a *nonplush*, but I'll show him the *differ*."

After this brag of war, Paddy whipped, Knockecroghery kicked; and Paddy, seemingly unconscious of danger, sat within reach of the kicking horse, twitching up first one of his legs, then the other, and shifting as the animal aimed his hoofs, escaping every time as it were by miracle. With a mixture of temerity and presence of mind, which made us alternately look upon him as a madman and a hero, he gloried in the danger, secure of success, and of the sympathy of the spectators.

"Ah! didn't I *compass* him cleverly then? Oh, the villain, to be browbating me! I'm too cute for him yet. See there, now, he's come to; and I'll be his bail he'll go *asy* enough wid me. Ogh! he has a fine spirit of his own, but it's I that can match him: 'twould be a poor case if a man like me cou'dn't match a horse any way, let alone a mare, which this is, or it never would be so vicious."

After this hard-fought battle, and suitable rejoicing for the victory, Paddy walked his subdued adversary on a few yards to allow us to pass him; but, to the dismay of my postilions, a hay-rope was at this instant thrown across the road, before our horses, by the road-makers, who, to explain this proceeding, cried out, "Plase your honour, the road is so dry, we'd expect a trifle to wet it."

"What do these fellows mean?" said I.

"It's only a tester or a hog they want, your honour, to give 'em to drink your honour's health," said Paddy.

"A hog to drink my health?"

"Ay, that is a thirteen, plase your honour; all as one as an English shilling."

I threw them a shilling: the hay-rope was withdrawn, and at last we went on. We heard no more of Paddy till evening. He came in two hours after us, and expected to be doubly paid *for driving my honour's gentlemen so well.*

I must say that on this journey, though I met with many delays and disasters; though one of my horses was lamed in shoeing by a smith, who came home drunk from a funeral; and though the back pannel of my carriage was broken by the pole of a chaise; and though one day I went without my dinner at a large desolate inn, where nothing was to be had but whiskey; and though one night I lay in a little smoky den, in which the meanest of my servants in England would have thought it impossible to sleep; and though I complained bitterly, and swore it was impracticable for a gentleman to travel in Ireland; yet I never remember to have experienced, on any journey, less ennui.78 I was out of patience twenty times a day, but I certainly felt no ennui; and I am convinced that the benefit some patients receive from a journey is in an inverse proportion to the ease and luxury of their mode of travelling. When they are compelled to exert their faculties, and to use their limbs, they forget their nerves, as I did. Upon this principle I should recommend to wealthy hypochondriacs a journey in Ireland, preferably to any country in the civilized world. I can promise them, that they will not only be moved to anger often enough to make their blood circulate briskly, but they will even, in the acme of their impatience, be thrown into salutary convulsions of laughter, by the comic concomitants of their disasters: besides, if they have hearts, their best feelings cannot fail to be awakened by the warm, generous hospitality they will receive in this country, from the cabin to the castle.

Late in the evening of the fourth day, we came to an inn on the verge of the county where my estate was situate. It was one of the wildest parts of Ireland. We could find no horses, nor accommodations of any sort, and we had several miles farther to go. For our only comfort, the dirty landlady, who had married the hostler, and wore gold drop ear-rings, reminded us, that, "Sure, if we could but wait an hour, and take a fresh egg, we should have a fine moon."

After many fruitless imprecations, my French cook was obliged to mount one of my saddle-horses; my groom was left to follow us the next day; I let my gentleman sit on the barouche box, and proceeded with my own tired horses. The moon, which my landlady had promised me, rose, and I had a full view of the face of the country. As we approached my maritime territories, the cottages were thinly scattered, and the trees had a stunted appearance; they all slanted one way, from the prevalent winds that blew from the ocean. Our road presently stretched along the beach, and I saw nothing to vary the prospect but rocks, and their huge shadows upon the water. The road being sandy, the feet of the horses made no noise, and nothing interrupted the silence of the night but the hissing sound of the carriage-wheels passing through the sand.

"What o'clock is it now, think you, John?" said one of my postilions to the other.

"Past twelve, for *sartain*," said John; "and this *bees* a strange Irish place," continued he, in a drawling voice; "with no possible way o' getting at it, as I see." John, after a pause, resumed, "I say, Timothy, to the best of my opinion, this here road is leading *on* us into the sea." John replied, "that he did suppose there might be such a thing as a boat farther on, but where, he could not say for *sartain*." Dismayed and helpless, they at last stopped to consult whether they had come the right road to the house. In the midst of their consultation there came up an Irish carman, whistling as he walked beside his horse and car.

"Honest friend, is this the road to Glenthorn Castle?"

"To Glenthorn, sure enough, your honour."

"Whereabouts is the castle?"

"Forenent you, if you go on to the turn."

"*Forenent* you!" As the postilions pondered upon this word, the carman, leaving his horse, and car, turned back to explain by action what he could not make intelligible by words.

"See, isn't here the castle?" cried he, darting before us to the turn of the road, where he stood pointing at what we could not possibly see, as it was hid by a promontory of rock. When we f reached the spot where he was stationed, we came full upon the view of Glenthorn Castle: it seemed to rise from the sea, abrupt and insulated, in all the gloomy grandeur of ancient times, with turrets and battlements, and a huge gateway, the pointed arch of which receded in perspective between the projecting towers.

"It's my lord himself, I'm fond to believe!" said our guide, taking off his hat; "I had best step on and tell 'em at the castle."

"No, my good friend, there is no occasion to trouble you farther; you had better go back to your horse and car, which you have left on the road."

"Oh! they are used to that, plase your honour; they'll go on very *quite*, and I'll run like a redshank with the news to the castle."

He ran on before us with surprising velocity, whilst our tired horses dragged us slowly through the sand. As we approached, the gateway of the castle opened, and a number of men, who appeared to be dwarfs when compared with the height of the building, came out with torches in their hands. By their bustle, and the vehemence with which they bawled to one another, one might have thought that the whole castle was in flames; but they were only letting down a drawbridge. As I was going over this bridge, a casement window opened in the castle; and a voice, which I knew to be old Ellinor's, exclaimed, "Mind the big hole in the middle of the bridge, God bless *yees!*"

I passed over the broken bridge, and through the massive gate, under an arched way, at the farthest end of which a lamp had just been lighted: then I came into a large open area, the court of the castle. The hollow sound of the horses' feet, and of the carriage rumbling over the drawbridge, was immediately succeeded by the strange and eager voices of the people, who filled the court with a variety of noises, contrasting, in the most striking manner, with the silence in which we had travelled over the sands. The great effect that my arrival instantaneously produced upon the multitude of servants and dependants, who issued from the castle, gave me an idea of my own consequence beyond any thing which I had ever felt in England. These people seemed "born for my use:" the officious precipitation with which they ran to and fro; the style in which they addressed me; some crying, "Long life to the Earl of Glenthorn!" some blessing me for coming to reign over them; all together gave more the idea of vassals than of tenants, and carried my imagination centuries back to feudal times.

The first person I saw on entering the hall of my castle was poor Ellinor: she pushed her way up to me—

"'Tis himself!" cried she. Then turning about suddenly, "I've seen him in his own castle—I've seen him; and if it pleases God this minute to take me to himself, I would die with pleasure."

"My good Ellinor," said I, touched to the heart by her affection, "my good Ellinor, I hope you will live many a happy year; and if I can contribute—"

"And himself to speak to me so kind before them all!" interrupted she. "Oh! this is too much—quite too much!" She burst into tears; and, hiding her face with her arm, made her way out of the hall.

The flights of stairs which I had to ascend, and the length of galleries through which I was conducted, before I reached the apartment where supper was served, gave me a vast idea of the extent of my castle; but I was too much fatigued to enjoy fully the gratifications of pride. To the simple pleasures of appetite I was more sensible: I ate heartily of one of the most profusely hospitable suppers that ever was prepared for a noble baron, even in the days when oxen were roasted whole. Then I grew so sleepy, that I was impatient to be shown to my bed. I was ushered through another suite of chambers and galleries; and, as I was traversing one of these, a door of some strange dormitory opened, and a group of female heads were thrust out, in the midst of which I could distinguish old Ellinor's face; but, as I turned my head, the door closed so quickly, that I had no time to speak: I only heard the words, "Blessings on him! that's he!"

I was so sleepy, that I rejoiced having escaped an occasion where I might have been called upon to speak, yet I was really grateful to my poor nurse for her blessing. The state tower, in which, after reiterated entreaties, I was at last left alone to repose, was hung with magnificent, but ancient tapestry. It was so like a room in a haunted castle, that if I had not been too much fatigued to think of any thing, I should certainly have thought of Mrs. Radcliffe. I am sorry to say that I have no mysteries, or even portentous omens, to record of this night; for the moment that I lay down in my antiquated bed, I fell into a profound sleep.

CHAPTER VII

When I awoke, I thought that I was on shipboard; for the first sound I heard was that of the sea booming against the castle walls. I arose, looked out of the window of my bedchamber, and saw that the whole prospect bore an air of savage wildness. As I contemplated the scene, my imagination was seized with the idea of remoteness from civilized society: the melancholy feeling of solitary grandeur took possession of my soul.

From this feeling I was relieved by the affectionate countenance of my old nurse, who at this instant put her head half in at the door.

"I only just made bold to look in at the fire, to see did it burn, because I lighted it myself, and would not be blowing of it for fear of wakening you."

"Come in, Ellinor, come in," said I. "Come quite in."

"I will, since you've nobody with you that I need be afraid of," said she, looking round satisfied, when she saw my own man was not in the room.

"You need never be afraid of any body, Ellinor, whilst I am alive," said I; "for I will always protect you. I do not forget your conduct, when you thought I was dead in the banqueting-room."

"Oh! don't be talking of that; thanks be to God there was nothing in it! I see you well now. Long life to you! Sure you must have been tired to death last night, for this morning early you lay so *quite*, sleeping like an angel; and I could see a great likeness in *yees* to what you were when you were a child in my arms."

"But sit down, sit down, my good Ellinor," said I, "and let us talk a little of your own affairs."

"And are not these my own affairs?" said she, rather angrily.

"Certainly; but I mean, that you must tell me how you are going on in the world, and what I can do to make you comfortable and happy."

"There's one thing would make me happy," said she.

"Name it," said I.

"To be let light your fire myself every morning, and open your shutters, dear."

I could not help smiling at the simplicity of the request. I was going to press her to ask something of more consequence, but she heard a servant coming along the gallery, and, starting from her chair, she ran and threw herself upon her knees before the fire, blowing it with her mouth with great vehemence.

The servant came to let me know that Mr. M'Leod, my agent, was waiting for me in the breakfast-room.

"And will I be let light your fire then every morning?" said Ellinor eagerly, turning as she knelt.

"And welcome," said I.

"Then you won't forget to speak about it for me," said she, "else may be I won't be let up by them English. God bless you, and don't forget to speak for me."

"I will remember to speak about it," said I; but I went down stairs and forgot it.

Mr. M'Leod, whom I found reading the newspaper in the breakfast-room, seemed less affected by my presence than any body I had seen since my arrival. He was a hard-featured, strong-built, perpendicular man, with a remarkable quietness of deportment: he spoke with deliberate distinctness, in an accent slightly Scotch; and, in speaking, he made use of no gesticulation, but held himself surprisingly still. No part of him but his eyes moved, and they had an expression of slow, but determined good sense. He was sparing of his words; but the few that he used said much, and went directly to the point. He pressed for the immediate examination and settlement of his accounts: he enumerated several things of importance, which he had done for my service: but he did this without pretending the slightest attachment to me; he mentioned them only as proofs of his having done his duty to his employer, for which he neither expected nor would accept of thanks. He seemed to be cold and upright in his mind as in his body. I was not influenced in his favour even by his striking appearance of plain-dealing, so strong was the general abhorrence of agents which Crawley's treachery had left in my mind. The excess of credulity, when convinced of its error, becomes the extreme of suspicion. Persons not accustomed to reason often argue absurdly, because, from particular instances, they deduce general conclusions, and extend the result of their limited experience of individuals indiscriminately to whole classes. The labour of thinking was so great to me, that, having once come to a conclusion upon any subject, I would rather persist in it, right or wrong, than be at the trouble of going over the process again to revise and rectify my judgment.

Upon this occasion national prejudice heightened the prepossession which circumstances had raised. Mr. M'Leod was not only an agent, but a Scotchman; and I had a notion that all Scotchmen were crafty: therefore I concluded that his blunt manner was assumed, and his plain-dealing but a more refined species of policy.

After breakfast he laid before me a general statement of my affairs; obliged me to name a day for the examination of his accounts; and then, without expressing either mortification or displeasure at the coldness of my behaviour, or at my evident impatience of his presence, he, unmoved of spirit, rang for his horse, wished me a good morning, and departed.

By this time my castle-yard was filled with a crowd of "great-coated suitors," who were all *come to see—could they see my lordship? or waiting just to say two words to my honour.* In various lounging attitudes, leaning against the walls, or pacing backwards and forwards before the window, to catch my eye, they, with a patience passing the patience of courtiers, waited, hour after hour, the live-long day, for their turn, or their chance, of an audience. I had promised myself the pleasure of viewing my castle this day, and of taking a ride through my grounds; but that was totally out of the question. I was no longer a man with a will of my own, or with time at my own disposal.

"Long may you live to reign over us!" was the signal that I was now to live, like a prince, only for the service of my subjects. How these subjects of mine had contrived to go on for so many years in my absence, I was at a loss to conceive; for, the moment I was present, it seemed evident that they could not exist without me.

One had a wife and six *childer,* and not a spot in the wide world to live in, if my honour did not let him live under me, in any bit of a skirt of the estate that would feed a cow.

Another had a brother in jail, who could not be *got out without me.*

Another had three lives dropped in a *lase* for ever; another wanted a renewal; another a farm; another a house; and one *expected* my lard would make his son an exciseman; and another that I would make him a policeman; and another was *racked,* if I did not settle the *mearing* between him and Corny Corkran; and half a hundred had given in *proposals* to the agent for lands that would be out next May; and half a hundred more came with legends of traditionary *promises from the old lord, my lordship's father that was*: and for hours I was forced to listen to long stories *out of the face,* in which there was such a perplexing and provoking mixture of truth and fiction, involved in language so figurative, and tones so new to my English ears, that, with my utmost patience and strained attention, I could comprehend but a very small portion of what was said to me.

Never were my ears so weary any day of my life as they were this day. I could not have endured the fatigue, if I had not been supported by the agreeable idea of my own power and consequence; a power seemingly next to despotic. This new stimulus sustained me for three days that I was kept a state-prisoner in my own castle, by the crowds who came to do me homage, and to claim my favour and protection. In vain every morning was my horse led about saddled and bridled: I never was permitted to mount. On the fourth morning, when I felt sure of having despatched all my tormentors, I was in astonishment and despair on seeing my levee crowded with a fresh succession of petitioners. I gave orders to my people to say that I was going out, and absolutely could see nobody. I supposed that they did not understand what my English servants said, for they never stirred from their posts. On receiving a second message, they acknowledged that they understood the first; but replied, that they could wait there till my honour came back from my ride. With difficulty I mounted my horse, and escaped from the closing ranks of my persecutors. At night I gave directions to have the gates kept shut, and ordered the porter not to admit any body at his peril. When I got up, I was delighted to see the coast clear; but the moment I went out, lo! at the outside of the gate, the host of besiegers were posted, and in my lawn, and along the road, and through the fields: they pursued me; and when I forbade them to speak to me when I was on horseback, the next day I found parties in ambuscade, who laid wait for me in silence, with their hats off, bowing and bowing, till I could not refrain from saying, "Well, my good friend, what do you stand bowing there for?" Then I was fairly prisoner, and held by the bridle for an hour.

In short, I found that I was now placed in a situation where I could hope neither for privacy nor leisure; but I had the joys of power, my rising passion for which would certainly have been extinguished in a short time by my habitual indolence, if it had not been kept alive by jealousy of Mr. M'Leod.

One day, when I refused to hear an importunate tenant, and declared that I had been persecuted with petitioners ever since my arrival, and that I was absolutely tired to death, the man answered, "True *for ye*, my lard; and it's a shame to be troubling you this way. Then, may be, it's to Mr. M'Leod I'll go? Sure the agent will do as well, and no more about it. Mr. M'Leod will do every thing the same way as usual."

"Mr. M'Leod will do every thing!" said I, hastily: "no, by no means."

"Who will we speak to, then?" said the man.

"To myself," said I, with as haughty a tone as Louis XIV. could have assumed, when he announced to his court his resolution to be his own minister. After this intrepid declaration to act for myself, I could not yield to my habitual laziness. So much had my pride been hurt, as well as my other feelings, by Captain Crawley's conduct, that I determined to show the world I was not to be duped a second time by an agent.

When, on the day appointed, Mr. M'Leod came to settle accounts with me, I, with an air of self-important capability, as if I had been all my life used to look into my own affairs, sat down to inspect the papers; and, incredible as it may appear, I went through the whole at a sitting, without a single yawn; and, for a man who never before had looked into an account, I understood the nature of debtor and creditor wonderfully well: but, with my utmost desire to evince my arithmetical sagacity, I could not detect the slightest error in the accounts; and it was evident that Mr. M'Leod was not Captain Crawley; yet, rather than believe that he could be both an agent and an honest man, I concluded, that if he did not cheat me out of my money, his aim was to cheat me out of power; and, fancying that he wished to be a man of influence and consequence in the county, I transferred to him instantly the feelings that were passing in my own mind, and took it for granted that he must be actuated by a love of power in every thing that he did apparently for my service.

About this time I remember being much disturbed in my mind, by a letter which Mr. M'Leod received in my presence, and of which he read to me only a part: I never rested till I saw the whole. The epistle proved well worth the trouble of deciphering: it related merely to the paving of my chicken-yard. Like the King of Prussia,79 who was said to be so jealous of power, that he wanted to regulate all the mousetraps in his dominions, I soon engrossed the management of a perplexing multiplicity of minute insignificant details. Alas! I discovered to my cost, that trouble is the inseparable attendant upon power: and many times, in the course of the first ten days of my reign, I was ready to give up my dignity from excessive fatigue.

CHAPTER VIII

Early one morning, after having passed a feverish night, tortured in my dreams by the voices and faces of the people who had surrounded me the preceding day, I was awakened by the noise of somebody lighting my fire. I thought it was Ellinor; and the idea of the disinterested affection of this poor woman came full into my mind, contrasted in the strongest manner with the recollection of the selfish encroaching people by whom, of late, I had been worried.

"How do you do, my good Ellinor?" said I; "I have not seen any thing of you this week past."

"It's not Ellinor at all, my lard," said a new voice.

"And why so? Why does not Ellinor light my fire?"

"Myself does not know, my lard."

"Go for her directly."

"She's gone home these three days, my lard."

"Gone! is she sick?"

"Not as I know *on*, my lard. Myself does not know what ailed her, except she would be jealous of my lighting the fire. But I can't say what ailed her; for she went away without a word good or bad, when she seen me lighting this fire, which I did by the housekeeper's orders."

I now recollected poor Ellinor's request, and reproached myself for having neglected to fulfil my promise, upon an affair which, however trifling in itself, appeared of consequence to her. In the course of my morning's ride I determined to call upon her at her own house, and make my apologies: but first I satisfied my curiosity about a prodigious number of *parks* and *towns* which I had heard of upon my estate. Many a ragged man had come to me, with the modest request that I would let him *one of the parks near the town*. The horse-park, the deer-park, the cow-park, were not quite sufficient to answer the ideas I had attached to the word *park*: but I was quite astonished and mortified when I beheld the bits and corners of land near the town of Glenthorn, on which these high-sounding titles had been bestowed:—just what would feed a cow is sufficient in Ireland to constitute a park.

When I heard the names of above a hundred towns on the Glenthorn estate, I had an exalted idea of my own territories; and I was impatient to make a progress through my dominions: but, upon visiting a few of these places, my curiosity was satisfied. Two or three cabins gathered together were sufficient to constitute a town, and the land adjoining thereto is called a town-land. The denominations of these town-lands having continued from generation to generation, according to ancient surveys of Ireland, it is sufficient to show the boundaries of a town-land, to prove that there must be a town; and a tradition of a town continues to be satisfactory, even when only a single cabin remains. I turned my horse's head away in disgust from one of these traditionary towns, and desired a boy to show me the way to Ellinor O'Donoghoe's house.

"So I will, plase your honour, my lard; sure I've a right to know, for she's my own granny."

The boy, or, as he was called, the *gossoon*, ran across some fields where there was abundance of fern and of rabbits. The rabbits, sitting quietly at the entrance of their holes, seemed to consider themselves as proprietors of the soil, and me and my horse as intruders. The boy apologized for the number of rabbit-holes on this part of the estate: "It would not be so, my lard, if I had a gun allowed me by the gamekeeper, which he would give me if he knew it would be plasing to your honour." The ingenuity with which even the young boys can introduce their requests in a favourable moment sometimes provoked me, and sometimes excited my admiration. This boy made his just at the time he was rolling out of my way a car that stopped a gap in the hedge; and he was so hot and out of breath with running in my service, that I could not refuse him *a token to the gamekeeper that he might get a gun* as soon as I understood what it meant.

We came to Ellinor's house, a wretched-looking, low, and mud-walled cabin; at one end it was propped by a buttress of loose stones, upon which stood a goat reared on his hind legs, to browse on the grass that grew on the house-top. A dung-hill was before the only window, at the other end of the house, and close to the door was a puddle of the dirtiest of dirty water, in which ducks were dabbling. At my approach there came out of the cabin a pig, a calf, a lamb, a kid, and two geese, all with their legs tied; followed by turkeys, cocks, hens, chickens, a dog, a cat, a kitten, a beggar-man, a beggar-woman with a pipe in her mouth, children innumerable, and a stout girl with a pitchfork in her hand; all together more than I, looking down upon the roof as I sat on horseback, and measuring the superficies with my eye, could have possibly supposed the mansion capable of containing. I asked if Ellinor O'Donoghoe was at home; but the dog barked, the geese cackled, the turkeys gobbled, and the beggars begged, with one accord, so loudly, that there was no chance of my being heard. When the *girl* had at last succeeded in appeasing them all with her pitchfork, she answered, that Ellinor O'Donoghoe was at home, but that she was out with the potatoes; and she ran to fetch her, after calling to *the lays, who was within in the room smoking,* to come out to his honour. As soon as they had crouched under the door, and were able to stand upright, they welcomed me with a very good grace, and were proud to see me in *the kingdom.* I asked if they were all Ellinor's sons?

"All entirely," was the first answer.

"Not one but one," was the second answer. The third made the other two intelligible.

"Plase your honour, we are all her sons-in-law, except myself, who am her lawful son."

"Then you are my foster-brother?"

"No, plase your honour, it's not me, but my brother, and he's not in it."

"*Not in it?*"

"No, plase your honour; becaase he's in the forge, up *abow.*"

"Abow!" said I; "what does he mean?"

"Sure he's the blacksmith, my lard."

"And what are you?"

"I'm Ody, plase your honour; the short for Owen."

"And what is your trade?"

"Trade, plase your honour! I was bred to none, more than another; but expects, only that my mother's not willing to part with me, to go into the militia next month; and I'm sure she'd let me, if your honour's lordship would spake a word to the colonel, to see to get me made a serjeant *immadiately.*"

As Ody made his request, all his companions came forward in sign of sympathy, and closed round my horse's head to make me *sinsible* of their expectations; but at this instant Ellinor came up, her old face colouring all over with joy when she saw me.

"So, Ellinor," said I, "you were affronted, I hear, and left the castle in anger?"

"In anger! And if I did, more shame for me—but anger does not last long with me any way; and against you, my lord, dear, how could it? Oh, think how good he is, coming to see me in such a poor place!"

"I will make it a better place for you, Ellinor," said I. Far from being eager to obtain promises, she still replied, that "all was good enough for her." I desired that she would come and live with me at the castle, till a better house than her present habitation could be built for her; but she seemed to prefer this hovel. I assured her that she should be permitted to light my fire.

"Oh, it's better for me not," said she; "better keep out of the way. I could not be asy if I got any one ill-will."

I assured her that she should be at liberty to do just as she liked: and whilst I rode home I was planning a pretty cottage for her near the porter's lodge. I was pleased with myself for my gratitude to this poor woman. Before I slept, I actually wrote a letter, which obtained for Ody the honour of being made a serjeant in the — — militia; and Ellinor, dazzled by this military glory, was satisfied that he should leave home, though he was her favourite.

"Well, let him leave me then," said she; "I won't stand in his light. I never thought of my living to see Ody a serjeant. Now, Ody, have done being wild, honey-dear, and be a credit to your family, and to his honour's commendation—God bless him for ever for it! From the very first I knew it was he that had the kind heart."

I am not sure that it was a very good action to get a man made a serjeant, of whom I knew nothing but that he was son to my nurse. Self-complacency, however, cherished my first indistinct feelings of benevolence. Though not much accustomed to reflect upon my own sensations, I think I remember, at this period, suspecting that the feeling of benevolence is a greater pleasure than the possession of *barouches*, and horses, and castles, and parks— greater even than the possession of power. Of this last truth, however, I had not as yet a perfectly clear conception. Even in my benevolence I was as impatient and unreasonable as a child. Money, I thought, had the power of Aladdin's lamp, to procure with magical celerity the gratification of my wishes. I expected that a cottage for Ellinor should rise out of the earth at my command. But the slaves of Aladdin's lamp were not Irishmen. The delays, and difficulties, and blunders, in the execution of my orders, provoked me beyond measure; and it would have been difficult for a cool spectator to decide whether I or my workmen were most in fault; they for their dilatory habits, or I for my impatient temper.

"Well, *plase* your honour, when the *pratees* are set, and the turf cut, we'll *fall-to* at Ellinor's house."

"Confound the potatoes and the turf! you must *fall-to*, as you call it, directly."

"Is it without the lime, and plase your honour? Sure that same is not drawn yet, nor the stones quarried, since it is of stone it will be—nor the foundations itself dug, and the horses were all putting out dung."

Then after the bog and the potatoes, came funerals and holidays innumerable. The masons were idle one week waiting for the mortar, and the mortar another week waiting for the stones, and then they were at a stand for the carpenter when they came to the door-case, and the carpenter was looking for the sawyer, and the sawyer was gone to have the saw mended. Then there was a *stop* again at the window-sills for the stone-cutter, and he was at the quarter-sessions, processing his brother for *tin and tinpence, hay-money*. And when, in spite of all delays and obstacles, the walls reached their destined height, the roof was a new plague; the carpenter, the slater, and the nailer, were all at variance, and I cannot tell which was the most provoking rogue of the three. At last, however, the house was roofed and slated: then I would not wait till the walls were dry before I plastered, and papered, and furnished it. I fitted it up in the most elegant style of English cottages; for I was determined that Ellinor's habitation should be such as had never been seen in this part of the world. The day when it was finished, and when I gave possession of it to Ellinor, paid me for all my trouble; I tasted a species of pleasure that was new to me, and which was the sweeter from having been earned with some difficulty. And now, when I saw a vast number of my tenants assembled at a rural feast which I gave on Ellinor's *installation*, my benevolence enlarged, even beyond the possibility of its gratification, and I wished to make all my dependants happy, provided I could accomplish it without much trouble. The method of doing good, which seemed to require the least exertion, and which I, therefore, most willingly practised, was giving away money. I did not wait to inquire, much less to examine into the merits of the claimants; but, without selecting proper objects, I relieved myself from the uneasy feeling of pity, by indiscriminate donations to objects apparently the most miserable.

I was quite angry with Mr. M'Leod, my agent, and considered him as a selfish, hard-hearted miser, because he did not seem to sympathize with me, or to applaud my generosity. I was so much irritated by his cold silence, that I could not forbear pressing him to say something.

"*I doubt*, then," said he, "since you desire me to speak my mind, my lord, *I doubt* whether the best way of encouraging the industrious is to give premiums to the idle."

"But, idle or not, these poor wretches are so miserable, that I cannot refuse to give them something; and, surely, when one can do it so easily, it is right to relieve misery. Is it not?"

"Undoubtedly, my lord; but the difficulty is, to relieve present misery, without creating more in future. Pity for one class of beings sometimes makes us cruel to others. I am told that there are some Indian Brahmins so very compassionate, that they hire beggars to let fleas feed upon them: I doubt whether it might not be better to let the fleas starve."

I did not in the least understand what Mr. M'Leod meant: but I was soon made to comprehend it, by crowds of eloquent beggars, who soon surrounded me: many who had been resolutely struggling with their difficulties, slackened their exertions, and left their labour for the easier trade of imposing upon my credulity. The money I had bestowed was wasted at the dram-shop, or it became the subject of family-quarrels; and those whom I had *relieved* returned to *my honour*, with fresh and insatiable expectations. All this time my industrious tenants grumbled, because no encouragement was given to them; and, looking upon me as a weak good-natured fool, they combined in a resolution to ask me for long leases, or reduction of rent.

The rhetoric of my tenants succeeded in some instances; and again I was mortified by Mr. M'Leod's silence. I was too proud to ask his opinion. I ordered, and was obeyed. A few leases for long terms were signed and sealed; and when I had thus my own way completely, I could not refrain from recurring to Mr. M'Leod's opinion.

"I doubt, my lord," said he, "whether this measure may be as advantageous as you hope. These fellows, these middle-men, will underset the land, and live in idleness, whilst they *rack* a parcel of wretched under-tenants."

"But they said they would keep the land in their own hands, and improve it; and that the reason why they could not afford to improve before was, that they had not long leases."

"It may be doubted whether long leases alone will make improving tenants; for in the next county to us, there are many farms of the dowager Lady Ormsby's land let at ten shillings an acre, and her tenantry are beggars: and the land now, at the end of the leases, is worn out, and worse than at their commencement."

I was weary listening to this cold reasoning, and resolved to apply no more for explanations to Mr. M'Leod; yet in my indolence I wanted the support of his approbation, at the very time I was jealous of his interference.

At one time I had a mind to raise the wages of labour; but Mr. M'Leod said, "*It might be doubted* whether the people would not work less, when they could with less work have money enough to support them."

I was puzzled: and then I had a mind to lower the wages of labour, to force them to work or starve. Still provoking Mr. M'Leod said, "It might be doubted whether it would not be better to leave them alone."

I gave marriage-portions to the daughters of my tenants, and rewards to those who had children; for I had always heard that legislators should encourage population. Still Mr. M'Leod hesitated to approve; he observed, "that my estate was so populous, that the complaint in each family was, that they had not land for the sons. *It might be doubted* whether, if a farm could support but ten people, it were wise to encourage the birth of twenty. *It might be doubted* whether it were not better for ten to live, and be well fed, than for twenty to be born, and to be half-starved."

To encourage manufactures in my town of Glenthorn, I proposed putting a clause in my leases, compelling my tenants to buy stuffs and linens manufactured at Glenthorn, and no where else. Stubborn M'Leod, as usual, began with, "*I doubt* whether that will not encourage the manufacturers at Glenthorn to make bad stuffs and bad linen, since they are sure of a sale, and without danger of competition."

At all events, I thought my tenants would grow rich and *independent*, if they made every thing *at home* that they wanted: yet Mr. M'Leod perplexed me by his "doubt whether it would not be better for a man to buy shoes, if he could buy them cheaper than he could make them." He added something about the division of labour, and Smith's Wealth of Nations; to which I could only answer—"Smith's a Scotchman."

I cannot express how much I dreaded Mr. M'Leod's *I doubt*—and—*It may be doubted.*

From the pain of doubt, and the labour of thought, I was soon most agreeably reprieved by the company of a Mr. Hardcastle, whose visits I constantly encouraged by a most gracious reception. Mr. Hardcastle was the agent of the dowager Lady Ormsby, who had a large estate in my neighbourhood: he was the very reverse of my Mr. M'Leod in his deportment and conversation. Talkative, self-sufficient, peremptory, he seemed not to know what it was *to doubt*; he considered doubt as a proof of ignorance, imbecility, or cowardice. "*Can any man doubt?*" was his usual beginning. On every subject of human knowledge, taste, morals, politics, economy, legislation; on all affairs, civil, military, or ecclesiastical, he decided at once in the most confident tone. Yet he "never read, not he!" he had nothing to do with books; he consulted only his own eyes and ears, and appealed only to common sense. As to theory, he had no opinion of theory; for his part, he only pretended to understand practice and experience—and his practice was confined steadily to his own practice, and his experience uniformly to what he had tried at New-town-Hardcastle.

At first I thought him a mighty clever man, and I really rejoiced to see my *doubter* silenced. After dinner, when he had finished speaking in this decisive manner, I used frequently to back him with a—*Very true—very fair—very clear*—though I understood what he said as little as he did himself; but it was an ease to my mind to have a disputed point settled—and I filled my glass with an air of triumph, whilst M'Leod never contradicted my assertions, nor controverted Mr. Hardcastle's arguments. There was still an air of content and quiet self-satisfaction in M'Leod's very silence, which surprised and vexed me.

One day, when Hardcastle was laying down the law upon several subjects in his usual dictatorial manner, telling us how he managed his people, and what order he kept them in, I was determined that M'Leod should not enjoy the security of his silence, and I urged him to give us his general opinion, as to the means of improving the poor people in Ireland.

"I doubt," said M'Leod, "whether any thing effectual can be done till they have a better education."

"Education!—Pshaw!—There it is now—these book-men," cried Hardcastle: "Why, my dear sir, can any man alive, who knows this country, doubt that the common people have already too much education, as it is called—a vast deal too much? Too many of them know how to read, and write, and cipher, which I presume is all you mean by education."

"Not entirely," said M'Leod; "a good education comprehends something more."

"The more the worse," interrupted Hardcastle. "The more they know, the worse they are, sir, depend on that; I know the people of this country, sir; I have *a good right* to know them, sir, being born amongst them, and bred amongst them; so I think I may speak with some confidence on these matters. And I give it as my decided humble opinion, founded on irrefragable experience, which is what I always build upon, that the way to ruin the poor of Ireland would be to educate them, sir. Look at the poor scholars, as they call themselves; and what are they? a parcel of young vagabonds in rags, with a book under their arm instead of a spade or a shovel, sir. And what comes of this? that they grow up the worst-disposed, and the most troublesome seditiousrascals in the community. I allow none of them about New-town-Hardcastle—none—banished them all. Useless vagrants—hornets, vipers, sir: and show me a quieter, better-managed set of people than I have made of mine. I go upon experience, sir; and that's the only thing to go upon; and I'll go no farther than New-town-Hardcastle: if that won't bring conviction home to you, nothing will."

"I never was at New-town-Hardcastle," said M'Leod, drily.

"Well, sir, I hope it will not be the case long. But in the mean time, my good sir, do give me leave to put it to your own common sense, what can reading or writing do for a poor man, unless he is to be a bailiff or an exciseman? and you know all men can't expect to be bailiffs or excisemen. Can all the book-learning in the world, sir, dig a poor man's potatoes for him, or plough his land, or cut his turf? Then, sir, in this country, where's the advantage of education, I humbly ask? No, sir, no, trust me—keep the Irish common people ignorant, and you keep 'em quiet; and that's the only way with them; for they are too quiet and smart, as it is, naturally. Teach them to read and write, and it's just adding fuel to fire—fire to gunpowder, sir. Teach them any thing, and directly you *set them up*: now it's our business to *keep them down*, unless, sir, you'd wish to have your throat cut. Education, sir! Lord bless your soul, sir! they have a great deal too much; they know too much already, which makes them so refractory to the laws, and so idle. I will go no farther than New-town-Hardcastle, to prove all this. So, my good sir," concluded he, triumphantly, "education, I grant you, is necessary for the rich; but tell me, if you can, what's the use of education to the poor?"

"Much the same, I apprehend, as to the rich," answered M'Leod. "The use of education, as I understand it, is to teach men to see clearly, and to follow steadily, their real interests. All morality, you know, is comprised in this definition; and—"

"Very true, sir; but all this can never apply to the poor in Ireland."

"Why, sir; are they not men?"

"Men, to be sure; but not like men in Scotland. The Irish know nothing of their interests; and as to morality, that's out of the question: they know nothing about it, my dear sir."

"That is the very thing of which I complain," said M'Leod. "They know nothing, because they have been taught nothing."

"They cannot be taught, sir."

"Did you ever try?"

"I *did*, sir, no later than last week. A fellow that I caught stealing my turf, instead of sending him to jail, I said to him, with a great deal of lenity, My honest fellow, did you never hear of the eighth commandment, 'Thou shalt not steal?' He confessed he had; but did not know it was the eighth. I showed it to him, and counted it to him myself; and set him, for a punishment, to get his whole catechism. Well, sir, the next week I found him stealing my turf again! and when I caught him by the wrist in the fact, he said, it was because the priest would not let him learn the catechism I gave him, because it was a Protestant one. Now you see, sir, there's a bar for ever to all education."

Mr. M'Leod smiled, said something about time and patience, and observed, "that one experiment was not conclusive against a whole nation." Any thing like a general argument Mr. Hardcastle could not comprehend. He knew every blade of grass within the reach of his tether, but could not reach an inch beyond. Any thing like an appeal to benevolent feelings was lost upon him; for he was so frank in his selfishness, that he did not even pretend to be generous. By sundry self-complacent motions he showed whilst his adversary spoke, that he disdained to listen almost as much as to read: but, as soon as M'Leod paused, he said, "What you observe, sir, may possibly be very true; but I have made up my mind." Then he went over and over again his assertions, in a louder and a louder voice, ending with a tone of interrogation that seemed to set all answer at defiance, "What have you to answer to me now, sir?—Can any man alive doubt this, sir?"

M'Leod was perfectly silent. The company broke up; and, as we were going out of the room, I maliciously asked M'Leod, why he, who could say so much in his own defence, had suffered himself to be so completely silenced? He answered me, in his low, deliberate voice, in the words of Moiré—"'Qu'est-ce que la raison avec un filet de voix contre une gueule comme celle-là?' At some other time," added Mr. M'Leod, "my sentiments shall be at your lordship's disposal."

Indolent persons love positive people, when they are of their own opinion; because they are saved the trouble of developing their thoughts, or supporting their assertions: but the moment the positive differs in sentiment from the indolent man, there is an end of the friendship. The indolent man then hates his pertinacious adversary as much as he loved his sturdy friend. So it happened between Mr. Hardcastle and me. This gentleman was a prodigious favourite with me, so long as his opinions were not in opposition to my own; but an accident happened, which brought his love of power and mine into direct competition, and then I found his peremptory mode of reasoning and his ignorance absurd and insufferable.

Before I can do justice to my part of this quarrel, I must explain the cause of the interest which I took in behalf of the persons aggrieved. During the time that my first hot fit of benevolence was on me, I was riding home one evening after dining with Mr. Hardcastle, and I was struck with the sight of a cabin, more wretched than any I had ever before beheld: the feeble light of a single rush-candle through the window revealed its internal misery.

"Does any body live in that hovel?" said I

"Ay, sure, does there: the Noonans, plase your honour," replied a man on the road. Noonans! I recollected the name to be that of the pugilist, who had died in consequence of the combat at which I had been present in London; who had, with his dying breath, besought me to convey his only half-guinea and his silk handkerchief to his poor father and sister. I alighted from my horse, asking the man, at the same time, if the son of this Noonan had not died in England.

"He had, sir, a son in England, Mick Noonan, who used to send him odd guineas, *I mind*, and was a *good lad to his father*, though wild; and there's been no account of him at-all-at-all this long while: but the old man has another boy, a sober lad, who's abroad with the army in the East Indies; and it's he that is the hope of the family. And there's the father—and old as he is, and poor, and a cripple, I'd engage there is not a happier man in the three counties at this very time speaking: for it is just now I seen young Jemmy Riley, the daughter's *bachelor*, go by with a letter. What news? says I. 'Great news!' says he: 'a letter from Tom Noonan to his father; and I'm going in to read it for him.'"

By the time my voluble informant had come to this period, I had reached the cabin door. Who could have expected to see smiles and hear exclamations of joy under such a roof?

I saw the father, with his hands clasped in ecstasy, and looking up to heaven, with the strong expression of delight in his aged countenance. I saw every line of his face; for the light of the candle was full upon it. The daughter, a beautiful girl, kneeling beside him, held the light for the young man, who was reading her brother's letter. I was sorry to interrupt them.

"Your honour's kindly welcome," said the old man, making an attempt to rise.

"Pray, don't let me disturb you."

"It was only a letter from a boy of mine that's over the seas, we was reading," said the old man. "A better boy to an ould father, that's good for nothing now in this world, never was, plase your honour. See what he has sent me: a draft here for ten guineas out of the little pay he has. God for ever bless him!—as he surely will."

After a few minutes' conversation, the old man's heart was so much opened towards me, that he talked as freely as if he had known me for years. I led to the subject of his other son Michael, who was mentioned in the letter as a wild chap. "Ah! your honour, that's what lies heaviest on my heart, and will, to my dying day, that Mick, before he died, which they say he did surely a twelvemonth ago, over there in England, never so much as sent me one line, good or bad, or his sister a token to remember him by even!"

"Had he but sent us the least bit of a word, or the least token in life, I had been content," said the sister, wiping her eyes: "we don't so much as know how he died."

I took this moment to relate the circumstances of Michael Noonan's death; and when I told them of his dying request about the half-guinea and the silk handkerchief, they were all so much touched, that they utterly forgot the ten-guinea draft, which I saw on the ground, in the dirt, under the old man's feet, whilst he contemplated the half-guinea which his *poor Michael* had sent him: repeating, "Poor fellow! poor fellow! 'twas all he had in the world. God bless him!—Poor Michael! he was a wild chap! but none better to his parents than he while the life was in him. Poor Michael!"

In no country have I found such strong instances of filial affection as in Ireland. Let the sons go where they may, let what will befall them, they never forget their parents at home: they write to them constantly the most affectionate letters, and send them a share of whatever they earn.

When I asked the daughter of this Noonan, why she had not married? the old man answered, "That's her own fault—if it be a fault to abide by an old father. She wastes her youth here, in the way your honour sees, tending him who has none other to mind him."

"Oh! let alone *that*," said the girl, with a cheerful smile; "we be too poor to think of marrying yet, by a great deal! so, father dear, you're no hinderance any way. For don't I know, and doesn't Jemmy there know, that it's a sin and a shame, as my mother used to say, for them that have nothing, to marry and set up house-keeping, like the rogue that ruined my father?"

"That's true," said the young man, with a heavy sigh; "but times will mend, or we'll strive and mend them, with the blessing of God."

I left this miserable but in admiration of the generosity of its inhabitants. I desired the girl to come to Glenthorn Castle the next day, that I might give her the silk handkerchief which her poor brother had sent her. The more I inquired into the circumstances of this family, the more cause I found for pity and approbation. The old man had been a good farmer in his day, as the traditions of the aged, and the memories of the young, were ready to witness; but he was unfortunately joined in *co-partnership* with a drunken rogue, who ran away, and left an arrear of rent, which ruined Noonan. Mr. Hardcastle, the agent, called upon him to pay it, and sold all that the old man possessed; and this being insufficient to discharge the debt, he was forced to give up his farm, and retire, with his daughter, to this hovel; and soon afterwards he lost the use of his side by a paralytic stroke.

I was so much pleased with the goodness of these poor people, that, in despite of my indolent disposition, I bestirred myself the very next day to find a better habitation for them on my own estate. I settled them, infinitely to their satisfaction, in a small farm; and the girl married her lover, who undertook to manage the farm for the old man. To my utter surprise, I found that Mr. Hardcastle was affronted by the part I took in this affair. He complained that I had behaved in a very ungentlemanlike manner, and had spirited the tenants away from Lady Ormsby's estate, against the regulation which he had laid down for all *the* tenants not to *emigrate* from *the estate*. Jemmy Riley, it seems, was one of the *cotters* on the Ormsby estate, a circumstance with which I was unacquainted; indeed I scarcely at that time understood what was meant by a *cotter*. Mr. Hardcastle's complaint, in matter and manner, was unintelligible to me; but I was quite content to leave off visiting him, as he left off visiting me—but here the matter did not stop. This over-wise and over-busy gentleman took upon him, amongst other offices, the regulation of the markets in the town of Ormsby; and as he apprehended, for reasons best and only known to himself, a year of scarcity, he thought fit to keep down the price of oats and potatoes. He would allow none to be sold in the market of Ormsby but at the price which he stipulated. The poor people grumbled, and, to remedy the injustice, made private bargains with each other. He had information of this, and seized the corn that was selling above the price he had fixed. Young Riley, Noonan's son-in-law, came to me to complain, that *his little oats were seized and detained.* I remonstrated. Hardcastle resented the appeal to me, and bid him wait and be damned. The young man, who was rather of a hasty temper, and who did not much like either to wait or be damned, seized his own oats, and was marching off, when they were recaptured by Hardcastle's bailiff, whom young Riley knocked down; and who, as soon as he got up again, went *straight* and swore examinations against Riley. Then I was offended, as I had a right to be, by the custom of the country, with the magistrate who took an examination against my tenant, without writing first to me. Then there was a race between the examinations of *my* justice of peace and *his* justice of peace. My indolence was conquered by my love of power: I supported the contest; the affair came before our grand jury: I conquered, and Mr. Hardcastle was ever after, of course, my enemy. To English ears the possessive pronouns *my* and *his* may sound extraordinary, prefixed to a justice of peace; but, in many parts of Ireland, this language is perfectly correct. A great man talks of *making* a justice of the peace with perfect confidence; a very great man talks with as much certainty of *making* a sheriff; and a sheriff makes the jury;

and the jury makes the law. We must not forget, however, that in England, during the reign of Elizabeth, a member of parliament defined a justice of peace to be "an animal, who for half a dozen chickens will dispense with half a dozen penal statutes." Time is necessary to enforce the sanctions of legislation and civilization—But I am anticipating reflections which I made at a much later period of my life. To return to my history.

My benevolence was soon checked by slight disappointments. Ellinor's cottage, which I had taken so much pains to build, became a source of mortification to me. One day I found my old nurse sitting at her wheel, in the midst of the wreck and litter of all sorts of household furniture, singing her favourite song of

> "There was a lady loved a swine:
>
> Honey! says she,
>
> I'll give ye a silver trough.
>
> Hunk! says he!"

Ellinor seemed, alas! to have as little taste for the luxuries with which I had provided her as the pig had for the silver trough. What I called conveniences were to her incumbrances: she had not been used to them; she was put out of her way; and it was a daily torment to one of her habits, to keep her house clean and neat.

There may be, as some philosophers assure us that there is, an innate love of order in the human mind; but of this instinctive principle my poor Ellinor was totally destitute. Her ornamented farm-house became, in a wonderfully short time, a scene of dirt, rubbish, and confusion. There was a partition between two rooms, which had been built with turf or peat, instead of bricks, by the wise economy I had employed. Of course, this was pulled down to get at the turf. The stairs also were pulled down and burned, though there was no scarcity of firing. As the walls were plastered and papered before they were quite dry, the paper grew mouldy, and the plaster fell off. In the hurry of finishing, some of the woodwork had but one coat of paint. In Ireland they have not faith in the excellent Dutch proverb, *"Paint costs nothing."* I could not get my workmen to give a second coat of paint to any of the sashes, and the wood decayed: divers panes of glass in the windows were broken, and their places filled up with shoes, an old hat, or a bundle of rags. Some of the slates were blown off one windy night: the slater lived at ten miles distance, and before the slates were replaced, the rain came in, and Ellinor was forced to make a bedchamber of the parlour, and then of the kitchen, retreating from corner to corner as the rain pursued, till, at last, when "it *would* come *every way* upon her bed," she petitioned me to let her take the slates off and thatch the house; for a slated-house, she said, was never so warm as a *tatched cabin*; and as there was no smoke, she was *kilt* with the *cowld*.

In my life I never felt so angry. I was ten times more angry than when Crawley ran away with my wife. In a paroxysm of passion, I reproached Ellinor with being a savage, an Irish-woman, and an ungrateful fool.

"Savage I am, for any thing I know; and *fool* I am, that's certain; but ungrateful I am not," said she, bursting into tears. She went home and took to her bed; and the next thing I heard from her son was, "that she was *lying in the rheumatism*, which had kept her awake many a long night, before she would come to complain to my honour of the house, in dread that I should blame myself for *sending of* her into it *afore* it was dry."

The rheumatism reconciled me immediately to Ellinor; I let her take her own way, and thatch the house, and have as much smoke as she pleased, and she recovered. But I did not entirely recover my desire to do good to my poor tenants. After forming, in the first enthusiasm of my benevolence, princely schemes for their advantage, my ardour was damped, and my zeal discouraged, by a few slight disappointments.

I did not consider, that there is often, amongst uncultivated people, a mixture of obstinate and lazy content, which makes them despise the luxuries of their richer neighbours; like those mountaineers, who, proud of their own hard fare,80 out of a singular species of contempt, call the inhabitants of the plains *mange-rotis*, "eaters of roast meat." I did not consider that it must take time to change local and national habits and prejudices; and that it is necessary to raise a taste for comforts, before they can be properly enjoyed.

In the pettishness of my disappointment, I decided that it was in vain to attempt to improve and civilize such people as the Irish. I did not recollect, perhaps at that time I did not know, that even in the days of the great Queen Elizabeth, "the greatest part of the buildings in the cities and good towns of England consisted only of timber, cast over with thick clay to keep out the wind. The new houses of the nobility were indeed either of brick or stone; and glass windows were then beginning to be used in England:"81 and clean rushes were strewed over the dirty floors of the royal palace. In the impatience of my zeal for improvement, I expected to do the work of two hundred years in a few months: and because I could not accelerate the progress of refinement in this miraculous manner, I was out of humour with myself and with a whole nation. So easily is the humanity of the rich and great disgusted and discouraged! as if any people could be civilized in a moment, and at the word of command of ignorant pride or despotic benevolence!

CHAPTER IX

"He saw—and but that admiration
Had been too active, too like passion,
Or had he been to ton less true,
Cupid had shot him through and through."

I have not thought it necessary to record every visit that I received from all my country neighbours; but I must now mention one, which led to important consequences; a visit from Sir Harry Ormsby, a very young dashing man of fortune, who, in expectation of the happy moment when he should be of age, resided with his mother, the dowager Lady Ormsby. Her ladyship had heard that there had been some disagreement between her agent, Mr. Hardcastle, and *my people*; but she took the earliest opportunity of expressing her wishes, that our families should be on an amicable footing.

Lady Ormsby was just come to the country, with a large party of her fashionable friends—some Irish, some English: Lord and Lady Kilrush; my Lady Kildangan, and her daughter the Lady Geraldine — — —; the knowing widow O'Connor; the English *dasher*, Lady Hauton; the interesting Mrs. Norton, *separated* but not *parted* from her husband; the pleasant Miss Bland; the three Miss Ormsbys, better known by the name of the Swanlinbar Graces; two English aides-de-camp from the Castle, and a brace of brigadiers; besides other men of inferior note.

I perceived that Sir Harry Ormsby took it for granted that I must be acquainted with the pretensions of all these persons to celebrity; his talkativeness and my taciturnity favoured me so fortunately, that he never discovered the extent of my ignorance. He was obligingly impatient to make me personally acquainted "with those of whom I must have heard so much in England." Observing that Ormsby Villa was too far from Glenthorn Castle for a morning visit, he pressed me to waive ceremony, and to do Lady Ormsby and him the honour of spending a week with them, as soon as I could make it convenient. I accepted this invitation, partly from a slight emotion of curiosity, and partly from my habitual inability to resist any reiterated importunity.

Arrived at Ormsby Villa, and introduced to this crowd of people, I was at first disappointed by seeing nothing extraordinary. I expected that their manners would have been as strange to me as some of their names appeared: but whether it was from my want of the powers of discrimination, or from the real sameness of the objects, I could scarcely, in this fashionable flock, discern any individual marks of distinction. At first view, the married ladies appeared much the same as those of a similar class in England, whom I had been accustomed to see. The young ladies I thought, as usual, "best distinguished by black, brown, and fair:" but I had not yet seen Lady Geraldine — — —; and a great part Of the conversation, the first day I was at Ormsby Villa, was filled with lamentations on the unfortunate tooth-ache, which prevented her ladyship from appearing. She was talked of so much, and as a person of such importance, and so essential to the amusement of society, that I could not help feeling a slight wish to see her. The next day at breakfast she did not appear; but, five minutes before dinner, her ladyship's humble companion whispered, "Now Lady Geraldine is coming, my lord." I was always rather displeased to be called upon to attend to any thing or any body, yet as Lady Geraldine entered, I gave one involuntary glance of curiosity. I saw a tall, finely-shaped woman, with the commanding air of a woman of rank; she moved well; not with feminine timidity, but with ease, promptitude, and decision. She had fine eyes and a fine complexion, yet no regularity of feature. The only thing that struck me as really extraordinary was her indifference when I was introduced to her. Every body had seemed extremely desirous that I should see her ladyship, and that her ladyship should see me; and I was rather surprised by her unconcerned air. This piqued me, and fixed my attention. She turned from me, and began to converse with others. Her voice was agreeable: she did not speak with the Irish accent; but, when I listened maliciously, I detected certain Hibernian inflections; nothing of the vulgar Irish idiom, but something that was more interrogative, more exclamatory, and perhaps more rhetorical, than the common language of English ladies, accompanied with much animation of countenance and demonstrative gesture. This appeared to me peculiar and unusual, but not affected. She was uncommonly eloquent, and yet, without action, her words were not sufficiently rapid to express her ideas. Her manner appeared foreign, yet it was not quite French. If I had been obliged to decide, I should, however, have pronounced it rather more French than English. To determine what it was, or whether I had ever seen any thing similar, I stood considering her ladyship with more attention than I had ever bestowed on any other woman. The words *striking—fascinating—bewitching,* occurred to me as I looked at her and heard her speak. I resolved to turn my eyes away, and shut my ears; for I was positively determined not to like her, I dreaded so much the idea of a second Hymen. I retreated to the farthest window, and looked out very soberly upon a dirty fish-pond. Dinner was announced. I observed Lady Kildangan manoeuvring to place me beside her daughter Geraldine, but Lady Geraldine counteracted this movement. I was again surprised and piqued. After yielding the envied position to one of the Swanlinbar Graces, I heard Lady Geraldine whisper to her next neighbour, "Baffled, mamma!"

It was strange to me to feel piqued by a young lady's not choosing to sit beside me. After dinner, I left the gentlemen as soon as possible, because the conversation wearied me. Lord Kilrush, the chief orator, was a courtier, and could talk of nothing but Dublin Castle, and my lord lieutenant's levees. The moment that I went to the ladies, I was seized upon by the officious Miss Bland: she could not speak of any thing but Lady Geraldine, who sat at so great a distance, and who was conversing with such animation herself, that she could not hear her *prôneuse*, Miss Bland, inform me, that "her friend, Lady Geraldine, was extremely clever; so clever, that many people were at first a little afraid of her; but that there was not the least occasion; for that, where she liked, nobody could be more affable and engaging." This judicious friend, a minute afterwards, told me, as a very great secret, that Lady Geraldine was an admirable mimic; that she could draw or speak caricatures; that she was also wonderfully happy in the invention of agnomens and cognomens, so applicable to the persons, that they could scarcely be forgotten or forgiven. I was a little anxious to know whether her ladyship would honour me with an agnomen. I could not learn this from Miss Bland, and I was too prudent to betray my curiosity: I afterwards heard it, however. Pairing me and Mr. M'Leod, whom she had seen together, her ladyship observed, that *Sawney* and *Yawney* were made for each other; and she sketched, in strong caricature, my relaxed elongation of limb, and his rigid rectangularity. A slight degree of fear of Lady Geraldine's powers kept my attention alert. In the course of the evening, Lady Kildangan summoned her daughter to the music-room, and asked me to come and hear an Irish song. I exerted myself so far as to follow immediately; but though summoned, Lady Geraldine did not obey. Miss Bland tuned the harp, and opened the music-books on the piano; but no Lady Geraldine appeared. Miss Bland was sent backwards and forwards with messages; but Lady Geraldine's ultimatum was, that she could not possibly sing, because she was afraid of the tooth-ache. God knows, her mouth had never been shut all the evening. "Well, but," said Lady Kildangan, "she can play for us, cannot she?" No; her ladyship was afraid of the cold in the music-room. "Do, my Lord Glenthorn, go and tell the dear capricious creature, that we are very warm here."

Very reluctantly I obeyed. The Lady Geraldine, with her circle round her, heard and answered me with the air of a princess.

"Do you the honour to play for you, my lord! Excuse me: I am no professor—I play so ill, that I make it a rule never to play but for my own amusement. If you wish for music, there is Miss Bland; she plays incomparably, and I dare say will think herself happy to oblige your lordship." I never felt so silly, or so much abashed, as at this instant. "This comes," thought I, "of acting out of character. What possessed me to exert myself to ask a lady to play? I, that have been tired to death of music! Why did I let myself be sent ambassador, when I had no interest in the embassy?"

To convince myself and others of my apathy, I threw myself on a sofa, and never stirred or spoke the remainder of the night. I presume I appeared fast asleep, else Lady Geraldine would not have said, within my hearing, "Mamma wants me to catch somebody, and to be caught by somebody; but that will not be; for, do you know, I think somebody is nobody."

I was offended as much as it was in my nature to be offended, and I began to meditate apologies for shortening my visit at Ormsby Villa: but, though I was shocked by the haughtiness of Lady Geraldine, and accused her, in my own mind, of want of delicacy and politeness, yet I could not now suspect her of being an accomplice with her mother in any matrimonial designs upon me. From the moment I was convinced of this, my conviction was, I suppose, visible to her ladyship's penetrating eyes, and from that instant she showed me that she could be polite and agreeable. Now, soothed to a state of ease and complacency, I might have sunk to indifference and ennui, but fresh singularities in this lady struck me, and kept my attention awake and fixed upon her character. If she had treated me with tolerable civility at first, I never should have thought about her. High-born and high-bred, she seemed to consider more what she thought of others than what others thought of her. Frank, candid, and affable, yet opinionated, insolent, and an egotist, her candour and affability appeared the effect of a naturally good temper, her insolence and egotism only those of a spoiled child. She seemed to talk of herself purely to oblige others, as the most interesting possible topic of conversation; for such it had always been to her fond mother, who idolized her ladyship as an only daughter, and the representative of an ancient house. Confident of her talents, conscious of her charms, and secure of her station, Lady Geraldine gave free scope to her high spirits, her fancy, and her turn for ridicule. She looked, spoke, and acted, like a person privileged to think, say, and do, what she pleased. Her raillery, like the raillery of princes, was without fear of retort. She was not ill-natured, yet careless to whom she gave offence, provided she produced amusement; and in this she seldom failed; for, in her conversation, there was much of the raciness of Irish wit, and the oddity of Irish humour. The singularity that struck me most about her ladyship was her indifference to flattery. She certainly preferred frolic. Miss Bland was her humble companion; Miss Tracey her *butt*. Her ladyship appeared to consider Miss Bland as a necessary appendage to her rank and person, like her dress or her shadow; and she seemed to think no more of the one than of the other. She suffered Miss Bland to follow her; but she would go in quest of n Miss Tracey. Miss Bland was allowed to speak; but her ladyship listened to Miss Tracey. Miss Bland seldom obtained an answer; but Miss Tracey never opened her lips without a repartee.

In describing Miss Tracey, Lady Geraldine said, "Poor simpleton! she cannot help imitating all she sees us do; yet, would you believe it, she really has starts of common sense, and some tolerable ideas of her own. Spoiled by bad company! In the language of the bird-fanciers, she has a few notes nightingale, and all the rest rubbish."

It was one of Lady Geraldine's delights to humour Miss Tracey's rage for imitating the fashions of fine people.

"Now you shall see Miss Tracey appear at the ball to-morrow, in every thing that I have sworn to her is fashionable. Nor have I cheated her in a single article: but the *tout ensemble* I leave to her better judgment; and you shall see her, I trust, a perfect monster, formed of every creature's best: Lady Kilrush's feathers, Mrs. Moore's wig, Mrs. O'Connor's gown, Mrs. Lighton's sleeves, and all the necklaces of all the Miss Ormsbys. She has no taste, no judgment; none at all, poor thing! but she can imitate as well as those Chinese painters, who, in their drawings, give you the flower of one plant stuck on the stalk of another, and garnished with the leaves of a third."

Miss Tracey's appearance the ensuing night justified all Lady Geraldine's predictions, and surpassed her ladyship's most sanguine hopes. Even I, albeit unused to the laughing mood, could not forbear smiling at the humour and ease with which her ladyship played off this girl's credulous vanity.

At breakfast the next morning, Lord Kilrush, in his grave manner (always too solemn by half for the occasion), declared, "that no man was more willing than himself to enter into a jest in proper time, and season, and measure, and so forth; but that it was really, positively, morally unjustifiable, in *his* apprehension, *the making* this poor girl so publicly ridiculous."

"My good lord," replied Lady Geraldine, "all the world are ridiculous some way or other: some in public, some in private. Now," continued she, with an appealing look to the whole company, "now, after all, what is there more extravagant in my Miss Tracey's delighting, at sixteen, in six yards of pink riband, than in your courtier sighing, at sixty, for three yards of blue riband? or what is there more ridiculous in her coming simpering into a ball-room, fancying herself the mirror of fashion, when she is a figure for a print-shop, than in the courtier rising solemnly in the House of Lords, believing himself an orator, and expecting to make a vast reputation, by picking up, in every debate, the very worst arguments that every body else let fall? There would be no living in this world, if we were all to see and expose one another's *ridicules*. My plan is much the best—to help my friends to expose themselves, and then they are infinitely obliged to me."

Satisfied with silencing all opposition, and seeing that the majority was with her, Lady Geraldine persisted in her course; and I was glad she was incorrigible, because her faults entertained me. As to love, I thought I was perfectly safe; because, though I admired her quickness and cleverness, yet I still, at times, perceived, or fancied I perceived, some want of polish, and elegance, and *tact*. She was not exactly cut out according to my English pattern of a woman of fashion; so I thought I might amuse myself without danger, as it was partly at her ladyship's expense. But about this time I was alarmed for myself by a slight twinge of jealousy. As I was standing lounging upon the steps at the hall-door, almost as ennuyé as usual, I saw a carriage at a distance, between the trees, driving up the *approach*; and, at the same instant, I heard Lady Geraldine's eager voice in the hall, "Oh! they are coming; he is coming; they are come. Run, Miss Bland, run, and give Lord Craiglethorpe my message before he gets out of the carriage—before any body sees him."

Afraid of hearing what I should not hear, I walked down the steps deliberately, and turned into a shrubbery-walk, to leave the coast clear. Out ran Miss Bland: and then it was that I felt the twinge—very slight, however. "Who is this Lord Craiglethorpe, with whom Lady Geraldine is on such favourable terms? I wonder what kind of looking man he is; and what could *the message* mean?—but, at all events, it cannot concern me; yet I am curious to see this Lord Craiglethorpe. I wonder any woman can like a man with so strange a name: but does she like him, after all?—Why do I plague myself about it?"

As I returned from my saunter, I was met by Miss Bland.

"A charming day, ma'am," said I, endeavouring to pass on.

"A charming day, my lord! But I must stop your lordship a moment. Oh, I am so out of breath—I went the wrong way——"

"The wrong way! Indeed! I am sorry. I am concerned you should have had so much trouble."

"No trouble in the world. Only I want to beg you'll keep our secret—my Lady Geraldine's secret."

"Undoubtedly, madam—a man of honour—Lady Geraldine cannot doubt—her ladyship's secret is perfectly safe."

"But do you know it? You don't know it yet, my lord."

"Pardon me; I was on the steps just now. I thought you saw me."

"I did, my lord—but I don't understand——"

"Nor I, neither," interrupted I, half laughing; for I began to think I was mistaken in my suspicions; "pray explain yourself, my dear Miss Bland: I was very rude to be so quick in interrupting you."

Miss Bland then made me the confidant of a charming scheme of Lady Geraldine's for quizzing Miss Tracey.

"She has never in her life seen Lord Craiglethorpe, who is an English lord travelling through Ireland," continued Miss Bland. "Now, you must know, that Miss Tracey is passionately fond of lords, let them be what they may. Now, Lord Craiglethorpe, this very morning, sent his groom with a note and excuse to Lady Ormsby, for not coming to us to-day; because, he said, he was bringing down in the chaise with him a surveyor, to survey his estate *near here*; and he could not possibly think of bringing the surveyor, who is a low man, to Ormsby Villa. But Lady Ormsby would take no apology, and wrote by the groom to beg that Lord Craiglethorpe would make no scruple of bringing the surveyor; for you know she is so polite and accommodating, and all that. Well, the note was scarcely gone, before Lady Geraldine thought of her charming scheme, and regretted, *of all things*, she had not put *it* into it."

"*It into it!*" repeated I to myself. "Ma'am," said I, looking a little bewildered.

"But," continued my clear narrator, "I promised to remedy all *that*, by running to meet the carriage, which was what I ran for when you saw me, my lord, in such a hurry."

I bowed—and was as wise as ever.

"So, my lord, you comprehend, that the surveyor, whose name, whose odious name, is Gabbitt, is to be my Lord Craiglethorpe, and my Lord Craiglethorpe is to be passed for Mr. Gabbitt upon Miss Tracey; and, you will see, Miss Tracey will admire Mr. Gabbitt prodigiously, and call him vastly genteel, when she thinks him a lord. Your lordship will keep our secret; and she is sure Lord Craiglethorpe will do any thing to oblige her, because he is a near connexion of hers. But, I assure you, it is not every body could get Lord Craiglethorpe to join in a joke; for he is very stiff, and cold, and high. Of course your lordship will know which is the real lord at first sight. He is a full head taller than Gabbitt."

Never was explanation finally more satisfactory: and whether the jest was really well contrived and executed, or whether I was put into a humour to think so, I cannot exactly determine; but, I confess, I was amused with the scenes that followed, though I felt that they were not quite justifiable even in jest.

The admiration of Miss Tracey for *the false Craiglethorpe*, as Lady Geraldine called Mr. Gabbitt; the awkwardness of Mr. Gabbitt with his title, and the awkwardness of Lord Craiglethorpe without it, were fine subjects of her ladyship's satirical humour.

In another point of view, Lord Craiglethorpe afforded her ladyship amusement; as an English traveller, full of English prejudices against Ireland and every thing Irish. Whenever Miss Tracey was out of the room, Lady Geraldine allowed Lord Craiglethorpe to be himself again; but he did not fare the better for this restoration to his honours. Lady Geraldine contrived to make him as ridiculous in his real as in his assumed character. Lord Craiglethorpe was, as Miss Bland had described him, very stiff, cold, and *high*. His manners were in the extreme of English reserve, and his ill-bred show of contempt for the Irish was sufficient provocation and justification of Lady Geraldine's ridicule. He was much in awe of his fair and witty cousin: she could easily put him out of countenance, for he was extremely bashful.

His lordship had that sort of bashfulness which makes a man surly and obstinate in his taciturnity; which makes him turn upon all who approach him, as if they were going to assault him; which makes him answer a question as if it were an injury, and repel a compliment as if it were an insult. Once, when he was out of the room, Lady Geraldine exclaimed, "That cousin Craiglethorpe of mine is scarcely an agreeable man: the awkwardness of *mauvaise honte* might be pitied and pardoned, even in a nobleman," continued her ladyship, "if it really proceeded from humility; but here, when I know it is connected with secret and inordinate arrogance, 'tis past all endurance. Even his ways of sitting and standing provoke me, they are so self-sufficient. Have you observed how he stands at the fire? Oh, the caricature of '*the English fire-side*' outdone! Then, if he sits, we hope that change of posture may afford our eyes transient relief: but worse again; bolstered up, with his back against his chair, his hands in his pockets, and his legs thrown out, in defiance of all passengers and all decorum, there he sits, in magisterial silence, throwing a gloom upon all conversation. As the Frenchman said of the Englishman, for whom even his politeness could not find another compliment, 'Il faut avouer que ce monsieur a un grand talent pour le silence;' he holds his tongue, till the people actually believe that he has something to say; a mistake they could never fall into if he would but speak."

Some of the company attempted to interpose a word or two in favour of Lord Craiglethorpe's timidity, but the vivacious and merciless lady went on.

"I tell you, my good friends, it is not timidity—it is all pride. I would pardon his dulness, and even his ignorance; for one, as you say, might be the fault of his nature, and the other of his education: but his self-sufficiency is his own fault, and that I will not, and cannot pardon. Somebody says, that nature may make a fool, but a coxcomb is always of his own making. Now, my cousin—(as he is my cousin, I may say what I please of him)—my cousin Craiglethorpe is a solemn coxcomb, who thinks, because his vanity is not talkative and sociable, that it's not vanity. What a mistake! his silent superciliousness is to me more intolerable than the most garrulous egotism that ever laid itself open to my ridicule."

Miss Bland and Miss Ormsby both confessed that Lord Craiglethorpe was vastly too silent.

"For the honour of my country," continued Lady Geraldine, "I am determined to make this man talk, and he shall say all that I know he thinks of us poor Irish savages. If he would but speak, one could answer him: if he would find fault, one might defend: if he would laugh, one might perhaps laugh again: but here he comes to hospitable, open-hearted Ireland; eats as well as he can in his own country; drinks better than he can in his own country; sleeps as well as he can in his own country; accepts all our kindness without a word or a look of thanks, and seems the whole time to think, that, 'Born for his use, we live but to oblige him.' There he is at this instant: look at him, walking in the park, with his note-book in his hand, setting down our faults, and conning them by rote. We are even with him. I understand, Lady Kilrush, that my bright cousin Craiglethorpe means to write a book, a great book, upon Ireland."

Lady Kilrush replied, that she understood Lord Craiglethorpe had it in contemplation to publish a Tour through Ireland, or a View of Ireland, or something of that nature.

"He! with his means of acquiring information!" exclaimed Lady Geraldine. "Posting from one great man's house to another, what can he see or know of the manners of any rank of people but of the class of gentry, which in England and Ireland is much the same? As to the lower classes, I don't think he ever speaks to them; or, if he does, what good can it do him? for he can't understand their modes of expression, nor they his: if he inquire about a matter of fact, I defy him to get the truth out of them, if they don't wish to tell it; and, for some reason or other, they will, nine times in ten, not wish to tell it to an Englishman. There is not a man, woman, or child, in any cabin in Ireland, who would not have wit and 'cuteness enough to make *my lard* believe just what they please. So, after posting from Dublin to Cork, and from the Giants' Causeway to Killarney; after travelling east, west, north, and south, my wise cousin Craiglethorpe will know just as much of the lower Irish as the cockney who has never been out of London, and who has never, *in all his born days,* seen an Irishman but on the English stage; where the representations are usually as like the originals, as the Chinese pictures of lions, drawn from description, are to the real animal."

"Now! now! look at his lordship!" cried Miss Bland; "he has his note-book out again."

"Mercy on us!" said Miss Callwell, "how he is writing!"

"Yes, yes, write on, my good cousin Craiglethorpe," pursued Lady Geraldine, "and nil the little note-book, which will soon turn to a ponderous quarto. I shall have a copy, bound in morocco, no doubt, *from the author,* if I behave myself prettily; and I will earn it, by supplying valuable information. You shall see, my friends, how I'll deserve well of my country, if you'll only keep my counsel and your own countenances."

Presently Lord Craiglethorpe entered the room, walking very pompously, and putting his note-book up as he advanced.

"Oh, my dear lord, open the book again; I have a bull for you."

Lady Geraldine, after putting his lordship in good humour by this propitiatory offering of a bull, continued to supply him, either directly or indirectly, by some of her confederates, with the most absurd anecdotes, incredible *facts,* stale jests, and blunders, such as were never made by true-born Irishmen; all which my Lord Craiglethorpe took down with an industrious sobriety, at which the spectators could scarcely refrain from laughing. Sometimes he would pause, and exclaim, "A capital anecdote! a curious fact! May I give my authority? may I quote your ladyship?"

"Yes, if you'll pay me a compliment in the preface," whispered Lady Geraldine: "and now, dear cousin, do go up stairs *and put it all in ink.*"

When she had despatched the noble author, her ladyship indulged her laughter. "But now," cried she, "only imagine a set of sober English readers studying my cousin Craiglethorpe's New View of Ireland, and swallowing all the nonsense it will contain!"

When Lord Kilrush remonstrated against the cruelty of letting the man publish such stuff, and represented it as a fraud upon the public, Lady Geraldine laughed still more, and exclaimed, "Surely you don't think I would use the public and my poor cousin so ill. No, I am doing him and the public the greatest possible service. Just when he is going to leave us, when the writing-box is packed, I will step up to him, and tell him the truth. I will show him what a farrago of nonsense he has collected as materials for his quarto; and convince him at once how utterly unfit he is to write a book, at least a book on Irish affairs. Won't this be deserving well of my country and of my cousin?"

Neither on this occasion, nor on any other, were the remonstrances of my Lord Kilrush of power to stop the course of this lady's flow of spirits and raillery.

Whilst she was going on in this manner with the real Lord Craiglethorpe, Miss Tracey was taking charming walks in the park with Mr. Gabbitt, and the young lady began to be seriously charmed with her false lord. This was carrying the jest farther, than Lady Geraldine had intended or foreseen; and her good-nature would probably have disposed her immediately to dissolve the enchantment, had she not been provoked by the interference of Lord Kilrush, and the affected sensibility of Miss Clementina Ormsby, who, to give me an exalted opinion of her delicacy, expostulated incessantly in favour of the deluded fair one. "But, my dear Lady Geraldine, I do assure you, it really hurts my feelings. This is going too far—when it comes to the heart. I can't laugh, I own—the poor girl's affections will be engaged—she is really falling in love with this odious surveyor."

"But now, my dear Clementina, I do assure you, it really hurts my feelings to hear you talk so childishly. 'When it comes to the heart!' 'affections engaged!' You talk of falling in love as if it were a terrible fall: for my part, I should pity a person much more for falling down stairs. Why, my dear, where is the mighty height from which Miss Tracey could fall? She does not live in the clouds, Clementina, as you do. No ladies live there now; for the best of all possible reasons, because there are no men there. So, my love, make haste and come down, before you are out of your teens, or you may chance to be left there till you are an angel or an old maid. Trust me, my dear, I, who have tried, tell you, there is no such thing as falling in love, now-a-days: you may slip, slide, or stumble; but to fall in love, I defy you."

I saw Lady Kildangan's eyes fix upon me as her daughter pronounced the last sentence.

"Geraldine, my dear, you do not know what you are talking about," said her ladyship. "Your time may come, Geraldine. Nobody should be too courageous. Cupid does not like to be defied."

Lady Kildangan walked away as she spoke, with a very well-satisfied air, leaving a party of us young people together. Lady Geraldine looked haughtily vexed. When in this mood, her wit gave no quarter; spared neither sex nor age.

"Every body says," whispered she, "that mamma is the most artful woman in the world; and I should believe it, only that every body says it: now, if it were true, nobody would know it."

Lady Geraldine's air of disdain towards me was resumed. I did not quite understand. Was it pride? was it coquetry? She certainly blushed deeply, and for the first time that I ever saw her blush, when her mother said, "Your time may come, Geraldine."

My week being now at an end, I resolved to take my leave. When I announced this resolution, I was assailed with the most pressing entreaties to stay a few days longer—one day longer. Lady Ormsby and Sir Harry said every thing that could be said upon the occasion: indeed, it seemed a matter of general interest to all, except to Lady Geraldine. She appeared wholly indifferent, and I was not even gratified by any apparent affectation of desiring my departure. Curiosity to see whether this would be sustained by her ladyship to the last, gave me resolution sufficient to resist the importunities of Sir Harry; and I departed, rejoicing that my indifference was equal to her ladyship's. As Tasso said of some fair one, whom he met at the carnival of Mantua, *I ran some risk of falling in love.* I had been so far roused from my habitual apathy that I actually made some reflections. As I returned home, I began to perceive that there was some difference between woman and woman, besides the distinctions of rank, fortune, and figure. I think I owe to Lady Geraldine my first relish for wit, and my first idea that a woman might be, if not a reasonable, at least a companionable animal. I compared her ladyship with the mere puppets and parrots of fashion, of whom I had been wearied; and I began to suspect that one might find, in a lady's "lively nonsense," a relief from ennui. These reflections, however, did not prevent me from sleeping the greatest part of the morning on my way home; nor did I dream of any thing that I can remember.

At the porter's lodge I saw Ellinor sitting at her spinning-wheel; and my thoughts took up my domestic affairs just where I had left them the preceding week.

CHAPTER X

In vain I attempted to interest myself in my domestic affairs; the silence and solitude of my own castle appeared to me intolerably melancholy, after my return from Ormsby Villa. There was a blank in my existence during a week, in which I can remember nothing that I did, said, or thought, except what passed during one ride, which Mr. McLeod compelled my politeness to take with him. He came with the same face to see me, and the same set of ideas, as those he had before I went to Ormsby Villa. He began to talk of my schemes for improving my tenantry, and of my wish that he should explain his notions relative to the education of the poor of Ireland, which, he said, as I now seemed to be at leisure, he was ready to do as concisely as possible. *As concisely as possible* were the only words of his address that I heard with satisfaction; but of course I bowed, said I was much obliged, and I should be happy to have the advantage of Mr. M'Leod's opinions and sentiments. What these were I cannot recollect, for I settled myself in a reverie soon after his voice began to sound upon my ear; but I remember at last he wakened me, by proposing that I should ride with him to see a school-house and some cottages, which he had built on a little estate of his own in my neighbourhood: "for," said he, "'tis better, my lord, to show you what can be done with these people, than to talk of what might be effected."

"Very true," said I, agreeing readily; because I wanted to finish a conversation that wearied me, and to have a refreshing ride. It was a delightful evening; and when we came on M'Leod's estate, I really could not help being pleased and interested. In an unfavourable situation, with all nature, vegetable and animal, against him, he had actually created a paradise amid the wilds. There was nothing wonderful in any thing I saw around me; but there was such an air of neatness and comfort, order and activity, in the people and in their cottages, that I almost thought myself in England; and I could not forbear exclaiming,—"How could all this be brought about in Ireland!"

"Chiefly by not doing and not expecting too much at first," said M'Leod. "We took time, and had patience. We began by setting them the example of some very slight improvements, and then, lured on by the sight of success, they could make similar trials themselves. My wife and I went among them, and talked to them in their cottages, and took an interest in their concerns, and did not want to have every thing our own way; and when they saw that, they began to consider which way was best; so by degrees we led where we could not have driven; and raised in them, by little and little, a taste for conveniences and comforts. Then the business was done; for the moment the taste and ambition were excited; to work the people went to gratify them; and according as they exerted themselves, we helped them. Perhaps it was best for them and for us, that we were not rich; for we could not do too much at a time, and were never tempted to begin grand schemes that we could not finish. There," said McLeod, pointing to a cottage with a pretty porch covered with woodbine, and a neat garden, in which many children were busily at work, "that house and that garden were the means of doing all the rest; that is our school-house. We could not expect to do much with the old, whose habits were fixed; but we tried to give the young children better notions, and it was a long time before we could bring that to bear. Twenty-six years we have been at this work; and in that time if we have done any thing, it was by beginning with the children: a race of our own training has now grown up, and they go on in the way they were taught, and prosper to our hearts' content, and, what is better still, to their hearts' content."

McLeod, habitually grave and taciturn, seemed quite enlivened and talkative this day; but I verily believe that not the slightest ostentation or vanity inspired him, for I never before or since heard him talk or allude to his own good deeds: I am convinced his motive was to excite me to persevere in my benevolent projects, by showing what had been done by small means. He was so truly in earnest that he never perceived how tired I was; indeed he was so little in the habit of expecting sympathy or applause, that he never missed even the ordinary expressions of concurrent complaisance.

"Religion," continued he, "is the great difficulty in Ireland. We make no difference between Protestants and Catholics; we always have admitted both into our school. The priest comes on Saturday morning, and the parish minister on Saturday evening, to hear the children belonging to each church their catechisms, and to instruct them in the tenets of their faith. And as we keep to our word, and never attempt making proselytes, nor directly or indirectly interfere with their religious opinions, the priests are glad to let us instruct the catholic children in all other points, which they plainly see must advance their temporal interests."

Mr. McLeod invited me to go in and look at the school. "In a hedge or ditch school," said he, "which I once passed on this road, and in which I saw a crowd of idle children, I heard the schoolmaster cry out, 'Rehearse! rehearse! there's company going by; and instantly all the boys snatched up their books, and began gabbling as fast as ever they could, to give an idea to the passenger of their diligence in repeating their lessons. But here, my lord," continued M'Leod, "you will not see any exhibitions *got up* for company. I hate such tricks. Walk in, my lord, if you please."

I walked in; but am ashamed to say, that I observed only that every thing looked as if it had been used for many years, and yet not worn out; and the whole school appeared as if all were in their places, and occupied and intent upon their business: but this general recollection is all I have retained. The enthusiasm for improvement had subsided in my mind; and though I felt a transient pleasure in the present picture of the happiness of these poor people and their healthy children, yet, as I rode home, the images faded away like a dream. I resolved, indeed, at some future period, to surpass all that Mr. M'Leod had done, or all that with his narrow income he could ever accomplish; and to this resolution I was prompted by jealousy of this man, rather than by benevolence. Before I had arranged, even in imagination, my plans, young Ormsby came one morning, and pressed me to return with him to Ormsby Villa. I yielded to his solicitations and to my own wishes. When I arrived, the ladies were all at their toilettes, except Miss Bland, who was in the book-room with the gentlemen, ready to receive me with her perpetual smile. Wherever Miss Bland went, she was always *l'amie de la maison*, accustomed to share with the lady of the house the labour of entertaining her guests. This *double* of Lady Ormsby talked to me most courteously of all the nothings of the day, and informed me of the changes which had taken place in the ever-varying succession of company at Ormsby Villa. The two brigadiers and one of the aides-de-camp were gone; but Captain Andrews, another castle aide-de-camp, was come, and my Lord O'Toole had arrived. Then followed a by-conversation between Miss Bland and some of the gentlemen, about the joy and sorrow which his lordship's arrival would create in the hearts of two *certain ladies*; one of whom, as I gathered from the innuendoes, was Lady Hauton, and the other Lady O'Toole. As I knew nothing of Dublin intrigues and scandal, I was little attentive to all this. Miss Bland, persisting in entertaining me, proceeded to inform me, that my Lord O'Toole had brought down with him Mr. Cecil Devereux, who was a wit and a poet, very handsome and gallant, and one of the most fashionable young men in Dublin. I determined not to like him—I always hated a flourish of trumpets; whoever enters, announced in this parading manner, appears to disadvantage. Mr. Cecil Devereux entered just as the flourish ceased. He was not at all the sort of person I was prepared to see: though handsome, and with the air of a man used to good company, there was nothing of a coxcomb in his manner; on the contrary, there was such an appearance of carelessness about himself, and deference towards others, that, notwithstanding the injudicious praise that had been bestowed on him, and my consequent resolution to dislike him, I was pleased and familiar with him before I had been ten minutes in his company. Lord Kilrush introduced him to me, with great pomposity, as a gentleman of talents, for whom he and his brother O'Toole interested themselves much. This air of patronage, I saw, disgusted Mr. Devereux; and instead of suffering himself to be *shown off*, he turned the conversation from his own poems to general subjects. He asked me some questions about a curious cavern, or subterraneous way, near Glenthorn Castle, which stretched from the sea-shore to a considerable distance under the rock, and communicated with an old abbey near the castle. Mr. Devereux said that such subterraneous places had been formerly used in Ireland as granaries by the ancient inhabitants; but a gentleman of the neighbourhood who was present observed, that the caverns on this coast had, within his memory, been used as hiding-places by smugglers: on this hint Lord Kilrush began a prosing dissertation upon smugglers and contraband traders, and talked to me a prodigious deal about exports and imports, and bounties, and the balance of trade. Not one word he said did I comprehend, and I question whether his lordship understood the subjects upon which he spoke so dictatorially; but he thought he succeeded in giving me an opinion of his wisdom and information. His brother O'Toole appeared next: he did not look like a man of gallantry, as I had been taught to expect from the hints thrown out respecting Lady Hauton; his lordship's whole soul seemed devoted to ambition, and he talked so much of great men, and state affairs, and court intrigues, and honours and preferments, that I began to fancy I had been buried alive, because I knew little of these things. I was tired of hearing him, yet mortified that I could not speak exactly in the same manner, and with the same air of being the best possible authority. I began to wish that I also had some interest at court. The cares and troubles of the ambitious man, so utterly repugnant to the indolence of my disposition, vanished in this moment of infatuation from my view, and I thought only of the pleasures of power. Such is the infectious nature of ambition!

Mr. Devereux helped me to throw off this dangerous contagion, before it did me any injury. He happened to stay in the room with me a quarter of an hour after the other gentlemen went to dress. Though not often disposed to conversation with a stranger, yet I was won by this gentleman's easy address: he politely talked of the English fashionable world, with which he knew that I was well acquainted; I, with equal politeness, recurred to the Irish great world: we fastened together upon Lord O'Toole, who took us to Dublin Castle; and I began to express my regret that I had not yet been at the Irish court, and that I had not earlier in life made myself of political consequence.

"Ambition," said I, "might help to keep a man awake and alive; all common pleasures have long since ceased to interest me—they really cannot make me stir."

"My lord," said Mr. Devereux, "you would do better to sit or lie still all your life than to toil for such vain objects.

> 'Full little knowest thou that hast not tried,
>
> What hell it is in sueing long to bide;'

Your lordship may remember Spenser's description of that hell?"

"Not exactly," said I, unwilling to lower the good opinion this gentleman seemed to have taken for granted of my literature. He took Spenser's poems out of the book-case, and I actually rose from my seat to read the passage; for what trouble will not even the laziest of mortals take to preserve the esteem of one by whom he sees that he is over-valued. I read the following ten lines without yawning!

> "Full little knowest thou that hast not tried,
>
> What hell it is in sueing long to bide;
>
> To lose good days, that might be better spent,
>
> To waste long nights in pensive discontent,
>
> To speed to-day, to be put back to-morrow,
>
> To feed on hope, to pine with fear and sorrow,
>
> To fret thy soul with crosses and with cares,
>
> To eat thy heart through comfortless despairs,
>
> To fawn, to crouch, to wait, to ride, to run,
>
> To spend, to give, to want, to be undone."

"Very strong, indeed," said I, with a competent air, as if used to judge of poetry.

"And it comes with still greater force, when we consider by whom it was written. A man, you know, my lord, who had been secretary to a lord lieutenant."

I felt my nascent ambition die away within me. I acknowledged it was better to spend an easy life. My determination was confirmed at this instant by the appearance of Lady Geraldine. Ambition and love, it is said, are incompatible passions. Neither of them had yet possession of my heart; but love and Lady Geraldine had perhaps a better chance than ambition and Lord O'Toole. Lady Geraldine appeared in high spirits; and, though I was not a vain man, I could not help fancying that my return to Ormsby Villa contributed to her charming vivacity. This gratified me secretly and soberly, as much as it visibly delighted her mother. Miss Bland, to pay her court to Lady Kildangan, observed that Lady Geraldine was in uncommonly fine spirits this evening. Lady Geraldine threw back a haughty frown over her left shoulder: this was the only time I ever saw her notice, in any manner, any thing that fell from her obsequious friend. To avert the fair one's displeasure, I asked for Miss Tracey and Mr. Gabbitt.

"Mr. Gabbitt," said her ladyship, resuming her good-humour instantly; "Mr. Gabbitt is gone off the happiest man in Ireland, with the hopes of surveying my Lord O'Toole's estate; a good job, which I was bound in honour to obtain for him, as a reward for taking a good joke. After mocking him with the bare imagination of a feast, you know the Barmecide in the Arabian Tales gave poor Shakabac a substantial dinner, a full equivalent for the jest."

"And Miss Tracey." said I, "what did your ladyship do for her?"

"I persuaded her mamma that the sweet creature was falling into an atrophy. So she carried the forlorn damsel post haste to the Black Rock for the recovery of her health, or her heart. Clementina, my dear, no reproachful looks; in your secret soul do not you know, that I could not do a young lady a greater favour than to give her a plausible excuse for getting away from home?"

I was afraid that Lady Geraldine would feel the want of her butt; however, I found that Miss Tracey's place was supplied by Captain Andrews, one of the Castle's aides-de-camp; and when Captain Andrews was out of the way, Lord Kilrush and his brother O'Toole were *good marks*. High and mighty as these personages thought themselves, and respectfully, nay obsequiously, as they were treated by most others, to this lady their characters appeared only a good *study*; and to laugh at them seemed only a *good practice*.

"Perhaps, my lord," said she to me, "you do not yet know my Lord O'Toole?"

"I have had the honour to be introduced to him."

"That's well; for he thinks that,

'Not to know him, argues yourself unknown.'

But as your lordship is a stranger in this country, you may be pardoned; and I will make you better acquainted with him. I suppose you know there are many Tooles in Ireland; some very ancient, respectable, and useful: this, however, is but a mere political tool, and the worst of all tools, a cat's paw. There's one thing to the credit of these brothers, they agree vastly well; for one delights in being always on the stage, and the other always behind the scenes. These brothers, with Captain Andrews—I hope they are none of them within hearing—form a charming trio, all admirable in their way. My Lord O'Toole is—artifice without art. My Lord Kilrush—importance without power. And Captain Andrews—pliability without ease. Poor Andrews! he's a defenceless animal—safe in impenetrable armour. Give him but time—as a man said, who once showed me a land-tortoise—give him but time to draw his head into his shell, and a broad-wheeled waggon may go over him without hurting him. Lord Glenthorn, did you ever observe Captain Andrews's mode of conversation?"

"No; I never heard him converse."

"Converse! nor I indeed; but you have heard him talk." "I have heard him say—*Very true*—and *Of course*."

"Lord Glenthorn is quite severe this evening," said Mrs. O'Connor.

"But though your lordship," continued Lady Geraldine, "may have observed Captain Andrews's wonderful economy of words, do you know whence it arises? Perhaps you think from his perception of his own want of understanding."

"Not from his perception of the want," said I.

"Again! again!" said Mrs. O'Connor, with an insulting tone of surprise; "Lord Glenthorn's quite witty this evening."

Lady Geraldine looked as if she were fully sensible of the want of politeness in Mrs. O'Connor's mode of praising. "But, my lord," pursued she, "you wrong Captain Andrews, if you attribute his monosyllabic replies either to stupidity or timidity. You have not guessed the reason why he never gives on any subject more than half an opinion."

"It was in the diplomatic school he was taught that art," said Mr. Devereux.

"You must know," pursued Lady Geraldine, "that Captain Andrews is only an aide-de-camp till a diplomatic situation can be found for him; and to do him justice, he has been so well trained in the diplomatic school, that he will not hazard an assertion on any subject; he is not certain of any thing, not even of his own identity."

"He assuredly wants," said Devereux, "the only proof of existence which Descartes would admit—*I think*, therefore I am."

"He has such a holy horror of committing himself," continued Lady Geraldine, "that if you were to ask him if the sun rose this morning, he would answer, with his sweet smile—*So I am told*—or—*So I am informed*."

"Begging your ladyship's pardon," cried Mr. Devereux, "that is much too affirmative. In the pure diplomatic style, impersonal verbs must ever be used in preference to active or passive. So I am told, lays him open to the dangerous questions, Who told you? or, By whom were you informed? Then he is forced into the imprudence of giving up his authorities; whereas he is safe in the impersonality of *So it is said*, or *So it is reported*."

"How I should like to see a meeting between two perfectly finished diplomatists!" cried Lady Geraldine.

"That is demonstrably impossible," said Mr. Devereux; "for in certain political, as well as in certain geometrical lines, there is a continual effort to approach, without a possibility of meeting."

Lady Geraldine's raillery, like all other things, would, perhaps, soon have become tiresome to me; but that there was infinite variety in her humour. At first I had thought her merely superficial, and intent solely upon her own amusement; but I soon found that she had a taste for literature, beyond what could have been expected in one who lived so dissipated a life; a depth of reflection that seemed inconsistent with the rapidity with which she thought; and, above all, a degree of generous indignation against meanness and vice, which seemed incompatible with the selfish character of a fine lady, and which appeared quite incomprehensible to the imitating tribe of her fashionable companions.

I mentioned a Mrs. Norton and Lady Hauton amongst the company of Ormsby Villa. These two English ladies, whom I had never met in any of the higher circles in London, who were persons of no consequence, and of no marked character in their own country, made, it seems, a prodigious *sensation* when they came over to Ireland, and turned the heads of half Dublin by the extravagance of their dress, the impertinence of their airs, and the audacity of their conduct. Fame flew before them to the remote parts of the country; and when they arrived at Ormsby Villa, all the country gentlemen and ladies were prepared to admire these celebrated fashionable belles. All worshipped them present, and abused them absent, except Lady Geraldine, who neither joined in the admiration nor inquired into the scandal. One morning Mrs. Norton and Lady Hauton had each collected her votaries round her: one group begging patterns of dress from Lady Hauton, who stood up in the midst of them, to have everything she wore examined and envied; the other group sat on a sofa apart, listening to Mrs. Norton, who, *sotto voce*, was telling interesting anecdotes of an English crim. con., which then occupied the attention of the fashionable world. Mrs. Norton had letters *from the best authorities* in London, which she was entreated by her auditors to read to them. Mrs. Norton went to look for the letters, Lady Hauton to direct her woman to furnish some patterns of I know not what articles of dress; and, in the mean time, all the company joined in canvassing the merits and demerits of the dress and characters of the two ladies who had just left the room. Lady Geraldine, who had kept aloof, and who was examining some prints at the farther end of the room, at this instant laid down her book, and looked upon the whole party with an air of magnanimous disdain; then smiling, as in scorn, she advanced towards them, and, in a tone of irony, addressing one of the Swanlinbar graces, "My dear Theresa," said her ladyship, "you are absolutely ashamed, I see, of not being quite naked; and you, my good Bess, will, no doubt, very soon be equally scandalized, at the imputation of being a perfectly modest woman. Go on, my friends; go on, and prosper; beg and borrow all the patterns and precedents you can collect of the newest fashions of folly and vice. Make haste, make haste; they don't reach our remote island fast enough. We Irish might live in innocence half a century longer, if you didn't expedite the progress of profligacy; we might escape the plague that rages in neighbouring countries, if we didn't, without any quarantine, and with open arms, welcome every *suspected* stranger; if we didn't encourage the importation of whole bales of tainted fineries, that will spread the contagion from Dublin to Cork, and from Cork to Galway!"

"La!" said Miss Ormsby, "how severe your ladyship is; and all only for one's asking for a pattern!"

"But you know," pursued Mrs. O'Connor, "that Lady Geraldine is too proud to take pattern from any body."

"Too proud am I? Well, then, I'll be humble; I'll abase myself—shall I?

'Proud as I am, I'll put myself to school;'

and I'll do what the ladies Hauton and Norton shall advise, to heighten my charms and preserve my reputation. I must begin, must not I, Mrs. O'Connor, by learning not to blush? for I observed you were ashamed for me yesterday at dinner, when I blushed at something said by one of our fair missionaries. Then, to whatever lengths flirtations and gallantry may go between unmarried or married people, I must look on. I may shut my eyes, if I please, and look down; but not from shame—from affectation I may as often as I please, or to show my eyelashes. Memorandum—to practise this before Clementina Ormsby, my mirror of fashion. So far, so good, for my looks; but now for my language. I must reform my barbarous language, and learn from Mrs. Norton, with her pretty accommodating voice, to call an intrigue *an arrangement*, and a crim. con. *an affair in Doctors' Commons*, or *that business before the Lords.*

'We never mention Hell to ears polite.'

How virtuous we shall be when we have no name for vice! But stay, I must mind my lessons—I have more, much more to learn. From the dashing Lady Hauton I may learn, if my head be but strong, and my courage intrepid enough, 'to touch the brink of all we hate,' without tumbling headlong into the gulf; and from the interesting Mrs. Norton, as I hear it whispered amongst you ladies, I may learn how, with the assistance of a Humane-society, to save a half-drowned reputation. It is, I understand, the glory of one class of fashionable females, to seem worse than they are; and of another class the privilege, to be worse than they seem."

Here clamorous voices interrupted Lady Geraldine—some justifying, some attacking, Lady Hauton and Mrs. Norton.

"Oh! Lady Geraldine, I assure you, notwithstanding all that was said about General —— and Mrs. Norton, I am convinced there was nothing in it."

"And, my dear Lady Geraldine, though Lady Hauton does go great lengths in coquetting with a certain lord, you must see that there's *nothing wrong*; and that she means nothing, but to provoke his lady's jealousy. You know his lordship is not a man to fall in love with."

"So, because Lady Hauton's passion is hatred instead of love, and because her sole object is to give pain to a poor wife, and to make mischief in families, all her sins are to be forgiven! Now, if I were forced to forgive any ill-conducted female, I would rather excuse the woman who is hurried on by love than she who is instigated by hatred."

Miss Bland now began to support her ladyship's opinion, that "Lady Hauton was much the worst of the two;" and all the scandal that was in circulation was produced by the partisans of each of these ladies.

"No matter, no matter, which is the worst," cried Lady Geraldine; "don't let us waste our time in repeating or verifying scandalous stories of either of them. I have no enmity to these ladies; I only despise them, or rather, their follies and their faults. It is not the sinner, but the sin we should reprobate. Oh! my dear countrywomen," cried Lady Geraldine, with increasing animation of countenance and manner—"Oh! my dear countrywomen, let us never stoop to admire and imitate these second-hand airs and graces, follies and vices. Let us dare to be ourselves!"

My eyes were fixed upon her animated countenance, and, I believe, I continued gazing even after her voice ceased. Mrs. O'Connor pointed this out, and I was immediately embarrassed. Miss Bland accounted for my embarrassment by supposing, that what Lady Geraldine had said of English crim. cons, had affected me. From a look and a whisper among the ladies,

I guessed this; but Lady Geraldine was too well-bred to suppose I could suspect her of ill-breeding and ill-nature, or that I could apply to myself what evidently was not intended to allude to my family misfortunes. By an openness of manner and sweetness of expression, which I cannot forget, she, in one single look, conveyed all this to me: and then resuming her conversation, "Pray, my lord," said she, "you who have lived so much in the great world in England, say, for you can, whether I am right or wrong in my suspicion, that these ladies, who have made such a noise in Ireland, have been little heard of in England?"

I confirmed her ladyship's opinion by my evidence. The faces of the company changed. Thus, in a few seconds, the empire of Lady Hauton and of Mrs. Norton seemed shaken to the foundation, and never recovered from this shock.

The warmth of Lady Geraldine's expressions, on this and many other occasions, wakened dormant feelings in my heart, and made me sensible that I had a soul, and that I was superior to the puppets with whom I had been classed.

One day Lady Kilrush, in her mixed mode, with partly the graces of a fine lady and partly the airs of a *bel esprit*, was talking of Mr. Devereux, whom she affected to patronise and *produce*.

"Here, Devereux!" cried she; "Cecil Devereux! What can you be thinking of? I am talking to you. Here's this epitaph of Francis the First upon Petrarch's Laura, that you showed me the other day: do you know, I dote upon it. I must have it translated: nobody can do it so well as you. I have not time; but I shall not sleep to-night if it is not done: and you are so quick: so sit down here, there's a dear man, and do it in your elegant way for me, whilst I go to my toilette. Perhaps you did not know that my name was Laura," said she, leaving the room with a very sentimental air.

"What will become of me!" cried Devereux. "Never was a harder task set by cruel patroness. I would rather 'turn a Persian tale for half-a-crown.' Read this, my lord, and tell me whether it will be easy to turn my Lady Kilrush into Petrarch's Laura."

"This sonnet, to be sure, is rather difficult to translate, or at least to modernize, as bespoke," said Lady Geraldine, after she had perused the sonnet;82 "but I think, Mr. Devereux, you brought this difficulty upon yourself. How came you to show these lines to such an amateur, such a fetcher and carrier of bays as Lady Kilrush? You might have been certain that, had they been trash, with the name of Francis the First, and with your fashionable approbation, and something to say about Petrarch and Laura, my Lady Kilrush would talk for ever, *et se pâmerait d'affectation*."

"Mr. Devereux," said I, "has only to abide by the last lines, as a good and sufficient apology to Lady Kilrush for his silence:

'Qui te pourra louer qu'en se taisant?

Car la parole est toujours réprimée

Quand le sujet surmonte le disant.'"

"There is no way to get out of my difficulties," said Mr. Devereux, with a very melancholy look; and with a deep sigh he sat down to attempt the translation of the poem. In a few minutes, however, he rose and left the room, declaring that he had the bad habit of not being able to do any thing in company.

Lady Geraldine now, with much energy of indignation, exclaimed against the pretensions of rich amateurs, and the mean and presumptuous manner in which some would-be great people affect to patronise genius.

"Oh! the baseness, the emptiness of such patronising ostentation!" cried she. "I am accused of being proud myself; but I hope—I believe—I am sure, that my pride is of another sort. Persons of any elevation or generosity of mind never have this species of pride; but it is your mean, second-rate folk, who imagine that people of talent are a sort of raree-show for their entertainment. At best, they consider men of genius only as artists formed for their use, who, if not in a situation to be paid with money, are yet to be easily recompensed by praise—by their praise—*their* praise! Heavens! what conceit! And these amateur-patrons really think themselves judges, and presume to advise and direct genius, and employ it to their petty purposes! Like that Pietro de Medici, who, at some of his entertainments, set Michael Angelo to make a statue of snow. My lord, did you ever happen to meet with Les Mémoires de Madame de Staël?"

"No: I did not know that they were published."

"You mistake me: I mean Madame de Staël of Louis the Fourteenth and the Regent's time, Mademoiselle de Launay."

I had never heard of such a person, and I blushed for my ignorance.

"Nay, I met with them myself only yesterday," said Lady Geraldine: "I was struck with the character of the Duchess de la Ferté, in which this kind of proud patronising ignorance is admirably painted from the life. It is really worth your while, my lord, to look at it. There's the book on that little table; here is the passage. You see, this Duchess de la Ferté is showing off to a sister-duchess a poor girl of genius, like a puppet or an ape.

"'Allons, mademoiselle, parlez—Madame, vous allez voir comme elle parle—Elle vit que j'hésitois à répondre, et pensa qu'il falloit m'aider comme une chanteuse à qui l'on indique ce qu'on désire d'entendre—Parlez un peu de religion, mademoiselle, vous direz ensuite autre chose.'

"This speech, Mr. Devereux tells me, has become quite proverbial in Paris," continued Lady Geraldine; "and it is often quoted, when any one presumes in the Duchess de la Ferte's style."

"Ignorance, either in high or low life, is equally self-sufficient, I believe," said I, exerting myself to illustrate her ladyship's remarks. "A gentleman of my acquaintance lately went to buy some razors at Packwood's. Mrs. Packwood alone was *visible*. Upon the gentleman's complimenting her on the infinite variety of her husband's ingenious and poetical advertisements, she replied, 'La! sir, and do you think husband has time to write them there things his-self? Why, sir, we keeps a poet to do all that there work.'"

Though Lady Geraldine spoke only in general of amateur-patrons and of men of genius, yet I could not help fancying, from the warmth with which she expressed herself, and from her dwelling on the subject so long, that her feelings were peculiarly interested for some individual of this description. Thus I discovered that Lady Geraldine had a heart; and I suspected that her ladyship and Mr. Devereux had also made the same discovery. This suspicion was strengthened by a slight incident, which occurred the following evening.

Lady Geraldine and Cecil Devereux, as we were drinking coffee, were in a recessed window, while some of the company stood round them, amused by their animated conversation. They went on, repartee after repartee, as if inspired by each other's spirits.

"You two," said a little girl of six years old, who was playing in the window, "go on singing to one another like two nightingales; and this shall be your cage," added she, drawing the drapery of the window-curtains across the recessed window. "You shall live always together in this cage: will you, pretty birds?"

"No, no; some birds cannot live in a cage, my dear," cried Lady Geraldine, playfully struggling to get free, whilst the child held her prisoner.

"Mr. Devereux seems tolerably quiet and contented in his cage," said the shrewd Mrs. O'Connor.

"I can't get out! I can't get out!" cried Devereux, in the melancholy tone of the starling in the Sentimental Journey.

"What is all this?" said my Lady Kildangan, sailing up to us.

"Only two birds," the child began.

"Singing-birds," interrupted Lady Geraldine, catching the little girl up in her arms, and stopping her from saying more, by beginning to sing most charmingly.

Lady Kildangan returned to the sofa without comprehending one word of what had passed. For my part, I now felt almost certain of the justice of my suspicions: I was a little vexed, but not by any means in that despair into which a man heartily in love would have been thrown by such a discovery.

Well, thought I, it is well it is no worse: it was very lucky that I did not fall quite in love with this fair lady, since it seems that she has given her heart away. But am I certain of this? I was mistaken once. Let me examine more carefully.

Now I had a new motive to keep my attention awake.

CHAPTER XI

To preserve the continuity of my story, and not to fatigue the reader with the journals of my comings and goings from Ormsby Villa to Glenthorn Castle, and from Glenthorn Castle to Ormsby Villa, I must here relate the observations I made, and the incidents that occurred, during various visits at Sir Harry Ormsby's in the course of the summer.

After the incident of the birds and cage, my sagacity was for some time at fault. I could not perceive any further signs of intelligence between the parties: on the contrary, all communication seemed abruptly to cease. As I was not well versed in such affairs, this quieted my suspicions, and I began to think that I had been entirely mistaken. Cecil Devereux spent his days shut up in his own apartment, immersed, as far as I could understand, in the study of the Persian language. He talked to me of nothing but his hopes of an appointment which Lord O'Toole had promised to procure for him in India. When he was not studying, he was botanizing or *mineralogizing* with O'Toole's chaplain. I did not envy him his new mode of life. Lady Geraldine took no notice of it. When they did meet, which happened as seldom as possible, there was an air of haughty displeasure on her part; on his, steady and apparently calm respect and self-satisfaction. Her spirits were exuberant, but variable; and, at times, evidently forced: his were not high, but even and certain. Towards me, her ladyship's manners were free from coquetry, yet politely gratifying, as she marked, by the sort of conversation she addressed to me, her opinion that I was superior in ability and capability to what she had at first thought me, and to what I had always thought myself.

Mr. Devereux, though with more effort, treated me with distinction, and showed a constant desire to cultivate my friendship. On every occasion he endeavoured to raise my opinion of myself: to give me ambition and courage to cultivate my mind. Once, when I was arguing in favour of natural genius, and saying that I thought no cultivation could make the abilities of one man equal to those of another, he, without seeming to perceive that I was apologizing at once for my own indolence and my intellectual inferiority, answered in general terms, "It is difficult to judge what are the natural powers of the mind, they appear so different in different circumstances. You can no more judge of a mind in ignorance than of a plant in darkness.

A philosophical friend told me, that he once thought he had discovered a new and strange plant growing in a mine. It was common sage; but so degenerated and altered, that he could not know it: he planted it in the open air and in the light, and gradually it resumed its natural appearance and character."

Mr. Devereux excited, without fatiguing, my mind by his conversation; and I was not yet sufficiently in love to be seriously jealous. I was resolved, however, to sound him upon the subject of Lady Geraldine, I waited for a good opportunity: at length, as we were looking together over the prints of Bürger's Lenore, he led to the sort of conversation that I desired, by telling me an anecdote relative to the poet, which he had lately heard from a German baron.

Burger was charmed with a sonnet, which an unknown fair one addressed to him, in praise of his poetry; he replied in equal strains; and they went on flattering one another, till both believed themselves in love: without ever having met, they determined to marry: they at length met, and married: they quarrelled and parted: in other words, the gentleman was terribly disappointed in his unknown mistress; and she consoled herself by running away from him with another lover.

The imprudence of this poetic couple led us to reflections on love and marriage in general. Keeping far away from all allusion to Lady Geraldine, I rallied Mr. Devereux about the fair Clementina, who was evidently a romantic admirer of his.

"Who, except Cupid, would barter his liberty for a butterfly?" said he; "and Cupid was a child. Men now-a-days are grown too wise to enslave themselves for women. Love occupies a vast space in a woman's thoughts, but fills a small portion in a man's life. Women are told, that 'The great, th' important business of their life, is love;' but men know that they are born for something better than to sing mournful ditties to a mistress's eyebrow. As to marriage, what a serious, terrible thing! Some quaint old author says, that man is of too smooth and oily a nature to climb up to heaven, if, to make him less slippery, there be not added to his composition the vinegar of marriage. This may be; but I will keep as long as possible from the vinegar."

"Really, Devereux," said I, smiling, "you talk so like a cynic and an old bachelor, and you look so little like either, that it is quite ridiculous."

"A man must be ridiculous sometimes," said he, "and bear to be thought so. No man ever distinguished himself, who could not bear to be laughed at."

Mr. Devereux left the room singing,

"No more for Amynta fresh garlands I wove;

Ambition, I said, will soon cure me of love."

I was uncertain what to think of all this. I inclined to believe that ambition was his ruling passion, notwithstanding the description of that Hell which he showed me in Spenser. His conduct to his patron-lords, by which a surer judgment of his character could be formed than by his professions, was not, however, that of a man merely intent upon rising in the world.

I remember once hearing Lord O'Toole attack a friend of this gentleman's, calling him, in a certain tone, *a philosopher*. Mr. Devereux replied, "that he could not consider that as a term of reproach; that where a false or pretended philosopher was meant, some other name should be used, equivalent to the Italian term of reproach, *filosofastro.*"

Lord O'Toole would by no means admit of this Italianism: he would make no distinctions: he deemed philosophers altogether a race of beings dangerous and inimical to states.

"For states read statesmen," said Devereux, who persisted in the vindication of his friend till Lord O'Toole grew pale with anger, while Captain Andrews smiled with ineffable contempt at the political *bévue*: Lady Geraldine glowed with generous indignation.

Afterwards, in speaking to me of Lord O'Toole, Devereux said, "His lordship's classification of men is as contracted as the savage's classification of animals: he divides mankind into two classes, knaves and fools; and when he meets with an honest man, he does not know what to make of him."

My esteem for Mr. Devereux was much increased by my daily observations upon his conduct: towards Lady Geraldine, I thought it particularly honourable: when her displeasure evidently merged in esteem, when her manners again became most winning and attractive, his continued uniformly the same; never passing the bounds of friendly respect, or swerving, in the slightest degree, from the line of conduct which he had laid down for himself. I thought I now understood him perfectly. That he liked Lady Geraldine I could scarcely doubt; but I saw that he refrained from aiming at the prize which he knew he ought not to obtain; that he perceived her ladyship's favourable disposition towards him, yet denied himself not only the gratification of his vanity, but the exquisite pleasure of conversing with her, lest he should stand in the way of her happier prospects. He frequently spoke to me of her ladyship in terms of the warmest approbation. He said, that all the world saw and admired her talents and beauty, but that he had had opportunities, as a relation, of studying her domestic life. "With all her vivacity, she has a heart formed for tenderness," said he; "a high sense of duty, the best security for a woman's conduct; and in generosity and magnanimity, I never found her superior in either sex. In short, I never saw any woman whose temper and disposition were more likely to make a man of sense and feeling supremely happy."

I could not forbear smiling, and asking Cecil Devereux how all this accorded with his late professions of hatred to marriage. "My professions were sincere," said he. "It would be misery to me to marry any inferior woman, and I am not in circumstances to marry as I could wish. I could not think of Lady Geraldine without a breach of trust, of which your lordship, I hope, cannot suspect me. Her mother places confidence in me. I am not only a relation, but treated as a friend of the family. I am not in love with Lady Geraldine. I admire, esteem, respect her ladyship; and I wish to see her united to a man, if such a man there be, who may deserve her. We understand one another now. Your lordship will have the goodness never more to speak to me on this subject." He spoke with much emotion, but with steadiness, and left me penetrated with feelings that were entirely new to me.

Much as I admired his conduct, I was yet undecided as to my own: my aversion to a second marriage was not yet conquered:—I was amused, I was captivated by Lady Geraldine; but I could not bring myself to think of making a distinct proposal. Captain Andrews himself was not more afraid of being committed than I was upon this tender subject. To gain time, I now thought it necessary to verify all the praises Mr. Devereux had bestowed on her ladyship. Magnanimity was a word that particularly struck my ear as extraordinary when applied to a female. However, by attending carefully to this lady, I thought I discovered what Mr. Devereux meant. Lady Geraldine was superior to manoeuvring little arts and petty stratagems to attract attention: she would not stoop, even to conquer. From gentlemen she seemed to expect attention as her right, as the right of her sex; not to beg or accept of it as a favour: if it were not paid, she deemed the gentleman degraded, not herself. Far from being mortified by any preference shown to other ladies, her countenance betrayed only a sarcastic sort of pity for the bad taste of the men, or an absolute indifference and look of haughty absence. I saw that she beheld with disdain the paltry competitions of the young ladies her companions: as her companions, indeed, she hardly seemed to consider them; she tolerated their foibles, forgave their envy, and never exerted any superiority, except to show her contempt of vice and meanness. To be in any degree excepted from the common herd; to be in any degree distinguished by a lady so proud, and with so many good reasons to be proud, was flattering to my self-love. She gave me no direct encouragement;

but I never advanced far enough to require encouragement, much less to justify repulse. Sometimes I observed, or I fancied, that she treated me with more favour when Mr. Devereux was present than at other times; perhaps—for she was a woman, not an angel—to pique Devereux, and try if she could move him from the settled purpose of his soul. He bore it all with surprising constancy: his spirits, however, and his health, began visibly to decline.

"If I do not intrude too much on your valuable time, Mr. Devereux," said her ladyship to him one evening, in her most attractive manner, "may I beg you to read to us some of these beautiful poems of Sir William Jones?"

There was a seat beside her ladyship on the sofa: the book was held out by the finest arm in the world.

"Nay," said Lady Geraldine, "do not look so respectfully miserable; if you have any other engagements, you have only to say so: or if you cannot speak you may bow: a bow, you know, is an answer to every thing. And here is my Lord Glenthorn ready to supply your place: pray, do not let me detain you prisoner. You shall not a second time say, *I can't get out.*"

Devereux made no further effort to escape, but took the book and his dangerous seat. He remained with us, contrary to his custom, the whole evening. Afterwards, as if he felt that some apology was necessary to me for the pleasure in which he had indulged himself, "Perhaps, my lord," said he, "another man in my situation, and with my feelings, would think it necessary to retreat, and prudent to secure his safety by flight; but flight is unworthy of him who can combat and conquer: the man who is sure of himself does not skulk away to avoid danger, but advances to meet it, armed secure in honesty."

This proud and rash security in his own courage, strength of mind, and integrity, was the only fault of Cecil Devereux. He never prayed not to be led into temptation, he thought himself so sure of avoiding evil. Unconscious of his danger, even though his disease was at its height, he now braved it most imprudently: he was certain that he should never pass the bounds of friendship; he had proved this to himself, and was satisfied: he told me that he could with indifference, nay, with pleasure, see Lady Geraldine mine. In the mean time, upon the same principle that he deemed flight inglorious, he was proud to expose himself to the full force of Love's artillery. He was with us now every day, and almost all day, and Lady Geraldine was more charming than ever. The week was fixed for her departure. Still I could not decide. I understood that her ladyship would pass the ensuing winter in Dublin, where she would probably meet with new adorers; and even if Mr. Devereux should not succeed, some adventurous knight might win and wear the prize. This was an alarming thought. It almost decided me to hazard the fatal declaration; but then I recollected that I might follow her ladyship to town the next winter, and that if the impression did not, as might be hoped, wear off during the intervening autumn, it would be time enough to *commit* myself when I should meet my fair one in Dublin. This was at last my fixed resolution. Respited from the agonies of doubt, I now waited very tranquilly for that moment to which most lovers look forward with horror, the moment of separation. I was sensible that I had accustomed myself to think about this lady so much, that I had gradually identified my existence with hers, and I thus found my *spirit of animation* much increased. I dreaded the departure of Lady Geraldine less than the return of ennui.

In this frame of mind I was walking one morning in the pleasure grounds with Lady Geraldine, when a slight accident made me act in direct contradiction to all my resolutions, and, I think, inconsistently with my character. But such is the nature of man! and I was doomed to make a fool of myself, even in the very temple of Minerva. Among the various ornamental buildings in the grounds at Ormsby Villa, there was a temple dedicated to this goddess, from which issued a troop of hoyden young ladies, headed by the widow O'Connor and Lady Kilrush, all calling to us to come and look at some charming discovery which they had just made in the temple of Minerva. Thither we proceeded, accompanied by the merry troop. We found in the temple only a poetical inscription of Lady Kilrush's, pompously engraved on a fine marble tablet. We read the lines with all the attention usually paid to a lady's poetry in the presence of the poetess. Lady Geraldine and I turned to pay some compliments on the performance, when we found that Lady Kilrush and all her companions were gone.

"Gone! all gone!" said Lady Geraldine; "and there they are, making their way very fast down to the temple of Folly! Lady Kilrush, you know, is so ba-a-ashful, she could not possibly stay to receive *nos hommages*. I love to laugh at affectation. Call them back, do, my lord, and you shall see the *fair author* go through all the evolutions of mock humility, and end by yielding quietly to the notion that she is the tenth Muse. But run, my lord, or they will be out of our reach."

I never was seen to run on any occasion; but to obey Lady Geraldine I walked as fast as I could to the door, and, to my surprise, found it fastened.

"Locked, I declare! Some of the witty tricks of the widow O'Connor, or the hoyden Miss Callwells!"

"How I hate hoydens!" cried Lady Geraldine: "but let us take patience; they will be back presently. If young ladies must perform practical jokes, because quizzing is the fashion, I wish they would devise something new. This locking-up is so stale a jest. To be sure it has lately to boast the authority of high rank in successful practice: but these bungling imitators never distinguish between cases the most dissimilar imaginable. Silly creatures! We have only to be wise and patient."

Her ladyship sat down to re-peruse the tablet. I never saw her look so beautiful.—The dignified composure of her manner charmed me; it was so unlike the paltry affectation of some of the fashionable ladies by whom I had been disgusted. I recollected the precedent to which she alluded. I recollected that the locking-up ended in matrimony; and as Lady Geraldine made some remarks upon the verses, I suppose my answers showed my absence of mind.

"Why so grave, my lord? why so absent? I assure you I do not suspect your lordship of having any hand in this vulgar manoeuvre. I acquit you honourably; therefore you need not stand any longer like a criminal."

What decided me at this instant I cannot positively tell: whether it was the awkwardness of my own situation, or the grace of her ladyship's manner: but all my prudential arrangements were forgotten, all my doubts vanished. Before I knew that the words passed my lips, I replied, "That her ladyship did me justice by such an acquittal; but that though I had no part in the contrivance, yet I felt irresistibly impelled to avail myself of the opportunity it afforded of declaring my real sentiments." I was at her ladyship's feet, and making very serious love, before I knew where I was. In what words my long-delayed declaration was made, I cannot recollect, but I well remember Lady Geraldine's answer.

"My lord, I assure you that you do not know what you are saying: you do not know what you are doing. This is all a mistake, as you will find half an hour hence. I will not be so cruelly vain as to suppose you serious."

"Not serious! no man ever was more serious."

"No, no—No, no, no."

I swore, of course, most fervently.

"Oh! rise, rise, I beseech you, my lord, and don't look so like a hero; though you have done an heroical action, I grant. How you ever brought yourself to it, I cannot imagine. But now, for your comfort, you are safe— Vous voilà quitte pour la peur! Do not, however, let this encourage you to venture again in the same foolish manner. I know but few, very few young ladies to whom Lord Glenthorn could offer himself with any chance or reasonable hope of being refused. So take warning: never again expect to meet with such another as my whimsical self."

"Never, never can I expect to meet with any thing resembling your charming self," cried I. This was a new text for a lover's rhapsody. It is not necessary, and might not be *generally* interesting to repeat all the ridiculous things I said, even if I could remember them.

Lady Geraldine listened to me, and then very calmly replied, "Granting you believe all that you are saying at this minute, which I must grant from common gratitude, and still more common vanity; nevertheless, permit me to assure you, my lord, that this is not love; it is only a fancy—only the nettle-rash, not the plague. You will not die this time. I will insure your life. So now jump out of the window as fast as you can, and unlock the door—you need not be afraid of breaking your neck—you know your life is insured. Come, take the lover's leap, and get rid of your passion at once."

I grew angry.

"Only a cloud," said Lady Geraldine—"it will blow over."

I became more passionate—I did not know the force of my own feelings, till they met with an obstacle; they suddenly rose to a surprising height.

"Now, my lord," cried Lady Geraldine with a tone and look of comic vexation, "this is really the most provoking thing imaginable; you have no idea how you distress me, nor of what exquisite pleasures you deprive me— all the pleasures of coquetry; legitimate pleasures, in certain circumstances, as I am instructed to think them by one of the first moral authorities. There is a case—I quote from memory, my lord; for my memory, like that of most other people, on subjects where I am deeply interested, is tolerably tenacious—there is a case, says the best of fathers, in his Legacy to the best of daughters—there is a case, where a woman may coquet justifiably to the utmost verge which her conscience will allow. It is where a gentleman purposely declines making his addresses, till such time as he thinks himself perfectly sure of her consent. Now, my lord, if you had had the goodness to do so, I might have made this delightful case my own; and what charming latitude I might have allowed my conscience! But now, alas! it is all over, and I must be as frank as you have been, under pain of forfeiting what I value more even than admiration—my own good opinion."

She paused, and was silent for a few moments; then suddenly changing her manner, she exclaimed, in a serious, energetic tone, "Yes, I must, I will be sincere; let it cost me what it may. I will be sincere. My lord, I never can be yours. My lord, you will believe me, even from the effort with which I speak:" her voice softened, and her face suffused with crimson, as she spoke. "I love another—my heart is no longer in my own possession; whether it will ever be in my power, consistently with my duty and his principles, to be united with the man of my choice, is doubtful—more than doubtful—but this is certain, that with such a prepossession, such a conviction in my mind, I never could nor ought to think of marrying any other person."

I pleaded, that however deserving of her preference the object of her favour might be, yet that if there were, as her own prudence seemed to suggest, obstacles, rendering the probability of her union with that person more than doubtful, it might be possible that her superior sense and strength of mind, joined to the persevering affection of another lover, who would spare no exertions to render himself worthy of her, might, perhaps, in time—

"No, no," said she, interrupting me; "do not deceive yourself. I will not deceive you. I give you no hopes that my sentiments may change. I know my own mind—it will not change. My attachment is founded on the firm basis of esteem; my affection has grown from the intimate knowledge of the principles and conduct of the man I love. No other man, let his merits be what they may, could have these advantages in my opinion. And when I say that the probability of our being united is more than doubtful, I do not mean to deny that I have distant hope that change of circumstances might render love and duty compatible. Without hope I know love cannot long exist. You see I do not talk romantic nonsense to you. All that you say of prudence, and time, and the effect of the attentions of another admirer, would be perfectly just and applicable, if my attachment were a fancy of yesterday—if it were a mere young lady's commonplace first love; but I am not a *very* young lady, nor is this, though a first love, commonplace. I do not, you see, in the usual style, tell you that the man I adore is an angel, and that no created form ever did, or ever can, resemble this *angel in green and gold*; but, on the contrary, do justice to your lordship's merit: and believing, as I do, that you are capable of a real love; still more, believing that such an attachment would rouse you to exertion, and bring to life and light a surprising number of good qualities; yet I should deceive you unpardonably, fatally for my own peace of mind, if not for yours, were I not frankly and decidedly to assure you, that I never could reward or return your affection. My attachment to—I trust entirely where I trust at all—my attachment to Mr. Devereux is for life."

"He deserves it—deserves it all," cried I, struggling for utterance; "that is as much as a rival can say."

"Not more than I expected from you, my lord."

"But your ladyship says there is a hope of duty and love being compatible. *Would* Lady Kildangan *ever* consent?"

She looked much disturbed.

"No, certainly; not unless—Lord O'Toole has promised—not that I depend on courtiers' promises—but Lord O'Toole is a relation of ours, and he has promised to obtain an appointment abroad, in India, for Mr. Devereux. If that were done, he might appear of more consequence in the eyes of the world. My mother might then, perhaps, be propitious. My lord, I give you the strongest proof of my esteem, by speaking with such openness. I have had the honour of your lordship's acquaintance only a few months; but without complimenting my own penetration, I may securely trust to the judgment of Mr. Devereux, and his example has taught me to feel confidence in your lordship. Your conduct now will, I trust, justify my good opinion, by your secrecy; and by desisting from useless pursuit you will entitle yourself to my esteem and gratitude. These, I presume, you will think worth securing."

My soul was so completely touched, that I could not articulate.

"Mr. Devereux is right—I see, my lord, that you have a soul that can be touched."

"Kissing hands, I protest!" exclaimed a shrill voice at the window. We turned, and saw Mrs. O'Connor and a group of tittering faces peeping in. "Kissing hands, after a good hour's tête-à-tête! Oh, pray, Lady Kildangan, make haste here," continued Mrs. O'Connor; "make haste, before Lady Geraldine's blushes are over."

"Were you ever detected in the crime of blushing, in your life, Mrs. O'Connor?" said I.

"I never was found out locked up with so fine a gentleman," replied Mrs. O'Connor.

"Then it hurts your conscience only to be found out, like all the rest of the vast family of the Surfaces," said Lady Geraldine, resuming her spirit.

"Found out!—Locked up!—bless me! bless me! What is all this?" cried Lady Kildangan, puffing up the hill. "For shame! young ladies; for shame!" continued her ladyship, with a decent suppression of her satisfaction, when she saw, or thought she saw, how matters stood. "Unlock the door, pray. Don't be vexed, my Geraldine. Fie! fie! Mrs. O'Connor. But quizzing is now so fashionable—nobody can be angry with any body. My Geraldine, consider we are all friends."

The door unlocked, and as we were going out, Lady Geraldine whispered to me—"For mercy's sake, my lord, don't break my poor mother's heart!

Never let her know that a coronet has been within my grasp, and that I have not clutched it."

Lady Kildangan, who thought that all was now approaching that happy termination she so devoutly wished, was so full of her own happy presentiments, that it was impossible for me to undeceive her ladyship. Even when I announced before her, to Sir Harry Ormsby, that I was obliged to return home immediately, on particular business, she was, I am sure, persuaded that I was going to prepare matters for marriage-settlements. When I mounted my horse, Mr. Devereux pressed through a crowd assembled on the steps at the hall-door, and offered me his hand, with a look and manner that seemed to say—Have you sufficient generosity to be still my friend? "I know the value of your friendship, Mr. Devereux," said I, "and I hope to deserve it better every year that I live."

For the effort which it cost me to say this I was rewarded. Lady Geraldine, who had retired behind her companions, at this instant approached with an air of mingled grace and dignity, bowed her head, and gave me a smile of grateful approbation. This is the last image left on my mind, the last look of the charming Geraldine—I never saw her again.

After I got home I did not shave for two days, and scarcely ever spoke. I should have taken to my bed to avoid seeing any human creature; but I knew that if I declared myself ill, no power would keep my old nurse Ellinor from coming to moan over me; and I was not in a humour to listen to stories of the Irish Black Beard, or the ghost of King O'Donoghoe; nor could I, however troublesome, have repulsed the simplicity of her affection. Instead of going to bed, therefore, I continued to lie stretched upon a sofa, ruminating sweet and bitter thoughts, after giving absolute orders that I should not be disturbed on any account whatever. Whilst I was in this state of reverie, one of my servants—an odd Irish fellow, who, under pretence of being half-witted, took more liberties than his companions—bolted into my presence.

"Plase your lordship, I thought it my duty, in spite of 'em all below, to come up to advertise to your lordship of the news that's going through the country. That they are all upside down at Ormsby Villa, all mad entirely— fighting and setting off through the kingdom, every one their own way; and, they say, it's all on account of something that Miss Clemmy Ormsby told, that Lady Geraldine said about my Lord O'Toole's being no better than a cat's paw, or something that way, which made his lordship quite mad; and he said, in the presence of Captain Andrews, and my Lady Kildangan, and Lady Geraldine, and all that were in it, something that vexed Lady Geraldine, which made Mr. Cecil Devereux mad next; and he said something smart in reply, that Lord O'Toole could not digest, he said, which made his lordship madder than ever, and he discharged Mr. Devereux from his favour, and he is not to get that place that was vacant, the lord-lieutenancy of some place in the Indies that he was to have had; this made Lady Geraldine mad, and it was found out she was in love with Mr. Devereux, which made her mother mad, the maddest of all, they say, so that none can hold her, and she is crying night and day how her daughter might have had the first coronet in the kingdom, *maning* you, my lard, if it had not been that she *preferred* a beggar-man, *maning* Mr. Cecil Devereux, who is as poor, they say, as a Connaughtman—and he's forbid to think of her, and she's forbid, under pain of bread and water, ever to set her eyes upon him the longest day ever she lives; so the horses and coaches are ordered, and they are all to be off with the first light for Dublin: and that's all, my lard; and all truth, not a word of lies I'm telling."

I was inclined not to credit a story so oddly told; but, upon inquiry, I found it true in its material points. My own words to Mr. Devereux, and the parting look of Lady Geraldine, were full in my recollection; I was determined, by an unexpected, exertion, to surprise both the lovers, and to secure for ever their esteem and gratitude. The appointment, which Mr. Devereux desired, was not yet given away; the fleet was to sail in a few days. I started up from my sofa—ordered my carriage instantly—shaved myself—sent a courier on before to have horses ready at every stage to carry me to Dublin—got there in the shortest time possible—found Lord O'Toole but just arrived. Though unused to diplomatic language and political negotiation, I knew pretty well on what they all *hinge*. I went directly to the point, and showed that it would be the interest of the party concerned to grant my request. By expressing a becoming desire that my boroughs, upon a question where a majority was required, should *strengthen the hands of government*, I obtained for my friend the favour he *deserved*. Before I quitted Lord O'Toole, his secretary, Captain Andrews, was instructed to write a letter, announcing to Mr. Devereux his appointment. A copy of the former letter of refusal now lay before me; it was in his lordship's purest diplomatic style—as follows:

"*Private.*

"Lord O'Toole is concerned to inform Mr. Devereux that he cannot feel himself justified in encouraging Mr. D., under the existing circumstances, to make any direct application relative to the last conversation his lordship had the honour to hold with Mr. Devereux."

"To Cecil Devereux, Esq. &c. Thursday — — —"

The letter which I obtained, and of which I took possession, ran as follows:

"*Private.*

"Lord O'Toole is happy to have it in command to inform Mr. Devereux, that his lordship's representations on the subject of their last conversation have been thought sufficient, and that an official notification of the appointment to India, which Mr. D. desired, will meet the wishes of Mr. Devereux.

"Captain Andrews has the honour to add his congratulations."

"To Cecil Devereux, Esq. &c. Thursday — — —"

Having despatched this business with a celerity that surprised all the parties concerned, and most myself, I called at the lodgings of Mr. Devereux, delivered the letter to his servant, and left town. I could not bear to see either Mr. Devereux or Lady Geraldine. I had the pleasure to hear, that the obtaining this appointment was followed by Lady Kildangan's consent to their marriage. Soon after my return to Glenthorn Castle, I received a letter of warm thanks from Devereux, and a polite postscript from Lady Geraldine, declaring that, though she felt much pleasure, she could feel no surprise in seeing her opinion of Lord Glenthorn justified; persuaded, as she and Mr. Devereux had always been, that only motive and opportunity were wanting to make his lordship's superior qualities known to the world, and, what was still more difficult, to himself. They left Ireland immediately afterwards in consequence of their appointment in India.

I was raised in my own estimation—I revelled a short time in my self-complacent reflections; but when nothing more remained to be done, or to be said—when the hurry of action, the novelty of generosity, the glow of enthusiasm, and the freshness of gratitude, were over, I felt that, though large motives could now invigorate my mind, I was still a prey to habitual indolence, and that I should relapse into my former state of apathy and disease.

CHAPTER XII

I remember to have heard, in some epilogue to a tragedy, that the tide of pity and of love, whilst it overwhelms, fertilizes the soul. That it may deposit the seeds of future fertilization, I believe; but some time must elapse before they germinate: on the first retiring of the tide, the prospect is barren and desolate. I was absolutely inert, and almost imbecile for a considerable time, after the extraordinary stimulus, by which I had been actuated, was withdrawn. I was in this state of apathy when the rebellion broke out in Ireland; nor was I roused in the least by the first news of the disturbances. The intelligence, however, so much alarmed my English servants, that, with one accord, they left me; nothing could persuade them to remain longer in Ireland. The parting with my English gentleman affected my lethargic selfishness a little. His loss would have been grievous to such a helpless being as I was, had not his place been immediately supplied by that half-witted Irishman, Joe Kelly, who had ingratiated himself with me by a mixture of drollery and simplicity, and by suffering himself to be continually my laughing-stock; for, in imitation of Lady Geraldine, I thought it necessary to have a butt. I remember he first caught my notice by a strange answer to a very simple question. I asked, "What noise is that I hear?" "My lard," said he, "it is only the singing in my ears; I have had it these six months." Another time, when I reproached him for having told me a lie, he answered, "Why, now indeed, and plase your honour, my lard, I tell as few lies as possibly I can." This fellow, the son of a bricklayer, had originally been intended for a priest, and he went, as he told me, to the College of Maynooth to study his *humanities*; but, unluckily, the charms of some Irish Heloise came between him and the altar. He lived in a cabin of love, till he was weary of his smoke-dried Heloise, and then thought it *convanient* to turn *sarving* man, as he could play on the flute, and brush a coat remarkably well, which he *larned* at Maynooth, by brushing the coats of the superiors. Though he was willing to be laughed at, Joe Kelly could in his turn laugh; and he now ridiculed, without mercy, the pusillanimity of the English *renegadoes*, as he called the servants who had just left my service; He assured me that, to his knowledge, there was no manner of danger, *excepted a man prefarred being afraid of his own shadow, which some did, rather than have nothing to talk of, or enter into resolutions about, with some of the spirited men in the chair.*

Unwilling to be disturbed, I readily believed all that lulled me in my security. I would not be at the trouble of reading the public papers; and when they were read to me, I did not credit any paragraph that militated against my own opinion. Nothing could awaken me. I remember, one day, lying yawning on my sofa, repeating to Mr. M'Leod, who endeavoured to open my eyes to the situation of the country, "Pshaw, my dear sir; there is no danger, be assured—none at all—none at all. For mercy's sake! talk to me of something more diverting, if you would keep me awake; time enough to think of these things when they come nearer to us."

Evils that were not immediately near me had no power to affect my imagination. My tenantry had not yet been contaminated by the epidemic infection, which broke out soon after with such violence as to threaten the total destruction of all civil order. I had lived in England—I was unacquainted with the causes and the progress of the disease, and I had no notion of my danger; all I knew was, that some houses had been robbed of arms, and that there was a set of desperate wretches called *defenders*; but I was *annoyed* only by the rout that was now made about them. Having been used to the regular course of justice which prevailed in England, I was more shocked at the summary proceedings of my neighbours than alarmed at the symptoms of insurrection. Whilst my mind was in this mood, I was provoked by the conduct of some of the violent party, which wounded my personal pride, and infringed upon my imagined consequence. My foster-brother's forge was searched for pikes, his house ransacked, his bed and *bellows*, as possible hiding places, were cut open; by accident, or from private malice, he received a shot in his arm; and, though not the slightest cause of suspicion could be found against him, the party left him with a broken arm, and the consolation of not being sent to jail as a defender. Without making any allowance for the peculiar circumstances of the country, my indignation was excited in the extreme, by the injury done to my foster-brother; his sufferings, the tears of his mother, the taunts of Mr. (now *Captain*) Hardcastle, and the opposition made by his party, called forth all the faculties of my mind and body. The poor fellow, who was the subject of this contest, showed the best disposition imaginable: he was excessively grateful to me for interesting myself to *get* him justice; but as soon as he found that parties ran high against me, he earnestly dissuaded me from persisting.

"Let it drop, and *plase* your honour; my lord, let it drop, and don't be making of yourself *inimies* for the likes of me. Sure, what signifies my arm? and, before the next assizes, sha'n't I be as well as ever, arm and all?" continued he, trying to appear to move the arm without pain. "And there's the new bellows your honour has *give* me; it does my heart good to look at 'em, and it won't be long before I will be blowing them again as stout as ever; and so God bless your honour, my lord, and think no more about it—let it drop entirely, and don't be bringing yourself into trouble."

"Ay, don't be bringing yourself into trouble, dear," added Ellinor, who seemed half distracted between her feelings for her son and her fears for me; "it's a shame to think of the way they've treated Christy—but there's no help now, and it's best not to be making bad worse; and so, as Christy says, let the thing drop, jewel, and don't be bringing yourself into trouble; you don't know the *natur* of them people, dear—you are too *innocent* for them entirely, and myself does not know the mischief they might do *yees*."

"True for ye," pursued Christy; "I wouldn't for the best cow ever I see that your honour ever larnt a sentence about me or my arm; and it is not for such as we to be minding every little accident—so God lend you long life, and don't be plaguing yourself to death! Let it drop, and I'll sleep well the night, which I did not do the week, for thinking of all the trouble you got, and would get, God presarve ye!"

This generous fellow's eloquence produced an effect directly contrary to what was intended; both my feelings and my pride were now more warmly interested in his cause. I insisted upon his swearing examinations before Mr. M'Leod, who was a justice of the peace. Mr. M'Leod behaved with the utmost steadiness and impartiality; and in this trying moment, when "it was infamy to seem my friend," he defended my conduct calmly, but resolutely, in private and in public, and gave his unequivocal testimony, in few but decided words, in favour of my injured tenant. I should have respected Mr. M'Leod more, if I had not attributed this conduct to his desire of being returned for one of my boroughs at the approaching election. He endeavoured, with persevering goodness, to convince me of the reality of the danger in the country. My eyes were with much difficulty forced open so far as to perceive that it was necessary to take an active part in public affairs to vindicate my loyalty, and to do away the prejudices that were entertained against me; nor did my incredulity, as to the magnitude of the peril, prevent me from making exertions essential to the defence of my own character, if not to that of the nation. How few act from purely patriotic and rational motives! At all events I acted, and acted with energy; and certainly at this period of my life I felt no ennui. Party spirit is an effectual cure for ennui; and perhaps it is for this reason that so many are addicted to its intemperance. All my passions were roused, and my mind and body kept in continual activity. I was either galloping, or haranguing, or fearing, or hoping, or fighting; and so long as it was said that I could not sleep in my bed, I slept remarkably well, and never had so good an appetite as when I was in hourly danger of having nothing to eat. *The rebels were up,* and *the rebels were down*—and Lord Glenthorn's spirited conduct in the chair, and indefatigable exertions in the field, were the theme of daily eulogium amongst my convivial companions and immediate dependants. But, unfortunately, my sudden activity gained me no credit amongst the violent party of my neighbours, who persisted in their suspicions; and my reputation was now still more injured, by the alternate charge of being a trimmer or a traitor. Nay, I was further exposed to another danger, of which, from my ignorance of the country, I could not possibly be aware. The disaffected themselves, as I afterwards found, really believed, that, as I had not begun by persecuting the poor, I must be a favourer of the rebels; and all that I did to bring the guilty to justice, they thought was only to give a *colour to the thing*, till the proper moment should come for my declaring myself. Of this absurd and perverse mode of judging I had not the slightest conception; and I only laughed when it was hinted to me. My treating the matter so lightly confirmed suspicion on both sides. At this time all objects were so magnified and distorted by the mist of prejudice, that no inexperienced eye could judge of their real proportions. Neither party could believe the simple truth, that my tardiness to act arose from the habitual *inertia* of my mind and body.

Whilst prepossessions were thus strong, the time, the important time, in Ireland the most important season of the year, the assizes, arrived. My foster-brother's cause, or, as it was now generally called, *Lord Glenthorn's* cause, came on to be tried. I spared no expense, I spared no exertions; I fee'd the ablest counsel; and not content with leaving them to be instructed by my attorney, I explained the affair to them myself with indefatigable zeal. One of the lawyers, whom I had seen, or by whom I had been seen, in my former inert state of existence, at some watering-place in England, could not refrain from expressing his astonishment at my change of character; he could scarcely believe that I was the same Lord Glenthorn, of whose indolence and ennui he had formerly heard and seen so much.

Alas! all my activity, all my energy, on the present occasion, proved ineffectual. After a dreadful quantity of false swearing, the jury professed themselves satisfied; and, without retiring from the box, acquitted the persons who had assaulted my foster-brother. The mortification of this legal defeat was not all that I had to endure; the victorious party mobbed me, as I passed some time afterwards through a neighbouring town, where Captain Hardcastle and his friends had been carousing. I was hooted, and pelted, and narrowly escaped with my life—*I* who, but a few months ago, had imagined myself possessed of nearly despotic power: but opinions had changed; and on opinion almost all power is founded. No individual, unless he possess uncommon eloquence, joined to personal intrepidity, can withstand the combination of numbers, and the force of prejudice.

Such was the result of my first public exertions! Yet I was now happier and better satisfied with myself than I had ever been before. I was not only conscious of having acted in a manly and generous manner, but the alarms of the rebels, and of the French, and of the loyalists, and the parading, and the galloping, and the quarrelling, and the continual agitation in which I was kept, whilst my character and life were at stake, relieved me effectually from the intolerable burden of ennui.

CHAPTER XIII

"And, for the book of knowledge fair,
Presented with an universal blank
Of Nature's works, to me expunged and rased."

Unfortunately *for me*, the rebellion in Ireland was soon quelled; the nightly scouring of our county ceased; the poor people returned to their duty and their homes; the occupation of upstart and ignorant *associators* ceased, and their consequence sunk at once. Things and persons settled to their natural level. The influence of men of property, and birth, and education, and character, once more prevailed. The spirit of party ceased to operate: my neighbours wakened, as if from a dream, and wondered at the strange injustice with which I had been treated. Those who had lately been my combined enemies were disunited, and each was eager to assure me that he had *always been privately my friend*, but that he was compelled to conceal his sentiments: each exculpated himself, and threw the blame on others: all apologized to me, and professed to be my most devoted humble servants. My popularity, my power, and my prosperity were now at their zenith, *unfortunately for me;* because my adversity had not lasted long enough to form and season my character. I had been driven to exertion by a mixture of pride and generosity; my understanding being uncultivated, I had acted from the virtuous impulse of the moment, but never from rational motive, which alone can be permanent in its operation. When the spur of the occasion pressed upon me no longer, I relapsed into my former inactivity. When the great interests and strong passions, by which I had been impelled to exertion, subsided, all other feelings, and all less objects, seemed stale, flat, and unprofitable. For the tranquillity which I was now left to enjoy I had no taste; it appeared to me a dead calm, most spiritless and melancholy.

I remember hearing, some years afterwards, a Frenchman, who had been in imminent danger of been guillotined by Robespierre, and who at last was one of those who arrested the tyrant, declare, that when the bustle and horror of the revolution were over, he could hardly keep himself awake; and that he thought it very insipid to live in quiet with his wife and family. He further summed up the catalogue of Robespierre's crimes, by exclaiming, "D'ailleurs c'étoit un grand philanthrope!" I am not conscious of any disposition to cruelty, and I heard this man's speech with disgust; yet upon a candid self-examination, I must confess, that I have felt, though from different causes, some degree of what he described. Perhaps *ennui* may have had a share in creating revolutions. A French author pronounces ennui to be "a moral indigestion, caused by a monotony of situations!"

I had no wife or family to make domestic life agreeable: nor was I inclined to a second marriage, my first had proved so unfortunate, and the recollection of my disappointment with Lady Geraldine was so recent. Even the love of power no longer acted upon me: my power was now undisputed. My jealousy and suspicions of my agent, Mr. M'Leod, were about this time completely conquered, by his behaviour at a general election. I perceived that he had no underhand design upon my boroughs; and that he never attempted or wished to interfere in my affairs, except at my particular desire. My confidence in him became absolute and unbounded; but this was really a misfortune to me, for it became the cause of my having still less to do. I gave up all business, and from all manner of trouble I was now free: yet I became more and more unhappy, and my nervous complaints returned. I was not aware that I was taking the very means to increase my own disease. The philosophical Dr. Cullen observes, that "whatever aversion to application of any kind may appear in hypochondriacs, there is nothing more pernicious to them than absolute idleness, or a vacancy from all earnest pursuit. It is owing to wealth admitting of indolence, and leading to the pursuit of transitory and unsatisfying amusements, or exhausting pleasures only, that the present times exhibit to us so many instances of hypochondriacism."

I fancied that change of air and change of place would do me good; and, as it was fine summer weather, I projected various parties of pleasure. The Giants' Causeway, and the Lake of Killarney, were the only things I had ever heard mentioned as worth seeing in Ireland. I suffered myself to be carried into the county of Antrim, and I saw the Giants' Causeway. From the description given by Dr. Hamilton of some of these wonders of nature, the reader may judge how much I *ought* to have been astonished and delighted.

In the bold promontory of Bengore, you behold, as you look up from the sea, a gigantic colonnade of basaltes, supporting a black mass of irregular rock, over which rises another range of pillars, "forming altogether a perpendicular height of one hundred and seventy feet, from the base of which the promontory, covered over with rock and grass, slopes down to the sea, for the space of two hundred feet more: making, in all, a mass of near four hundred feet in height, which, in the beauty and variety of its colouring, in elegance and novelty of arrangement, and in the extraordinary magnificence of its objects, cannot be rivalled."

Yet I was seized with a fit of yawning, as I sat in my pleasure-boat, to admire this sublime spectacle. I looked at my watch, observed that we should be late for dinner, and grew impatient to be rowed back to the place where we were to dine; not that I was hungry, but I wanted to be again set in motion. Neither science nor taste expanded my view; and I saw nothing worthy of my admiration, or capable of giving me pleasure. The watching a straw floating down the tide was the only amusement I recollect to have enjoyed upon this excursion.

I was assured, however, by Lady Ormsby, that I could not help being enchanted with the Lake of Killarney. The party was arranged by this lady, who, having the preceding summer seen me captivated by Lady Geraldine, and pitying my disappointment, had formed the obliging design of restoring my spirits, and marrying me to one of her near relatives. She calculated, that as I had been charmed by Lady Geraldine's vivacity, I must be enchanted with the fine spirits of Lady Jocunda Lawler. So far were the thoughts of marriage from my imagination, that I only was sorry to find a young lady smuggled into our party, because I was afraid she would be troublesome: but I resolved to be quite passive upon all occasions, where attentions to the fair sex are sometimes expected. My arm, or my hand, or my assistance, in any manner, I was determined not to offer: the lounging indifference which some fashionable young men affect towards ladies, I really felt; and, besides, nobody minds unmarried women! This fashion was *most convenient to my indolence. In my state of torpor I was* not, however, long left in peace. Lady Jocunda was a high-bred romp, who made it a rule to say and do whatever she pleased. In a hundred indirect ways I was called upon to admire her charming spirits: but the rattling voice, loud laughter, flippant wit, and hoyden gaiety, of Lady Jocunda, disgusted me beyond expression. A thousand times on my journey I wished myself quietly asleep in my own castle. Arrived at Killarney, such blowing of horns, such boating, such seeing of prospects, such prosing of guides, all telling us what to admire! Then such exclamations, and such clambering! I was walked and talked till I was half-dead. I wished the rocks, and the hanging-woods, and the glens, and the water-falls, and the arbutus, and the myrtles, and the upper and lower lakes, and the islands, and Mucruss, and Mucruss Abbey, and the purple mountain, and the eagle's nest, and the Grand Turk, and the lights and the shades, and the echoes, and, above all, the Lady Jocunda, fairly at the devil.

A nobleman in the neighbourhood had the politeness to invite us to see a stag-hunt upon the water. The account of this diversion, which I had met with in my Guide to the Lakes,83 promised well. I consented to stay another day: that day I really was revived by this spectacle, for it was new.

The sublime and the beautiful had no charms for me: novelty was the only power that could waken me from my lethargy; perhaps there was in this spectacle something more than novelty. The Romans had recourse to shows of wild beasts and gladiators to relieve their ennui. At all events, I was kept awake this whole morning, though I cannot say that I felt in *such ecstasies as to be in any imminent danger of jumping out of the boat.*

Of our journey back from Killarney I remember nothing, but my being discomfited by Lady Jocunda's practical jests and overpowering gaiety. When she addressed herself to me, my answers were as constrained and as concise as possible; and, as I was afterwards told, I seemed, at the close of my reply to each interrogative of her ladyship's, to answer with Odin's prophetess,

> *"Now my weary lips I close;*
>
> *Leave me, leave me to repose."*

This she never did till we parted; and, at that moment, I believe, my satisfaction appeared so visible, that Lady Ormsby gave up all hopes of me. Arrived at my own castle, I threw myself on my bed quite exhausted. I took three hours' additional sleep every day for a week, to recruit my strength, and rest my nerves, after all that I had been made to suffer by this young lady's prodigious animal spirits.

CHAPTER XIV

I could now boast that I had travelled all over Ireland, from north to south; but, in fact, I had seen nothing of the country or of its inhabitants. In these commodious parties of pleasure, every thing had been provided to prevent the obstacles that roused my faculties. Accustomed by this time to the Hibernian tone, I fancied that I knew all that could be known of the Irish character; familiarized with the comic expressions of the lower class of people, they amused me no longer. On this journey, however, I recollect making one observation, and once laughing at what I thought a practical bull. We saw a number of labourers at work in a bog, on a very hot day, with a fire lighted close to them. When I afterwards mentioned, before Mr. M'Leod, this circumstance, which I had thought absurd, he informed me that the Irish labourers often light fires, that the smoke may drive away or destroy those myriads of tiny flies, called *midges*, by which they are often tormented so much, that without this remedy, they would, in hot and damp weather, be obliged to abandon their work. Had I been sufficiently active during my journey to pen a journal, I should certainly, without further inquiry, have noted down, that the Irish labourers *always* light fires in the hottest weather to cool themselves; and thus I should have added one more to the number of cursory travellers, who expose their own ignorance, whilst they attempt to ridicule local customs, of which they have not inquired the cause, or discovered the utility.

A foreigner, who has lately written Letters on England, has given a laughable instance of this promptitude of misapprehension. He says, he had heard much of the venality of the British parliament, but he had no idea of the degree to which it extended, till he actually was an eye-witness of the scene. The moment the minister entered the House, all the members ran about exclaiming, "Places! places!" which means, Give us places—give us places.

My heavy indolence fortunately preserved me from exposing myself, like these volatile tourists. I was at least secure from the danger of making mistakes in telling what I never saw.

As to the mode of living of the Irish, their domestic comforts or grievances, their habits and opinions, their increasing or decreasing ambition to better their condition, the proportion between the population and the quantity of land cultivated or capable of cultivation, the difference between the profits of the husbandman and the artificer, the relation between the nominal wages of labour and the actual command over the necessaries of life;—these were questions wholly foreign to my thoughts, and, at this period of my life, absolutely beyond the range of my understanding. I had travelled through my own country without making even a single remark upon the various degrees of industry and civilization visible in different parts of the kingdom. In fact, it never occurred to me that it became a British nobleman to have some notion of the general state of that empire, in the legislation of which he has a share; nor had I the slightest suspicion that political economy was a study requisite or suitable to my rank in life or situation in society. Satisfied with having seen all that is worth seeing in Ireland, the Giants' Causeway and the Lake of Killarney, I was now impatient to return to England. During the rebellion, I could not, with honour, desert my post; but now that tranquillity was apparently restored, I determined to quit a country of which my partial knowledge had in every respect been unfortunate. This resolution of mine to leave Ireland threw Ellinor into despair, and she used all her eloquence to dissuade me from the journey. I was quite surprised by the agony of grief into which she was thrown by the dread of my departure. I felt astonished that one human being could be so attached to another, and I really envied her sensibility. My new man, Joe Kelly, also displayed much reluctance at the thoughts of leaving his native country; and this sentiment inclined Ellinor to think more favourably of him, though she could not quite forgive him for being a Kelly of Ballymuddy.

"Troth," said she to him one day, in my presence, "none of them Kellys of Ballymuddy but what are a bad clan! Joey, is not there your own *broder's* uncle lying in the jail of — — — at this present time for the murder of a woman?"—"Well," replied Joe, "and if he was so unfortunate to be *put up*, which was not *asy* done neither, is it not better and more *creditabler* to lie in a jail for a murder than a robbery, I ask you?" This new scale of crimes surprised me; but Joe spoke what was the sense of many of his countrymen at that period.

By various petty attentions, this man contrived to persuade me of the sincerity of his attachment: chiefly by the art of appearing to be managed by me in all things, he insensibly obtained power over my pride; and, by saving me daily trouble, secured considerable influence over my indolence. More than any one whom I had ever seen, he had the knack of seeming half-witted—too simple to overreach, and yet sufficiently acute and droll to divert his master. I liked to have him about me, as uncultivated kings like to have their fools. One of our ancient monarchs is said to have given three parishes to his *joculator*; I gave only three farms to mine. I had a sort of mean pride in making my favourite an object of envy: besides, I fell into the common mistake of the inexperienced great, who fancy that attachment can be purchased, and that gratitude can be secured, by favours disproportioned to deserts. Joe Kelly, by sundry manoeuvres too minute for description, contrived to make me delay, from day to day, the preparations for my journey to England. From week to week it was put off till the autumn was far advanced. At length Kelly had nothing left to *suggest*, but that it would be best to wait for answers from my English steward to the letters that had been written to inquire whether every thing was ready for my reception. During this interval, I avoided every human creature (except Joe Kelly), and was in great danger of becoming a misanthrope from mere indolence. I did not hate my fellow-creatures, but I dreaded the trouble of talking to them. My only recreation, at this period, was sauntering out in the evening beside the sea-shore. It was my regular practice to sit down upon a certain large stone, at the foot of a rock, to watch the ebbing of the tide. There was something in the contemplation of the sea and of the tides which was fascinating to my mind. I could sit and look at the ocean whole hours together; for, without any exertion of my own, I beheld a grand operation of nature, accompanied with a sort of vast monotony of motion and sound, which lulled me into reverie.

Late one evening, as I was seated on my accustomed stone, my attention was slightly diverted from the sea by the sight of a man descending the crag above me, in rather a perilous manner. With one end of a rope coiled round his body, and the other fastened to a stake driven into the summit of the rock, he let himself half-way down the terrible height. One foot now rested on a projecting point, one hand held the rope, and hanging thus midway in the air, he seemed busy searching in the crevices of the rock, for the eggs of water-fowl. This dangerous trade I had seen frequently plied on this coast, so that I should scarcely have regarded the man if he had not turned, from time to time, as if to watch me. When he saw that he had fixed my eye, he threw down, as I thought, a white stone, which fell nearly at my feet. I stooped to examine it; the man waited till he saw it in my hands, then coiled himself swiftly up his rope to the summit of the rock, and disappeared. I found a paper tied round the stone, and on this paper, in a hand-writing that seemed to be feigned, were written these words:—

"Your life and caracter, one or t'other—say both, is in danger. Don't be walking here any more late in the evening, near them caves, nor don't go near the old abbey, any time—And don't be trusting to Joe Kelly any way— Lave the kingdom entirely; the wind sarves.

"So prays your true well-wisher.

"P.S. Lave the castle the morrow, and say nothing of this to Joe Kelly, or you'll repent when it's all over wid you."

I was startled a little by this letter at first, but in half an hour I relapsed into my apathy. Many gentlemen in the country had received anonymous letters: I had been tired of hearing of them during the rebellion. This, I thought, might be only a *quiz*, or a trick to hurry me out of the kingdom, contrived by some of those who desired my absence. In short, the labour of *thinking* about the matter fatigued me. I burned the letter as soon as I got home, and resolved not to puzzle or plague myself about it any more. My steward's answer came the next morning from England; Kelly made no difficulty, when I ordered him to be ready to set out in three days. This confirmed me in my opinion that the letter was malicious, or a jest. Mr. M'Leod came to take leave of me. I mentioned the circumstance to him slightly, and in general terms: he looked very serious, and said, "All these things are little in themselves, but are to be heeded, as marking the unsettled minds of the people—straws that show which way the wind blows. I apprehend we shall have a rough winter again, though we have had so still a summer. The people about us are too *hush* and too prudent—it is not their natures—there's something contriving among them: they don't break one another's heads at fairs as they used to do; they keep from whiskey; there must be some strong motive working this change upon them—good or bad, 'tis hard to say which. My lord, if we consider the condition of these poor people, and if we consider the causes—"

"Oh! for Heaven's sake, do not let us consider any more about it now; I am more than half asleep already," said I, yawning; "and our considering about it can do no good, to *me* at least; for you know I am going out of the kingdom; and when I am gone, M'Leod, you, in whom I have implicit confidence, must manage as you always used to do, you know, and as well as you can."

"True," said M'Leod, calmly, "that is what I shall do, indubitably; for that is my duty, and since your lordship has implicit confidence in me, my pleasure. I wish your lordship a good night and a good journey."

"I shall not set out in the morning; not till the day after to-morrow, I believe," said I; "for I feel consumedly tired to-night: they have plagued me about so many things to-day; so much business always before one can get away from a place; and then Joe Kelly has no head."

"Have a care he has not too much head, my lord, as your anonymous correspondent hints—he may be right there: I told you from the first I would not go security for Joe Kelly's honesty; and where there is not strict honesty, I conceive there ought not to be implicit confidence."

"Oh, hang it! as to honesty, they are none of them honest; I know that: but would you have me plague myself till I find a strictly honest servant? Joe's as honest as his neighbours, I dare say: the fellow diverts me, and is attached to me, and that's all I can expect. I must submit to be cheated, as all men of large fortunes are, more or less."

Mr. M'Leod listened with stubborn patience, and replied, that if I thought it necessary to submit to be cheated he could make no objection, except where it might come under his cognizance, and then he must take the liberty to remonstrate, or to give up his agency to some of the many, who could play better than he could the part of the dog in the fable, *pretending* to guard his master's meat.

The cold ungracious integrity of this man, even in my own cause, at once excited my spleen and commanded my respect. After shaking my leg, as I sat for two minutes in silence, I called after M'Leod, who moved towards the door, "Why, what can I do, Mr. M'Leod? What would you have me do? Now, don't give me one of your dry answers, but let me have your notions as a friend: you know, M'Leod, I cannot help having the most perfect confidence in you."

He bowed, but rather stiffly.

"I am proud to hear you cannot help that, my lord," said he. "As to a friend, I never considered myself upon that footing till now: but, as you at present honour me so far as to ask my counsel, I am free to give it. Part with Joe Kelly to-night; and whether you go or stay, you are safer without him. Joe's a rogue: he can do no good, and may do harm."

"Then," said I, "you are really frightened by this anonymous letter?"

"Cannot a man take prudent precautions without being frightened?" said M'Leod.

"But have you any particular reason to believe—in short to—to think, there can be any real danger for my life?"

"No particular reason, my lord; but the general reasons I have mentioned, the symptoms among the common people lead me to apprehend there may be fresh *risings* of the people soon; and you, as a man of fortune and rank, must be in danger. Captain Hardcastle says that he has had informations of seditious meetings; but, he being a prejudiced man, I don't trust altogether to what he says."

"Trust altogether to what he says!" exclaimed I; "no, surely; for my part, I do not trust a word he says; and his giving it as his opinion that the people are ill-inclined would decide me to believe the exact contrary."

"It would hardly be safe to judge that way either," said M'Leod; "for that method of judging by contraries might make another's folly the master of one's own sense."

"I don't comprehend you now. Safe way of judging or not, Captain Hardcastle's opinion shall never lead mine. When I asked for your advice, Mr. M'Leod, it was because I have a respect for your understanding; but I cannot defer to Captain Hardcastle's. I am now decided in my own opinion, that the people in this neighbourhood are perfectly well-disposed; and as to this anonymous letter, it is a mere trick, depend upon it, my good sir. I am surprised that a man of your capacity should be the dupe of such a thing; I should not be surprised if Hardcastle himself, or some of his people, wrote it."

"I should," said M'Leod, coolly.

"You should!" cried I, warmly. "Why so? And why do you pronounce so decidedly, my good friend? Have not I the same means of judging as you have? unless, indeed, you have some private reason with which I am unacquainted. Perhaps," cried I, starting half up from the sofa on which I lay, charmed with a bright idea, which had just struck me, "perhaps, M'Leod, you wrote the letter yourself for a jest. Did you?"

"That's a question, my lord," said M'Leod, growing suddenly red, and snatching up his hat with a quicker motion than I ever saw from him before, "that's a question, my lord, which I must take leave not to answer; a question, give me leave to add, my Lord Glenthorn," continued he, speaking in a broader Scotch accent than I had ever heard from him before, "which I should knock my equal *doon* for putting to me. A M'Leod, my lord, in jest or in earnest, would scorn to write to any man breathing that letter to which he would not put his name; and more, a M'Leod would scorn to write or to say that thing, to which he ought not to put his name. Your humble servant, my Lord Glenthorn," said he, and, making a hasty bow, departed.

I called after him, and even followed him to the head of the stairs, to explain and apologize; but in vain: I never saw him angry before.

"It's very weel, my lord, it's very weel; if you say you meant nothing offensive, it's very weel; but if you think fit, my lord, we will sleep upon it before we talk any more. I am a wee bit warmer than I could wish, and your lordship has the advantage of me, in being cool. A M'Leod is apt to grow warm, when he's touched on the point of honour; and there's no wisdom in talking when a man's not his own master."

"My good friend," said I, seizing his hand as he was buttoning up his coat, "I like you the better for this warmth; but I won't let you sleep upon your wrath: you must shake hands with me before that hall-door is opened to you."

"Then so I do, for there's no standing against this frankness; and, to be as frank with you, my lord, I was wrong myself to be so testy—I ask pardon, too. A M'Leod never thought it a disgrace to crave a pardon when he was wrong."

We shook hands, and parted better friends than ever. I spoke the exact truth when I said that I liked him the better for his warmth: his anger wakened me, and gave me something to think of, and some emotion for a few minutes. Joe Kelly presently afterwards came, with the simplest face imaginable, to inquire what I had determined about the journey.

"To put it off till the day after to-morrow," said I. "Light me to bed."

He obeyed; but observed, that "it was not his fault now if there was puttings-off; for his share, every thing was ready, and he was willing and ready to follow me, at a moment's warning, to the world's end, as he had a good right to do, let alone inclination; for, parting me, he could never be right in himself: and though loth to part his country, he had rather part that *nor* 84 me."

Then, without dwelling upon these expressions of attachment, he changed to a merry mood, and by his drolleries diverted me all the time I was going to bed, and at last fairly talked me asleep.

CHAPTER XV

When the first grey light of morning began to make objects indistinctly visible, I thought I saw the door of my apartment open very softly. I was broad awake, and kept my eyes fixed upon it—it opened by very slow degrees; my head was so full of visions, that I expected a ghost to enter—but it was only Ellinor.

"Ellinor!" cried I; "is it you at this time in the morning?"

"Hush! hush!" said she, shutting the door with great precaution, and then coming on tiptoe close to my bedside; "for the love of God, speak softly, and make no stir to awake them that's asleep near and too near you. It's unknown to all that I come up; for may be, when them people are awake and about, I might not get the opportunity to speak, or they might guess I knew something by my looks."

Her looks were full of terror—I was all amazement and expectation. Before she would say a word more, she searched the closets carefully, and looked behind the tapestry, as if she apprehended that she might be overheard: satisfied that we were alone, she went on speaking, but still in a voice that, with my utmost strained attention, I could but just hear.

"As you hope to live and breathe," said she, "never go again after nightfall any time walking in that lone place by the sea-shore. It's a mercy you escaped as you did; but if you go again you'll never come back alive—for never would they get you to do what they want, and to be as wicked as themselves the wicked villains!"

"Who?" said I. "What wicked villains? I do not understand you; are you in your right senses?"

"That I am, and wish you was as much in yours; but it's time yet, by the blessing of God! What wicked villains am I talking of? Of three hundred that have sworn to make you their captain, or, in case you refuse, to have your life this night. What villains am I talking of? Of him, the wickedest of all, who is now living in the very house with you, that is now lying in the very next room to you."

"Joe Kelly?"

"That same. From the first minute I saw him in the castle, I should have hated him, but for his causing you for to put off the journey to England. I never could abide him; but that blinded me, or I am sure I would have found him out long ago."

"And what have you found out concerning him?"

"That he is (speaking very low) a *united-man*, and stirring up the *rubbles* again here; and they have their meetings at night in the great cave, where the smugglers used to hide formerly, under the big rock, opposite the old abbey—and there's a way up into the abbey, that you used to be so fond of walking to, dear."

"Good Heavens! can this be true?"

"True it is, and too true, dear."

"But how did you find all this out, Ellinor?"

"It was none of I found it, nor ever could any such things have come into my head—but it pleased God to make the discovery of all by one of the *childer*—my own grandson—the boy you gave the gun to, long and long ago, to shoot them rabbits. He was after a hare yesterday, and it took him a chase over that mountain, and down it went and took shelter in the cave, and in went the boy after it, and as he was groping about, he lights on an old great coat; and he brought it home with him, and was showing it, as I was boiling the potatoes for their dinner yesterday, to his father forenent me; and turning the pockets inside out, what should come up but the broken head of a pipe; then he *sarches* in the other pocket, and finds a paper written all over—I could not read it—thank God, I never could read none of them wicked things, nor could the boy—by very great luck he could not, being no scholar, or it would be all over the country before this."

"Well, well! but what was in the paper after all? Did any body read it?"

"Ay, did they—that is, Christy read it—none but Christy—but he would not tell us what was in it—but said it was no matter, and he'd not be wasting his time reading an old song—so we thought no more, and he sent the boy up to the castle with a bill for smith's work, as soon as we had eat the potatoes, and I thought no more about any thing's being going wrong, no more than a child; and in the evening Christy said he must go to the funeral of a neighbour, and should not be home till early in the morning, may be; and it's not two hours since he came home and wakened me, and told me where he had been, which was not to the funeral at all, but to the cave where the coat was found; and he put the coat and the broken head of the pike, and the papers all in the pockets, just as we found it, in the cave—and the paper was a list of the names of them *rubbles* that met there, and a letter telling how they would make Lord Glenthorn their captain, or have his life; this was what made Christy to try and find out more—so he hid hisself in a hole in the side of the cave, and built hisself up with rubbish, only just leaving a place for hisself to breathe—and there he stayed till nightfall; and then on till midnight, God help us! so sure enough, them villains all come filling fast into the cave. He had good courage, God bless him for it—but he always had—and there he heard and saw all—and this was how they were talking:—First, one began by saying, how they must not be delaying longer to show themselves; they must make a rising in the country—then named the numbers in other parts that would join, and that they would not be put down so *asy* as afore, for they would have good leaders—then some praised you greatly, and said they was sure you favoured them in your heart, by all the ill-will you got in the county the time of the last 'ruction. But, again, others said you was milk and water, and did not go far enough, and never would, and that it was not in you, and that you was a sleepy man, and not the true thing at all, and neither beef nor *vael*. Again, thim that were for you spoke and said you would show yourself soon—and the others made reply, and observed you must now spake out, or never spake more; you must either head 'em, or be tramped under foot along with the rest, so it did not signify talking, and Joey Kelly should not be fribbling any more about it; and it was a wonder, said they, he was not the night at the meeting. And what was this about your being going off for England—what would they do when you was gone with M'Leod the Scotchman, to come in over them again agent, who was another guess sort of man from you, and never slept at all, and would scent 'em out, and have his corps after 'em, and that once M'Leod was master, there would be no making any head again his head; so, not to be tiring you too much with all they said, backward and forward, one that was a captain, or something that way, took the word, and bid 'em all hold their peace, for they did not know what they was talking on, and said that Joey Kelly and he had settled it all, and that the going to England was put off by Joe, and all a sham, and that when you would be walking out to-morrow at nightfall, in those lone places by the sea-side or the abbey, he and Joe was to seize upon you, and when you would be coming back near the abbey, to have you down through the trap-door into the cave, and any way they would swear you to join and head them, and if you would not, out with you, and shove you into the sea, and no more about it, for it would be give out you drown' yourself in a fit of the melancholy lunacy, which none would question, and it would be proved too you made away wid yourself, by your hat and gloves lying on the bank—Lord save us! What are you laughing at in that, when it is truth every word, and Joe Kelly was to find the body, after a great search. Well, again, say you would swear and join them, and head them, and do whatever they pleased, still that would not save you in the end; for they would quarrel with you at the first turn, because you would not be ruled by them as captain, and then they would shoot or pike you (God save the mark, dear), and give the castle to Joe Kelly, and the plunder all among 'em entirely. So it was all laid out, and they are all to meet in the cave to-morrow evening—they will go along bearing a funeral, seemingly to the abbey-ground. And now you know the whole truth, and the Lord preserve you! And what will be done? My poor head has no more power to think for you no more than an infant's, and I'm all in a tremble ever since I heard it, and afraid to meet any one lest they should see all in my face. Oh, what will become of *yees* now—they will be the death of you, whatever you do!"

By the time she came to these last words, Ellinor's fears had so much overpowered her, that she cried and sobbed continually, repeating—"What will be done now! What will be done! They'll surely be the death of you, whatever you do." As to me, the urgency of the danger wakened my faculties: I rose instantly, wrote a note to Mr. M'Leod, desiring to see him immediately on particular business. Lest my note should by any accident be intercepted or opened, I couched it in the most general and guarded terms; and added a request, that he would bring his last settlement of accounts with him; so that it was natural to suppose my business with him was of a pecuniary nature. I gradually quieted poor Ellinor by my own appearance of composure: I assured her, that we should take our measures so as to prevent all mischief—thanked her for the timely warning she had given me—advised her to go home before she was observed, and charged her not to speak to any one this day of what had happened. I desired that as soon as she should see Mr. M'Leod coming through the gate, she would send Christy after him to the castle, to get his bill paid; so that I might then, without exciting suspicion, talk to him in private, and we might learn from his own lips the particulars of what he saw and heard in the cavern.

Ellinor returned home, promising to obey me exactly, especially as to my injunction of secrecy—to make sure of herself she said "she would go to bed straight, and have the rheumatism very bad all day; so as not to be in a way to talk to none who would call in." The note to M'Leod was despatched by one of my grooms, and I, returning to bed, was now left at full leisure to finish my morning's nap.

Joe Kelly presented himself at the usual hour in my room; I turned my head away from him, and, in a sleepy tone, muttered that I had passed a bad night, and should breakfast in my own apartment.

Some time afterwards Mr. M'Leod arrived, with an air of sturdy pride, and produced his accounts, of which I suffered him to talk, till the servant who waited upon us had left the room; I then explained the real cause of my sending for him so suddenly. I was rather vexed, that I could not produce in him, by my wonderful narrative, any visible signs of agitation or astonishment. He calmly observed—"We are lucky to have so many hours of daylight before us. The first thing we have to do is to keep the old woman from talking."

I answered for Ellinor.

"Then the next thing is for me, who am a magistrate, to take the examinations of her son, and see if he will swear to the same that he says."

Christy was summoned into our presence, and he came with his *bill for smith's work done*; so that the servants could have no suspicion of what was going forward. His examinations were taken and sworn to in a few minutes: his evidence was so clear and direct, that there was no possibility of doubting the truth. The only variation between his story and his mother's report to me was as to the numbers he had seen in the cavern—her fears had turned thirteen into three hundred.

Christy assured us that there were but thirteen at this meeting, but that they said there were three hundred ready to join them.

"You were a very bold fellow, Christy," said I, "to hazard yourself in the cave with these villains; if you had been found out in your hiding-place, they would have certainly murdered you."

"True for me." said Christy; "but a man must die some way, please your honour; and where's the way I could die better? Sure, I could not but remember how good you was to me that time I was shot, and all you suffered for it! It would have been bad indeed if I would stay quiet, and let 'em murder you after all. No, no, Christy O'Donoghoe would not do that— any way. I hope, if there's to be any fighting, your honour would not wrong me so much as not to give me a blunderbush, and let me fight a bit along wid de rest for yees."

"We are not come to that yet, my good fellow," said Mr. M'Leod, who went on methodically; "if you are precipitate, you will spoil all. Go home to your forge, and work as usual, and leave the rest to us; and I promise that you shall have your share, if there is any fighting."

Very reluctantly Christy obeyed. Mr. M'Leod then deliberately settled our plan of operations. I had a fishing-lodge at a little distance, and a pleasure-boat there: to this place M'Leod was to go, as if on a fishing-party with his nephew, a young man, who often went there to fish. They were to carry with them some yeomen in coloured clothes, as their attendants, and more were to come as their guests to dinner. At the lodge there was a small four-pounder, which had been frequently used in times of public rejoicing; a naval victory, announced in the papers of the day, afforded a plausible pretence for bringing it out. We were aware that the rebels would be upon the watch, and therefore took every precaution to prevent their suspecting that we had made any discovery. Our fishing-party was to let the mock-funeral pass them quietly, to ask some trifling questions, and to give money for pipes and tobacco. Towards evening the boat, with the four-pounder on board, was to come under shore, and at a signal given by me was to station itself opposite to the mouth of the cave.

At the same signal a trusty man on the watch was to give notice to a party hid in the abbey, to secure the trap-door above. The signal was to be my presenting a pistol to the captain of the rebels, who intended to meet and seize me on my return from my evening's walk. Mr. M'Leod at first objected to my hazarding a meeting with this man; but I insisted upon it, and I was not sorry to give a public proof of my loyalty, and my personal courage. As to Joe Kelly, I also undertook to secure him.

Mr. M'Leod left me, and went to conduct his fishing-party. As soon as he was gone, I sent for Joe Kelly to play on the flute to me. I guarded my looks and voice as well as I could, and he did not see or suspect any thing—he was too full of his own schemes. To disguise his own plots he affected great gaiety; and to divert me, alternately played on the flute, and told me good stories all the morning. I would not let him leave me the whole day. Towards evening I began to talk of my journey to England, proposed setting out the next morning, and sent Kelly to look for some things in what was called *the strong closet*—a closet with a stout door and iron-barred windows, out of which no mortal could make his escape. Whilst he was busy searching in a drawer, I shut the door upon him, locked it, and put the key into my pocket. As I left the castle, I said in a jesting tone to some of the servants who met me—"I have locked Joe Kelly up in the strong room; if he calls to you to let him out never mind him; he will not get out till I come home from my walk—I owe him this trick." The servants thought it was some jest, and I passed on with my loaded pistols in my pocket. I walked for some time by the sea-shore, without seeing any one. At last I espied our fishing-boat, just peering out, and then keeping close to the shore. I was afraid that the party would be impatient at not seeing my signal, and would come out to the mouth of the cave, and show themselves too soon. If Mr. M'Leod had not been their commander, this, as I afterwards learned, would have infallibly happened; but he was so punctual, cool, and peremptory, that he restrained the rest of the party, declaring that, if it were till midnight, he would wait till the signal agreed upon was given. At last I saw a man creeping out of the cave—I sat down upon my wonted stone, and yawned as naturally as I could; then began to describe figures in the sand with my stick, as I was wont to do, still watching the image of the man in the water as he approached. He was muffled up in a frieze great coat; he sauntered past, and went on to a turn in the road, as if looking for some one. I knew well for whom he was looking. As no Joe Kelly came to meet him, he returned in a few minutes towards me. I had my hand upon the pistol in my pocket.

"You are my Lard Glenthorn, I presume," said he.

"I am."

"Then you will come with me, if you plase, my lard," said he.

"Make no resistance, or I will shoot you instantly," cried I, presenting my pistol with one hand, and seizing him by the collar with the other. I dragged him (for I had force enough, now my energy was roused) to the spot appointed for my signal. The boat appeared opposite the mouth of the cave. Every thing answered my expectation.

"There," said I, pointing to the boat, "there are my armed friends; they have a four-pounder—the match is ready lighted—your plot is discovered. Go in to your confederates in that cave; tell them so. The trap-door is secured above; there is no escape for them: bid them surrender: if they attempt to rush out, the grape shot will pour upon them, and they are dead men."

I cannot say that my rebel captain showed himself as stout as I could have wished, for the honour of my victory. The surprise disconcerted him totally: I felt him tremble under my grasp. He obeyed my orders—went into the cave to bring his associates to submission. His parley with them, however, was not immediately successful: I suppose there were some braver fellows than he amongst them, whose counsel might be for open war. In the mean time our yeomen landed, and surrounded the cave on all sides, so that there was no possibility of escape for those within. At last they yielded themselves our prisoners. I am sorry I have no bloody battle for the entertainment of such of my readers as like horrors; but so it was, that they yielded without a drop of blood being spilled, or a shot fired. We let them out of their hiding-place one by one, searching each as he issued forth, to be secure that they had no concealed weapons. After they had given up the arms which were concealed in the cave, the next question was, what to do with our prisoners. As it was now late, and they could not all be examined and committed with due legal form to the county gaol, Mr. M'Leod advised that we should detain them in the place they had chosen for themselves till morning. Accordingly, in the cave we again stowed them, and left a guard at each entrance to secure them for the night. We returned to the castle. I stopped at the gate to tell Ellinor and Christy that I was safe. They were sitting up watching for the news. The moment Ellinor saw me, she clasped her hands in an ecstasy of joy, but could not speak. Christy was voluble in his congratulations; but, in the midst of his rejoicing, he could not help reproaching me with forgetting to give him the *blunderbush*, and to let him have a bit of the fighting. "Upon my honour," said I, "there was none, or you should have been there."

"Oh, don't be plaguing and gathering round him now," said Ellinor: "sure he is tired, and look how hot—no wonder—let him get home and to bed: I'll run and warm it with the pan myself, and not be trusting them."

She would not be persuaded that I did not desire to have my bed warmed, but, by some short cut, got in before us. On entering the castle-hall, I found her, with the warming-pan in her hand, held back by the inquisitive servants, who were all questioning her about the news, of which she was the first, and not very intelligible enunciator.

I called for bread and water for my prisoner in the strong-room, and then I heard various exclamations of wonder.

"Ay, it is all true! it is no jest! Joe is at the bottom of all. *I* never liked Joe Kelly—*I* always knew Joe was not the right thing—and *I* always said so; and I, and I, and I. And it was but last week I was saying so: and it was but yesterday *I* said so and so."

I passed through the gossiping crowd with bread and water for my culprit. McLeod instantly saw and followed me.

"I will make bold to come with you," said he; "a pent rat's a dangerous animal."—I thanked him, and acquiesced; but there was no need for the precaution. When we opened the door, we found the conscience or terror-struck wretch upon his knees, and in the most abject terms he implored for mercy. From the windows of the room, which looked into the castle-yard, he had heard enough to guess all that had happened. I could not bear to look at him. After I had set down his food, he clung to my knees, crying and whining in a most unmanly manner. McLeod, with indignation, loosened him from me, threw him back, and locked the door.

"Cowardice and treachery," said he, "usually go together."

"And courage and sincerity," said I. "And now we'll go to supper, my good friends. I hope you are all as hungry as I am."

I never did eat any meal with so much appetite.

"'Tis a pity, my lord," said McLeod, "but that there was a conspiracy against you every day of your life, it seems to do you so much good."

CHAPTER XVI

"What new wonders? What new misfortunes, Ellinor?" said I, as Ellinor, with a face of consternation, appeared again in the morning in my room, just as I was going down to breakfast: "what new misfortunes, Ellinor?"

"Oh! the worst that could befall me!" cried she, wringing her hands; "the worst, the very worst!—to be the death of my own child!" said she, with inexpressible horror. "Oh! save him! save him! for the love of heaven, dear, save him! If you don't save him, 'tis I shall be his death."

She was in such agony, that she could not explain herself farther for some minutes.

"It was I gave the information against them all to you. But how could I ever have thought Owen was one of them? My son, my own son, the unfortunate cratur; I never thought but what he was with the militia far away. And how could it ever come into my head that Owen could have any hand in a thing of the kind?"

"But I did not see him last night," interrupted I.

"Oh! he was there! One of his own friends, one of the military that went with you, saw him among the prisoners, and came just now to tell me of it. That Owen should be guilty of the like!—Oh! what could have come over him! He must have been out of his *rason*. And against you to be plotting! That's what I never will believe, if even I'd hear it from himself. But he's among them that were taken last night. And will I live to see him go to gaol?—and will I live to see—No, I'd rather die first, a thousand and a thousand times over. Oh! for mercy's sake!" said she, dropping on her knees at my feet, "have pity on me, and don't let the blood of my own child be upon me in my old days."

"What would you have me do, Ellinor?" said I, much moved by her distress.

"There is but one thing to do," said she. "Let him off: sure a word from you would be enough for the soldiers that are over them on guard. And Mr. McLeod has not yet seen him; and if he was just let escape, there would be no more about it; and I'd I engage he shall fly the country, the unfortunate cratur! and never trouble you more. This is all I ask: and sure, dear, you can't refuse it to your own Ellinor; your old nurse, that carried ye in her arms, and fed ye with her milk, and watched over ye many's the long night, and loved ye; ay, none ever loved, or could love ye so well."

"I am sensible of it; I am grateful," interrupted I; "but what you ask of me, Ellinor, is impossible—I cannot let him escape; but I will do my utmost."

"Troth, nothing will save him, if you would not say the word for him now. Ah! why cannot you let him off, then?"

"I should lose my honour; I should lose my character. You know that I have been accused of favouring the rebels already—you saw the consequences of my protecting your other son, though he was innocent and injured, and bore an excellent character."

"Christy; ay, true: but poor Owen, unlucky as he is, and misguided, has a better claim upon you."

"How can that be? Is not the other my foster-brother, in the first place?"

"True for him."

"And had not I proofs of his generous conduct and attachment to me?"

"Owen is naturally fonder of you by a great deal," interrupted she; "I'll answer for that."

"What! when he has just been detected in conspiring against my life?"

"That's what I'll never believe," cried Ellinor, vehemently: "that he might be drawn in, may be, when out of his *rason*—he was always a wild boy—to be a united-man, and to hope to get you for his captain, might be the case, and bad enough that; but, jewel, you'll find he did never conspire against you: I'd lay down my life upon that."

She threw herself again at my feet, and clung to my knees.

"As you hope for mercy yourself in this world, or the world to come, show some now, and do not be so hard-hearted as to be the death of both mother and son."

Her supplicating looks and gestures, her words, her tears, moved me so much, that I was on the point of yielding; but recollecting what was due to justice and to my own character, with an effort of what I thought virtuous resolution, I repeated, "It is impossible: my good Ellinor, urge me no farther: ask any thing else, and it shall be granted, but this is impossible."

As I spoke, I endeavoured to raise her from the ground; but with the sudden force of angry despair, she resisted.

"No, you shall not raise me," cried she. "Here let me lie, and break my heart with your cruelty! 'Tis a judgment upon me—it's a judgment, and it's fit I should feel it as I do. But you shall feel too, in spite of your hard heart. Yes, your heart is harder than the marble: you want the natural touch, you do; for your mother has knelt at your feet, and you have denied her prayer."

"My mother!"

"And what was her prayer?—to save the life of your brother."

"My brother! Good heavens! what do I hear?"

"You hear the truth: you hear that I am your lawful mother. Yes, you are my son. You have forced that secret from me, which I thought to have carried with me to my grave. And now you know all: and now you know how wicked I have been, and it was all for you; for you that refused me the only thing ever I asked, and that, too, in my greatest distress, when my heart was just breaking: and all this time too, there's Christy—poor good Christy; he that I've wronged, and robbed of his rightful inheritance, has been as a son, a dutiful good son to me, and never did he deny me any thing I could ask; but in you I have found no touch of tenderness. Then it's fit I should tell you again, and again, and again, that he who is now slaving at the forge, to give me the earnings of his labour; he that lives, and has lived all his days, upon potatoes and salt, and is content; he who has the face and the hands so disguised with the smoke and the black, that yourself asked him t'other day did he ever wash his face since he was born—I tell ye, he it is who should live in this castle, and sleep on that soft bed, and be lord of all here—he is the true and real Lord Glenthorn, and to the wide world I'll make it known. Ay, be pale and tremble, do; it's your turn now: I've touched you now: but it's too late. In the face of day I shall confess the wrong I've done; and I shall call upon you to give back to him all that by right is his own."

Ellinor stopped short, for one of my servants at this instant came into the room.

"My lord, Mr. McLeod desires me to let you know the guard has brought up the prisoners, and he is going to commit them to gaol, and would be glad to know if you choose to see them first, my lord."

Stupified by all I had just heard, I could only reply, that I would come presently. Ellinor rushed past the servant,—"Are they come?" cried she. "Where will I get a sight of them?" I stayed for a few minutes alone, to decide upon what I ought to say and do. A multitude of ideas, more than had ever come in my mind in a twelvemonth, passed through it in these few minutes.

As I was slowly descending the great staircase, Ellinor came running, as fast as she could run, to the foot of the stairs, exclaiming, "It's a mistake! it's all a mistake, and I was a fool to believe them that brought me the word.

Sure Ody's not there at all! nor ever was in it. I've seen them all, face to face; and my son's not one of them, nor ever was: and I was a fool from beginning to end—and I beg your pardon entirely," whispered she, coming close to my ear: "I was out of my reason at the thought of that boy's being to suffer, and I, his mother, the cause of it. Forgive all I said in my passion, my own best jewel: you was always good and tender to me, and be the same still, dear. I'll never say a word more about it to any one living: the secret shall die with me. Sure, when my conscience has borne it so long, it may strive and bear it a little longer for your sake: and it can't be long I have to live, so that will make all easy. Hark! they are asking for you. Do you go your ways into the great parlour, to Mr. McLeod, and think no more of any thing at all but joy. My son's not one of them! I must go to the forge, and tell Christy the good news."

Ellinor departed, quite satisfied with herself, with me, and with all the world. She took it for granted that she left me in the same state of mind, and that I should obey her injunctions, and *think of nothing but joy*. Of what happened in the great parlour, and of the examinations of the prisoners, I have but a confused recollection. I remember that Mr. McLeod seemed rather surprised by my indifference to what concerned me so nearly; and that he was obliged to do all the business himself. The men were, I believe, all committed to gaol, and Joe Kelly turned king's evidence; but as to any further particulars, I know no more than if I had been in a dream. The discovery which Ellinor had just made to me engrossed all my powers of attention.

CHAPTER XVII

"Le vrai n'est pas toujours vraisemblable," says an acute observer of human affairs. The romance of real life certainly goes beyond all other romances; and there are facts which few writers would dare to put into a book, as there are skies which few painters would venture to put into a picture.

When I had leisure to reflect, I considered, that as yet I had no proof of the truth of Ellinor's strange story, except her own assertions. I sent for her again, to examine her more particularly. I was aware that, if I alarmed her, I should so confuse her imagination, that I should never obtain the truth; therefore I composed myself, and assumed my usual external appearance of nonchalance. I received her lolling upon my sofa, as usual, and I questioned her merely as if to gratify an idle curiosity.

"Troth, dear," said she, "I'll tell you the whole story how it was, to make your mind asy, which, God knows, mine never was, from that minute it first came into my head, till this very time being. You mind the time you got the cut in your head—no, not you, jewel; but the little lord that was then, Christy there below that is.—Well, the cut was a terrible cut as ever you seen, got by a fall on the fender from the nurse's arms, that was drunk, three days after he was born."

"I remember to have heard my father talk of some accident of this sort, which happened to me when I was an infant."

"Ay, sure enough it did, and that was what first put him in the notion of taking the little lord out of the hands of the Dublin nurse-tenders, and them that were about my Lady Glenthom, and did not know how to manage her, which was the cause of her death: and he said he'd have his own way about his son and heir any way, and have him nursed by a wholesome woman in a cabin, and brought up hardy, as he, and the old lord, and all the family, were before him. So with that he sends for me, and he puts the young lord; God bless him, into my arms himself, and a *donny* thing he was that same time to look at, for he was but just out of the surgeon's hands, the head just healed and scarred over like; and my lord said there should be no more doctors never about him. So I took him, that is, Christy, and you, to a house at the sea, for the salt water, and showed him every justice; and my lord often came to see him whilst he was in the country; but then he was off, after a time, to Dublin, and I was in a lone place, where nobody came, and the child was very sick with me, and you was all the time as fine and thriving a child as ever you see; and I thought, to be sure, one night, that he would die wid me. He was very bad, very bad indeed; and I was sitting up in bed, rocking him backwards and forwards this ways: I thought with myself, what a pity it was, the young lord should die, and he an only son and heir, and the estate to go out of the family the Lord knows where; and then the grief the father would be in: and then I thought how happy he would be if he had such a fine *babby* as you, dear; and you was a fine *babby* to be sure: and then I thought how happy it would be for you, if you was in the place of the little lord: and then it came into my head, just like a shot, where would be the harm to change you? for I thought the real lord would surely die; and then, what a gain it would be to all, if it was never known, and if the dead child was carried to the grave, since it must go, as only poor Ellinor O'Donoghoe's, and no more about it. Well, if it was a wicked thought, it was the devil himself put it in my head, to be sure; for, only for him, I should never have had the sense to think of such a thing, for I was always innocent like, and not worldly given. But so it was, the devil put it in my head, and made me do it, and showed me how, and all in a minute. So, I mind, your eyes and hair were both of the very same colour, dear; and as to the rest, there's no telling how those young things alter in a few months, and my lord would not be down from Dublin in a hurry, so I settled it all right; and as there was no likelihood at all the real lord would live, that quieted my conscience; for I argued, it was better the father should have any sort of child at all than none. So, when my lord came down, I carried him the child to see, that is you, jewel. He praised me greatly for all the care I had taken of his boy; and said, how finely you was come on! and I never see a father in greater joy; and it would have been a sin, I thought, to tell him the truth, after he took the change that was put upon him so well, and it made him so happy like. Well, I was afeard of my life he'd pull off the cap to search for the scar, so I would not let your head be touched any way, dear, saying it was tinder and soft still with the fall, and you'd cry if the cap was stirred; and so I made it out indeed, very well; for, God forgive me, I twitched the string under your chin, dear, and made you cry like mad, when they would come to touch you. So there was no more about it, and I had you home to myself, and, all in good time, the hair grew, and fine thick hair it was, God bless you; and so there was no more about it, and I got into no trouble at all, for it all fell out just as I had laid it out, except that the real little young lord did not die as I thought; and it was a wonder but he did, for you never saw none so near death, and backwards and forwards, what turns of sickness he took with me for months upon months, and year after year, so that none could think, no more than me, there was any likelihood at all of rearing him to man's estate. So that kept me easier in my mind concerning what I'd done; for as I kept saying to myself, better the family should have an heir to the estate, suppose not the right, than none at all; and if the father, nor nobody, never found it out, there was he and all the family made happy for life, and my child made a lord of, and none the wiser or the worse. Well, so I down-argued my conscience; and any way I took to little Christy, as he was now to be called—and I loved him, all as one as if he was my own—not that he was ever as well-looking as Ody, or any of the childer I had, but I never made any differ betwixt him and any of my own—he can't say as I did, any how, and he has no reason to complain of my being an unnat'ral mother to him, and being my foster-child I had a right to love him as I did, and I never wronged him in any way, except in the one article of changing him at nurse, which he being an infant, and never knowing, wa" never a bit the worse for, nor never will, now. So all's right^ dear, and make your mind asy, jewel; there's the whole truth of the story, for you."

"But it is a very strange story, Ellinor, after all, and—and I have only your word for it, and may be you are only taking advantage of my regard for you to make me believe you."

"What is it, plase your honour?" said she, stepping forward, as if she did not hear or understand me.

"I say, Ellinor, that after all I have no proof of the truth of this story, except your word."

"And is not that enough? and where's the use of having more? but if it will make you asy, sure I can give you proof—sure need you go farther than the scar on his head? If he was shaved to-morrow, I'd engage you'd see it fast enough. But sure, can't you put your hand up to your head this minute, and feel there never was no scar there, nor if all the hair you have, God save the mark, was shaved this minute, never a bit of a scar would be to be seen: but proof is it you want?—why, there's the surgeon that dressed the cut in the child's head, before he ever came to me; sure he's the man that can't forget it, and that will tell all: so to make your mind asy, see him, dear; but for your life don't let him see your head to feel it, for he'd miss the scar, and might suspect something by your going to question him."

"Where does he live?" interrupted I.

"Not above twelve miles off."

"Is he alive?"

"Ay, if he been't dead since Candlemas."

At first I thought of writing to this man; but afterwards, being afraid of committing myself by writing, I went to him: he had long before this time left off business, and had retired to enjoy his fortune in the decline of life. He was a whimsical sort of character; he had some remains of his former taste for anatomy, and was a collector of curiosities. I found him just returned from a lake which he had been dragging for a moose-deer's horns, to complete the skeleton of a moose-deer, which he had mounted in his hall. I introduced myself, desiring to see his museum, and mentioned to him the thigh-bone of a giant found in ray neighbourhood; then by favour of this bone I introduced the able cure that he had made of a cut in my head, when I was a child.

"A cut in your head, sir? Yes, my lord, I recollect perfectly well, it was a very ugly cut, especially in an infant's head; but I am glad to find you feel no bad effects from it. Have you any cicatrice on the place?—Eleven feet high, did you say? and is the giant's skeleton in your neighbourhood?"

I humoured his fancy, and by degrees he gave me all the information I wanted without in the least suspecting my secret motives. He described the length, breadth, and depth, of the wound to me; showed me just where it was on the head, and observed that it must have left an indelible mark, but that my fine hair covered it. When he seemed disposed to search for it, I defended myself with the giant's thigh-bone, and warded off his attacks most successfully. To satisfy myself upon this point, I affected to think that he had not been paid: he said he had been amply paid, and he showed me his books to prove it. I examined the dates, and found that they agreed with Ellinor's precisely. On my return home, the first thing I did was to make Christy a present of a new wig, which I was certain would induce him to shave his head; for the lower Irish agree with the beaux and belles of London and Paris, in preferring wigs to their own hair. Ellinor told me, that I might safely let his head be shaved, because to her certain knowledge, he had scars of so many cuts which he had received at fairs upon his skull, that there would appear nothing particular *in one more or less*. As soon as the head was shaved, and the wig was worn, I took an opportunity one day of stopping at the forge to have one of my horse's shoes changed; and whilst this was doing, I took notice of his new wig, and how well it fitted him. As I expected, he took it off to show it me better, and to pay his own compliments to it.

"Sure enough, you are a very fine wig," said he, apostrophising it as he held it up on the end of his hammer; "and God bless him that give it me, and it fits me as if it was nailed to my head."

"You seem to have had a good many nails in your head already, Christy," said I, "if one may judge by all these scars."

"Oh yes, please your honour, my lord," said he, "there's no harm in them neither; they are scratches got when I was no wiser than I should be, at fairs, fighting with the boys of Shrawd-na-scoob."

Whilst he fought his battles o'er again, I had leisure to study his head; and I traced precisely all the boundary lines. The situation, size, and figure of the cicatrice, which the surgeon and Ellinor had described to me, were so visible and exact, that no doubt could remain in my mind of Christy's being the real son of the late Lord and Lady Glenthorn. This conviction was still more impressed upon my mind a few days afterwards. I recollected having seen a file of family pictures in a lumber-room in the castle; and I rummaged them out to see if I could discover amongst them any likeness to Christy: I found one; the picture of my grandfather,—I should say, of *his* grandfather, to which Christy bore a striking resemblance, when I saw him with his face washed, and in his Sunday clothes.

My mind being now perfectly satisfied of the truth of Ellinor's story, I was next to consider how I ought to act. To be or not to be Lord Glenthorn, or, in other words, to be or not to be a villain, was now the question. I could not dissemble to my conscience this plain state of the case, that I had no right to keep possession of that which I knew to be another's lawful property; yet, educated as I had been, and accustomed to the long enjoyment of those luxuries, which become necessaries to the wealthy; habituated to attendance as I had been; and, even amongst the dissipated and idle, notorious for extravagance the most unbounded and indolence the most inveterate; how was I at once to change my habits, to abdicate my rank and power, to encounter the evils of poverty? I was not compelled to make such sacrifices; for though Ellinor's transient passion had prompted her to threaten me with a public discovery, yet I knew that she would as soon cut off her own right hand as execute her threats. Her affection for me, and her pride in my consequence, were so strong, that I knew I might securely rely upon her secrecy. The horrid idea of being the cause of the death of one of her own children had for a moment sufficient power to balance her love for me; yet there was but little probability that any similar trial should occur, nor had I reason to apprehend that the reproaches of her conscience should induce her to make a voluntary discovery; for all her ideas of virtue depended on the principle of fidelity to the objects of her affection, and no scrupulous notions of justice disturbed her understanding or alarmed her self-complacency. Conscious that she would willingly sacrifice all she had in the world for any body she loved, and scarcely comprehending that any one could be selfish, she, in a confused way, applied the maxim of "Do as you would be done by," and was as generous of the property of others as of her own. At the worst, if a law-suit commenced against me, I knew that possession was nine points of the law. I also knew that Ellinor's health was declining, and that the secret would die with her. Unlawful possession of the wealth I enjoyed could not, however, satisfy my own mind; and, after a severe conflict between my love of ease and my sense of right—between my tastes and my principles—I determined to act honestly and honourably, and to relinquish what I could no longer maintain without committing injustice, and feeling remorse. I was, perhaps, the more ready to do rightly because I felt that I was not compelled to it. The moment when I made this virtuous decision was the happiest I had at that time ever felt: my mind seemed suddenly relieved from an oppressive weight; my whole frame glowed with new life; and the consciousness of courageous integrity elevated me so much in my own opinion, that titles, and rank, and fortune, appeared as nothing in my estimation. I rang my bell eagerly, and ordered that Christy O'Donoghoe should be immediately sent for. The servant went instantly; but it seemed to me an immoderately long time before Christy arrived. I walked up and down the room impatiently, and at last threw myself at full length upon the sofa: the servant returned.

"The smith is below in the hall, my lord."

"Show him up."—He was shown up into the ante-chamber.

"The smith is at the door, my lord."

"Show him in, cannot you? What detains him?"

"My brogues, my lord! I'd be afraid to come in with 'em on the carpet." Saying this, Christy came in, stepping fearfully, astonished to find himself in a splendid drawing-room.

"Were you never in this room before, Christy?" said I.

"Never, my lord, plase your honour, barring the day I mended the bolt."

"It is a fine room, is not it, Christy?"

"Troth, it is the finest ever I see, sure enough."

"How should you like to have such a room of your own, Christy?"

"Is it I, plase your honour?" replied he, laughing; "what should I do with the like?"

"How should you feel if you were master of this great castle?"

"It's a poor figure I should make, to be sure," said he, turning his head over his shoulder towards the door, and resting upon the lock: "I'd rather be at the forge by a great *dale*."

"Are you sure of that, Christy? Should not you like to be able to live without working any more, and to have horses and servants of your own?"

"What would I do with them, plase your honour, I that have never been used to them? sure they'd all laugh at me, and I'd not be the better o' that, no more than of having nothing to do; I that have been always used to the work, what should I do all the day without it? But sure, my lord," continued he, changing his voice to a more serious tone, "the horse that I shod yesterday for your honour did not go lame, did he?"

"The horse is very well shod, I believe; I have not ridden him since: I know nothing of the matter."

"Because I was thinking, may be, it was that made your honour send for me up in the hurry—I was afeard I'd find your honour mad with me; and I'd be very sorry to disoblige you, my lord; and I'm glad to see your honour looking so well after all the trouble you've been put to by them *rubbles*, the villains, to be *consarting* against you under-ground. But, thanks be to God, you have 'em all in gaol now. I thought my mother would have died of the fright she took, when the report came that Ody was one of them. I told her there could not be no truth in it at all, but she would not mind me: it would be a strange unnatural thing, indeed, of any belonging to her to be plotting against your honour. I knew Ody could not be in it, and be a brother of mine; and that's what I kept saying all the time but she never heeded me: for, your honour knows, when the women are frighted, and have taken a thing into their heads, you can't asy get it out again."

"Very true: but to return to what I was saying, should not you like to change places with me, if you could?"

"Your honour, my lord, is a very happy jantleman, and a very good jantleman, there's no doubt, and there's few but would be proud to be like you in any thing at all."

"Thank you for that compliment. But now, in plain English, as to yourself, would you like to be in my place—to change places with me?"

"In your honour's place—I! I would *not*, my lord; and that's the truth, now," said he, decidedly. "I would not: no offence—your honour bid me to speak the truth; for I've all I want in the world, a good mother, and a good wife, and good *childer*, and a reasonable good little cabin, and my little *pratees*, and the grazing of the cow, and work enough always, and not called on to slave, and I get my health, thank God for all; and what more could I have if I should be made a lord to-morrow? Sure, my good woman would never make a lady; and what should I do with her? I'd be grieved to see her the laughing-stock of high and low, besides being the same myself, and my boy after me. That would never answer for me; so I am not like them that would overturn all to get uppermost; I never had any hand, art, or part, in a thing of the kind; I always thought and knew I was best as I am; not but what, if I was to change with any, it is with you, my lord, I would be proud to change; because if I was to be a jantleman at all, I'd wish to be of a *ra-al* good *ould* family born."

"You are then what you wish to be?" said I.

"Och!" said he, laughing and scratching his head, "your honour's jesting me about them kings of Ireland, that they say the O'Donoghoes was once: but that's what I never think *on*, that's all idle talk for the like of me, for sure that's a long time ago, and what use going back to it? One might as well be going back to Adam, that was the father of all, but which makes no differ now."

"But you do not understand me," interrupted I; "I am not going back to the kings of Ireland: I mean to tell you, that you were born a gentleman—nay, I am perfectly serious; listen to me."

"I do, plase your honour, though it is mocking me, I know you are; I would be sorry not to take a joke as well as another."

"This is no joke; I repeat that I am serious. You are not only a gentleman, but a nobleman: to you this castle and this great estate belongs, and to you they shall be surrendered."

He stood astonished; and, his eyes opening wide, showed a great circle of white in his black face.

"Eh!" cried he, drawing that long breath, which astonishment had suppressed. "But how can this be?"

"Your mother can explain better than I can: your mother, did I say? she is not your mother; Lady Glenthorn was your mother."

"I can't understand it at all—I can't understand it at all. I'll lave it all to your honour," said he, making a motion with his hands, as if to throw from him the trouble of comprehending it.

"Did you never hear of such a thing as a child's being changed at nurse?"

"I did, plase your honour; but *my* mother would never do the like, I'll answer for *her*, any way; and them that said any thing of the kind, belied her; and don't be believing them, my lord."

"But Ellinor was the person who told me this secret."

"Was she so? Oh, she must have been *draaming*; she was always too good a mother to me to have sarved me so. But," added he, struggling to clear his intellects, "you say it's not my mother she is; but whose mother is she then? Can it be that she is yours? 'tis not possible to think such a great lord was the son of such as her, to look at you both: and was you the son of my father Johnny O'Donoghoe? How is that again?"

He rubbed his forehead; and I could scarcely forbear laughing at his odd perplexity, though the subject was of such serious importance. When he clearly understood the case, and thoroughly believed the truth, he did not seem elated by this sudden change of fortune; he really thought more of me than of himself.

"Well, I'll tell you what you will do then," continued he, after a pause of deep reflection; "say nothing to nobody, but just keep asy on, even as we are. Don't let there be any surrendering at all, and I'll speak to my mother, that is, Ellinor O'Donoghoe, and settle it so; and let it be so settled, in the name of God, and no more about it: and none need never be the wiser; 'tis so best for all. A good day to your honour, and I'll go shoe the mare."

"Stay," said I; "you may hereafter repent of this sudden determination. I insist upon your taking four-and-twenty hours—no, that would be too little—take a month to consider of it coolly, and then let me know your final determination."

"Oh! plase your honour, I will say the same then as now. It would be a poor thing indeed of me, after all you done for me and mine, to be putting you to more trouble. It would be a poor thing of me to forget how you liked to have lost your life all along with me at the time of the 'ruction. No, I'll not take the fortin from you, any how."

"Put gratitude to me out of the question," said I. "Far be it from me to take advantage of your affectionate temper. I do not consider you as under any obligations to me; nor will I be paid for doing justice."

"Sure enough, your honour desarved to be born a gentleman," said Christy.

"At least I have been bred a gentleman," said I. "Let me see you again this day month, and not till then."

"You shall not—that is, you *shall*, plase your honour: but for fear any one would suspect any thing, I'd best go shoe the mare, any way."

CHAPTER XVIII

"What riches give us, let us then inquire—

Meat, fire, and clothes—What more?—Meat, clothes, and fire."

The philosophy we learn from books makes but a faint impression upon the mind, in comparison with that which we are taught by our own experience; and we sometimes feel surprised to find that what we have been taught as maxims of morality prove true in real life. After having had, for many years, the fullest opportunities of judging of the value of riches, when I reflected upon my past life, I perceived that their power of conferring happiness is limited, nearly as the philosophic poet describes; that all the changes and modifications of luxury must, in the sum of actual physical enjoyment, be reduced to a few elementary pleasures, of which the industrious poor can obtain their share: a small share, perhaps; but then it is enjoyed with a zest that makes it equal in value perhaps to the largest portion offered to the sated palate of ennui. These truths are as old as the world; but they appeared quite new to me, when I discovered them by my own experience.

During the month which I had allowed to my foster-brother for reflection, I had leisure to philosophize, and my understanding made a rapid progress. I foresaw the probability of Christy's deciding to become Earl of Glenthorn; notwithstanding that his good sense had so clearly demonstrated to him in theory, that, with his education and habits, he must be happier working in his forge than he could be as lord of Glenthorn Castle. I was not dismayed by the idea of losing my wealth and rank; I was pleased with myself for my honest conduct, and conscious of a degree of pleasure from my own approbation, superior to what my riches had ever procured.

The day appointed for Christy's final determination arrived. I knew by the first motion of his shoulder as he came into the room, what his decision would be.

"Well, Christy," said I, "you will be Earl of Glenthorn, I perceive. You are glad now that I did not take you at your word, and that I gave you a month's time for consideration."

"Your honour was always considerate; but if I'd wish now to be changing my mind," said he, hesitating, and shifting from leg to leg, "it is not upon my own account, any way, but upon my son Johnny's."

"My good friend," said I, "no apology is necessary. I should be very unjust if I were offended by your decision, and very mean if, after the declarations I have made, I could, for an instant, hesitate to restore to you that property which it is your right and your choice to reclaim."

Christy made a low bow, and seemed much at a loss what he was to say next.

"I hope," continued I, "that you will be as happy when you are Earl of Glenthorn, as you have been as Christy O'Donoghoe."

"May be not, plase your honour; but I trust my childer will be happy after me; and it's them and my wife I'm thinking of, as in duty bound. But it is hard your honour should be astray for want of the fortin you've been bred to; and this weighs with me greatly on the other side. If your honour could live on here, and share with us—But I see your honour's displeased at my naming *that*. It was my wife thought o' that; I knew it could not do. But then, what I think is, that your honour should name what you would be pleased to keep to live upon: for, to be sure, you have a right to live as a gentleman, that have always lived as one, as every body knows, and none better than I. Would your honour be so kind, then, as just to put down on a bit of paper what you'd wish to keep; and that same, whatever it is, none shall touch but yourself; and I would not own a child for mine that would begrudge it you. I'll step down and wait below while your honour writes what you plase."

The generosity of this man touched me to the heart. I accepted from him three hundred a year; and requested that the annuity I allowed to the unfortunate Lady Glenthorn might be continued; that the house which I had built for Ellinor, and the land belonging to it, might be secured to her rent-free for life; and that all my debts should be paid. I recommended Mr. M'Leod in the strongest manner, as an agent whose abilities and integrity would be to him an invaluable treasure.

Christy, when I gave him the paper on which I had stated these requests, took a pen instantly, and would have signed his name without reading it; but to this I absolutely objected.

"Well, then," said he, "I'll take it home, and read it over, and take time, as you desire, to consider. There's no danger of my changing my mind about this: I hope your honour can't think there is."

The next day, on returning it to me, he observed, that it was making very little of him to put down only such a trifle; and he pressed me to make the hundreds thousands:—this I refused.

"But I hope your honour won't object to what I am going to propose. Is not there a house in London? and is not there another in England, in the country? and, sure, I and mine can't live there and here and every where at once: if you'd just condescend to occupy one of them, you'd do me a great pleasure, and a great sarvice too; for every thing would be right, instead of going wrong, as it might under an agent, and me at a distance, that does not know well how to manage such great estates. I hope you'll not refuse me that, if it's only to show me I don't lose your honour's good-will."

The offer was made with so much earnestness, and even delicacy, that I could not abruptly refuse it at the moment, though one of these magnificent houses could be of no use tome with an income of 300*l. per annum.*

"As to the annuity," continued Christy, "that shall be paid as punctual as the day: Mr. M'Leod will pay it; and he shall have it all settled right, and put upon a stamp, by the lawyers, in case any thing should happen me. Then, as to Ellinor, sure, she is my mother, for I never can think of her any other way; and, except in that single article of changing me at nurse, was always the best of mothers to me. And even that same trick she played me, though very wicked, to be sure, was very nat'ral—ay, very nat'ral—to *prefar* her own flesh and blood if she could: and no one could be more sorry for the wrong she did me than she is now: there she is crying at home, ready to break her heart: but as I tell her, there's no use in repenting a thing when once it is done; and as I forgive her, none can ever bring it up against her: and as to the house and farm, she shall surely have that, and shall never want for any thing. So I hope your honour's mind will be asy on that matter; and whatever else you recollect to wish, *that* shall be done, if in my power."

It is with pleasure that I recollect and record all these instances of goodness of heart in poor Christy, which, notwithstanding the odd mixture of absurdity and sense in his language and ideas, will, I make no doubt, please my readers, though they cannot affect them as much as they affected me. I now prepared for my departure from Glenthorn Castle, never more to return. To spare me from unnecessary mortification, Christy had the wonderful self-command to keep the secret faithfully, so that none of the people in the neighbourhood, nor even my servants, had the slightest idea of the truth. Having long talked of returning to England, the preparations for my journey excited no surprise. Every thing went on as usual, except that Christy, instead of being at the forge, was almost every day at the whiskey-shop.

I thought it proper to speak openly of my affairs to Mr. M'Leod: he was the only person who could make out a correct list of my debts. Besides, I wished to recommend him as agent to the future earl, to whom an honest and able agent would be peculiarly necessary, ignorant, as he was, both of the world and of business; and surrounded, as he must probably be, on his accession to his estate, by a herd of vulgar and designing flatterers.

Albeit not easily moved to surprise, Mr. M'Leod really did, for an instant, look astonished, when I informed him that Christy O'Donoghoe was Earl of Glenthorn. But I must resolve not to stop to describe the astonishment that each individual showed upon this occasion, else I shall never have finished my story.

It was settled that Mr. M'Leod should continue agent; and, for his credit, I must observe that, after he was made acquainted with my loss of rank and fortune, he treated me with infinitely more respect and regard than he had ever shown me whilst he considered me only as his employer. Our accounts were soon settled; and when this was done, and they were all regularly signed, Mr. M'Leod came up to me, and, in a low voice of great emotion, said, "I am not a man of professions; but when I say I am a man's friend, I hope I shall ever be found to be so, as far as can be in my power: and I cannot but esteem and admire the man who has acted so nobly as you have done."

M'Leod wrung my hand as he spoke, and the tears stood in his eyes. I knew that the feeling must indeed be strong, which could extort from him even these few words of praise, and this simple profession of regard; but I did not know, till long afterwards, the full warmth of his affections and energy of his friendship. The very next day, unfortunately for me, he was obliged to go to Scotland, to his mother, who was dying: and at this time I saw no more of him.

In due legal form I now made a surrender of all claim upon the hereditary property of the Earl of Glenthorn, and every thing was in readiness for my journey. During this time poor Ellinor never appeared at the castle. I went to see her, to comfort her about my going away; but she was silent, and seemingly sullen, and would not be comforted.

"I've enough to grieve me," said she: "I know what will be the end of all; I see it as plain as if you'd told me. There's no hiding nothing from a mother: no, there's no use in striving to comfort me." Every method which I tried to console her seemed to grieve her more.

The day before that which was fixed for my departure, I sent to desire to see her. This request I had repeatedly made; but she had, from day to day, excused herself, saying that she was unwell, and that she would be up on the morrow. At last she came; and though but a few days had elapsed since I had seen her, she was so changed in her appearance, that I was shocked the moment I beheld her countenance.

"You don't look well, Ellinor," said I: "sit down."

"No matter whether I sit or stand," said she, calmly; "I'm not long for this world: I won't live long after you are gone, that's one comfort."

Her eyes were fixed and tearless; and there was a dead unnatural tranquillity in her manner.

"They are making a wonderful great noise nailing up the boxes, and I seen them cording the trunks as I came through the hall. I asked them, could I be of any use: but they said I could be of none, and that's true; for, when I put my hand to the cord, to pull it, I had no more strength than an infant. It was seven-and-twenty years last Midsummer-day since I first had you an infant in my arms. I was strong enough then, and you—was a sweet babby. Had I seen that time all that would come to pass this day! But that's over now. I have done a wicked thing; but I'll send for Father Murphy, and get absolution before I die."

She sighed deeply, then went on speaking more quickly.

"But I can do nothing until you go. What time will you go in the morning, dear? It's better go early. Is it in the coach you'll go? I see it in the yard. But I thought you must leave the coach, with all the rest, to the rightful heir. But my head's not clear about it all, I believe—and no matter."

Her ideas rambled from one subject to another in an unconnected manner. I endeavoured in vain to recall her understanding by speaking of her own immediate interests; of the house that was secured to her for life; and of the promise that had been made me, that she should never *want for any thing*, and that she should be treated with all possible kindness. She seemed to listen to me; but showed that she did not comprehend what I said, by her answers; and, at every pause I made, she repeated the same question—

"What time will you go in the morning, dear?"

At last I touched her feelings, and she recovered her intellect, when I suddenly asked, if she would accompany me to England the next morning.

"Ay, that I will," cried she, "go with you through the wide world."

She burst into tears, and wept bitterly for some time.

"Ah! now I feel right again," said she; "this is what I wanted; but could not cry this many a day—never since the word came to me that you was going, and all was lost."

I assured her that I now expected to be happier than I had ever been.

"Oh!" cried she: "and have you never been happy all this time? What a folly it was for me, then, to do so wicked a thing! and all my comfort was, the thinking you was happy, dear. And what will become of you now? And is it on foot you'll go?"

Her thoughts rambled again.

"Whatever way I go, you shall go with me," said I. "You are my mother; and now that your son has done what he knows to be honest and just, he will prosper in the world, and will be truly happy; and so may you be happy, now that you have nothing more to conceal."

She shook her head.

"It's too late," said she, "quite too late. I often told Christy I would die before you left this place, dear; and so I will, you will see. God bless you! God bless you! and pray to him to forgive me! None that could know what I've gone through would ever do the like; no, not for their own child, was he even such as you, and that would be hard to find. God bless you, dear; I shall never see you more! The hand of death is upon me—God for ever bless you, dear!"

She died that night; and I lost in her the only human being who had ever shown me warm, disinterested affection. Her death delayed for a few days my departure from Glenthorn Castle. I stayed to see her laid in the grave. Her funeral was followed by crowds of people: by many, from the general habit of attending funerals; by many, who wished to pay their court to me, in showing respect to the memory of my nurse.

When the prayers over the dead were ended, and the grave closed, just as the crowd were about to disperse, I stood up on a monument belonging to the Glenthorn family; and the moment it was observed that I wished to address the multitude, the moving waves were stilled, and there was a dead silence. Every eye was fixed upon me with eager expectation. It was the first time in my life that I had ever spoken before numbers; but as I was certain that I had something to say, and quite indifferent about the manner, words came without difficulty. Amazement appeared in every face when I declared myself to be the son of the poor woman whom we had just interred. And when I pointed to the real Earl of Glenthorn, and when I declared that I relinquished to him his hereditary title and lawful property, my auditors looked alternately at me and at my foster-brother, seeming to think it impossible that a man, with face and hands so black as Christy's usually were known to be, could become an earl.

When I concluded my narrative, and paused, the silence still continued; all seemed held in mute astonishment.

"And now, my good friends," continued I, "let me bid you farewell; probably you will never see or hear of me more; but, whether he be rich or poor, or high or low-born, every honest man must wish to leave behind him a fair character. Therefore, when I am gone, and, as it were, dead to you, speak of me, not as of an impostor, who long assumed a name and enjoyed a fortune that was not his own; but remember that I was bred to believe myself heir to a great estate, and that, after having lived till the age of seven-and-twenty, in every kind of luxury, I voluntarily gave up the fortune I enjoyed, the moment I discovered that it was not justly mine."

"*That* you did, indeed," interrupted Christy; "and of that I am ready to bear witness for you in this world and in the next. God bless and prosper you wherever you go! and sure enough he will, for he cannot do other than prosper one that deserves it so well. I never should have known a sentence of the secret," continued he, addressing his neighbours, "if it had not been for *his* generosity to tell it me; and even had I found it out by any *maracle*, where would have been the gain of that to me? for you know he could, had he been so inclined, have kept me out of all by the law—ay, baffled me on till my heart was sick, and till my little substance was wasted, and my bones rotten in the ground; but, God's blessing be upon him! he's an honest man, and *done* that which many a lord in his place would not have done; but a good conscience is a kingdom in itself, and *that* he cannot but have, wherever he goes—and all which grieves me is that he is going away from us. If he'd be prevailed with by me, he'd stay where he is, and we'd share and share alike; but he's too proud for that—and no wonder—he has a right to be proud; for no matter who was his mother, he'll live and die a gentleman, every inch of him. Any man, you see, may be made a lord; but a gentleman, a man must make himself. And yourselves can witness, has not he reigned over us like a gentleman, and a *raal* gentleman; and shown mercy to the poor, and done justice to all, as well as to me? and did not he take me by the hand when I was persecuted, and none else in the wide world to *befrind* me; and did not he stand up for me against the tyrants that had the sway then; ay, and did not he put himself to trouble, day and night, go riding here and there, and *spaking* and writing for me? Well, as they say, he loves his ease, and that's the worse can be said of him; he took all this pains for a poor man, and had like to have lost his life by it. And now, wherever he is and whatever, can I help loving and praying for him? or could you? And since you will go," added he, turning to me with tears in his eyes, "take with you the blessings of the poor, which, they say, carry a man straight to heaven, if any thing can."

The surrounding crowd joined with one voice in applauding this speech: "It is he that has said what we all think," cried they, following me with acclamations to the castle. When they saw the chaise at the door which was to carry me away, their acclamations suddenly ceased—"But is he going?—But can't he stay?—And is he going this minute? troth it's a pity, and a great pity!"

Again and again these honest people insisted upon taking leave of me, and I could not force myself away without difficulty. They walked on beside my carriage, Christy at their head; and in this species of triumph, melancholy indeed, but grateful to my heart, I quitted Glenthorn Castle, passed through that park which was no longer mine, and at the verge of the county shook hands for the last time with these affectionate and generous people. I then bid my postilion drive on fast; and I never looked back, never once cast a lingering look at all I left behind. I felt proud of having executed my purpose, and conscious I had not the insignificant, inefficient character that had formerly disgraced me. As to the future, I had not distinctly arranged my plans, nor was my mind during the remainder of the day sufficiently tranquil for reflection. I felt like one in a dream, and could scarcely persuade myself of the reality of the events, that had succeeded each other with such astonishing rapidity. At night I stopped at an inn where I was not known; and having no attendants or equipage to command respect from hostlers, waiters, and inn-keepers, I was made immediately sensible of the reality, at least of the change in my fortune; but I was not mortified—I felt only as if I were travelling incognito. And I contrived to go to bed without a valet-de-chambre, and slept soundly, for I had earned a sound sleep by exertion both of body and mind.

CHAPTER XIX

In the morning I awoke with a confused notion that something extraordinary had happened; but it was a good while before I recollected myself sufficiently to be perfectly sensible of the absolute and irrevocable change in my circumstances. An inn may not appear the best possible place for meditation, especially if the moralizer's bedchamber be next the yard where carriages roll, and hostlers swear perpetually; yet so situated, I, this morning as I lay awake in my bed, thought so abstractedly and attentively, that I heard neither wheels nor hostlers. I reviewed the whole of my past life; I regretted bitterly my extravagance, my dissipation, my waste of time; I considered how small a share of enjoyment my wealth had procured, either for myself or others; how little advantage I had derived from my education, and from all my opportunities of acquiring knowledge. It had been in my power to associate with persons of the highest talents, and of the best information, in the British dominions; yet I had devoted my youth to loungers, and gamesters, and epicures, and knew that scarcely a trace of my existence remained in the minds of those selfish beings, who once called themselves my friends. I wished that I could live my life over again; and I felt that, were it in my power, I should live in a manner very different from that in which I had fooled away existence. In the midst of my self-reproaches, however, I had some consolation in the idea that I had never been guilty of any base or dishonourable action. I recollected, with satisfaction, my behaviour to Lady Glenthorn, when I discovered her misconduct; I recollected that I had always shown gratitude to poor Ellinor for her kindness; I recollected with pleasure, that when trusted with power I had not used it tyrannically. My exertions in favour of my foster-brother, when he was oppressed, I remembered with much satisfaction; and the steadiness with which I behaved, when a conspiracy was formed against my life, gave me confidence in my own courage; and, after having sacrificed my vast possessions to a sense of justice, no mortal could doubt my integrity: so that upon the whole, notwithstanding my past follies, I had a tolerably good opinion of myself, or rather good hopes for the future. I was certain, that there was more in me than the world had seen; and I was ambitious of proving that I had some personal merit, independently of the adventitious circumstances of rank and fortune. But how was I to distinguish myself?

Just as I came to this difficult question, the chambermaid interrupted my reverie, by warning me in a shrill voice, that it was very late, and that she had called me above two hours before.

"Where's my man! send up my man. Oh! I beg your pardon—nothing at all: only, my good girl, I should be obliged to you if you could let me have a little warm water, that I may shave myself."

It was new and rather strange to me to be without attendants; but I found that, when I was forced to it, I could do things admirably well for myself, that I had never suspected I could perform without assistance. After I had travelled two days without servants, how I had travelled with them was the wonder. I once caught myself saying of myself, "that careless blockhead has forgotten my nightcap." For some time I was liable to make odd blunders about my own identity; I was apt to mistake between my old and my new habits, so that when I spoke in the tone and imperative mood in which Lord Glenthorn had been accustomed to speak, people stared at me as if I were mad, and I in my turn was frequently astonished by their astonishment, and perplexed by their ease of behaviour in my presence.

Upon my arrival in Dublin, I went to a small lodging which Mr. M'Leod had recommended to me; it was such as suited my reduced finances; but, at first view, it was not much to my taste; however, I ate with a good appetite my very frugal supper, upon a little table, covered with a little table-cloth, on which I could not wipe my mouth without stooping low. The mistress of the house, a North-country woman, was so condescending as to blow my fire, remarking, at the same time, that coals were *a very scarce article*; she begged to know whether I would choose a fire in my bed-room, and what quantity of coals she should lay in; she added many questions about boarding, and small-beer, and tea, and sugar, and butter, and blankets, and sheets, and washerwomen, which almost overwhelmed my spirits.

"And must I think of all these things for myself?" said I, in a lamentable tone, and I suppose with a most deplorable length of face, for the woman could not refrain from laughing: as she left the room, I heard her exclaim, "Lord help him, he looks as much astray as if he was just new from the Isle of Skye."

The cares of life were coming fast upon me, and I was terrified by the idea of a host of petty evils; I sat ruminating, with my feet upon the bars of the grate, till past midnight, when my landlady, who seemed to think it incumbent upon her to supply me with common sense, came to inform me that there was a good fire burning to waste in the bed-room, and that I should find myself a great deal better there than sitting over the cinders. I suffered myself to be removed to the bedchamber, and again established my feet upon the upper bar of the grate.

"Lack! sir, you'll burn your boots," said my careful landlady; who, after bidding me good night, put her head back into the room, to beg I would be sure to rake the fire, and throw up the ashes safe, before I went to bed. Left to my own meditations, I confess I did feel rather forlorn. I reflected upon my helplessness in all the common business of life; and the more I considered that I was totally unfit for any employment or profession, by which I could either earn money, or distinguish myself, the deeper became my despondency. I passed a sleepless night, vainly regretting the time that never could be recalled.

In the morning, my landlady gave me some letters, which had been forwarded for me from Glenthorn Castle; the direction to the Earl of Glenthorn scratched out, and in its place inserted my new address, "C. O'Donoghoe, Esq., No. 6, Duke-street, Dublin." I remember, I held the letters in my hand, contemplating the direction for some minutes, and at length reading it aloud repeatedly, to my landlady's infinite amusement:—she knew nothing of my history, and seemed in doubt whether to think me extremely silly or mad. One of my letters was from Lord Y——, an Irish nobleman, with whom I was not personally acquainted, but for whose amiable character and literary reputation I had always, even during my days of dissipation, peculiar respect. He wrote to me to make inquiries respecting the character of a Mr. Lyddell, who had just proposed himself as tutor to the son of one of his friends. Mr. Lyddell had formerly been my favourite tutor, the man who had encouraged me in every species of ignorance and idleness. In my present state of mind I was not disposed to speak favourably of this gentleman, and I resolved that I would not be instrumental in placing another young nobleman under his guidance. I wrote an explicit, indignant, and I will say eloquent letter upon this occasion; but, when I came to the signature, I felt a repugnance to signing myself, C. O'Donoghoe; and I recollected, that as my history could not yet be public, Lord Y—— would be puzzled by this strange name, and would be unable to comprehend this answer to his letter. I therefore determined to wait upon his lordship, and to make my explanations in person: besides my other reasons for determining on this visit, I had a strong desire to become personally acquainted with a nobleman of whom I had heard so much. His lordship's porter was not quite so insolent as some of his brethren; and though I did not come in a showy equipage, and though I had no laced footmen to enforce my rights, I gained admission. I passed through a gallery of fine statues, to a magnificent library, which I admired till the master of the house appeared, and from that moment he commanded, or rather captivated, my attention.

Lord Y— — was at this time an elderly gentleman. In his address, there was a becoming mixture of ease and dignity; he was not what the French call *maniéré*; his politeness was not of any particular school, but founded on those general principles of good taste, good sense, and good-nature, which must succeed in all times, places, and seasons. His desire to please evidently arose not from vanity but benevolence. In his conversation, there was neither the pedantry of a recluse, nor the coxcombry of a man of the world: his knowledge was select; his wit without effort, the play of a cultivated imagination: the happiness of his expressions did not seem the result of care; and his allusions were at once so apposite and elegant, as to charm both the learned and the unlearned: all he said was sufficiently clear and just to strike every person of plain sense and natural feeling, while to the man of literature it had often a further power to please, by its less obvious meaning. Lord Y— —'s superiority never depressed those with whom he conversed; on the contrary, they felt themselves raised by the magic of politeness to his level; instead of being compelled to pay tribute, they seemed invited to share his intellectual dominion, and to enjoy with him the delightful pre-eminence of genius and virtue.

I shall be forgiven for pausing in my own insignificant story, to dwell on the noble character of a departed friend. That he permitted me to call him my friend, I think the greatest honour of my life. But let me, if I can, go on regularly with my narrative.

Lord Y— — took it for granted, during our first half-hour's conversation, that he was speaking to the Earl of Glenthorn: he thanked me with much warmth for putting him on his guard against the character of Mr. Lyddell: and his lordship was also pleased to thank me for making him acquainted, as he said, with my own character; for convincing him how ill it had been appreciated by those who imagined that wealth and title were the only distinctions which the Earl of Glenthorn might claim. This compliment went nearer to my heart than Lord Y— — could guess.

"My character," said I, "since your lordship encourages me to speak of myself with freedom, my character has, I hope, been much changed and improved by circumstances; and perhaps those which might at present be deemed the most unfortunate, may ultimately prove of the greatest advantage, by urging me to exertion.—Your lordship is not aware of what I allude to; a late event in my singular history," continued I, taking up the newspapers which lay on his library table—"my singular history has not yet, I fancy, got into the public newspapers. Perhaps you will hear it most favourably from myself."

Lord Y— — was politely, benevolently attentive, whilst I related to him the sudden and singular change in my fortune: when I gave an account of the manner in which I had conducted myself after the discovery of my birth, tears of generous feeling filled his eyes; he laid his hand upon mine when I paused—

"Whatever you have lost," said he, "you have gained a friend. Do not be surprised," continued he, "by this sudden declaration. Before I saw you this morning, your real character was better known to me than you imagine. I learnt it from a particular friend of mine, of whose judgment and abilities I have the highest opinion, Mr. Cecil Devereux; I saw him just after his marriage; and the very evening before they sailed, I remember, when Lady Geraldine and he were talking of the regret they felt in leaving Ireland, among the friends whom they lamented that they should not see again, perhaps for years, you were mentioned with peculiar esteem and affection. They called you their generous benefactor, and fully explained to me the claim you had to this title—a title which never can be lost. But Mr. Devereux was anxious to convince me that he was not influenced by the partiality of gratitude in his opinion of his benefactor's talents. He repeated an assertion, that was supported with much energy by the charming Lady Geraldine, that Lord Glenthorn had *abilities to be any thing Tie pleased*; and the high terms in which they spoke of his talents, and the strong proofs they adduced of the generosity of his character, excited in my mind a warm desire to cultivate his acquaintance; a desire which has been considerably increased within this last hour. May I hope that the Irish rapidity with which I have passed from acquaintance to friendship may not shock English habits of reserve; and may not induce you to doubt the sincerity of the man, who has ventured with so little hesitation or ceremony to declare himself your friend?"

I was so much moved by this unexpected kindness, that, though I felt how much more was requisite, I could answer only with a bow; and I was glad to make my retreat as soon as possible. The very next day, his lordship returned my visit, to my landlady's irrecoverable astonishment; and I had increasing reason to regard him with admiration and affection. He convinced me, that I had interested him in my concerns, and told me, I must forgive him if he spoke to me with the freedom of a friend: thus I was encouraged to consult him respecting my future plans. Plans, indeed, I had none regularly formed; but Lord Y— —, by his judicious suggestions, settled and directed my ideas without overpowering me by the formality of advice. My ambition was excited to deserve his friendship, and to accomplish his predictions. The profession of the law was that to which he advised me to turn my thoughts: he predicted, that, if for five years I would persevere in application to the necessary preparatory studies, I should afterwards distinguish myself at the bar, more than I had ever been distinguished by the title of Earl of Glenthorn. Five years of hard labour! the idea alarmed, but did not utterly appal my imagination; and to prevent my dwelling upon it too long at the first, Lord Y— — suddenly changed the conversation; and, in a playful tone, said, "Before you immerse yourself in your studies, I must, however, claim some of your time. You must permit me to carry you home with me to-day, to introduce you to two ladies of my acquaintance: the one prudent and old—if a lady can ever be old; the other, young, and beautiful, and graceful, and witty, and wise, and reasonable. One of these ladies is much prepossessed in your favour, the other strongly prejudiced against you—for the best of all possible reasons, because she does not know you."

I accepted Lord Y— —'s invitation; not a little curious to know whether it was the old and prudent, or the young, beautiful, graceful, witty, wise, and reasonable lady, who was much prepossessed in my favour. Notwithstanding my usual indifference to the whole race of *very agreeable young ladies*, I remember trying to form a picture in my imagination of this all-accomplished female.

CHAPTER XX

Upon my arrival at Y—— house, I found two ladies in the drawing-room, in earnest conversation with Lady Y——. In their external appearance they were nearly what my friend had described; except that the beauty of the youngest infinitely surpassed my expectations. The elegance of her form, and the charming expression of her countenance, struck me with a sort of delightful surprise, that was quickly succeeded by a most painful sensation.

"Lady Y——, give me leave to introduce to you Mr. O'Donoghoe."

Shocked by the sound of my own name, I was ready to recoil abashed. The elderly lady turned her eyes upon me for an instant, with that indifference with which we look at an uninteresting stranger. The young lady seemed to pity my confusion; for though so well and so long used to varieties of the highest company, when placed in a situation that was new to me, I was unaccountably disconcerted. Ah! thought I, how differently should I be received were I still Earl of Glenthorn!

I was rather angry with Lord Y——, for not introducing me, as he had promised, to this fair lady; and yet the repetition of my name would have increased my vexation. In short, I was unjust, and felt an impatience and irritability quite unusual to my temper. Lady Y——addressed some conversation to me, in an obliging manner, and I did my best to support my part till she left me: but my attention was soon distracted, by a conversation that commenced at another part of the room, between her and the elderly lady.

"My dear Lady Y——, have you heard the extraordinary news? the most incredible thing that ever was heard! For my part, I cannot believe it yet, though we have the intelligence from the best authority. Lord Glenthorn, that is to say, the person we always called Lord Glenthorn, turns out to be the son of the Lord knows who—they don't mention the name."

At this speech I was ready to sink into the earth. Lord Y—— took my arm, and led me into another room. "I have some cameos," said he, "which are thought curious; would you like to look at them?"

"Can you conceive it?" continued the elderly lady, whose voice I still heard, as the folding-doors of the room were open: "Changed at nurse! One hears of such things in novels, but, in real life, I absolutely cannot believe it. Yet here, in this letter from Lady Ormsby, are all the particulars: and a blacksmith is found to be Earl of Glenthorn, and takes possession of Glenthorn castle, and all the estates. And the man is married, to some vulgarian of course: and he has a son, and may have half a hundred, you know; so there is an end of our hopes; and there is an end too of all my fine schemes for Cecilia."

I felt myself change colour again. "I believe," said I to Lord Y——, "I ought not to hear this. If your lordship will give me leave, I will shut the door."

"No, no," said he, smiling, and stopping me; "you ought to hear it, for it will do you a great deal of good. You know I have undertaken to be your guide, philosopher, and friend; so you must let me have my own way: and if it should so happen, hear yourself abused patiently.—Is not this a fine bust of Socrates?"

Some part of the conversation in the next room I missed, whilst his lordship spoke. The next words I heard were—

"But my dear Lady Y——, look at Cecilia.—Would not any other girl be cast down and miserable in Cecilia's place? yet see, see how provokingly happy and well she looks."

"Yes," replied Lady Y——, "I never saw her appear better: but we are not to judge of her by what any other young lady would be in her place, for I know of none at all comparable to Miss Delamere."

"Miss Delamere!" said I to Lord Y——. "Is this the Miss Delamere who is heiress at law to——"

"The Glenthorn estate. Yes—do not let the head of Socrates fall from your hands," said his lordship, smiling.

I again lost something that was said in the next room; but I heard the old lady going on with—

"I only say, my dear, that if the man had been really what he was said to be, you could not have done better."

"Dearest mother, you cannot be serious," replied the sweetest voice I ever heard. "I am sure that you never were in earnest upon this subject: you could not wish me to be united to such a man as Lord Glenthorn was said to be."

"Why? what was he said to be, my dear?—a little dissipated, a little extravagant only: and if he had a fortune to support it, child, what matter?" pursued the mother: "all young men are extravagant now-a-days—you must take the world as it goes."

"The lady who married Lord Glenthorn, I suppose, acted upon that principle; and you see what was the consequence."

"Oh, my dear, as to her ladyship, it ran in the blood: let her have married whom she would, she would have done the same: and I am told Lord Glenthorn made an incomparably good husband. A cousin of Lady Glenthorn's assured me that she was present one day, when her ladyship expressed a wish for a gold chain to wear round her neck, or braid her hair, I forget for what; but that very hour Lord Glenthorn bespoke for her a hundred yards of gold chain, at ten guineas a yard. Another time she longed for an Indian shawl, and his lordship presented her next day with three dozen real India shawls. There's a husband for you, Cecilia!"

"Not for me, mamma," said Cecilia, laughing.

"Ah, you are a strange romantic girl, and never will be married after all, I fear."

"Never to a fool, I hope," said Cecilia.

"Miss Delamere will, however, allow," said Lady Y— —, "that a man may have his follies, without being a fool, or wholly unworthy of her esteem; otherwise, what a large portion of mankind she would deprive of hope!"

"As to Lord Glenthorn, he was no fool, I promise you," continued the mother: "has not he been living prudently enough these three years? We have not heard of late of any of his *extraordinary landaus*."

"But I have been told," said Cecilia, "that he is quite uninformed, without any taste for literature, and absolutely incapable of exertion—a victim to ennui. How miserable a woman must be with such a husband!"

"But," said Lady Y— —, "what could be expected from a young nobleman bred up as Lord Glenthorn was?"

"Nothing," said Cecilia; "and that is the very reason I never wished to see him."

"Perhaps Miss Delamere's opinion might be changed if she had known him," said Lady Y— —,

"Ay, for he is a very handsome man, I have heard," said the mother. "Lady Jocunda Lawler told me so, in one of her letters; and Lady Jocunda was very near being married to him herself, I can tell you, for he admired her prodigiously."

"A certain proof that he never would have admired me," said Cecilia; "for two women, so opposite in every respect, no man could have loved."

"Lord bless you, child! how little you know of the matter! After all, I dare say, if you had been acquainted with him, you might have been in love yourself with Lord Glenthorn."

"Possibly," said Cecilia, "if I had found him the reverse of what he is reported to be."

Company came in at this instant. Lord Y— — was called to receive them, and I followed; glad, at this instant, that I was not Lord Glenthorn. At dinner the conversation turned upon general subjects; and Lord Y— —, with polite and friendly attention, *drew me out*, without seeming to do so, in the kindest manner possible.

I had the pleasure to perceive that Cecilia Delamere did not find me a fool. I never, even in the presence of Lady Geraldine, exerted myself so much to avoid this disgrace.

After all the company, except Mrs. and Miss Delamere, were gone, Lord Y— — called me aside.

"Will you pardon," said he, "the means I have taken to convince you how much superior you are to the opinion that has been commonly formed of Lord Glenthorn? Will you forgive me for convincing you that when a man has sufficient strength of mind to rely upon himself, and sufficient energy to exert his abilities, he becomes independent of common report and vulgar opinion? He secures the suffrages of the best judges; and they, in time, lead all the rest of the world. Will you permit me now to introduce you to your prudent friend and your fair enemy? Mrs. Delamere—Miss Delamere—give me leave to introduce to you the late Earl of Glenthorn."

Of the astonishment in the opening eyes of Mrs. Delamere I have some faint recollection. I can never forget the crimson blush that instantaneously spread over the celestial countenance of Cecilia. She was perfectly silent; but her mother went on talking with increased rapidity.

"Good Heavens! the late Lord Glenthorn! Why, I was talking—but he was not in the room." The ladies exchanged looks, which seemed to say, "I hope he did not hear all we said of him."

"My dear Lord Y— —, why did not you tell us this before? Suppose we had spoken of his lordship, you would have been answerable for all the consequences."

"Certainly," said Lord Y— —.

"But, seriously," said the old lady, "have I the pleasure to speak to Lord Glenthorn, or have I not? I believe I began, unluckily, to talk of a strange story I had heard; but perhaps all this is a mistake, and my country correspondent may have been amusing herself at the expense of my credulity. I assure you I was not imposed upon; I never believed half the story."

"You may believe the whole of it, madam," said I; "the story is perfectly true."

"Oh! my good sir, how sorry I am to hear you say it is all true! And the blacksmith is really Earl of Glenthorn, and has taken possession of the castle, and is married, and has a son! Lord bless me, how unfortunate! Well, I can only say, sir, I wish, with all my heart, you were Earl of Glenthorn still."

After hearing from Lord Y— — the circumstances of what he was pleased to call my generous conduct, Mrs. Delamere observed, that I had acted very generously, to be sure, but that few in my place would have thought themselves bound to give up possession of an estate, which I had so long been taught to believe was my own. To have and to hold, she observed, always went together in law; and she could not help thinking I had done very injudiciously and imprudently not to let the law decide for me.

I was consoled for Mrs. Delamere's reprehensions by her daughter's approving countenance. After this visit, Lord Y— — gave me a general invitation to his house, where I frequently saw Miss Delamere, and frequently compared her with my recollection of Lady Geraldine — — —. Cecilia Delamere was not so entertaining, but she was more interesting than Lady Geraldine: the flashes of her ladyship's wit, though always striking, were sometimes dangerous; Cecilia's wit, though equally brilliant, shone with a more pleasing and inoffensive light. With as much generosity as Lady Geraldine could show in great affairs, she had more forbearance and delicacy of attention on every-day occasions. Lady Geraldine had much pride, and it often gave offence; Cecilia, perhaps, had more pride, but it never appeared, except upon the defensive: without having less candour, she had less occasion for it than Lady Geraldine seemed to have; and Cecilia's temper had more softness and equability. Perhaps Cecilia was not so fascinating, but she was more attractive. One had the envied art of appearing to advantage in public—the other, the more desirable power of being happy in private. I admired Lady Geraldine long before I loved her; I loved Cecilia long before I admired her.

Whilst I possibly could, I called what I felt for Miss Delamere only esteem; but when I found it impossible to conceal from myself that I loved, I resolved to avoid this charming woman. How happy, thought I, would the fortune I once possessed now make me! but in my present circumstances what have I to hope? Surely my friend Lord Y— — has not shown his usual prudence in exposing me to such a temptation; but it is to be supposed, he thinks that the impossibility of my obtaining Miss Delamere will prevent my thinking of her, or perhaps he depends on the inertness and apathy of my temper. Unfortunately for me, my sensibility has increased since I have become poor; for many years, when I was rich, and could have married easily, I never wished to marry, and now that I have not enough to support a wife, I immediately fall desperately in love.

Again and again I pondered upon my circumstances: three hundred a-year was the amount of all my worldly possessions; and Miss Delamere was not rich, and she had been bred expensively; for it had never been absent from her mother's mind, that Cecilia would be heiress to the immense Glenthorn estate. The present possessor was, however, an excellent life, and he had a son stout and healthy, so all these hopes of Mrs. Delamere's were at an end; and as there was little chance, as she said (laughing), of persuading her daughter to marry Johnny, the young lord and heir apparent, it was now necessary to turn her views elsewhere, and to form for Cecilia some suitable alliance. Rank and large fortune were, in Mrs. Delamere's opinion, indispensable to happiness. Cecilia's ideas were far more moderate; but, though perfectly disinterested and generous, she was not so romantic, or so silly, as to think of marrying any man without the probability of his being able to support her in the society of her equals: nor, even if I could have thought it possible to prevail upon Miss Delamere to make an unbecoming and imprudent choice, would I have taken advantage of the confidence reposed in me by Lord Y— —, to destroy the happiness of a young friend, for whom he evidently had a great regard. I resolved to see her no more— and for some weeks I kept my resolution; I refrained from going to Y— — house. I deem this the most virtuous action of my life; it certainly was the most painful sacrifice I ever made to a sense of duty. At last, Lord Y— — came to me one morning, and after reproaching me, in a friendly manner, for having so long absented myself from his house, declared that he would not be satisfied with any of those common excuses, which might content a mere acquaintance; that his sincere anxiety for my welfare gave him a right to expect from me the frankness of a friend. It was a relief to my mind to be encouraged in this manner. I confessed with entire openness my real motive: Lord Y— — heard me without surprise.

"It is gratifying to me," said his lordship, "to be convinced that I was not mistaken in my judgment, either of your taste, or your integrity; permit me to assure you, that I foresaw exactly how you would feel, and precisely how you would act. There are certain moral omens, which old experience never fails to interpret rightly, and from which unerring predictions of the future conduct, and consequently of the future fate of individuals, may be formed. I hold that we are the artificers of our own fortune. If there be any whom the gods wish to destroy, these are first deprived of understanding; whom the gods wish to favour, they first endow with integrity, inspire with understanding, and animate with activity. Have I not seen integrity in you, and shall I not see activity? Yes; that supineness of temper or habit with which you reproach yourself has arisen, believe me, only from want of motive; but you have now the most powerful of motives, and in proportion to your exertions will be your success. In our country, you know, the highest offices of the state are open to talents and perseverance; a man of abilities and application cannot fail to secure independence, and obtain distinction. Time and industry are necessary to prepare you for the profession, to which you will hereafter be an honour, and you will courageously submit.

—'Time and industry, the mighty two,
Which bring our wishes nearer to our view.'

As to the probability that your present wishes may be crowned with success, I can judge only from my general knowledge of the views and disposition of the lady whom you admire. I know that her views with respect to fortune are moderate; and that her disposition and excellent understanding will, in the choice of a husband, direct her preference to the essential good qualities, and not to the accidental advantages, of the candidates for her favour. As to the mother's influence, that will necessarily yield to the daughter's superior judgment. Cecilia possesses over her mother that witchcraft of gentle manners, which in the female sex is always irresistible, even over violent tempers. Prudential considerations have a just, though not exclusive, claim to Miss Delamere's attention. But her relations, I fancy, could find means of providing against any pecuniary embarrassments, if she should think proper to unite herself to a man who can be content, as she would be, with a competence, and who should *have proved himself able, by his own exertions, to maintain his wife in independence.* On this last condition I must dwell with emphasis, because it is indispensable; and I am convinced that without it Miss Delamere's consent, even after she is of age, and at liberty to judge for herself, could never be obtained. You perceive, then, how much depends upon your own exertions; and this is the best hope, and the best motive, that I can give to a strong and generous mind. Farewell—Persevere and prosper."

Such was the general purport of what Lord Y—— said to me; indeed, I believe that I have repeated his very words, for they made a great and ineffaceable impression upon my mind. From this day I date the commencement of a new existence. Fired with ambition,—I hope generous ambition,—to distinguish myself among men, and to win the favour of the most amiable and the most lovely of women, all the faculties of my soul were awakened: I became active, permanently active. The enchantment of indolence was dissolved, and the demon of ennui was cast out for ever.

CHAPTER XXI

If, among those who maybe tempted to peruse my history, there should be any mere novel readers, let me advise them to throw the book aside at the commencement of this chapter; for I have no more wonderful incidents to relate, no more changes at nurse, no more sudden turns of fortune. I am now become a plodding man of business, poring over law-books from morning till night, and leading a most monotonous life: yet occupation, and hope, and the constant sense of approaching nearer to my object, rendered this mode of existence, dull as it may seem, infinitely more agreeable than many of my apparently prosperous days, when I had more money, and more time, than I knew how to enjoy. I resolutely persevered in my studies.

About a month after I came to town, the doors of my lodging were blockaded by half a dozen cars, loaded with huge packing-cases, on which I saw, in the hand-writing which I remembered often to have seen in my blacksmith's bills, a direction to *Christopher O'Donoghoe, Esquire—this side upwards: to be kept dry.*

One of the carmen fumbled in what he called his pocket, and at last produced a very dirty note.

"My dear and honourable foster-brother, larning from Mr. M'Leod that you are thinking of *studdeing*, I send you inclosed by the bearer, who is to get nothing for the *carrige*, all the bookes from the big booke-room at the castle, which I hope, being of not as much use as I could wish to me, your honour will not scorn to accept, with the true veneration of

"Your ever-loving foster-brother, and grateful humble servant, *to command.*

"P.S. No name needful, for you will not be astray about the hand."

This good-natured fellow's present was highly valuable and useful to me.

Among my pleasures at this studious period of my life, when I had few events to break the uniform tenor of my days, I must mention letters which I frequently received from Mr. Devereux and Lady Geraldine, who still continued in India. Mr. Devereux was acquainted with almost all the men of eminence at the Irish bar; men who are not mere lawyers, but persons of literature, of agreeable manners, and gentlemanlike habits. Mr. Desvereux wrote to his friends so warmly in my favour, that, instead of finding myself a stranger in Dublin, my only difficulty was how to avoid the numerous invitations which tempted me from my studies.

Those gentlemen of the bar who were intimate with Mr. Devereux honoured me with particular attention, and their society was peculiarly useful, as well as agreeable, to me: they directed my industry to the best and shortest means of preparing myself for their profession; they put into my hands the best books; told me all that experience had taught them of the art of distinguishing, in the mass of law-precedents, the useful from the useless: instructed me in the methods of indexing and common-placing; and gave me all those advantages, which solitary students so often want, and the want of which so often makes the study of the law appear an endless maze without a plan. When I found myself surrounded with books, and reading assiduously day and night, I could scarcely believe in my own identity; I could scarcely imagine that I was the same person, who, but a few months before this time, lolled upon a sofa half the day, and found it an intolerable labour to read or think for half an hour together. Such is the power of motive! During the whole time I pursued my studies, and kept my terms, in Ireland, the only relaxation I allowed myself was in the society at Lord Y——'s house in Dublin, and, during my vacations, in excursions which I made with his lordship to different parts of the country. Lord Y—— had two country-seats in the most beautiful parts of Ireland. How differently the face of nature appeared to me now! with what different sensations I beheld the same objects!

> *"No brighter colours paint th' enamell'd fields,*
> *No sweeter fragrance now the garden yields;*
> *Whence then this strange increase of joy?*
> *Is it to love these new delights I owe?"*

It was not to love that I owed these new delights, for Cecilia was not there; but my powers of observation were awakened, and the confinement and labour to which I had lately submitted gave value to the pleasures of rest and liberty, and to the freshness of country air, and the beautiful scenes of nature. So true it is, that all our pleasures must be earned, before they can be enjoyed. When I saw on Lord Y——'s estates, and on those of several other gentlemen, which he occasionally took me to visit, the neat cottages, the well-cultivated farms, the air of comfort, industry, and prosperity, diffused through the lower classes of the people, I was convinced that much may be done by the judicious care and assistance of landlords for their tenantry. I saw this with mixed sensations of pleasure and of pain—of pain, for I reflected how little I had accomplished, and how ill I had done even that little, whilst the means of doing good to numbers had been in my power. For the very trifling services I did to some of my poor tenants, I am sure I had abundant gratitude; and I was astonished and touched by instances of this shown to me after I had lost my fortune, and when I scarcely had myself any remembrance of the people who came to thank me. Trivial as it is, I cannot forbear to record one of the many instances of gratitude I met with from a poor Irishman.

Whilst I was in Dublin, as I was paying a morning visit to Lord Y— —, sitting with him in his library, we heard some disturbance in the inner court; and looking out of the window, we saw a countryman with a basket on his arm, struggling with the porter and two footmen.

"He is here; I know to a certainty he is here, and I *shall* see him, say what you plase now!"

"I tell you my lord is not at home," said the porter.

"What's the matter?" said Lord Y— —, opening the window.

"See, there's my lord himself at the window: are not you ashamed of yourself now?" said the footman.

"And why would I be ashamed that am telling no lies, and hindering no one?" said the countryman, looking up to us with so sudden a motion that his hat fell of. I knew his face, but could not recollect his name.

"Oh! there he is, his own honour; I've found him, and *axe* pardon for my boldness; but it's because I've been all day yesterday, and this day, running through Dublin after *yees*; and when certified by the lady of the lodgings you was in it here, I could not lave town without my errand, which is no more than a cheese from my wife of her own making, to be given to your honour's own hands, and she would not see me if I did not do it."

"Let him come up," said Lord Y— —. "This," continued his lordship, turning to me, "reminds me of Henry the Fourth, and the Gascon peasant with his *fromages de boeuf.*"

"But our countryman brings his offering to an abdicated monarch," said I.

The poor fellow presented his wife's cheese to me with as good a grace as any courtier could have made his offering. Unembarrassed, his manners and his words gave the natural and easy expression of a grateful heart. He assured me that he and his wife were the happiest couple in all Ireland; and he hoped I would one day be as happy myself in a wife as I *desarved*, who had made others so; and there were many on the estate remembered as well as he did the good I did to the poor during *my reign.*

Then stepping up closer to me, he said, in a lower voice, "I'm Jimmy Riley, that married *ould* Noonan's daughter; and now that it is all over I may tell you a bit of a *secret*, which made me so eager to get to the speech of your honour, that I might tell it to your own ear alone—no offence to this gentleman, before whom I'd as soon say it as yourself, *becaase* I see he is all as one as another yourself. Then the thing is—does your honour remember the boy with the cord round his body, looking for the birds' eggs in the rock, and the 'nonymous bit of a letter that you got? 'Twas I wrote it, and the *gossoon* that threw it to your honour was a cousin of my own that I sent, that nobody, nor yourself even, might not know him: and the way I got the information I never can tell till I die, and then only to the priest, *becaase* I swore I would not never. But don't go for to think it was by being a *rubble* any way; no man can, I thank my God, charge me with indifference. So rejoiced to see you the same, I wish you a good morrow, and long life, and a happy death—when it comes."

About this time I frequently used to receive presents to a considerable amount, and of things which were most useful to me, but always without any indication by which I could discover to whom I was indebted for them: at last, by means of my Scotch landlady, I traced them to Mr. M'Leod. His kindness was so earnest and peremptory, that it would admit neither thanks nor refusals; and I submitted to be obliged to a man for whom I felt such high esteem. I looked upon it as not the least of his proofs of regard, that he gave me what I knew he valued more than any thing else—his time. Whenever he came to Dublin, though he was always hurried by business, so that he had scarcely leisure to eat or sleep, he used constantly to come to see me in my obscure lodgings; and when in the country, though he hated all letter-writing, except letters of business, yet he regularly informed me of every thing that could be interesting to me. Glenthorn Castle he described as a scene of riotous living, and of the most wasteful vulgar extravagance. My poor foster-brother, the best-natured and most generous fellow in the world, had not sufficient prudence or strength of mind to conduct his own family; his wife filled the castle with tribes of her vagabond relations; she chose to be descended from one of the kings of Ireland; and whoever would acknowledge her high descent, and whoever would claim relationship with her, were sure to have their claims allowed, and were welcome to live in all the barbaric magnificence of Glenthorn Castle. Every instance that she could hear of the former Lady Glenthorn's extravagance or of mine—

and, alas! there were many upon record, she determined to exceed. Her diamonds, and her pearls, and her finery, surpassed every thing but the extravagance of some of the Russian favourites of fortune. Decked out in the most absurd manner, this descendant of kings, as Mr. M'Leod assured me, often indulged in the pleasures of the banquet, till, no longer able to support the regal diadem, she was carried by some of the meanest of her subjects to her bed. The thefts committed during these interregnums were amazing in their amount, and the jewels of the crown were to be replaced as fast as they were stolen. Poor Christy all this time was considered as a mean-spirited *cratur*, who had no notion of living like a prince; and whilst his wife and her relations were revelling in this unheard-of manner, he was scarcely considered as the master of the house: he lived by the fireside disregarded in winter, and in summer he spent his time chiefly in walking up and down his garden, and picking fruit. He once made an attempt to amuse himself by mending the lock of his own room door; but he was detected in the fact, and exposed to such loud ridicule by his lady's favourites, that he desisted, and sighing said to Mr. M'Leod—"And isn't it now a great hardship upon a man like me to have nothing to do, or not to be let do any thing? If it had not been for my son Johnny's sake, I never would have quit the forge; and now all will be spent in *coshering*, and Johnny, at the last, will never be a penny the better, but the worse for my consinting to be lorded; and what grieves me more than all the rest, *she* is such *a negre*,85 that I haven't a guinea I can call my own to send, as I'd always laid out to do at odd times, such little tokens of my love and duty, as would be becoming to my dear foster-brother there in Dublin. And now, you tell me, he is going away too, beyond sea to England, to finish making a lawyer of himself in London; and what friends will he find there, without money in his pocket? and I had been thinking this while past, ever since you gave me notice of his being to quit Ireland, that I would go up to Dublin myself to see him, and wish him a good journey kindly before he would go; and I had a little *compliment* here, in a private drawer, that I had collected *unknownst* to my wife; but here last night she *lit* upon it, and now that her hand has closed upon it, not a guinea of it shall I ever see more, nor a farthing the better of it will my dear foster-brother ever be, for it or for me; and this is what grieves me more than all, and goes to the quick of my heart."

When Mr. M'Leod repeated to me these lamentations of poor Christy, I immediately wrote to set his heart at ease, as much as I could, by the assurance that I was in no distress for money; and that my three hundred a year would support me in perfect comfort and independence, while "I was making a lawyer of myself in London." I farther assured my good foster-brother, that I was so well convinced of his affectionate and generous disposition towards me, that it would be quite unnecessary ever to send me tokens of his regard. I added a few words of advice about his wife and his affairs, which, like most words of advice, were, as I afterwards found, absolutely thrown away.

Though I had taken care to live with so much economy, that I was not in any danger of being in pecuniary embarrassments, yet I felt much distress of another kind in leaving Ireland. I left Miss Delamere surrounded with admirers; her mother using her utmost art and parental influence to induce Cecilia to decide in favour of one of these gentlemen, who was a person of rank and of considerable fortune. I had seen all this going on, and was bound in honour the whole time to remain passive, not to express my own ardent feelings, not to make the slightest attempt to win the affections of the woman who was the object of all my labours, of all my exertions. The last evening that I saw her at Lord Y——'s, just before I sailed for England, I suffered more than I thought it was in my nature to feel, especially at the moment when I went up to make my bow, and take leave of her with all the cold ceremony of a common acquaintance. At parting, however, in the presence of her mother and of Lord Y——, Cecilia, with her sweet smile, and, I think, with a slight blush, said a few words, upon which I lived for months afterwards.

"I sincerely wish you, sir, the success your perseverance so well deserves."

The recollection of these words was often my solace in my lonely chambers in the Temple; and often, after a day's hard study, the repeating them to myself operated as a charm that dissipated all fatigue, and revived at once my exhausted spirits. To be sure, there were moments when my fire was out, and my candle sinking in the socket, and my mind over-wearied saw things in the most gloomy point of view; and at these times I used to give an unfavourable interpretation to Cecilia's words, and I fancied that they were designed to prevent my entertaining fallacious hopes, and to warn me that she must yield to her mother's authority, or perhaps to her own inclinations, in favour of some of her richer lovers. This idea would have sunk me into utter despondency, and I should have lost, with my motive, all power of exertion, had not I opposed to this apprehension the remembrance of Lord Y——'s countenance, at the moment Cecilia was speaking to me. I then felt assured, that his lordship, at least, understood the words in a favourable sense, else he would have suffered for me, and would not certainly have allowed me to go away with false hopes. Re-animated by this consideration, I persevered—for it was by perseverance alone that I could have any chance of success.

It was fortunate for me, that, stimulated by a great motive, I thus devoted my whole time and thoughts to my studies, otherwise I must, on returning to London, have felt the total neglect and desertion of all my former associates in the fashionable world; of all the vast number of acquaintance who used to lounge away their hours in my company, and partake of the luxuries of my table and the festivities of my house. Some, whom I accidentally met in the street, just at my re-appearance in town, thought proper, indeed, to know me again at first, that they might gratify their curiosity about the paragraphs which they had seen in the papers, and the reports which they had heard of my extraordinary change of fortune; but no sooner had they satisfied themselves that all they had heard was true, than their interest concerning me ceased. When they found, that, instead of being Earl of Glenthorn, and the possessor of a large estate, I was now reduced to three hundred a year, lodging in small chambers in the Temple, and studying the law, they never more thought me worthy of their notice. They affected, according to their different humours, either to pity me for my misfortunes, or to blame me for my folly in giving up my estate; but they unanimously expressed astonishment at the idea of my becoming a member of any active profession. They declared that it was impossible that I could ever endure the labour of the law, or succeed in such an arduous career. Their prophecies intimidated me not; I was conscious that these people did not in the least know me; and I hoped and believed that I had powers and a character which they were incapable of estimating: their contempt rather excited than depressed my mind, and their pity I returned with more sincerity than it was given. I had lived their life, knew thoroughly what were its pleasures and its pains; I could compare the ennui I felt when I was a Bond-street lounger with the self-complacency I enjoyed now that I was occupied in a laborious but interesting and honourable pursuit. I confess, I had sometimes, however, the weakness to think the worse of human nature, for what I called the desertion and ingratitude of these my former companions and flatterers; and I could not avoid comparing the neglect and solitude in which I lived in London, where I had lavished my fortune, with the kindness and hospitalities I had received in Dublin, where I lived only when I had no fortune to spend. After a little time, however, I became more reasonable and just; for I considered that it was my former dissipated mode of life, and imprudent choice of associates, which I should blame for the mortifications I now suffered from the desertion of companions, who were, in fact, incapable of being friends. In London I had lived with the most worthless, in Dublin with the best company; and in each place I had been treated as, in fact, I deserved. But, leaving the history of my feelings, I must proceed with my narrative.

One night, after I had dined with an Irish gentleman, a friend of Lord Y— —'s, at the west end of the town, as I was returning late to my lodgings, I was stopped for some time by a crowd of carriages, in one of the fashionable streets. I found that there was a masquerade at the house of a lady, with whom I had been intimately acquainted. The clamours of the mob, eager to see the dresses of those who were alighting from their carriages, the gaudy and fantastic figures which I beheld by the light of the flambeaux, the noise and the bustle, put me in mind of various similar nights of my past life, and it seemed to me like a dream, or reminiscence of some former state of existence. I passed on as soon as the crowd would permit, and took my way down a narrow street, by which I hoped to get, by a shorter way than usual, to my quiet lodgings. The rattling of the carriages, the oaths of the footmen, and the shouts of the mob still sounded in my ears; and the masquerade figures had scarcely faded from my sight, when I saw, coming slowly out of a miserable entry, by the light of a few wretched candles and lanterns, a funeral. The contrast struck me: I stood still to make way for the coffin; and I heard one say to another, "What matter how she's buried! I tell you, be at as little expense as possible, for he'll never pay a farthing." I had a confused recollection of having heard the voice before: as one of the bearers lifted his lantern, I saw the face of the woman who spoke, and had a notion of having seen her before. I asked whose funeral it was; and I was answered, "It is one Mrs. Crawley's—Lady Glenthorn that was," added the woman. I heard no more: I was so much shocked, that I believe I should have fallen in the street, if I had not been immediately supported by somebody near me. When I recovered my recollection, I saw the funeral had moved on some paces, and the person who supported me, I now found, was a clergyman. In a mild voice, he told me that his duty called him away from me at present, but he added, that if I would tell him where I could be found, he would see me in the morning, and give me any information in his power, as he supposed that I was interested for this unfortunate woman. I put a card with my address into his hands, thanked him, and got home as well as I could. In the morning, the clergyman called upon me—a most benevolent man, unknown to fame; but known to all the wretched within the reach of his consolatory religion. He gave me a melancholy account of the last days of the unhappy woman, whose funeral I had just seen. I told him who I was, and what she had been to me. She had, almost in her last moments, as he assured me, expressed her sense of, what she called, my generosity to her, and had shown deep contrition for her infidelity. She died in extreme poverty and wretchedness, with no human being who was, or even seemed, interested for her, but a maid-servant (the woman whose voice I recollected), whose services were purchased to the last, by presents of whatever clothes or trinkets were left from the wreck of her mistress's fortune. Crawley, it seems, had behaved brutally to his victim. After having long delayed to perform his promise of marrying her, he declared that he could never think of a woman who had been divorced in any other way than a mistress: she, poor weak creature, consented to live with him on any terms; but, as his passions and his interest soon turned to new objects, he cast her off without scruple, refusing to pay any of the tradesmen, who had supplied her while she bore his name. He refused to pay the expenses even of her funeral, though she had shared with him her annuity, and every thing she possessed. I paid the funeral expenses, and some arrears of the maid's wages, together with such debts for necessaries as I had reason to believe were justly due: the strict economy with which I had lived for three years, and the parting with a watch and some other trinkets too fine for my circumstances, enabled me to pay this money without material inconvenience, and it was a satisfaction to my mind. The good clergyman who managed these little matters became interested for me, and our acquaintance with each other grew every day more intimate and agreeable. When he found that I was studying the law, he begged to introduce me to a brother of his, who had been one of the most eminent special pleaders in London, and who now, on a high salary, undertook to prepare students for the bar. I was rather unwilling to accept of this introduction, because I was not rich enough to become a pupil of this gentleman's; but my clergyman guessed the cause of my reluctance, and told me that his brother had charged him to overrule all such objections. "My brother and I," continued he, "though of different professions, have in reality but one mind between us: he has heard from me all the circumstances I know of you, and they have interested him so much, that he desires, in plain English, to be of any service he can to you."

This offer was made in earnest; and if I had given him the largest salary that could have been offered by the most opulent of his pupils, I could not have met with more attention, or have been instructed with more zeal than I was, by my new friend the special pleader. He was also so kind as to put me at ease by the assurance, that whenever I should begin to make money by my profession, he would accept of remuneration. He jestingly said, that he would make the same bargain with me that was made by the famous sophist Protagoras of old with his pupil, that he should have the profits of the first cause I should win—certain that I would not, like his treacherous pupil Evathlus, employ the rhetorician's arms against himself, to cheat him out of his promised reward. My special pleader was not a mere man of forms and law *rigmaroles*; he knew the reason for the forms he used: he had not only a technical, but a rational knowledge of his business; and, what is still more uncommon, he knew how to teach what he had learnt. He did not merely set me down at a desk, and leave me skins after skins of parchment to pore over in bewildered and hopeless stupidity; he did not use me like a mere copying machine, to copy sheet after sheet for him, every morning from nine till four, and again every evening from five till ten. Mine was a law tutor of a superior sort. Wherever he could, he gave me a clue to guide me through the labyrinth; and when no reason could be devised for what the law directs, he never puzzled me by attempting to explain what could not be explained; he did not insist upon the total surrender of my rational faculties, but with wonderful liberality would allow me to call nonsense, nonsense; and would, after two or three hours' hard scrivening, as the case might require—for this I thank him more than all the rest—permit me to yawn, and stretch, and pity myself, and curse the useless repetitions of lawyers, sinking under the weight of *declarations*, and *replications*, and *double pleas*, and *dilatory, pleas*;

"*Of horse pleas, traverses, demurrers,*

Jeofails, imparlances, and errors.

Averments, bars, and profestandoes.'"

O! Cecilia, what pains did I endure to win your applause! Yet, that I may state the whole truth, let me acknowledge, that even these, my dullest, hardest tasks, were light, compared with the burden I formerly bore of ennui. At length my period of probation in my pleader's office was over; I escaped from the dusky desk, and the smell of musty parchments, and the close smoky room; I finished *eating my terms* at the Temple, and returned, even, as the captain of the packet swore, "in the face and teeth of the wind," to Dublin.

But, in my haste to return, I must not omit to notice, for the sake of poetical equity, that just when I was leaving England, I heard that slow but sure-paced justice at last overtook that wretch Crawley. He was detected and convicted of embezzling considerable sums, the property of a gentleman in Cheshire, who had employed him as his agent. I saw him, as I passed through Chester, going to prison, amidst the execrations of the populace.

CHAPTER XXII

As I was not, as formerly, asleep in my carriage on deck, when we came within sight of the Irish shore, I saw, and hailed with delight, the beautiful bay of Dublin. The moment we landed, instead of putting myself out of humour, as before, with every thing at the Marine Hotel, I went directly to my friend Lord Y——'s. I made my *sortie* from the hotel with so much extraordinary promptitude, that a slip-shod waiter was forced to pursue me, running or shuffling after me the whole length of the street, before he could overtake me with a letter, which had been "waiting for my honour, at the hotel, since yesterday's Holyhead packet." This was a mistake, as the letter had never come or gone by any Holyhead packet; it was only a letter from Mr. M'Leod, to welcome me to Ireland again; and to tell me, that he had taken care to secure good well-aired lodgings for me: he added an account of what was going on at Glenthorn Castle. The extravagance of *my lady* had by this time reduced the family to great difficulties for ready money, as they could neither sell nor mortgage any part of the Glenthorn estate, which was settled on the son. My poor foster-brother had, it seems, in vain attempted to restrain the wasteful folly of his wife, and to persuade Johnny, the young heir-apparent, to *larn* to be a *jantleman*: in vain Christy tried to prevail on his lordship to "refrain drinking whisky *preferably* to claret:" the youth pleaded both his father's and mother's examples; and said, that as he was an only son, and his father had but a life-interest in the estate, he *expected* to be indulged; he repeated continually "a short life and a merry one for me." Mr. M'Leod concluded this letter by observing, "that far from its being a merry life, he never saw any thing more sad than the life this foolish boy led; and that Glenthorn Castle was so melancholy and disgusting a scene of waste, riot, and intemperance, that he could not bear to go there." I was grieved by this account, for the sake of my poor foster-brother; but it would have made a deeper impression upon me at any other time. I must own that I forgot the letter, and all that it contained, as I knocked at Lord Y——'s door.

Lord Y—— received me with open arms; and, with all the kindness of friendship, anticipated the questions I longed, yet feared, to ask.

"Cecilia Delamere is still unmarried—Let these words be enough to content you for the present; all the rest is, I hope, in your own power."

In my power!—delightful thought! yet how distant that hope! For I was now, after all my labours, but just called to the bar; not yet likely, for years, to make a guinea, much less a fortune, by my profession. Many of the greatest of our lawyers have gone circuit for ten or twelve years, before they made a *Fashionable Life*. hundred a year; and I was at this time four-and-thirty. I confessed to my Lord Y— —, that these reflections alarmed and depressed me exceedingly: but he encouraged me by this answer—"Persevere— deserve success; and trust the rest, not to fortune, but to your friends. It is not required of you to make ten thousand or one thousand a year at the bar, in any given time; but it is expected from you to give proofs that you are capable of conquering the indolence of your disposition or of your former habits. It is required from you to give proofs of intellectual energy and ability. When you have convinced me that you have the knowledge and assiduity that ought to succeed at the bar, I shall be certain that only time is wanting to your actual acquisition of a fortune equal to what I ought to require for my fair friend and relation. When it comes to that point, it will, my dear sir, be time enough for me to say more. Till it comes to that point, I have promised Mrs. Delamere that you will not even attempt to see her daughter. She blames me for having permitted Cecilia and you to see so much of each other, as you did in this house when you were last in Ireland. Perhaps I was imprudent, but your conduct has saved me from my own reproaches, and I fear no other. I end where I began, with 'Persevere—and may the success your perseverance deserves be your reward.' If I recollect right, these were nearly Miss Delamere's own words at parting with you."

In truth, I had not forgotten them; and I was so much excited by their repetition at this moment, and by my excellent friend's encouraging voice, that all difficulties, all dread of future labours or evils, vanished from my view. I went my first circuit, and made two guineas, and was content; for Lord Y— — was not disappointed: he told me it would, it must be so. But though I made no money, I obtained gradually, amongst my associates at the bar, the reputation for judgment and knowledge. Of this they could judge by my conversation, and by the remarks on the trials brought on before us. The elder counsel had been prepared in my favour, first by Mr. Devereux, and afterwards by my diligence in following their advice, during my studies in Dublin: they perceived that I had not lost my time in London, and that *my mind was in my possession*. They prophesied, that from the moment I began to be employed, I should rise rapidly. Opportunity, they told me, was now all that I wanted, and for that I must wait with patience. I waited with as much patience as I could. I had many friends; some among the judges, some among a more powerful class of men, the attorneys: some of these friends made for me by Mr. Devereux and Lady Geraldine; some by Lord

Y——; some, may I say it? by myself. Yet the utmost that even the highest patronage from the bench can do for a young barrister is, to give him an opportunity of distinguishing himself in preference to other competitors. This was all I hoped; and I was not deceived in this hope. It happened that a cause of considerable moment, which had come on in our circuit, and to the whole course of which I had attended with great care, was removed, by an appeal, to Dublin. I fortunately, I should say prudently, was in the habit of constant attendance at the courts: the counsel who was engaged to manage this cause was suddenly taken ill, and was disabled from proceeding. The judge called upon me; the attorneys, and the other counsel, were all agreed in wishing me to take up the business, for they knew I was prepared, and competent to the question. The next day the cause, which was then to be finally decided, came on. I sat up all night to look over my documents, and to make myself sure of my points. Ten years before this, if any one had prophesied this of me, how little could I have believed them!

The trial came on—I rose to speak. How fortunate it was for me, that I did not know my Lord Y—— was in the court! I am persuaded that I could not have uttered three sentences, if he had caught my eye in the exordium of this my first harangue. Every man of sensibility—and no man without it can be an orator—every man of sensibility knows that it is more difficult to speak in the presence of one anxious friend, of whose judgment we have a high opinion, than before a thousand auditors who are indifferent, and are strangers to us. Not conscious who was listening to me, whose eyes were upon me, whose heart was beating for me, I spoke with confidence and fluency, for I spoke on a subject of which I had previously made myself completely master; and I was so full of the matter, that I thought not of the words. Perhaps this, and my having the right side of the question, were the causes of my success. I heard a buzz of thanks and applause round me. The decree was given in our favour. At this moment I recollected my bargain, and my debt to my good master the special pleader. But all bargains, all debts, all special pleaders, vanished the next instant from my mind; for the crowd opened, Lord Y—— appeared before me, seized my hand, congratulated me actually with tears of joy, carried me away to his carriage, ordered the coachman to drive home—fast! fast!

"And now," said he to me, "I am satisfied. Your trial is over—successfully over—you have convinced me of your powers and your perseverance. All the hopes of friendship are fulfilled: may all the hopes of love be accomplished! You have now my free and full approbation to address my ward and relation, Cecilia Delamere. You will have difficulties with her mother, perhaps; but none beyond what we good and great lawyers shall, I trust, be able to overrule. Mrs. Delamere knows, that, as I have an unsettled estate, and but one son, I have it in my power to provide for her daughter as if she were my own. It has always been my intention to do so: but if you marry Miss Delamere, you will still find it necessary to pursue your profession diligently, to maintain her in her own rank and style of life; and now that you have felt the pleasures of successful exertion, you will consider this necessity as an additional blessing. From what I have heard this day, there can be no doubt, that, by pursuing your profession, you can secure, in a few years, not only ease and competence, but affluence and honours—honours of your own earning. How far superior to any hereditary title!"

The carriage stopped at Lord Y——'s door. My friend presented me to Cecilia, whom I saw this day for the first time since my return to Ireland. From this hour I date the commencement of my life of real happiness. How unlike that life of *pleasure*, to which so many give erroneously the name of happiness! Lord Y——, with his powerful influence, supported my cause with Mrs. Delamere, who was induced, though with an ill grace, to give up her opposition.

"Cecilia," she said, "was now three-and-twenty, an age to judge for herself; and Lord Y——'s judgment was a great point in favour of Mr. O'Donoghoe, to be sure. And no doubt Mr. O'Donoghoe might make a fortune, since he had made a figure already at the bar. In short, she could not oppose the wishes of Lord Y——, and the affections of her daughter, since they were so fixed. But, after all," said Mrs. Delamere, "what a horrid thing it will be to hear my girl called Mrs. O'Donoghoe! Only conceive the sound of—Mrs. O'Donoghoe's carriage there!—Mrs. O'Donoghoe's carriage stops the way!"

"Your objection, my dear madam," replied Lord Y——, "is fully as well founded as that of a young lady of my acquaintance, who could not prevail on her delicacy to become the wife of a merchant of the name of *Sheepshanks*. He very wisely, or very gallantly, paid five hundred pounds to change his name. I make no doubt that your future son-in-law will have no objection to take and bear the name and arms of Delamere; and I think I can answer for it, that a king's letter may be obtained, empowering him to do so. With this part of the business allow me to charge myself."

I spare the reader the protracted journal of a lover's hopes and fears. Cecilia, convinced, by the exertions in which I had so long persevered, that my affection for her was not only sincere and ardent, but likely to be permanent, did not torture me by the vain delays of female coquetry. She believed, she said, that a man capable of conquering habitual indolence could not be of a feeble character; and she therefore consented, without hesitation, to entrust her happiness to my care.

I hope my readers have, by this time, too favourable an opinion of me to suspect, that, in my joy, I forgot him who had been my steady friend in adversity. I wrote to M'Leod, as soon as I knew my own happiness, and assured him that it would be incomplete without his sympathy. I do not think there was at our wedding a face of more sincere, though sober joy, than M'Leod's. Cecilia and I have been now married above a twelvemonth, and she permits me to say, that she has never, for a moment, repented her choice. That I have not relapsed into my former habits, the judicious and benevolent reader will hence infer: and yet I have been in a situation to be spoiled; for I scarcely know a wish of my heart that remains ungratified, except the wish that my friend Mr. Devereux and Lady Geraldine should return from India, to see and partake of that happiness of which they first prepared the foundation. They first awakened my dormant intellects, made me know that I had a heart, and that I was capable of forming a character for myself. The loss of my estate continued the course of my education, forced me to exert my own powers, and to rely upon myself. My passion for the amiable and charming Cecilia was afterwards motive sufficient to urge me to persevering intellectual labour: fortunately my marriage has obliged me to continue my exertions, and the labours of my profession have made the pleasures of domestic life most delightful. The rich, says a philosophic moralist, are obliged to labour, if they would be healthy or happy; and they call this labour exercise.

Whether, if I were again a rich man, I should have sufficient voluntary exertion to take a due portion of mental and bodily exercise, I dare not pretend to determine, nor do I wish to be put to the trial. Desiring nothing in life but the continuance of the blessings I possess, I may here conclude my memoirs, by assuring my readers, that after a full experience of most of what are called the pleasures of life, I would not accept of all the Glenthorn and Sherwood estates, to pass another year of such misery as I endured whilst I was "stretched on the rack of a too easy chair."

The preceding memoirs were just ready for publication, when I received the following letter:

"HONOURED FOSTER-BROTHER,

"Since the day I parted yees, nothing in life but misfortins has happened me, owing to my being overruled by my wife, who would be a lady, all I could say again it. But that's over, and there's no help; for all and all that ever she can say will do no good. The castle's burnt down all to the ground, and my Johnny's dead, and I wish I was dead in his place. The occasion of his death was owing to drink, which he fell into from getting too much money, and nothing to do—and a snuff of a candle. When going to bed last night, a little in liquor, what does he do but takes the candle, and sticks it up against the head of his bed, as he used oftentimes to do, without detriment, in the cabin where he was reared, against the mud-wall. But this was close to an ould window curtain, and a deal of ould wood in the bed, which was all in a smother, and he lying asleep after drinking, when he was ever hard to wake, and before he waked at all, it appears the unfortunit *cratur* was smothered, and none heard a sentence of it, till the ceiling of my room, the blue bedchamber, with a piece of the big wood cornice, fell, and wakened me with terrible uproar, and all above and about me was flame and smoke, and I just took my wife on my back, and down the stairs with her, which did not give in till five minutes after, and she screeching, and all them relations she had screeching and running every one for themselves, and no thought in any to save any thing at all, but just what they could for themselves, and not a sarvant that was in his right rason. I got the ladder with a deal of difficulty, and up to Johnny's room, and there was a sight for me—he a corpse, and how even to get the corpse out of that, myself could not tell, for I was bewildered, and how they took me down, I don't well know. When I came to my sinses, I was lying on the ground in the court, and all confusion and screaming still, and the flames raging worse than ever. There's no use in describing all—the short of it is, there's nothing remaining of the castle but the stones; and it's little I'd think o' that, if I could have Johnny back—such as he used to be in my good days; since he's gone, I am no good. I write this to beg you, being married, of which I give you joy, to Miss Delamere, that is the *hare* at law, will take possession of all immediately, for I am as good as dead, and will give no hindrance. I will go back to my forge, and, by the help of God, forget at my work what has passed; and as to my wife, she may go to her own kith and kin, if she will not abide by me. I shall not trouble her long. Mr. M'Leod is a good man, and will follow any directions you send;

and may the blessing of God attind, and come to reign over us again, when you will find me, as heretofore,

"Your loyal foster-brother,

"CHRISTY DONOGHOE"

Glenthorn Castle is now rebuilding; and when it is finished, and when I return thither, I will, if it should be desired by the public, give a faithful account of my feelings. I flatter myself that I shall not relapse into indolence; my understanding has been cultivated—I have acquired a taste for literature, and the example of Lord Y—— convinces me that a man may at once be rich and noble, and active and happy.

Written in 1804. Printed in 1809.

THE DUN

"Horrible monster! hated by gods and men." — PHILLIPS.

"In the higher and middle classes of society," says a celebrated writer, "it is a melancholy and distressing sight to observe, not unfrequently, a man of a noble and ingenuous disposition, once feelingly alive to a sense of honour and integrity, gradually sinking under the pressure of his circumstances, making his excuses at first with a blush of conscious shame, afraid to see the faces of his friends from whom he may have borrowed money, reduced to the meanest tricks and subterfuges to delay or avoid the payment of his just debts, till, ultimately grown familiar with falsehood, and at enmity with the world, he loses all the grace and dignity of man."

Colonel Pembroke, the subject of the following story, had not, at the time his biographer first became acquainted with him, "grown familiar with falsehood;" his conscience was not entirely callous to reproach, nor was his heart insensible to compassion; but he was in a fair way to get rid of all troublesome feelings and principles. He was connected with a set of selfish young men of fashion, whose opinions stood him in stead of law, equity, and morality; to them he appealed in all doubtful cases, and his self-complacency being daily and hourly dependent upon their decisions, he had seldom either leisure or inclination to consult his own judgment. His amusements and his expenses were consequently regulated by the example of his companions, not by his own choice. To follow them in every absurd variety of the mode, either in dress or, equipage, was his first ambition; and all their factitious wants appeared to him objects of the first necessity. No matter how good the boots, the hat, the coat, the furniture, or the equipage might be, if they had outlived the fashion of the day, or even of the hour, they were absolutely worthless in his eyes. *Nobody* could be seen in such things — then of what use could they be to *any body*? Colonel Pembroke's finances were not exactly equal to the support of such *liberal* principles; but this was a misfortune which he had in common with several of his companions. It was no check to their spirit — they could live upon credit — credit, "that talisman, which realizes every thing it imagines, and which can imagine every thing." [See Des Casaux sur le Méchanisme de la Société.] Without staying to reflect upon the immediate or remote consequences of this system, Pembroke, in his first attempts, found it easy to reduce it to practice: but, as he proceeded, he experienced some difficulties. Tradesmen's bills accumulated, and applications for payment became every day more frequent and pressing. He defended himself with much address and ingenuity, and practice perfected him in all the Fabian arts of delay. *"No faith with duns"* became, as he frankly declared, a maxim of his morality. He could now, with a most plausible face, protest to a *poor devil,* upon the honour of a gentleman, that he should be paid to-morrow; when nothing was farther from his intentions or his power than to keep his word: and when *to-morrow* came, he could, with the most easy assurance, *damn the rascal* for putting a gentleman in mind of his promises. But there were persons more difficult to manage than *poor devils.* Colonel Pembroke's tailor, who had begun by being the most accommodating fellow in the world, and who had in three years run him up a bill of thirteen hundred pounds, at length began to fail in complaisance, and had the impertinence to talk of his large family, and his urgent calls for money, etc. And next, the colonel's shoe and boot-maker, a man from whom he had been in the habit of taking two hundred pounds' worth of shoes and boots every year, for himself and his servants, now pretended to be in distress for ready money, and refused to furnish more goods upon credit. "Ungrateful dog!" Pembroke called him; and he actually believed his creditors to be ungrateful and insolent, when they asked for their money; for men frequently learn to believe what they are in the daily habit of asserting [Rochefoucault], especially if their assertions be not contradicted by their audience. He knew that his tradesmen overcharged him in every article he bought, and therefore he thought it but just to delay payment whilst it suited his convenience. "Confound them, they can very well afford to wait!" As to their pleas of urgent demands for ready money, large families, &c., he considered these merely as words of course, tradesmen's cant, which should make no more impression upon a gentleman than the whining of a beggar.

One day when Pembroke was just going out to ride with some of his gay companions, he was stopped at his own door by a pale, thin, miserable-looking boy, eight or nine years old, who presented him with a paper, which he took for granted was a petition; he threw the child half-a-crown. "There, take that," said he, "and stand out of the way of my horse's heels, I advise you, my little fellow."

The boy, however, still pressed closer; and, without picking up the half-crown, held the paper to Colonel Pembroke, who had now vaulted into his saddle.

"O no! no! That's too much, my lad—I never read petitions—I'd sooner give half-a-crown at any time than read a petition."

"But, sir, this is not a petition—indeed, sir, I am not a beggar."

"What is it then?—Heyday! a bill!—Then you're worse than a beggar—a dun!—a dun! in the public streets, at your time of life! You little rascal, why what will you come to before you are your father's age?" The boy sighed. "If," pursued the colonel, "I were to serve you right, I should give you a good horse-whipping. Do you see this whip?"

"I do, sir," said the boy; "but——"

"But what? you insolent little dun!—But what?"

"My father is dying," said the child, bursting into tears, "and we have no money to buy him bread, or any thing."

Struck by these words, Pembroke snatched the paper from the boy, and looking hastily at the total and title of the bill, read—"Twelve pounds fourteen—John White, weaver."—"I know of no such person!—I have no dealings with weavers, child," said the colonel, laughing: "My name's Pembroke—Colonel Pembroke."

"Colonel Pembroke—yes, sir, the very person Mr. Close, the tailor, sent me to!"

"Close the tailor! D—n the rascal: was it he sent you to dun me? For this trick he shall not see a farthing of my money this twelvemonth. You may, tell him so, you little whining hypocrite!—And, hark you! the next time you come to me, take care to come with a better story—let your father and mother, and six brothers and sisters, be all lying ill of the fever—do you understand?"

He tore the bill into bits as he spoke, and showered it over the boy's head. Pembroke's companions laughed at this operation, and he facetiously called it "powdering a dun." They rode off to the Park in high spirits; and the poor boy picked up the half-crown, and returned home. His home was in a lane in Moorfields, about three miles distant from this gay part of the town. As the child had not eaten any thing that morning, he was feeble, and grew faint as he was crossing Covent Garden. He sat down upon the corner of a stage of flowers.

"What are you doing there?" cried a surly man, pulling him up by the arm; "What business have you lounging and loitering here, breaking my best balsam?"

"I did not mean to do any harm—I am not loitering, indeed, sir,—I'm only weak," said the boy, "and hungry."

"Oranges! oranges! fine China oranges!" cried a woman, rolling her barrow full of fine fruit towards him. "If you've a two-pence in the world, you can't do better than take one of these fine ripe China oranges."

"I have not two-pence of my own in the world," said the boy.

"What's that I see through the hole in your waistcoat pocket?" said the woman; "is not that silver?"

"Yes, half-a-crown; which I am carrying home to my father, who is ill, and wants it more than I do."

"Pooh! take an orange out of it—it's only two-pence—and it will do you good—I'm sure you look as if you wanted it badly enough."

"That may be; but father wants it worse.—No, I won't change my half-crown," said the boy, turning away from the tempting oranges.

The gruff gardener caught him by the hand.

"Here, I've moved the balsam a bit, and it is not broke, I see; sit ye down, child, and rest yourself, and eat this," said he, putting into his hand half a ripe orange, which he just cut.

"Thank you!—God bless you, sir!—How good it is!—But," said the child, stopping after he had tasted the sweet juice, "I am sorry I have sucked so much; I might have carried it home to father, who is ill; and what a treat it would be to him!—I'll keep the rest."

"No—that you sha'n't," said the orange-woman. "But I'll tell you what you shall do—take this home to your father, which is a better one by half—I'm sure it will do him good—I never knew a ripe China orange do harm to man, woman, or child."

The boy thanked the good woman and the gardener, as only those can thank who have felt what it is to be in absolute want. When he was rested, and able to walk, he pursued his way home. His mother was watching for him at the street-door.

"Well, John, my dear, what news? Has he paid us?"

The boy shook his head.

"Then we must bear it as well as we can," said his mother, wiping the cold dew from her forehead.

"But look, mother, I have this half-crown, which the gentleman, thinking me a beggar, threw to me."

"Run with it, love, to the baker's. No—stay, you're tired—I'll go myself; and do you step up to your father, and tell him the bread is coming in a minute."

"Don't run, for you're not able, mother; don't hurry so," said the boy, calling after her, and holding up his orange: "see, I have this for father whilst you are away."

He clambered up three flights of dark, narrow, broken stairs, to the room in which his father lay. The door hung by a single hinge, and the child had scarcely strength enough to raise it out of the hollow in the decayed floor into which it had sunk. He pushed it open, with as little noise as possible, just far enough to creep in.

Let those forbear to follow him whose fine feelings can be moved only by romantic, elegant scenes of distress, whose delicate sensibility shrinks from the revolting sight of real misery. Here are no pictures for romance, no stage effect to be seen, no poetic language to be heard; nothing to charm the imagination,—every thing to disgust the senses.

This room was so dark, that upon first going into it, after having been in broad daylight, you could scarcely distinguish any one object it contained; and no one used to breathe a pure atmosphere could probably have endured to remain many minutes in this garret. There were three beds in it: one on which the sick man lay; divided from it by a tattered rug was another, for his wife and daughter; and a third for his little boy in the farthest corner. Underneath the window was fixed a loom, at which the poor weaver had worked hard many a day and year—too hard, indeed—even till the very hour he was taken ill. His shuttle now lay idle upon his frame. A girl of about sixteen—his daughter—was sitting at the foot of his bed, finishing some plain work.

"Oh, Anne! how your face is all flushed!" said her little brother, as she looked up when he came into the room.

"Have you brought us any money?" whispered she: "don't say *No* loud, for fear father should hear you." The boy told her in a low voice all that had passed.

"Speak out, my dear, I'm not asleep," said his father. "So you are come back as you went?"

"No, father, not quite—there's bread coming for you."

"Give me some more water, Anne, for my mouth is quite parched."

The little boy cut his orange in an instant, and gave a piece of it to his father, telling him, at the same time, how he came by it The sick man raised his hands to heaven, and blessed the poor woman who gave it to him.

"Oh, how I love her! and how I hate that cruel, unjust, rich man, who won't pay father for all the hard work he has done for him!" cried the child: "how I hate him!"

"God forgive him!" said the weaver. "I don't know what will become of you all, when I'm gone; and no one to befriend you, or even to work at the loom. Anne, I think if I was up," said he, raising himself, "I could still contrive to do a little good."

"Dear father, don't think of getting up; the best you can do for us is to lie still and take rest."

"Rest! I can take no rest, Anne. Rest! there's none for me in this world. And whilst I'm in it, is not it my duty to work for my wife and children? Reach me my clothes, and I'll get up."

It was in vain to contend with him, when this notion seized him that it was his duty to work till the last. All opposition fretted and made him worse; so that his daughter and his wife, even from affection, were forced to yield, and to let him go to the loom, when his trembling hands were scarcely able to throw the shuttle. He did not know how weak he was till he tried to walk. As he stepped out of bed, his wife came in with a loaf of bread in her hand: at the unexpected sight he made an exclamation of joy; sprang forward to meet her, but fell upon the floor in a swoon, before he could put one bit of the bread which she broke for him into his mouth. Want of sustenance, the having been overworked, and the constant anxiety which preyed upon his spirits, had reduced him to this deplorable state of weakness. When he recovered his senses, his wife showed him his little boy eating a large piece of bread; she also ate, and made Anne eat before him, to relieve his mind from that dread which had seized it—and not without some reason—that he should see his wife and children starve to death.

"You find, father, there's no danger for to-day," said Anne; "and to-morrow I shall be paid for my plain work, and then we shall do very well for a few days longer; and I dare say in that time Mr. Close the tailor will receive some money from some of the great many rich gentlemen who owe him so much; and you know he promised that as soon as ever he was able he would pay us."

With such hopes, and the remembrance of such promises, the poor man's spirits could not be much raised; he knew, alas! how little dependence was to be placed on them. As soon as he had eaten, and felt his strength revive, he insisted upon going to the loom; his mind was bent upon finishing a pattern, for which he was to receive five guineas in ready money: he worked and worked, then lay down and rested himself,—then worked again, and so on during the remainder of the day; and during several hours of the night he continued to throw the shuttle, whilst his little boy and his wife by turns wound spools for him.

He completed his work, and threw himself upon his bed quite exhausted, just as the neighbouring clock struck one.

At this hour Colonel Pembroke was in the midst of a gay and brilliant assembly at Mrs. York's, in a splendid saloon, illuminated with wax-lights in profusion, the floor crayoned with roses and myrtles, which the dancers' feet effaced, the walls hung with the most expensive hot-house flowers; in short, he was surrounded with luxury in all its extravagance. It is said that the peaches alone at this entertainment amounted to six hundred guineas. They cost a guinea a-piece: the price of one of them, which Colonel Pembroke threw away because it was not perfectly ripe, would have supported the weaver and his whole family for a week.

There are political advocates for luxury, who assert, perhaps justly, that the extravagance of individuals increases the wealth of nations. But even upon this system, those who by false hopes excite the industrious to exertion, without paying them their just wages, commit not only the most cruel private injustice, but the most important public injury. The permanence of industry in any state must be proportioned to the certainty of its reward.

Amongst the masks at Mrs. York's were three who amused the company particularly; the festive mob followed them as they moved, and their bon-mots were applauded and repeated by all the best, that is to say, the most fashionable male and female judges of wit. The three distinguished characters were a spendthrift, a bailiff, and a dun. The spendthrift was supported with great spirit and *truth* by Colonel Pembroke, and two of his companions were *great* and *correct* in the parts of the bailiff and the dun. The happy idea of appearing in these characters this night had been suggested by the circumstance that happened in the morning. Colonel Pembroke gave himself great credit, he said, for thus "striking novelty even from difficulty;" and he rejoiced that the rascal of a weaver had sent his boy to dun him, and had thus furnished him with diversion for the evening as well as the morning. We are much concerned that we cannot, for the advantage of posterity, record any of the innumerable *good things* which undoubtedly were uttered by this trio. Even the newspapers of the day could speak only in general panegyric. The probability, however, is, that the colonel deserved the praises that were lavished upon his manner of supporting his character. No man was better acquainted than himself with all those anecdotes of men of fashion, which could illustrate the spendthrift system. At least fifty times he had repeated, and always with the same *glee*, the reply of a great character to a creditor, who, upon being asked when his *bond* debts were likely to be paid, answered, "On the day of judgment."

Probably the admiration which this and similar sallies of wit have excited, must have produced a strong desire in the minds of many young men of spirit to perform similar feats; and though the ruin of innumerable poor creditors may be the consequence, that will not surely be deemed by a certain class of reasoners worthy of a moment's regret, or even a moment's thought. Persons of tender consciences may, perhaps, be shocked at the idea of committing injustice and cruelty by starving their creditors, but they may strengthen their minds by taking an enlarged political view of the subject.

It is obvious, that whether a hundred guineas be in the pocket of A or B, the total sum of the wealth of the nation remains the same; and whether the enjoyments of A be as 100, and those of B as 0,—or whether these enjoyments be equally divided between A and B,—is a matter of no importance to the political arithmetician, because in both cases it is obvious that the total sum of national happiness remains the same. The happiness of individuals is nothing compared with the general mass.

And if the individual B should fancy himself ill-used by our political arithmetician, and should take it into his head to observe, that though the happiness of B is nothing to the general mass, yet that it is every thing to him, the politician of course takes snuff, and replies, that his observation is foreign to the purpose—that the good of the whole society is the object in view. And if B immediately accede to this position, and only ask humbly whether the good of the whole be not made up of the good of the parts, and whether as a part he have not some right to his share of good, the dexterous logical arithmetician answers, that B is totally out of the question, because B is a negative quantity in the equation. And if obstinate B, still conceiving himself aggrieved, objects to this total annihilation of himself and his interests, and asks why the lot of extinction should not fall upon the debtor C, or even upon the calculator himself, by whatever letter of the alphabet he happens to be designated, the calculator must knit his brow, and answer— any thing he pleases—except, *I don't know*—for this is a phrase below the dignity of a philosopher. This argument is produced, not as a statement of what is really the case, but as a popular argument against political sophistry.

Colonel Pembroke, notwithstanding his success at Mrs. York's masquerade in his character of a spendthrift, could not by his utmost wit and address satisfy or silence his impertinent tailor. Mr. Close absolutely refused to give further credit without valuable consideration; and the colonel was compelled to pass his bond for the whole sum which was claimed, which was fifty pounds more than was strictly due, in order to compound with the tailor for the want of ready money. When the bond was fairly signed, sealed, and delivered, Mr. Close produced the poor weaver's bill.

"Colonel Pembroke," said he, "I have a trifling bill here—I am really ashamed to speak to you about such a trifle—but as we are settling all accounts—and as this White, the weaver, is so wretchedly poor, that he or some of his family are with me every day of my life dunning me to get me to speak about their little demand—"

"Who is this White?" said Mr. Pembroke.

"You recollect the elegant waistcoat pattern of which you afterwards bought up the whole piece, lest it should become common and vulgar?—this White was the weaver from whom we got it."

"Bless me! why that's two years ago: I thought that fellow was paid long ago!"

"No, indeed, I wish he had been; for he has been the torment of my life this many a month—I never saw people so eager about their money."

"But why do you employ such miserable, greedy creatures? What can you expect but to be dunned every hour of your life?"

"Very true, indeed, colonel; it is what I always, on that principle, avoid as far as possibly I can: but I can't blame myself in this particular instance; for this White, at the time I employed him first, was a very decent man, and in a very good way, for one of his sort: but I suppose he has taken to drink, for he is worth not a farthing now."

"What business has a fellow of his sort to drink? He should leave that for his betters," said Colonel Pembroke, laughing. "Drinking's too great a pleasure for a weaver. The drunken rascal's money is safer in my hands, tell him, than in his own."

The tailor's conscience twinged him a little at this instant, for he had spoken entirely at random, not having the slightest grounds for his insinuation that this poor weaver had ruined himself by drunkenness.

"Upon my word, sir," said Close, retracting, "the man may not be a drunken fellow for any thing I know positively—I purely surmised *that* might be the case, from his having fallen into such distress, which is no otherwise accountable for, to my comprehension, except we believe his own story, that he has money due to him which he cannot get paid, and that this has been his ruin."

Colonel Pembroke cleared his throat two or three times upon hearing this last suggestion, and actually took up the weaver's bill with some intention of paying it; but he recollected that he should want the ready money he had in his pocket for another indispensable occasion; for he was *obliged* to go to Brookes's that night; so he contented his humanity by recommending it to Mr. Close to pay White and have done with him.

"If you let him have the money, you know, you can put it down to my account, or make a memorandum of it at the back of the bond. In short, settle it as you will, but let me hear no more about it. I have not leisure to think of such trifles—Good morning to you, Mr. Close."

Mr. Close was far from having any intention of complying with the colonel's request. When the weaver's wife called upon him after his return home, he assured her that he had not seen the colour of one guinea, or one farthing, of Colonel Pembroke's money; and that it was absolutely impossible that he could pay Mr. White till he was paid himself—that it could not be expected he should advance money for any body out of his own pocket—that he begged he might not be pestered and dunned any more, for that *he really had not leisure to think of such trifles.*

For want of this trifle, of which neither the fashionable colonel nor his fashionable tailor had leisure to think, the poor weaver and his whole family were reduced to the last degree of human misery—to absolute famine. The man had exerted himself to the utmost to finish a pattern, which had been bespoken for a tradesman who promised upon the delivery of it to pay him five guineas in hand. This money he received; but four guineas of it were due to his landlord for rent of his wretched garret, and the remaining guinea was divided between the baker, to whom an old bill was due, and the apothecary, to whom they were obliged to have recourse, as the weaver was extremely ill. They had literally nothing now to depend upon but what the wife and daughter could earn by needlework; and they were known to be so miserably poor, that the *prudent* neighbours did not like to trust them with plain work, lest it should not be returned safely. Besides, in such a dirty place as they lived in, how could it be expected that they should put any work out of their hands decently clean? The woman to whom the house belonged, however, at last procured them work from Mrs. Carver, a widow lady, who she said was extremely charitable. She advised Anne to carry home the work as soon as it was finished, and to wait to see the lady herself, who might perhaps be as charitable to her as she was to many others. Anne resolved to take this advice: but when she carried home her work to the place to which she was directed, her heart almost failed her; for she found Mrs. Carver lived in such a handsome house, that there was little chance of a poor girl being admitted by the servants farther than the hall-door or the kitchen. The lady, however, happened to be just coming out of her parlour at the moment the hall-door was opened for Anne; and she bid her come in and show her work—approved of it—commended her industry—asked her several questions about her family—seemed to be touched with compassion by Anne's account of their distress—and after paying what she had charged for the work, put half-a-guinea into her hand, and bid her call the next day, when she hoped that she should be able to do something more for her. This unexpected bounty, and the kindness of voice and look with which it was accompanied, had such an effect upon the poor girl, that if she had not caught hold of a chair to support herself she would have sunk to the ground. Mrs. Carver immediately made her sit down—"Oh, madam! I'm well, quite well now—it was nothing—only surprise," said she, bursting into tears. "I beg your pardon for this foolishness—but it is only because I'm weaker to-day than usual, for want of eating."

"For want of eating! my poor child! How she trembles! she is weak indeed, and must not leave my house in this condition."

Mrs. Carver rang the bell, and ordered a glass of wine; but Anne was afraid to drink it, as she was not used to wine, and as she knew that it would affect her head if she drank without eating. When the lady found that she refused the wine, she did not press it, but insisted upon her eating something.

"Oh, madam!" said the poor girl, "it is long, long indeed, since I have eaten so heartily; and it is almost a shame for me to stay eating such dainties, when my father and mother are all the while in the way they are. But I'll run home with the half-guinea, and tell them how good you have been, and they will be so joyful and so thankful to you! My mother will come herself, I'm sure, with me to-morrow morning—she can thank you so much better than I can!"

Those only who have known the extreme of want can imagine the joy and gratitude with which the half-guinea was received by this poor family. Half-a-guinea!—Colonel Pembroke spent six half-guineas this very day in a fruit-shop, and ten times that sum at a jeweller's on seals and baubles for which he had no manner of use.

When Anne and her mother called the next morning to thank their benefactress, she was not up; but her servant gave them a parcel from his mistress: it contained a fresh supply of needlework, a gown, and some other clothes, which were directed *for Anne*. The servant said, that if she would call again about eight in the evening, his lady would probably be able to see her, and that she begged to have the work finished by that time. The work was finished, though with some difficulty, by the appointed hour; and Anne, dressed in her new clothes, was at Mrs. Carver's door just as the clock struck eight. The old lady was alone at tea; she seemed to be well pleased by Anne's punctuality; said that she had made inquiries respecting Mr. and Mrs. White, and that she heard an excellent character of them; that therefore she was disposed to do every thing she could to serve them. She added, that she "should soon part with her own maid, and that perhaps Anne might supply her place." Nothing could be more agreeable to the poor girl than this proposal: her father and mother were rejoiced at the idea of seeing her so well placed; and they now looked forward impatiently for the day when Mrs. Carver's maid was to be dismissed. In the mean time the old lady continued to employ Anne, and to make her presents, sometimes of clothes, and sometimes of money. The money she always gave to her parents; and she loved her "good old lady," as she always called her, more for putting it in her power thus to help her father and mother than for all the rest. The weaver's disease had arisen from want of sufficient food, from fatigue of body, and anxiety of mind; and he grew rapidly better, now that he was relieved from want, and inspired with hope. Mrs. Carver bespoke from him two pieces of waistcoating, which she promised to dispose of for him most advantageously, by a raffle, for which she had raised subscriptions amongst her numerous acquaintance. She expressed great indignation, when Anne told her how Mr. White had been ruined by persons who would not pay their just debts; and when she knew that the weaver was overcharged for all his working materials, because he took them upon credit, she generously offered to lend them whatever ready money might be necessary, which she said Anne might repay, at her leisure, out of her wages.

"Oh, madam!" said Anne, "you are too good to us, indeed—too good! and if you could but see into our hearts, you would know that we are not ungrateful."

"I am sure *that* is what you never will be, my dear," said the old lady; "at least such is my opinion of you."

"Thank you, ma'am! thank you, from the bottom of my heart!—We should all have been starved, if it had not been for you. And it is owing to you that we are so happy now—quite different creatures from what we were."

"Quite a different creature indeed, you look, child, from what you did the first day I saw you. To-morrow my own maid goes, and you may come at ten o'clock; and I hope we shall agree very well together—you'll find me an easy mistress, and I make no doubt I shall always find you the good, grateful girl you seem to be."

Anne was impatient for the moment when she was to enter into the service of her benefactress; and she lay awake half the night, considering how she should ever be able to show sufficient gratitude. As Mrs. Carver had often expressed her desire to have Anne look neat and smart, she dressed herself as well as she possibly could; and when her poor father and mother took leave of her, they could not help observing, as Mrs. Carver had done the day before, that "Anne looked quite a different creature from what she was a few weeks ago." She was, indeed, an extremely pretty girl; but we need not stop to relate all the fond praises that were bestowed upon her beauty by her partial parents. Her little brother John was not at home when she was going away; he was at a carpenter's shop in the neighbourhood mending a wheelbarrow, which belonged to that good-natured orange-woman who gave him the orange for his father. Anne called at the carpenter's shop to take leave of her brother. The woman was there waiting for her barrow— she looked earnestly at Anne when she entered, and then whispered to the boy, "Is that your sister?"—"Yes," said the boy, "and as good a sister she is as ever was born."

"Maybe so," said the woman; "but she is not likely to be good for much long, in the way she is going on now."

"What way—what do you mean?" said Anne, colouring violently.

"Oh, you understand me well enough, though you look so innocent."

"I do not understand you in the least."

"No!—Why, is not it you that I see going almost every day to that house in Chiswell-street?"

"Mrs. Carver's?—Yes."

"Mrs. Carver's indeed!" cried the woman, throwing an orange-peel from her with an air of disdain—"a pretty come-off indeed! as if I did not know her name, and all about her, as well as you do."

"Do you?" said Anne; "then I am sure you know one of the best women in the world."

The woman looked still more earnestly than before in Anne's countenance; and then, taking hold of both her hands, exclaimed, "You poor young creature! what are you about? I do believe you don't know what you are about—if you do, you are the greatest cheat I ever looked in the face, long as I've lived in this cheating world."

"You frighten my sister," said the boy: "do pray tell her what you mean at once, for look how pale she turns!"

"So much the better, for now I have good hope of her. Then to tell you all at once—no matter how I frighten her, it's for her good—this Mrs. Carver, as you call her, is only Mrs. Carver when she wants to pass upon such as you for a good woman."

"To pass for a good woman!" repeated Anne, with indignation. "Oh, she is, she is a good woman—you do not know her as I do."

"I know her a great deal better, I tell you: if you choose not to believe me, go your ways—go to your ruin—go to your shame—go to your grave— as hundreds have gone, by the same road, before you. Your Mrs. Carver keeps two houses, and one of them is a bad house—and that's the house you'll soon go to, if you trust to her: now you know the whole truth."

The poor girl was shocked so much, that for several minutes she could neither speak nor think. As soon as she had recovered sufficient presence of mind to consider what she should do, she declared that she would that instant go home and put on her rags again, and return to the wicked Mrs. Carver all the clothes she had given her.

"But what will become of us all?—She has lent my father money—a great deal of money. How can he pay her?—Oh, I will pay her all—I will go into some honest service, now I am well and strong enough to do any sort of hard work, and God knows I am willing."

Full of these resolutions, Anne hurried home, intending to tell her father and mother all that had happened; but they were neither of them within. She flew to the mistress of the house, who had first recommended her to Mrs. Carver, and reproached her in the most moving terms which the agony of her mind could suggest. Her landlady listened to her with astonishment, either real or admirably well affected—declared that she knew nothing more of Mrs. Carver but that she lived in a large fine house, and that she had been very charitable to some poor people in Moorfields—that she bore the best of characters—and that if nothing could be said against her but by an orange-woman, there was no great reason to believe such scandal.

Anne now began to think that the whole of what she had heard might be a falsehood, or a mistake; one moment she blamed herself for so easily suspecting a person who had shown her so much kindness; but the next minute the emphatic words and warning looks of the woman recurred to her mind; and though they were but the words and looks of an orange-woman, she could not help dreading that there was some truth in them. The clock struck ten whilst she was in this uncertainty. The woman of the house urged her to go without farther delay to Mrs. Carver's, who would undoubtedly be displeased by any want of punctuality; but Anne wished to wait for the return of her father and mother.

"They will not be back, either of them, these three hours, for your mother is gone to the other end of the town about that old bill of Colonel Pembroke's, and your father is gone to buy some silk for weaving—he told me he should not be home before three o'clock."

Notwithstanding these remonstrances, Anne persisted in her resolution: she took off the clothes which she had received from Mrs. Carver, and put on those which she had been used to wear. Her mother was much surprised, when she came in, to see her in this condition; and no words can describe her grief, when she heard the cause of this change.

She blamed herself severely for not having made inquiries concerning Mrs. Carver before she had suffered her daughter to accept of any presents from her; and she wept bitterly, when she recollected the money which this woman had lent her husband.

"She will throw him into jail, I am sure she will—we shall be worse off a thousand times than ever we were in our worst days. The work that is in the loom, by which he hoped to get so much, is all for her, and it will be left upon our hands now; and how are we to pay the woman of this house for the lodgings?——Oh! I see it all coming upon us at once," continued the poor woman, wringing her hands. "If that Colonel Pembroke would but let us have our own!—But there I've been all the morning hunting him out, and at last, when I did see him, he only swore, and said we were all a family of *duns*, or some such nonsense. And then he called after me from the top of his fine stairs, just to say, that he had ordered Close the tailor to pay us; and when I went to him there was no satisfaction to be got from him—his shop was full of customers, and he hustled me away, giving me for answer, that when Colonel Pembroke paid him, he would pay us, and no sooner. Ah! these purse-proud tradesfolk, and these sparks of fashion, what do they know of all we suffer? What do they care for us?—It is not for charity I ask any of them—only for what my own husband has justly earned, and hardly toiled for too; and this I cannot get out of their hands. If I could, we might defy this wicked woman—but now we are laid under her feet, and she will trample us to death."

In the midst of these lamentations, Anne's father came in: when he learned the cause of them, he stood for a moment in silence; then snatched from his daughter's hand the bundle of clothes, which she had prepared to return to Mrs. Carver.

"Give them to me; I will go to this woman myself," cried he with indignation: "Anne shall never more set her foot within those doors."

"Dear father," cried Anne, stopping him as he went out of the door, "perhaps it is all a mistake: do pray inquire from somebody else before you speak to Mrs. Carver—she looks so good, she has been so kind to me, I cannot believe that she is wicked. Do pray inquire of a great many people before you knock at the door."

He promised that he would do all his daughter desired.

With most impatient anxiety they waited for his return: the time of his absence appeared insupportably long, and they formed new fears and new conjectures every instant. Every time they heard a footstep upon the stairs, they ran out to see who it was: sometimes it was the landlady—sometimes the lodgers or their visitors—at last came the person they longed to see; but the moment they beheld him, all their fears were confirmed. He was pale as death, and his lips trembled with convulsive motion. He walked directly up to his loom, and without speaking one syllable, began to cut the unfinished work out of it.

"What are you about, my dear?" cried his wife. "Consider what you are about—this work of yours is the only dependence we have in the world."

"You have nothing in this world to depend upon, I tell you," cried he, continuing to cut out the web with a hurried hand—"you must not depend on me—you must not depend on my work—I shall never throw this shuttle more whilst I live—think of me as if I was dead—to-morrow I shall be dead to you—I shall be in a jail, and there must lie till carried out in my coffin. Here, take this work just as it is to our landlady—she met me on the stairs, and said she must have her rent directly—that will pay her—I'll pay all I can. As for the loom, that's only hired—the silk I bought to-day will pay the hire—I'll pay all my debts to the uttermost farthing, as far as I am able—but the ten guineas to that wicked woman I cannot pay—so I must rot in a jail. Don't cry, Anne, don't cry so, my good girl—you'll break my heart, wife, if you take on so. Why! have not we one comfort, that let us go out of this world when we may, or how we may, we shall go out of it honest, having no one's ruin to answer for, having done our duty to God and man, as far as we are able?—My child," continued he, catching Anne in his arms, "I have you safe, and I thank God for it!"

When this poor man had thus in an incoherent manner given vent to his first feelings, he became somewhat more composed, and was able to relate all that had passed between him and Mrs. Carver. The inquiries which he made before he saw her sufficiently confirmed the orange-woman's story; and when he returned the presents which Anne had unfortunately received, Mrs. Carver, with all the audacity of a woman hardened in guilt, avowed her purpose and her profession—declared that whatever ignorance and innocence Anne or her parents might now find it convenient to affect, she was "confident they had all the time perfectly understood what she was about, and that she would not be cheated at last by a parcel of swindling hypocrites." With horrid imprecations she then swore, that if Anne was kept from her she would have vengeance—and that her vengeance should know no bounds. The event showed that these were not empty threats—the very next day she sent two bailiffs to arrest Anne's father. They met him in the street, as he was going to pay the last farthing he had to the baker. The wretched man in vain endeavoured to move the ear of justice by relating the simple truth. Mrs. Carver was rich—her victim was poor. He was committed to jail; and he entered his prison with the firm belief, that there he must drag out the remainder of his days.

One faint hope remained in his wife's heart—she imagined that if she could but prevail upon Colonel Pembroke's servants, either to obtain for her a sight of their master, or if they would carry to him a letter containing an exact account of her distress, he would immediately pay the fourteen pounds which had been so long due. With this money she could obtain her husband's liberty, and she fancied all might yet be well. Her son, who could write a very legible hand, wrote the petition. "Ah, mother!" said he, "don't hope that Colonel Pembroke will read it—he will tear it to pieces, as he did one that I carried him before."

"I can but try," said she; "I cannot believe that any gentleman is so cruel, and so unjust—he must and will pay us when he knows the whole truth."

Colonel Pembroke was dressing in a hurry, to go to a great dinner at the Crown and Anchor tavern. One of Pembroke's gay companions had called, and was in the room waiting for him. It was at this inauspicious time that Mrs. White arrived. Her petition the servant at first absolutely refused to take from her hands; but at last a young lad, whom the colonel had lately brought from the country, and who had either more natural feeling, or less acquired power of equivocating, than his fellows, consented to carry up the petition, when he should, as he expected, be called by his master to report the state of a favourite horse that was sick. While his master's hair was dressing, the lad was summoned; and when the health of the horse had been anxiously inquired into, the lad with country awkwardness scratched his head, and laid the petition before his master, saying—"Sir, there's a poor woman below waiting for an answer; and if so be what she says is true, as I take it to be, 'tis enough to break one's heart."

"Your heart, my lad, is not seasoned to London yet, I perceive," said Colonel Pembroke, smiling; "why, your heart will be broke a thousand times over by every beggar you meet."

"No, no; I be too much of a man for that," replied the groom, wiping his eyes hastily with the back of his hand—"not such a noodle as that comes to, neither—beggars are beggars, and so to be treated—but this woman, sir, is no common beggar, not she; nor is she begging any ways—only to be paid her bill—so I brought it, as I was coming up."

"Then, sir, as you are going down, you may take it down again, if you please," cried Colonel Pembroke; "and in future, sir, I recommend it to you to look after your horses, and to trust me to look after my own affairs."

The groom retreated; and his master gave the poor woman's petition, without reading it, to the hair-dresser, who was looking for a piece of paper to try the heat of his irons.

"I should be pestered with bills and petitions from morning till night, if I did not frighten these fellows out of the trick of bringing them to me," continued Colonel Pembroke, turning to his companion. "That blockhead of a groom is but just come to town; he does not yet know how to drive away a dun—but he'll learn. They say that the American dogs did not know how to bark, till they learnt it from their civilized betters."

Colonel Pembroke habitually drove away reflection, and silenced the whispers of conscience, by noisy declamation, or sallies of wit.

At the bottom of the singed paper, which the hair-dresser left on the table, the name of White was sufficiently visible. "White!" exclaimed Colonel Pembroke, "as I hope to live and breathe, these Whites have been this half-year the torment of my life." He started up, rang the bell, and gave immediate orders to his servant, that *these Whites* should never more be let in, and that no more of their bills and petitions in any form whatever should be brought to him. "I'll punish them for their insolence—I won't pay them one farthing this twelvemonth: and if the woman is not gone, pray tell her so—I bid Close the tailor pay them: if he has not, it is no fault of mine. Let me not hear a syllable more about it—I'll part with the first of you who dares to disobey me."

"The woman is gone, I believe, sir," said the footman; "it was not I let her in, and I refused to bring up the letter."

"You did right. Let me hear no more about the matter. We shall be late at the Crown and Anchor. I beg your pardon, my dear friend, for detaining you so long."

Whilst the colonel went to his jovial meeting, where he was the life and spirit of the company, the poor woman returned in despair to the prison where her husband was confined.

We forbear to describe the horrible situation to which this family were soon reduced. Beyond a certain point, the human heart cannot feel compassion.

One day, as Anne was returning from the prison, where she had been with her father, she was met by a porter, who put a letter into her hands, then turned down a narrow lane, and was out of sight before she could inquire from whom he came. When she read the letter, however, she could not be in doubt—it came from Mrs. Carver, and contained these words:—

"You can gain nothing by your present obstinacy—you are the cause of your father's lying in jail, and of your mother's being as she is, nearly starved to death. You can relieve them from misery worse than death, and place them in ease and comfort for the remainder of their days. Be assured, they do not speak sincerley to you, when they pretend not to wish that your compliance should put an end to their present sufferings. It is you that are cruel to them—it is you that are cruel to yourself, and can blame nobody else. You might live all your days in a house as good as mine, and have a plentiful table served from one year's end to another, with all the dainties of the season, and you might be dressed as elegantly as the most elegant lady in London (which, by-the-bye, your beauty deserves), and you would have servants of your own, and a carriage of your own, and nothing to do all day long but take your pleasure. And after all, what is asked of you?— only to make a person happy, whom half the town would envy you, that would make it a study to gratify you in every wish of your heart. The person alluded to you have seen, and more than once, when you have been talking to me of work in my parlour. He is a very rich and generous gentleman. If you come to Chiswell-street about six this evening, you will find all I say true—if not, you and yours must take the consequences."

Coarse as the eloquence of this letter may appear, Anne could not read it without emotion: it raised in her heart a violent contest. Virtue, with poverty and famine, were on one side—and vice, with affluence, love, and every worldly pleasure, on the other.

Those who have been bred up in the lap of luxury; whom the breath of heaven has never visited too roughly; whose minds from their earliest infancy have been guarded even with more care than their persons; who in the dangerous season of youth are surrounded by all that the solicitude of experienced friends, and all that polished society, can devise for their security; are not perhaps competent to judge of the temptations by which beauty in the lower classes of life may be assailed. They who have never seen a father in prison, or a mother perishing for want of the absolute necessaries of life—they who have never themselves known the cravings of famine, cannot form an adequate idea of this poor girl's feelings, and of the temptation to which she was now exposed. She wept—she hesitated— and "the woman that deliberates is lost." Perhaps those who are the most truly virtuous of her sex will be the most disposed to feel for this poor creature, who was literally half famished before her good resolutions were conquered. At last she yielded to necessity. At the appointed hour she was in Mrs. Carver's house. This woman received her with triumph—she supplied Anne immediately with food, and then hastened to deck out her victim in the most attractive manner. The girl was quite passive in her hand. She promised, though scarcely knowing that she uttered the words, to obey the instructions that were given to her, and she suffered herself without struggle, or apparent emotion, to be led to destruction. She appeared quite insensible—but at last she was roused from this state of stupefaction, by the voice of a person with whom she found herself alone. The stranger, who was a young and gay gentleman, pleasing both in his person and manners, attempted by every possible means to render himself agreeable to her, to raise her spirits, and calm her apprehensions. By degrees his manner changed from levity to tenderness. He represented to her, that he was not a brutal wretch, who could be gratified by any triumph in which the affections of the heart have no share; and he assured her, that in any connexion which she might be prevailed upon to form with him, she should be treated with honour and delicacy.

Touched by his manner of speaking, and overpowered by the sense of her own situation, Anne could not reply one single word to all he said—but burst into an agony of tears, and sinking on her knees before him, exclaimed, "Save me! save me from myself!—Restore me to my parents, before they have reason to hate me."

The gentleman seemed to be somewhat in doubt whether this was *acting* or nature: but he raised Anne from the ground, and placed her upon a seat beside him. "Am I to understand, then, that I have been deceived, and that our present meeting is against your own consent?"

"No, I cannot say that—oh, how I wish that I could!—I did wrong, very wrong, to come here—but I repent—I was half-starved—I have a father in jail—I thought I could set him free with the money——but I will not pretend to be better than I am—I believe I thought that, beside relieving my father, I should live all my days without ever more knowing what distress is—and I thought I should be happy—but now I have changed my mind—I never could be happy with a bad conscience—I know—by what I have felt this last hour."

Her voice failed; and she sobbed for some moments without being able to speak. The gentleman, who now was convinced that she was quite artless and thoroughly in earnest, was struck with compassion; but his compassion was not unmixed with other feelings, and he had hopes that, by treating her with tenderness, he should in time make it her wish to live with him as his mistress. He was anxious to hear what her former way of life had been; and she related, at his request, the circumstances by which she and her parents had been reduced to such distress. His countenance presently showed how much he was interested in her story—he grew red and pale—he started from his seat, and walked up and down the room in great agitation, till at last, when she mentioned the name of Colonel Pembroke, he stopped short, and exclaimed, "I am the man—I am Colonel Pembroke—I am that unjust, unfeeling wretch! How often, in the bitterness of your hearts, you must have cursed me!"

"Oh, no—my father, when he was at the worst, never cursed you; and I am sure he will have reason to bless you now, if you send his daughter back again to him, such as she was when she left him."

"That shall be done," said Colonel Pembroke; "and in doing so, I make some sacrifice, and have some merit. It is time I should make some reparation for the evils I have occasioned," continued he, taking a handful of guineas from his pocket: "but first let me pay my just debts."

"My poor father!" exclaimed Anne; "to-morrow he will be out of prison."

"I will go with you to the prison, where your father is confined—I will force myself to behold all the evils I have occasioned."

Colonel Pembroke went to the prison; and he was so much struck by the scene, that he not only relieved the misery of this family, but in two months afterwards his debts were paid, his race-horses sold, and all his expenses regulated, so as to render him ever afterwards truly independent. He no longer spent his days, like many young men of fashion, either in DREADING or in DAMNING DUNS.

Edgeworthstown, 1802.

FOOTNOTES

1 ["The cloak, or mantle, as described by Thady, is of high antiquity. Spenser, in his 'View of the State of Ireland,' proves that it is not, as some have imagined, peculiarly derived from the Scythians, but that most nations of the world anciently used the mantle; for the Jews used it, as you may read of Elias's mantle, &c.; the Chaldees also used it, as you may read in Diodorus; the Egyptians likewise used it, as you may read in Herodotus, and may be gathered by the description of Berenice in the Greek Commentary upon Callimachus; the Greeks also used it anciently, as appeared by Venus's mantle lined with stars, though afterward they changed the form thereof into their cloaks, called Pallai, as some of the Irish also use: and the ancient Latins and Romans used it, as you may read in Virgil, who was a great antiquary, that Evander when Aeneas came to him at his feast, did entertain and feast him sitting on the ground, and lying on mantles: insomuch that he useth the very word mantile for a mantle,

'— — —Humi mantilia sternunt:'

so that it seemeth that the mantle was a general habit to most nations, and not proper to the Scythians only."

Spenser knew the convenience of the said mantle, as housing, bedding, and clothing.

"*Iren.* Because the commodity doth not countervail the discommodity; for the inconveniences which thereby do arise are much more many; for it is a fit house for an outlaw, a meet bed for a rebel, and an apt cloak for a thief. First, the outlaw being, for his many crimes and villanies, banished from the towns and houses of honest men, and wandering in waste places, far from danger of law, maketh his mantle his house, and under it covereth himself from the wrath of Heaven, from the offence of the earth, and from the sight of men. When it raineth, it is his penthouse; when it bloweth, it is his tent; when it freezeth, it is his tabernacle. In summer he can wear it loose; in winter he can wrap it close; at all times he can use it; never heavy, never cumbersome. Likewise for a rebel it is as serviceable; for in this war that he maketh (if at least it deserves the name of war), when he still flieth from his foe, and lurketh in the *thick woods (this should be black bogs)* and straight passages, waiting for advantages, it is his bed, yea, and almost his household stuff."]

2 [These fairy-mounts are called ant-hills in England. They are held in high reverence by the common people in Ireland. A gentleman, who in laying out his lawn had occasion to level one of these hillocks, could not prevail upon any of his labourers to begin the ominous work. He was obliged to take a *loy* from one of their reluctant hands, and began the attack himself. The labourers agreed, that the vengeance of the fairies would fall upon the head of the presumptuous mortal, who first disturbed them in their retreat. See Glossary [K].]

3 [The Banshee is a species of aristocratic fairy, who, in the shape of a little hideous old woman, has been known to appear, and heard to sing in a mournful supernatural voice under the windows of great houses, to warn the family that some of them are soon to die. In the last century every great family in Ireland had a Banshee, who attended regularly; but latterly their visits and songs have been discontinued.]

4 [*Childer:* this is the manner in which many of Thady's rank, and others in Ireland, *formerly* pronounced the word *children.*]

5 [*Middle men.*—There was a class of men termed middle men in Ireland, who took large farms on long leases from gentlemen of landed property, and let the land again in small portions to the poor, as under-tenants, at exorbitant rents. The *head landlord,* as he *was* called, seldom saw his *under-tenants;* but if he could not get the *middle man* to pay him his rent punctually, he *went to his land, and drove the land for his rent,* that is to say, he sent his steward or bailiff, or driver, to the land to seize the cattle, hay, corn, flax, oats, or potatoes, belonging to the under-tenants, and proceeded to sell these for his rents: it sometimes happened that these unfortunate tenants paid their rent twice over, once to *the middle man,* and once to the *head landlord.*

The characteristics of a middle man *were,* servility to his superiors, and tyranny towards his inferiors: the poor detested this race of beings. In speaking to them, however, they always used the most abject language, and the most humble tone and posture—*"Please your honour; and please your honour's honour"* they knew must be repeated as a charm at the beginning and end of every equivocating, exculpatory, or supplicatory sentence; and they were much more alert in doffing their caps to these new men, than to those of what they call *good old families.* A witty carpenter once termed these middle men *journeymen gentlemen.*]

6 [This part of the history of the Rackrent family can scarcely be thought credible; but in justice to honest Thady, it is hoped the reader will recollect the history of the celebrated Lady Cathcart's conjugal imprisonment.—The editor was acquainted with Colonel M'Guire, Lady Cathcart's husband; he

has lately seen and questioned the maid-servant who lived with Colonel M'Guire during the time of Lady Cathcart's imprisonment. Her ladyship was locked up in her own house for many years; during which period her husband was visited by the neighbouring gentry, and it was his regular custom at dinner to send his compliments to Lady Cathcart, informing her that the company had the honour to drink her ladyship's health, and begging to know whether there was any thing at table that she would like to eat? the answer was always, "Lady Cathcart's compliments, and she has every thing she wants." An instance of honesty in a poor Irish woman deserves to be recorded:—Lady Cathcart had some remarkably fine diamonds, which she had concealed from her husband, and which she was anxious to get out of the house, lest he should discover them. She had neither servant nor friend to whom she could entrust them; but she had observed a poor beggar woman, who used to come to the house; she spoke to her from the window of the room in which she was confined; the woman promised to do what she desired, and Lady Cathcart threw a parcel, containing the jewels, to her. The poor woman carried them to the person to whom they were directed; and several years afterwards, when Lady Cathcart recovered her liberty, she received her diamonds safely.

At Colonel M'Guire's death her ladyship was released. The editor, within this year, saw the gentleman who accompanied her to England after her husband's death. When she first was told of his death, she imagined that the news was not true, and that it was told only with an intention of deceiving her. At his death she had scarcely clothes sufficient to cover her; she wore a red wig, looked scared, and her understanding seemed stupified; she said that she scarcely knew one human creature from another: her imprisonment lasted above twenty years. These circumstances may appear strange to an English reader; but there is no danger in the present times, that any individual should exercise such tyranny as Colonel M'Guire's with impunity, the power being now all in the hands of government, and there being no possibility of obtaining from parliament an act of indemnity for any cruelties.]

7 [Boo! boo! an exclamation equivalent to *pshaw* or *nonsense.*]

8 [*Pin,* read *pen.* It formerly was vulgarly pronounced *pin* in Ireland.]

9 [*Her mark.* It *was* the custom in Ireland for those who could not write to make a cross to stand for their signature, as was formerly the practice of our English monarchs. The Editor inserts the fac-simile of an Irish *mark,* which may hereafter be valuable to a judicious antiquary—

     Her

Judy   X   *M'Quirk,*

Mark.

In bonds or notes, signed in this manner, a witness is requisite, as the name is frequently written by him or her.]

10 [*Vows.*—It has been maliciously and unjustly hinted, that the lower classes of the people in Ireland pay but little regard to oaths; yet it is certain that some oaths or vows have great power over their minds. Sometimes they swear they will be revenged on some of their neighbours; this is an oath that they are never known to break. But, what is infinitely more extraordinary and unaccountable, they sometimes make and keep a vow against whiskey; these vows are usually limited to a short time. A woman who has a drunken husband is most fortunate if she can prevail upon him to go to the priest, and make a vow against whiskey for a year, or a month, or a week, or a day.]

11 [*Gossoon*, a little boy—from the French word *garçon*. In most Irish families there *used* to be a barefooted gossoon, who was slave to the cook and butler, and who in fact, without wages, did all the hard work of the house. Gossoons were always employed as messengers. The Editor has known a gossoon to go on foot, without shoes or stockings, fifty-one English miles between sunrise and sunset.]

12 [At St. Patrick's meeting, London, March, 1806, the Duke of Sussex said he had the honour of bearing an Irish title, and, with the permission of the company, he should tell them an anecdote of what he had experienced on his travels. When he was at Rome, he went to visit an Irish seminary, and when they heard who he was, and that he had an Irish title, some of them asked him, "Please you Royal Highness, since you are an Irish peer, will you tell us if you ever trod upon Irish ground?" When he told them he had not, "Oh, then," said one of the order, "you shall soon do so". They then spread some earth, which had been brought from Ireland, on a marble slab, and made him stand upon it.]

13 [This was actually done at an election in Ireland.]

14 [*To put him up*—to put him in gaol.]

15 [*My little potatoes*—Thady does not mean, by this expression, that his potatoes were less than other people's, or less than the usual size—*little* is here used only as an Italian diminutive, expressive of fondness.]

16 [*Kith and kin*—family or relations. *Kin* from *kind*; *kith* from we know not what.]

17 [Wigs were formerly used instead of brooms in Ireland, for sweeping or dusting tables, stairs, &c. The Editor doubted the fact, till he saw a labourer of the old school sweep down a flight of stairs with his wig; he

afterwards put it on his head again with the utmost composure, and said, "Oh, please your honour, it's never a bit the worse."

It must be acknowledged, that these men are not in any danger of catching cold by taking off their wigs occasionally, because they usually have fine crops of hair growing under their wigs. The wigs are often yellow, and the hair which appears from beneath them black; the wigs are usually too small, and are raised up by the hair beneath, or by the ears of the wearers.]

18 [A wake in England is a meeting avowedly for merriment; in Ireland it is a nocturnal meeting avowedly for the purpose of watching and bewailing the dead; but, in reality, for gossiping and debauchery. See Glossary [C2].]

19 [Shebean-house, a hedge alehouse. Shebcan properly means weak small-beer, taplash.]

20 [At the coronation of one of our monarchs, the king complained of the confusion which happened in the procession. The great officer who presided told his majesty, "That it should not be so next time."]

21 [*Kilt and smashed.*—Our author is not here guilty of an anti-climax. The mere English reader, from a similarity of sound between the words *kilt* and *killed*, might be induced to suppose that their meanings are similar, yet they are not by any means in Ireland synonymous terms. Thus you may hear a man exclaim, "I'm kilt and murdered!" but he frequently means only that he has received a black eye, or a slight contusion.—*I'm kilt all over* means that he is in a worse state than being simply *kilt*. Thus, *I'm kilt with the cold*, is nothing to *I'm kilt all over with the rheumatism.*]

22 [*The room*—the principal room in the house.]

23 [*Tester*—sixpence; from the French word, tête, a head: a piece of silver stamped with a head, which in old French was called "un testion," and which was about the value of an old English sixpence. Tester is used in Shakspeare.]

24 [Natural History, century iii. p. 191.—*Bacon produces it to show that echoes will not readily return the letter S..*]

25 ["Un savant écrivoit à un ami, et un importun étoit à côté de lui, qui regardoit par dessus l'épaule ce qu'il écrivoit. Le savant, qui s'en apperçut, écrivit ceci à la place: 'Si un impertinent qui est à mon côté ne regardoit pas ce que j'écris, je vous écrirois encore plusieurs choses qui ne doivent être sues que de vous et de moi.' L'importun, qui lisoit toujours, prit la parole et dit: 'Je vous jure que je n'ai regardé ni lû ce que vous écriviez.' Le savant repartit, 'Ignorant, que vous êtes, pourquoi me dites-vous donc ce que vous

dites?'" *Les Paroles Remarquables des Orientaux; traduction de leurs ouvrages en Arabe, en Persan, et en Turc (suivant la copie imprimée à Paris), à la Haye, chez Louis et Henry Vandole, marchands libraires, dans le Pooten, à l'enseigne du Port Royal, M.DC.XCIV.*]

26 ["Le bailli nous donne an diable, et nous nous recommandons à vous, monseigneur."]

27 [On faisoit compliment à madame Denis de la façon dont elle venoit de jouer Zaïre. "Il faudroit," dit elle, "être belle et jeune." "Ah, madame!" reprit le complimenteur naïvement, "vous êtes bien la preuve du contraire."]

28 [Locke's Essay concerning the Human Understanding, fifteenth edit. vol. i. p. 292.]

29 [*"De moi je commence à douter tout de ben.*

Pourtant quand je me tâte, et quand je me rappelle,

Il me semble que je suis moi."]

30 [*"So Indian murd'rers hope to gain*

The powers and virtues of the slain,

Of wretches they destroy."]

31 [Vide Mémoires du Cardinal de Retz.]

32 [Vide Sir W. Hamilton's account of an eruption of Mount Vesuvius.]

33 [This fact, *we believe*, is mentioned in a letter of Mrs. Cappe's on parish schools.]

34 [Vide Mrs. Piozzi's English Synonymy.]

35 [John Lydgate.]

36 [Iliad, 6th book, l. 432, Andromache says to Hector, "You will make your son an orphan, and your wife a widow."]

37 [Lord Chesterfield.]

38 [Essay on Chemical Nomenclature, by S. Dickson, M.D.; in which are comprised observations on the same subject, by R. Kirwan, Pres. R.I.A,— Vide pages 21, 22, 23, &c.]

39 [This conjuror, whose name was Broadstreet, was a native of the county of Longford, in Ireland: he by this hit pocketed 200*l.*, and proved himself to be more knave than fool.]

40 [A gripe or fast hold.]

41 [An oak stick, supposed to be cut from the famous wood of Shilala.]

42 [This is nearly verbatim from a late Irish complainant.]

43 ["Pleurez, pleurez, mes yeux, et fondez vous en eau, La moitié de ma vie a mis l'autre au tombeau."]

44 ["Il pover uomo che non sen' era accorto, Andava combattendo, ed erà morto."]

45 [See his account of the siege of Gibraltar.]

46 [Life of Hyder Ali Khan, vol. ii. p. 231.]

47 [See the advice of Cleomenes to Crius. HERODOTUS EBATO.]

48 [It is said that the waters of the Garonne are famed for a similar virtue.]

49 [The stomach.]

50 [This ancient old man, we fear, was more knave than fool. History informs us, that the Bishop of Rochester had diverted the revenue, appropriated for keeping Sandwich harbour in repair, to the purpose of building a steeple. — Vide Fuller's Worthies of England, page 65.]

51 [Baskets.]

52 [Vide Robertson's History of Scotland.]

53 [Slink calf.]

54 [This was written down a few minutes after it had been spoken.]

55 [James Adams, S.R.E.S., author of a book entitled, "The Pronunciation of the English Language vindicated from imputed Anomaly and Caprice; with an Appendix on the Dialects of Human Speech in all Countries, and an analytical Discussion and Vindication of the Dialect of Scotland."]

56 [Vide Illustrations on Sublimity, in his Essays.]

57 [The glossary to the Lancashire dialect informs us, that 'lieve me comes from beleemy, believe me; from belamy, my good friend, old French.]

58 [Gawmbling (Anglo-Saxon, gawmless), stupid.]

59 ["Every thing speaks against us, even our silence."]

60 [Lord Chatham.]

61 [Your hands alone have a right to conquer the unconquerable.]

62 [And when Caesar was the only emperor within the dominion of Rome, he suffered me to be another.]

63 [This bull was really made.]

64 [Castle Rackrent.]

65 [Il y a des nations dont l'une semble faite pour être soumise à l'autre. Les Anglois ont toujours eu sur les Irlandois la superiorite du génie, des richesses, et des armes. *La supériorite que les blancs ont sur les noirs.*]

66 ["On lisait dans les premières éditions, *la supèriorità que les blancs ont sur les négres.* M. de Voltaire effaça cette expression injurieuse. L'état presque sauvage ou étoit l'Irlande lorsqu'elle fut conquise, la superstition, l'oppression exercée par les Anglois, le fanatisme religieux qui divise les Irlandois en deux nations ennemies, telles sont les causes qui ont retenues ce peuple dans l'abaissement et dans la foiblesse. Les haines religieuses se sont assoupies, et elle a repris sa liberté. *Les Irlandois ne le cédent plus aux Anglois, ni en industrie ni en lumières.*"]

67 [See O'Halloran's History of Ireland.]

68 [Author of Chiysal, or Adventures of a Guinea.]

69 [Author of the beautiful moral tale Nourjahad.]

70 [Marmontel.]

71 [Emilius and Sophia.]

72 [Vide Duchess of Marlborough's Apology.]

73 [Clodius Albinus.]

74 [I was not the nobleman who laid a wager, that he could ride a fine horse to death in fifteen minutes. Indeed, I must do myself the justice to say, that I rejoiced at this man's losing his bet. He *blew* the horse in four minutes, and killed it; but it did not die within the time prescribed by the bet.]

75 [If any one should think it impossible that a man of Lord Glenthorn's consequence should, at the supposed moment of his death, thus be neglected, let them recollect the scenes that followed the death of Tiberius—of Henry the Fourth of France—of William Rufus, and of George the Second.]

76 ["For fostering, I did never hear or read, that it was in use or reputation in any country, barbarous or civil, as it hath been, and yet is, in Ireland.... In the opinion of this people, fostering hath always been a stronger alliance than blood; and the foster-children do love and are beloved of their foster-fathers and their sept (or *clan*) more than of their natural parents and kindred; and do participate of their means more frankly, and do adhere unto them, in all fortunes, with more affection and constancy.... Such a general custom in a kingdom, in giving and taking children to foster, making such a firm alliance as it doth in Ireland, was never seen or heard of in any other country of the world beside."—DAVIES.

See in Lodge's Peerage of Ireland an account of an Irish nurse, who went from Kerry to France, and from France to Milan, to see her foster-son, the Lord Thomas Fitzmaurice; and to warn him that his estate was in danger from an heir-at-law, who had taken possession of it in his absence. The nurse, being very old, died on her return home.]

77 [Verbatim.]

78 [Since Lord Glenthorn's Memoirs were published, the editor has received letters and information from the east, west, north, and south of Ireland, on the present state of posting in that country. The following is one of the many, which is vouched by indisputable authority as a true and recent anecdote, given in the very words in which it was related to the editor ... Mr. — — —, travelling in Ireland, having got into a hackney chaise, was surprised to hear the driver knocking at each side of the carriage. "What are you doing?" — "A'n't I nailing your honour up?" — "Why do you nail me up? I don't wish to be nailed up." — "Augh! would your honour have the doors fly off the hinges?" When they came to the end of the stage, Mr. — — — begged the man to unfasten the doors. "Ogh! what would I he taking out the nails for, to be racking the doors?" — "How shall I get out then?" — "Can't your honour get out of the window like any other *jantleman?*" Mr. — — — began the operation; but, having forced his head and shoulder out, could get no farther, and called again to the postilion. "Augh! did any one ever see any one get out of a chay head foremost? Can't your honour put out your feet first, like a Christian?"

Another correspondent from the south relates, that when he refused to go on till one of the four horses, who wanted a shoe, was shod, his two postilions in his hearing commenced thus: "Paddy, where *will* I get a shoe, and no smith nigh hand?" — "Why don't you see yon *jantleman's* horse in the field? can't you go and unshoe him?" — "True for ye," said Jem; "but that horse's shoe will never fit him." — "Augh! you can but try it," said Paddy. — So the gentleman's horse was actually unshod, and his shoe put upon the hackney horse; and, fit or not fit, Paddy went off with it.

Another gentleman, travelling in the north of Ireland in a hackney chaise during a storm of wind and rain, found that two of the windows were broken, and two could not by force or art of man be pulled up: he ventured to complain to his Paddy of the inconvenience he suffered from the storm pelting in his face. His consolation was, "Augh! God bless your honour, and can't you get out and *set* behind the carriage, and you'll not get a drop at all, I'll engage."]

79 [Mirabeau—Secret Memoirs.]

80 [See Philosophical Transactions, vol. lxvii. part ii., Sir George Shuckburgh's observations to ascertain the height of mountains—for a full account of the cabin of a couple of Alpine shepherdesses.]

81 [See Harrison.]

82 [*"En petit compris vous pouvez voir*

Ce qui comprend beaucoup par renommé,

Plume, labeur, la langue, et le devoir

Furent vaincus par l'amant de l'aimée.

O gentille ame, étant toute estimée!

Qui te pourra louer, qu'en se taisant?

Car la parole est toujours réprimée

Quand le sujet surmonte le disant."]

83 ["The stag is roused from the woods that skirt Glenaa mountain, in which there are many of these animals that run wild; the bottoms and sides of the mountains are covered with woods, and the declivities are so long and steep that no horse could either make his way to the bottom, or climb these impracticable hills. It is impossible to follow the hunt, either on foot or on horseback. The spectator enjoys the diversion on the lake, where the cry of hounds, the harmony of the horn, resounding from the hills on every side, the universal shouts of joy along the valleys and mountains, which are often lined with foot-people, who come in vast numbers to partake and assist at the diversion, re-echo from hill to hill, and give the highest glee and satisfaction that the imagination can conceive possible to arise from the chase, and perhaps can nowhere be enjoyed with that spirit and sublime elevation of soul, that a thorough-bred sportsman feels at a stag-hunt on the Lake of Killarney. There is, however, one imminent danger which awaits him; that in his raptures and ecstasies he may forget himself and jump out of the boat. When hotly pursued, and weary with the constant difficulty of making his way with his ramified antlers through the woods, the stag, terrified at the cry of his open-mouthed pursuers, almost at his heels, now looks toward the lake as his last resource—then pauses and looks upwards;

but the hills are insurmountable, and the woods refuse to shelter him—the hounds roar with redoubled fury at the sight of their victim—he plunges into the lake. He escapes but for a few minutes from one merciless enemy to fall into the hands of another—the shouting boat-men surround their victim—throw cords round his majestic antlers—he is haltered and dragged to shore; while the big tears roll down his face, and his heaving sides and panting flanks speak his agonies, the keen searching knife drinks his blood, and savages exult at his expiring groan."]

84 [Than.]

85 [An Irishman in using this word has some confused notion that it comes from *negro*; whereas it really means niggard.]